THE GOLDEN WEST

ALSO BY DANIEL FUCHS

Summer in Williamsburg (1934)

Homage to Blenholt (1936)

Low Company (1937)

Stories (1956)
(with Jean Stafford, John Cheever, and William Maxwell)

West of the Rockies (1971)

The Apathetic Bookie Joint (1979)

Selected by CHRISTOPHER CARDUFF

Introduction by JOHN UPDIKE

THE
GOLDEN WEST

HOLLYWOOD STORIES

BY DANIEL FUCHS

A BLACK SPARROW BOOK
DAVID R. GODINE · *Publisher*
Boston

This is
A Black Sparrow Book
published in 2005 by
David R. Godine · *Publisher*
Post Office Box 450
Jaffrey, New Hampshire 03452
www.blacksparrowbooks.com

These stories and essays first appeared in *Cinema Arts, Collier's, Commentary,
The New York Times,* and *The New Yorker,* and in books published by Methuen
and Alfred A. Knopf, Inc. A detailed list of sources and acknowledgments
begins on page 255.

The Black Sparrow Books pressmark is by Julian Waters
www.waterslettering.com
Book composition and design by Carl W. Scarbrough

LIBRARY OF CONGRESS CATALOGING-IN-PUBLICATION DATA

Fuchs, Daniel, 1909–1993
The golden West : Hollywood stories / by Daniel Fuchs ;
selected by Christopher Carduff ; introduction by John Updike.— 1st ed.
    p.   cm.
"A Black Sparrow book."
ISBN 1-57423-205-3 (hardcover : alk. paper)
1. Hollywood (Los Angeles, Calif.)—Fiction. 2. Motion picture authorship—
Fiction. 3. Motion picture industry—Fiction. 4. Screenwriters—Fiction.
I. Carduff, Christopher. II. Title.
PS3511.U27A6   2005
813'.52—dc22
2004029888

SECOND PRINTING, 2005
PRINTED IN THE UNITED STATES OF AMERICA

CONTENTS

INTRODUCTION

When films ceased to be silent, a migration of Eastern writers, play-wrights, and wits swarmed to the Golden State, to write scripts for the studios. Though it wasn't exactly the Donner Party, its annals are not happy ones. One thinks of Fitzgerald and his quixotic, dashed hopes of bringing his brand of literary refinement and glamour to film; of Faulkner sneaking back to Mississippi as soon as one of his raids on the studio coffers had yielded its loot; of Dorothy Parker complaining that Hollywood money melted like snow and embracing communism, perhaps in protest. Novels from Nathanael West's *The Day of the Locust* (1939) to Bruce Wagner's *Force Majeure* (1991) and *I'm Losing You* (1996) portray a nearly apocalyptic community of grotesque losers— schemers and dreamers driven mad by the wealth and fame apparently to be had all around them. The insider's view, as painted by Hollywood offspring Budd Schulberg and Leslie Epstein, is scarcely rosier. Even as benign a visitor as Ludwig Bemelmans struck off a novel, *Dirty Eddie* (1947), despairing of the screenwriter's lucrative but thankless lot.

What can we make, then, of long-term Tinseltown denizen Daniel Fuchs, who in 1937 left behind a schoolteacher's job in Brooklyn, three quite brilliant novels produced in his twenties, and a career of frequent acceptances of his short fiction by *The New Yorker*, *The Saturday Evening Post*, and *Collier's* to become one of RKO's scribbling minions, and who never looked back with regret? In "The Aftershock" Fuchs extols southern California as he found it in 1937, "still undeveloped . . . fresh and brimming and unawakened, at the beginning . . . everything in this new land wonderfully solitary, burning, and kind." For him, "the studios exude an excitement, a sense of life, a reach and hope, to an extent hard to describe." With delight he wanders the studio back lots, their elaborate fabrications of Western streets and bygone fishing villages, and watches "the studio bravos in their costumes at their perpetual play, folk coming from backgrounds unknown to me, people with a smiling, generous style." He relishes, as the years go by, the uncanny cleanliness and health of his growing, tanned children. Looking back on thirty-four years of residence, he thanks the gods of filmdom

> for the boon of work; for the joy of leisure, the happy, lazy days; for the castles and drowsy back lots; for the stalwarts I've come to know, John and Bob and Sam; for the parties at Barney's, the times at Phil's, the flowers, the sycamores, the blessings of the sun.

No sour grapes on these vines. In his long story "Triplicate," Fuchs lets a character assert with admitted exaggeration but without contradiction,

> "What people don't understand about this place is that the whole idea is not to make great pictures but to enjoy life in the sun. They keep asking for works of art, but the picture-making from the beginning was secondary, starting with the Fairbanks–Pickford days when they entertained visiting royalty and statesmen. That's why the pictures had their worldwide success. They were made without strain by happy, unneurotic people who were busy having a good time and who worked naturally out of their instincts, and audiences everywhere were intelligent enough to perceive this and treasure it. It's the climate, the desert. It comes with the locality."

His fiction tells a somewhat more complicated and qualified story, of feverish rises and falls, rousing successes and creeping failures, of neurosis and frustration amid the sunshine and bougainvillea. The three stories he wrote in the 1930s, soon after his arrival, are Kafkaesque, show-ing the screenwriter's Hollywood as a nightmare of aborted projects and inscrutable higher powers. But the longest of them, "Florida" (originally titled "Toilers of the Screen"), ends with a decision to stay in this "screwy, heartbreaking" place, and Fuchs remains a rarity, a literary Easterner who never opted out or badmouthed the crass hands that fed him. The equanimity, the pervasive amused sympathy, with which he regarded the waifs and gangsters of Brooklyn's tough Williamsburg section and of New York's racing crowd—*Low Company*, one of his novels is titled —extended to the movie crowd, whose brand of flamboyance and voiced desperation fills to overflowing the party scenes of "Triplicate" and "The Golden West." Fuchs resembles Bellow in his admiration of energy, how-ever ill expended. He anticipated Bellow's rapid easy tumble of imagery and dialogue, with its sometimes breathtakingly fresh adjectives: "this world of celebrity, of fast movement and shiny living"; "the larceny in his eyes, as he devoted himself to the girl, wooing her and getting her rosy." There is the same acceptance, both offhand and religious, of people as the messy, troublesome spirits they are. Bellow, however, sometimes takes positions, presses a point—Herzog writing all those querulous letters to the mighty—where Fuchs maintains an unblemished cool, an unblink-ing, unblaming candor and, with all his street smarts, an innocence.

His alter ego Rosengarten, the detached writer-witness of "Tripli-cate," explains that "what was of most importance in a piece of writing was a certain exhilaration, a life, a liveliness, a sense of well-being aris-ing from the scene and the people, hard for him to describe or even to understand clearly, and yet the thing that gave him a sinking terror when it was missing, when he knew it wasn't there." Farther down the page, he falls into self-exhortation:

"Make something that didn't exist before," he said to himself, "a thing, a fact, your own, absolute, unassailable. Do something with it. Don't let it just stand there. Make something happen—an ela-tion, a joy."

The first thing by Daniel Fuchs I ever read was a paragraph typed and posted on the bulletin board of William Maxwell, a fiction editor at *The New Yorker,* when I worked in the magazine's offices in the mid-fifties. Maxwell, Fuchs's editor, had loved this paragraph—something about clowns and balloons, in my dim memory—enough to type it up and pin it up as an epitome of elation and joy in prose. (It was Maxwell, I believe, to whom Fuchs was referring, in the introduction to his collection *The Apathetic Bookie Joint*, as "the most urbane and kindliest man I have ever known.") The copyright credits for *The Apathetic Bookie Joint* list a number of *New Yorker* short stories after 1937, but they stop in 1942, to resume, briefly, with four titles, in 1953–54. I once heard Brendan Gill say, of this resumption, "Boy, didn't he come out of the West with his six-guns blazing!" They were wonderful stories, including "The Golden West" in this volume. Fuchs's demonstration, after a decade's silence, of so much vitality, subtlety, clairvoyance, and edginess in the short-story form made him something of a legend in Eastern literary circles. How could the writer of such fiction be content with the drudgery, the compromises, the abasement of screenwriting?

In "Strictly Movie," his 1989 Letter from Hollywood, he himself wrote:

> Critics and bystanders who concern themselves with the plight of the Hollywood screenwriter don't know the real grief that goes with the job. The worst is the dreariness in the dead sunny afternoons when you consider the misses, the scripts you've labored on and had high hopes for and that wind up on the shelf, when you think of the mountains of failed screenplays on the shelf at the different movie companies; in all my time at the studios, I managed to get my name on a little more than a dozen pictures, most unmemorable, one a major success.

Little more than a dozen pictures, most with shared credits, in all those decades seems a bleak harvest. The "major success," for which Fuchs received an Academy Award, was *Love Me or Leave Me*. Fuchs credits its success to Joe Pasternak's getting James Cagney to act the part of the crippled thug Moe Snyder; he doesn't mention the sensation of the picture, what the crowds paid to see—Doris Day's playing a tough girl, the singer Ruth Etting, smoking and drinking and getting knocked around and standing spread-legged in a spangly little flapper dress and singing "Come on, Big Boy—ten cents a dance!" Fuchs follows his description of the screenwriter's sorrows with the demur, "It's the same when you write for publication, on your own.... Of course, the difference is that in the movies you get paid when you fail and there is that to carry you over." This ignores the likelihood that the print-writer, if he possesses Fuchs's distinction and contacts, will wind up with a published book, a work all his own, warped by no actor or director or producer or studio head, available for years to come in libraries if not in bookstores, a virtually everlasting personal testament.

In fact, Fuchs was dissatisfied with writing for print before Hollywood beckoned. His three novels had received some good notices but didn't sell, and would have sold less if his fellow-schoolteachers hadn't loyally bought a number. He accepted an ill-fated invitation from the Broadway producer Jed Harris (who appears in "Triplicate" as the provocative, self-destructive Rogers Hammet) to adapt his novel *Homage to Blenholt*, and the experience, though it ended in rejection, left Fuchs with an appetite for outsize showbiz personalities: "He put on a continuous show. It had been a revelation, all new to me—the recklessness, his commitment to his star, the fierce expenditure of energy and the turbulence he created around him." This quotation comes from a remarkably full account of himself that Fuchs wrote in 1987 for Gale's *Contemporary Authors Autobiography Series*. In the same piece he describes his growing distrust of his own writing, its humor, its comedy: "The brave jollity —it increasingly seemed to me—was an evasion; it dodged and skidded around the truth and would not meet it fairly.... I was, in the end, in the peculiar position of a writer whose forte was a quality he secretly disliked and wanted to lean on less and less and not at all, and who, on the other hand, had no other special talent or great idea to offer in its place."

He found refuge, it would seem, in the collaborative craft of movie-making. Like few other veterans of the script mills, he unfailingly communicates respect for the industrial process, the many-sided group effort. "Writing for the Movies," his 1962 Letter from Hollywood, compellingly describes his first assignment: trying to save a film, already in rough cut, from the stubbornly unsuitable acting of the lead, a thinly disguised George Raft. In this salvage operation the youthful, awe-struck Fuchs had as his collaborator a writer "who was no less than one of perhaps the ten most important literary figures in the world"—William Faulkner. The two can't communicate, the task seems impossible, and yet, at last, "abruptly, miraculously, everything was calm. The fever was over. Everything that needed to be done was done. . . . The wonder was the picture. It was whole now, sound—the myriad nerve-lines of continuity in working order, the conglomeration of effects artfully re-juggled, brisk and full of urgent meaning." Fuchs sees no shame in shaping a product for a mass audience; rather, he sees wizardry, and a special kind of truth:

> It had to have an opulence; or an urbanity; or a gaiety; a strength and assurance; a sense of life with its illimitable reach and promise. As a matter of fact, it didn't even have to be the truth.

He finds good words to say about tyrants of the industry like Louis B. Mayer and Harry Cohn, men who, however misguided, lived for the movies, who demanded *the work*. "It was always surprising how underneath the outcries and confusion the work steadily went on. They never slackened; fighting the *malach ha-moves* [the Hebrew Angel of Death] and the dingy seepage of time, they beat away to the limits of their strength and endowments, striving to get it right, to run down the answers, to realize and secure the picture." Twenty-seven years later, in "Strictly Movie," he still praises the work:

> You get absorbed in the picture-making itself. It's a large-scale, generous art or occupation, and you're grateful to be part of it. . . . What impressed me about the people on the set as I looked on was the intensity with which they worked. . . . They were artists or talented people—the photographers, set designers, editors, and others whose names you see on the credit lists. They worked with the assiduity and worry of artists, putting in the effort to secure the effect needed by the story, to go further than that and enhance the story, and not mar it.

The fiction writer works as a solitary, to please himself and, usually, a modest audience; the "large-scale, generous" corporate enterprise of motion-picture-making touched, amid all the scuffling of egos, an idealistic chord within Fuchs, a yearning for absorption in something bigger, something mass-oriented.

In an ideological decade, with fascism and communism both urging the sublimation of individual identity, Fuchs's renunciation of New York–style fiction for the Hollywood mills was a political act, a vote for the everymen and everywomen who filled the seats of the movie theaters. At the same time, it provided him with bourgeois comfort in an idyllic climate and exposed to his admiration the vivacity, intensity, and fantasy of Hollywood's immigrants from the East and Europe. There were "shenanigans and excesses" on the studio lots; there were the endless, free-form weekend parties that figure in his fiction as Chekhovian orgies of lamentation and hope and comically confessed folly.

The longest piece of fiction here, the short novel "West of the Rockies," concerns one of the technical problems that arise in the industry and threaten to mar the work—the star breakdown, the overload of narcissistic anxiety and self-medication that short-circuits the Marilyn Monroes and Judy Garlands of the film world and stops production. Adele Hogue, overwhelmed by "the clamor in her," has fled the set and holed up in Palm Springs. Fuchs, both tender and impatient with his heroine, limns her humble beginnings and fierce scramble into celebrity, her "fanatic energy" and "the fury in her, the rage of disbelief and bewilderment, now that all this which she had fought for so desperately was so soon being taken away from her." She is aging, fattening: her body is guilty of "the widening at the waist—that thickening which, it had been surveyed and studied in the business, the young people in the movie houses spotted and resented, perhaps without even knowing what they resented, which from their vantage point and youth they found repellent and wouldn't accept." Yet she still "was a big name, one of the handful who really brought people into the movie house." A jaded talent agent, a former athlete and her sometime lover, Burt Claris, sees her as worth rescuing, and at the novel's end she silently mouths "I love you, I love you, I love you" at him as they announce their engagement to the press. The author closes by musing on how "we are each of us precious to ourselves and wouldn't exchange ourselves, the being in us, with any other." The novel, published when Fuchs was in his sixties, feels hurried, written in uncharacteristic run-on sentences, and the author's manner of glimmering diffidence verges on boredom when the plot arrives at its well-prepared climactic scenes; and yet this tale of deals forged out of weaknesses is his most limpid attempt to plumb movie magic, its human essence, the sway stars hold over an audience when mounted in a sufficiently well-engineered story, one lubricated with what Fuchs calls (in a passing homage to the obstreperous Harry Cohn) "those secret elixirs, hideously slippery and intangible, that make a work of the imagination go." The word "elixir" recurs in a brief fit of literary introspection in 1989—"What is the secret elixir that we must look for, the thing that gives a story life?... It's the melodic line—when it all comes together, when it sings." Fuchs in his modesty and optimism construed his tortuous Hollywood labors, with their dozen credited scripts, as a species of singing.

—JOHN UPDIKE

THE GOLDEN WEST

WRITING FOR THE MOVIES: A LETTER FROM HOLLYWOOD, 1962

Dear Editors:

Thank you for your kind letter and compliments. Yes, your hunch was right, I would like very much to tell about the problems and values I've encountered, writing for the movies all these years. I'm so slow in replying to you because I thought it would be a pleasant gesture—in return for your warm letter—to send you the completed essay. But it's taken me longer than I thought it would. I've always been impressed by the sure, brimming conviction of people who attack Hollywood, and this even though they may never have been inside the business and so haven't had the chance of knowing how really onerous and exacerbating the conditions are. But for me the subject is more disturbing, or else it is that I like to let my mind wander and that I start from a different bias, or maybe I've just been here too long.

When I came to California twenty-five years ago, I was taken with the immense, brilliantly clean sunshine that hovered over everything. I wrote troubled pieces about Hollywood—a diary that I actually kept, an article titled "Dream City, or The Drugged Lake." The studio where I worked, RKO on Gower Street, seemed drenched and overpowered by the sun. The studio paths were empty; you heard a composer somewhere listlessly working up a tune for a musical picture: "Oh, I ADORE you, ADORE you, ADORE you—you WONDERFUL thing!" The people stayed hidden inside their offices, and what they did there, I didn't know. I was made welcome to the community with a grace I somehow hadn't expected—by the wonderful Epstein brothers, who broke the way for me and looked out for me; by Dorothy Parker, who telephoned and introduced me to a glittering group of people, or a group I thought glittering; by John Garfield, with his honest and whole-hearted happy spirits; and by a man named Barney Glazer, now dead, at one time head of Paramount Studios. Mr. Glazer had a beautiful home on Chevy Chase Drive in Beverly Hills. It was surrounded by carefully tended grounds— gardens and strawberry patches, patios, a championship enclosed tennis court, a championship swimming pool, dressing rooms, a gymnasium. After the week's work, starting with Saturday afternoon, guests assembled there and a sort of continuous party went on until Monday morning. Mr. Glazer trotted through the assemblage, ignoring the entertainment and the championship tennis court, bent on his own pursuits. He was interested in fine china and *objets d'art*, in carpentry work, in watching over his dogs who were getting old and decrepit and kept falling into the swimming pool; the dogs, when they hurt themselves, would huddle motionless and just wait until Mr. Glazer came hurrying up, to scold and take care of them. With his open generosity, he took pains to make sure I felt easy among the company at those parties, and I visited his home often, appearing on most of the weekends. Many kinds of people were there, but mainly the old-timers, men who were firmly a part of the movie business—grizzled and heavy-eyed, patient, pestered by arthritis, sciatica, and other vexations. They smiled at me. They were amused by my inexperience and newness to their community. They liked me and I think they wanted to be liked. But they would never parry my questions. They wouldn't respond to my inquiries and doubts. They knew that if I was to learn anything about their way of living and working, it would be no good unless I found it out by myself. "I would argue with you," one of them said to me, "but if I win the argument, what do I win?" They had their minds set on other things, and time was short.

*   *   *

Not long after I came to Hollywood, I was asked by my studio—not RKO, another studio—to help work on a picture which was shot and done, which was in a rough cut, but which had gone awry along the road. The picture was a mystery spy-thriller, the kind of story the English write so expertly. Our English novelist was one of the best; his novel had been adapted by an able, conscientious screenwriter; the producer and director were also thoroughly seasoned and professional. The trouble lay in the star. If you examine these English spy-thrillers, you find that they're almost invariably concerned with an innocent: the hero is guileless and sweet, he is suddenly assaulted by a bewildering collection of circumstances; he gropes, is buffeted; he holds on, out of a perverse stubbornness; he digs in, perseveres; little by little the truths are revealed to him; he is chastened, matured, and the picture is over. That's how these stories go. But our star would have nothing to do with innocence. He adamantly refused to play the part as written. There was no use in blaming him. He had built up a personal identity over the years as a trenchcoated, hardboiled character who knew the world; he believed in this characterization and had prospered with it; and from his point of view it would have been senseless to jettison everything for the sake of a single picture. Nor could you fairly blame the studio management— there are just so many stars around and you take the best one you can get. So I could understand the star, I could understand the studio; I was inside the business now, and knew these were realities that had to be met. But the essential conflict between the star and his part produced a chaos—when the picture was put together—that was amazingly complex and convoluted. Every story value was bewitched. The film raced on its sprocket holes; people glided about, as in dreams; telling points were certainly being made, except that you didn't know what they told, you didn't know what you were supposed to think or feel. I was confounded. I didn't know even how to begin. To add to my predicament, by a quirk of fortune, I was thrown into this assignment by the studio, required to work in tandem with a collaborator who was no less than one of perhaps the ten most important literary figures in the world. I was paralyzed by awe. It happened that I had a deep, longtime admiration for this man and his achievement. I couldn't blurt out my esteem. It was almost impossible for me to hold conferences with him, to exchange notions and story ideas in the free, knockabout way that is our

the situation might be. I was bereft. I liked my collaborator, and was failing him. I had seen enough of the people at Mr. Glazer's home to be genuinely respectful. I was touched by their quality; I wondered at them and was attracted and wanted some day to be part of them. And yet they were failing me, or I was failing them. Out of my haplessness and distress, I became furtive. I started keeping out of sight. I slipped off the lot. They say the first delivery is the hardest, but in our case, with my wife and me, it was the second—we were having a new baby at the time. I received sudden emergency calls, and bolted. Toward the end I stayed close to the hospital and was gone from the studio for days at a stretch. And then abruptly, miraculously, everything was calm. The fever was over. Everything that needed to be done was done. The scenes had been photographed; the picture was re-assembled; the front office was pleased. Suddenly, late one Saturday afternoon, I found myself with my collaborator sitting in the producer's office, the producer there thanking us for our contributions to the job, still apologizing because he had unavoidably neglected us. All endings are sad, no matter what they are the ending to, and few places are as peaceful and benign as a movie lot when the work has halted and everyone has left. The producer was mellow, worn and humble in spirit, as we are after a crisis.

"I'll think of you," he said to my collaborator—my collaborator was leaving us, on his way back to his home in the heart of the nation.

"I'll think of you too," my collaborator said, eyeing us both somberly, thinking no doubt of the turmoil, the business with the sound stage; my peculiar behavior, and the mysterious phone calls. "I'll think of you too," he said, implacable and without mercy to the last, "in the middle of the night."

The wonder was the picture. It was whole now, sound—the myriad nerve-lines of continuity in working order, the conglomeration of effects artfully re-juggled, brisk and full of urgent meaning. With the unsettling irrelevance of life everywhere, when I was in the Navy years later, during the war, I was assigned to the OSS, the intelligence agency, and on one of the first days this old spy-thriller movie was duly shown to us in the official course of our orientation. My collaborator, talented but benighted, had been mistrustful. He had been discomfited by the things we had seen, was affronted and disapproving, and passed on. But for me what had taken place was now in the nature of a phenomenon. I knew a massive exertion had been put forth. I knew it was a head-breaking feat of will and strength, a feat certainly beyond me. I thought of the producer, overworked and beset on all sides, doggedly bearing down on his task, never once letting himself lose heart. My mind went back to the director, with his scarf, with his erect, courtly posture and reticence, with his accumulation of who knew what special lore within him. "Isn't Fitzwilliam wonderful?" his bride had burst out impetuously to a group of us waiting in the anteroom, that morning of our first meeting. She was entranced, glowing. "He's shooting his next picture in Tahiti, and he's taking me along. He's so good to me. Oh, I love him. He is the only man in the world I could ever care for." He was sixty; he lived, we had heard, in a mansion under dark pines near the mansions of Hearst and Doheny, raced thoroughbreds from Ireland, had been to sea and had wrangled horses in Wyoming in his youth. Working in private, disregarding sightseers, outsiders, and all other distractions, this elegant, strange man had struggled with the film with a dedication and intensity that I could well imagine but couldn't fathom, and hadn't rested until he had conquered it.

We tested our pictures in Huntington Park, in out-of-the-way small towns, towns still undeveloped and straggling. This was what the studios went by—the audience's reaction. It was bedrock for them, holy writ— the rest, all other criteria, they waved aside with a blunt, contemptuous indifference. Banks of lights were set up on top of the marquee—MAJOR STUDIO PREVIEW TONITE—and the people would come gathering in the chill of evening, drifting up to the theater, to the blaze of light, in their jeans and stiff cotton house dresses, their eyes wavering and uncertain. They were field hands, workers in the citrus groves; they were miscellaneous day laborers, filling-station attendants, people newly resettled from Oklahoma and Arkansas. I saw them in our great drugstores, wandering through the gaudy aisles, staring in silence at the gewgaws and confections on the shelves, spending their money on objects which, when they took them home, they must have surely realized were unneeded and a waste. I used to stand in front of the theater and look at their loose, yielding faces, and wonder what kind of pictures could be given to them; if it was possible to reach them in any important, meaningful way; if it even made sense to try. And yet, once they were inside the movie house, a transformation occurred. Others have remarked on it. In the dark, forming a mass, they lost their individual disabilities and insufficiencies. They became informed; they became larger than themselves; a separate entity appeared, an entity that was knowing and complete. Unfamiliar and demanding as the material might be, no matter how deeply probing or delicate and sophisticated the treatment, if the picture was good, they were unfailingly affected by it and gave it its full measure of appreciation. I witnessed it again and again, with the unlikeliest pictures, so that I was soon able to understand why the studios put such store on these sneak previews, so that I began to share their faith, so that I myself have now come secretly to believe—secretly, since I know it isn't so—that good pictures will always command a mass audience; that if a picture fails to find this mass following, then it is in reality spurious and without substance. In an interview in *Life* magazine, Joseph L. Mankiewicz said (I quote freely, from memory): "The most electrifying thing happens in the movie house when you give the audience the truth." I knew exactly what he meant. You could almost tell the instant the picture took hold. An excitement filled into the theater, a thralldom. The people forgot they were sitting on the seats; they forgot themselves, their bodies. They lived only in the film. They were tumbled, swept along, possessed. Of course Mr. Mankiewicz didn't mean it could be just any truth. It had to be a carefully selected truth, carefully aligned and ordered. It had to be a truth that was worthy and could legitimately engage an audience. It had to have an opulence; or an urbanity; or a gaiety; a strength and assurance; a sense of life with its illimitable reach and promise. As a matter of fact, it didn't even have to be the truth. Properly stated, the sentence should have read: "The most electrifying thing happens in the movie house when you give the audience—"

No one knew. Wizardry was involved. The studio people, with their unrelenting practicality, held solely with the instinct of the audience. These standards were basic, material, solid; everything else was frippery and phoniness. The product here was tested, exposed. There was no opportunity for illusion or deception. You saw the proof. And yet the exasperating dilemma remained that what you were to give the audience was a quantity really indefinable, ephemeral, everlastingly elusive. Here was the heart of the problem, the problem that was to plague and occupy me in all my time in the studios. It lay at the bottom of the com-

motion that went on in these places. It accounted for much of the puzzling behavior—the excesses, the hi-jinx, the strife and alarms, the wild,
demented flights. It was a tantalizing, almost constantly frustrating pursuit, and the movie people gave themselves over to it with a tenacity that
amounted to a kind of devotion.

We screenwriters shifted about from studio to studio, staying on one
lot for a spell until a disenchantment set in and we were let go or left of
our own volition and moved on to the next. Traveling around the studios, listening to the gossip at the different writers' tables in the commis-
saries, I heard stories about a certain outstanding movie executive who
soon caught hold in my imagination and with whom I eventually became
entangled. He was one of the industry's pioneers, had built his studio
from the street up. Like the courtly director to whom for the sake of convenience I gave the fictitious name of Fitzwilliam, he also had come out
of a dim, adventurous background. He had been a bootlegger, a prizefighter, had participated in mean, degrading enterprises, had also roamed
through the solitary towns of the Far West fifty years back. The studios,
most of them, were not prepossessing establishments; they had been put
together haphazardly over the years, additions stuck on to existing structures, projection rooms interspersed among the wardrobe and accounting departments, the whole clutter connected by a maze of stairways,
ramps, crosswalks, balconies—and this movie executive prowled rest-
lessly at all hours through the maze at his studio, looking for employees
to pounce upon, for lights that should have been turned out and were
left burning, to make trouble in general. He was a low-slung, pugnacious
man, thoroughly hated, grasping and always dissatisfied. "Your husband's
just like me, we both don't care for money," he said to my wife one
evening at a party—this was later, when I had become mixed up with him
and he and I knew each other—and my wife shrieked with glee from the
shock. It was a totally unexpected, bizarre remark, coming from him.
"He put more people in the cemetery than all the rest of them com-
bined," a man once told me about him, sincerely marveling, big-eyed
and solemn. The way I came to meet him, I was calling on a friend of
mine, a much sought-after director who was making a picture at his studio; my friend and I were weaving through the maze of staircases, going
out to the street, when the movie executive, coursing on his rounds there,

saw us and promptly nabbed us. It was my friend's birthday that day, and the executive—courting him aggressively at the time, the disenchant-ment not yet having set in—insisted on celebrating the occasion, on having a drink with him, and so he dragged him back up to his office, I tagging along. Upstairs in the office, he was rattling around the room, working on my friend and putting on a show, when he suddenly broke off and turned to me. "What kind of a writer are you anyway?" he said harshly, hurriedly, getting it in. "Some people tell me you're good, other people tell me you stink."

I winced, confused and dazed, not so much offended—confused to think, in the flurry of the moment, that he had heard of me, that he knew who I was, and let down because he had expressed himself so dismally. He went right on with his shenanigans, but he had seen that wince on my face and it irked him, I could tell—it was in him to be affected because I was disappointed in him, that he had been rushed and hadn't been able to do well by himself. It stayed in his mind and rankled. From that meeting on, he kept having me brought over to his office to offer me a number of picture assignments, assignments which for one reason or another were unsuitable and I couldn't accept. He put himself out for my benefit. He became impish, teased me, revealed the softer side to his nature. "Keep quiet," he said to the coterie of assistants who surrounded him, shushing them. He wanted to do all the talking. "He didn't come up here to hear you. He heard the legend—now let him see the man," he said, and turned and faced me, grinning.

"What's the matter, you don't like my money?" he chided me, as I passed up his assignments. "You got a better job some place else? What are you trying to prove to me, that you're a fine rabbi? You giving me the con, getting me fat and sweet, and then you'll move in and make a killing?" He couldn't believe a writer would turn down an assignment just because the material was unsuitable. He thought there had to be a deeper, intricate motivation. He thought that I was maneuvering. "Every-body that walks into this office is a prostitute," he said. "They don't come in here unless they're out for something. Everybody cares only for their self-interest. Here, I'll show you—I got it right in my desk . . ." He pulled the paper out. It was a garish act of betrayal by some close relative, a son or a brother. They had manipulated stock against him, had labored in an effort to push him out of his company. The betrayal had occurred many years ago, but he always kept the letter of dismissal with him—it was a comfort, he needed to believe that people were base and abject.

The funny thing was there was some substance to his suspicions about me. His studio owned a story, the basis of a story, which I liked very much and kept secretly angling for. During those turbulent interviews in his office, in the ebb and rise, I would persistently refer to this story property, mentioning what a fine picture I thought it would make, murmuring how I would be pleased to be allowed to work on it.

"You don't want to do that story," he ground out at me. "You just want to hit me for a big pot of money. If you really want to write it, if you got your heart and soul so set on it, then why don't you write it—who's stopping you?"

He had me. I didn't know how to answer him, and one day, after a difficult session, sawing back and forth, listening to his explosions and the flow of his bitter cynicisms, I finally agreed to go in with him in some loose, percentage arrangement, proceeding more or less on a speculative basis; and so that was how I came to work for him, that was why he told my wife I didn't care for money. I did, in fact, have my heart in the story. I sometimes think a successful motion-picture story is so complex and impossibly constituted that you don't really write them—that they already exist and that you *find* them, that they're either there, somewhere, or else you're doomed. This was one of those stories, touched with grace and blessed. It went kindly. It became vigorous and spunky with life. I found, and firmly, the dramatic incubus, that enveloping cloud of anxiety against which a man moment by moment pits himself and which thereby gives a story its never-ceasing, insidious thrust. I found the theatrical image of my hero, the humor—that dancing bundle of slants, deceits, stratagems by which a man conceals his despair and which gives him an instantaneous hold on the attention of the audience. Best of all, what delighted me, was a lyricism—I caught, and was able to show, those innermost dreams and raptures the steady dissolution of which infuses a man's despair with meaning and a piercing, significant emotion.

"It's a wonderful story," he told me, when I had finished it and had turned it in. He had stayed up all night with the script, I knew; he had studied it meticulously, section by section. I sang inside of me. He knew the story perfectly, savored each value, each shading. "It's the story of you and your wife," he twitted me. "It's autobiographical. You can't make up things like this. They have to happen. It's the best story I ever read," he said, crashing down on me. "I wouldn't touch it with a ten-foot pole—it'll be a colossal flop."

He wouldn't touch it because nobody was interested in horse-race betting (if we assume the subject of this story had to do with the horses), but he flung that out carelessly, on the run; because it was different, fluky; because it wasn't enough for a picture to be original—just because a picture was new and different, it didn't necessarily mean it would go; because it was ambitious and hard to manage and fragile; because if a story like this one miscarried, it would splatter and become a hideous, total fiasco; because a screenplay was nothing but a blueprint, a declaration of hopes and intentions; because it needed actors, handlers, diviners who would know surely what to do with it and who could be counted on to bring it off. "Get me a big star," he said, in spite of his arguments, reversing himself, "and I'll do it. Get me a big director," he told his subordinates, and they in turn came hurrying to tell me; and it struck me, so that it remains with me still, how this harsh, rampaging man, who was universally detested, whose fingers were fearfully twisted with arthritis, who just recently had undergone surgery for cancer (a secret, which I knew only through the indiscretion of a friend, a doctor), although, oddly, it was a heart seizure that took him off a year and a half later—it struck me how he fiercely persevered with his obsession, asking no quarter, staying up all night in the dead quiet of his studio.

While I was at the studio on this bout, it happened that an old acquaintance was simultaneously working there. He was brought in on a one-picture deal, a picture that he had initiated and was to produce for the management. As could be predicted, he quickly became embroiled with the executive, and I had an inside view of their curious, intensive battle over the stretch of months. This acquaintance was a man I knew from earlier days in New York; he was a brilliant Broadway producer with a distinguished record of successes, who also at intervals busied himself in motion pictures and who—I never clearly understood why, because he said I reminded him of all his uncles—had befriended me and took a continuing, fitful interest in my welfare. He was a vivid individual, with a surging, autocratic style. He had made fortunes, had lost them, acted on fancy and was always on the move. He would come swooping down on me in Hollywood, find out what I was doing, immediately rant and lash out at me for wasting my time; he would call up my agent and fire him, call up the heads of the studios where I was working (people who most often didn't even know I was in their employ), drub them in the most forceful, intemperate language—"He's working for *you*? You should be working for *him*"—hang up and go spinning off again, to resume his journeyings. "Don't, *don't* write short stories about me," he would say, grimacing with distaste, after he had read in a magazine some piece of disguised fiction I had written about him, "novels, *novels!*" He lived in a cocoon. "A son is a fantasy," he would say, his eyes shining, believing in children, in whatever would enhance life. "You don't have to excite yourself and try to show me how bright, how talented you are—just listen," he would say, when I would think of something to add to the conversation. He wanted to do all the talking too. "Read *Life on the Mississippi*." "Never write about people who can't manipulate their destinies." And he would hustle out to the airport, get himself settled in his sleeping berth on the plane, take a dose of sleeping tablets, tuck the blankets tidily around him, and be wafted off to London or Peru.

But during this period I'm writing of, he was anchored, in disgrace with fortune, obliged to work out a term at the studio, and so this made two of them, my friend and the executive. They went at it hammer and tongs, the executive with a grinning relish, almost grateful, it seemed to me, to have such a willing, supple adversary at hand. They fought over the casting, over hairdressers, over gowns, over lines of dialogue, over each separate word. I watched them cut each other up almost daily when they met at lunch in the studio's private dining room. But underneath the clash of wills and the tumulting, what was really provoking them, if the truth was known, was the old basic problem of the picture, the familiar welter of uncertainties and indecisions. The mind became cauterized; it was a torment to hold on to the over-all vision of the picture—the lines of the continuity, the component sequences, the proper working place of everything in the design. It wasn't enough to go on hope or intuition or instinct. You could take nothing on sufferance. You had to *know* every moment what was happening in the picture; you had perpetually to control and understand each stroke and effect—and it was easier for them to hack away at themselves in these senseless spasms than to go on wrestling with the riddles. Just as Mr. Louis B. Mayer over at Metro had a sentimental attachment to chicken-noodle soup and provided it at less than cost at his studio's commissary, so, similarly, pickles meant something to our executive; once a week or once every two weeks, whichever it was, the great black truck from the pickle-works drew up to the curb with its terrible smell, bringing us fresh supplies—and my friend, boring in assiduously, fiendishly belabored the executive on the score of this human frailty, taking a ruthless advantage of every opening. "You're common. You fill yourself with junk. You come from a low-class, first-generation tenement life and you're still stuck away there in that Yiddish *pippik*. That's why you're worth only a measly five or six million. You have no taste, no sense of literature."

At the time the contracts were worked up, there had been a hard wrangle over the control of the picture—my friend was determined not to let the executive have the say-so over him. The executive had craftily agreed, conceding the point, stipulating only that he, the executive, was to be brought in as arbiter in cases where my friend had differences with the other principals—the stars, the director. It proved to be a peculiarly constraining condition—a straitjacket, an affliction. My friend, who thought that he and only he alone saw the picture true, was unable to flash fire and impose orders; he had to cajole, plead—there were even excruciating instances when he had to give ground. His chest broke out in a profusion of boils. I can remember the sight of him, hurtling blindly from wall to wall in the murky maze of the staircases. I can see him now as he once went slamming over the pavement of the parking lot, panting and clawing at his chest, vowing that he wouldn't be beaten, that he would stick it out no matter what the cost. "I'll get along with everyone," he affirmed breathlessly, lost in his fervor. "Nobody'll be able to say I'm temperamental. I'll be sweet. I'll be charming—they won't even recognize it's me." As the weeks rolled on, his madness broke loose and he went past all rational behavior. He communicated with the executive in a series of wicked, fanatically labored-over, anti-Semitic memos. As the picture neared completion and everyone could see it would be at last a wonderful, resplendent hit, as the New York office of the film company tried to entice him and keep him at the studio for further commitments, he flared out into the most searing, impossible demands—that the executive was to be forbidden ever to speak to him, that the executive was to keep himself out of view. "If I walk into the private dining room and he's sitting there eating, he has to get up and leave." He wanted that put into the contract. But the New York office, in courting him, trying to keep him at the studio, was only speaking for the executive; it was the executive who was really courting him—in spite of the vilification, in spite of the pickles and the wretched memos.

It was a strange preoccupation they had, my friend and the executive, and it chivvied them in countless ways, without let-up. Passing along through the studios in the game of musical chairs we played, I continually met with this ferment, with this reckless expenditure of energy and clamor. I never knew Mr. Mayer, was only introduced to him three or four times; but he was of course a stalwart figure, no doubt the most obstreperous of the breed, and I often glimpsed him in action, moving here and there with his retinue, vigilantly attending to everything. He walked like a czar. Jules Dassin—then beginning as a director, treading carefully—once made a photographic study of his leading lady, shading her face with the flickering play of leaves, and Mr. Mayer swiftly had him on the carpet for the shot, upbraiding him for the shadows, wanting nothing that would mar the clear, crystalline beauty of his company's stars. He lectured Jules severely on the point, so that Jules told me of the incident, startled by the older man's vehemence, by his notions, by his odd possessive insistence. It was deep personal involvement with Mr. Mayer, a seemingly life-and-death concern. When I returned to Metro on an assignment after the war, they were making *The Postman Always Rings Twice*, a picture of the violent category to which Mr. Mayer was powerfully opposed; and I was seriously cautioned for my own good never to speak of this picture aloud—it was in production on the lot and we were all to behave as though it wasn't there, he wasn't to hear of it. Years later, when the dice had taken another roll and he was out of the studio, fallen from favor, I saw him one evening at a party—idling by himself on the fringes now, no one any longer obliged to listen to him. I was again introduced to him, Miss Lillian Burns plucking me by the sleeve and bringing me over to him. He smiled graciously, in spite of adversity; he started to offer me his hand; and then Miss Burns, a vivacious lady with an impudent, mischievous bent, went on to mention the name of a picture I was at that particular time associated with, a big hit which was also of the category he despised—and he instantly took his hand back, turned on his heel and stalked off, still haughty, still fierce, indomitable. . . .

I knew of a certain director, a veteran, master moviemaker, well-tempered and suave, who one day—in the heat and struggle—suddenly went raving wild at his writer (thank God, not me), raging that the writer didn't know his craft, that he hadn't applied himself, that he hadn't been willing to dig into the *bones* of the work, that he hadn't broken his head enough at those devastating sneak previews which were our testing grounds.

I remember a curious experience with Billy Wilder: I had seen his *Sunset Boulevard* twice, was greatly moved by this work of art, sent him a fan letter. A little while later it happened that I met him for the first time, and to my astonishment he spent the greater part of our meeting inquiring into a section of the film—the section in which the hero first wanders into that gauzy, soft-lit mansion of Norma Desmond, the faded movie star. The picture was out, playing in the houses, acclaimed, but the sequence still vexed Mr. Wilder. He didn't know what was working there, why it should be sound. He wasn't on top of it, couldn't rationalize it; and he worried away at the problem, probing and trying to reassure himself. In another case, not far from the studio where *Sunset Boulevard* was made, a writer-director—who had finally rationalized his picture, who knew in his heart he controlled and was on top of it—was nevertheless engaged in a furious running feud with the head of his studio (always the same pattern, always somehow that grueling, drawn-out battle between the two). "I'm so sure this will be the biggest disaster we've ever had in the history of the studio, that I'm putting it in writing," the head of the studio wrote him, dating and signing his memo. The writer-director swept on, uncaring. They tested their picture in some small town up north, Sausalito or San Anselmo—and the audience howled it down, they ripped it to pieces. Everything went wrong. The writer-director disappeared for days. No one knew where he was or what was happening to him. But then there he was back at the studio again, locked up in the cutting room, working over the Moviola, grim and spinning and searching, never pausing until he got it right. He won out in the end—the picture became one of the all-time classics, the studio was festooned with honors. . . .

It was always surprising how underneath the outcries and confusion the work steadily went on. They never slackened; fighting the *malach ha-moves* and the dingy seepage of time, they beat away to the limits of their strength and endowments, striving to get it right, to run down the answers, to realize and secure the picture. I was once brought in with a producer and director, a famous mismatched pair who were noted for their rows and the rigors of their professional efforts, and so this time I was in the eye of the storm, caught up in the middle between them. This producer's trouble was his compassion, his kindliness and understanding. He had lived five lifetimes in one, was intelligent, sensitive, and had a ready, inundating sorrow. "Darling, sweetheart, why are you blue?" he would beseech his gifted partner, pursuing him. "Do you want my beach house? Do you want my boat, my car?" In retaliation, the director—who was the one I was supposed to work with—savagely turned himself inside out to think up new ways of torturing him. He was harrowed enough with the dilemmas of the script—"they expect us to work up a screenplay out of a ketchup label." He contrived mean, elaborate practical jokes. We took off in all directions, traveling by train and plane—ostensibly for purposes of research, to scout locations. We crisscrossed the country. We were gone for weeks and the weeks turned into months. The director entertained royally wherever we went, holding big drinking parties every day before and after dinner, sitting down thirty and forty guests at a clip for dinner, everything charged to the producer. The producer wept and fumed at long range, laying the blame on me.

"That's why I put you in with him—to watch out and be a restraining influence," he reproached me piercingly over the phone, all hot and scrambled. "Him we knew for a lunatic, that was foregone. But you are a family man, with responsibilities—why do you conspire with him against me?"

"*I'll* speak to him," the director said to me that day in the hotel room, taking the phone from me. "Ben," he declaimed into the mouthpiece, speaking in his hearty, royal way, "how are you?"

"Don't ask me how I am; never mind how I am!" the producer railed at him, his voice whirling aloft, and for a minute or two I could hear him carrying on there in his frenzy three thousand miles away.

"Ben, I've got good news for you and bad," the director boomed, unperturbed.

"Don't tell the bad!" the producer wailed. "Bad news I got, all I can use. I don't need more. Only tell me the good—what is the good?"

"Ben, we are leaving New Orleans tonight."

"Darling, sweetheart!" the producer cried, ecstatic, gushing, everything changed—bygones would be bygones; they would forget what transpired; they would go forward now only in harmony. "So what is the bad news—what can be bad?"

"We're going to New York," the director said.

It went on like that on that trip and on other trips, for a number of years, in great capitals and over four continents. I dropped out, to work for other directors and producers, but they skirmished along, harassing each other day by day, the director systematically making the producer's life a hell, the two of them evolving in the meantime between them a group of the most beguilingly rare, iridescent productions—until at last the director shamed himself irreparably before the producer and was forced to bring their relationship to a permanent end. "Darling, sweetheart," I can still hear the producer crying, desolate and engulfed, his eyes hungering to forgive, to forget, to let bygones be bygones. But the director had offended too deeply and there was no going back for him. "If I could only find an honest Ben So-and-so," he often mutters to himself, pining for his friend, disconsolate and wretched.

They knew the wandering lassitude of the will, the essential human servitude and unworthiness. They knew how loathsome it was to be obliged to transgress, to commit iniquity and betray, and that the pity was with the wrongdoer. They were a chastened crew, with a wry, flickering wisdom. Coming out of their raw, bustling background, combing the earth with their energy and avid need for pleasure, they had the kind of education you get in the prize ring—not from hearsay or from precept. They knew the *guderim*. Isn't it true that a good deal of what we know of the world comes from these men—from their pictures, from their lore? Isn't it true that they have had an amazingly penetrating effect, people in countries all over the globe running eagerly to see their pictures, to share in their virility, in their realism and gusto and command of life? I think it is a foolish scandal that we have the habit of deriding these men and their industry, that it is the mode. Is it fitting to pass by so indifferently the work of Ford, Stevens, Wilder, Mankiewicz, Huston, Zinnemann, William Wellman, Howard Hawks, Sam Wood, Clarence Brown,

Victor Fleming, Willard Van Dyke, King Vidor, Raoul Walsh, Henry Hathaway, Henry King, Chaplin, Lubitsch, Goldwyn, Selznick, Milestone, Capra, Wyler, Cukor, Kazan? They were a gaudy company, rambunctious and engrossed. What they produced, roistering along in those sun-filled, sparkling days, was a phenomenon, teeming with vitality and ardor, as indigenous as our cars or skyscrapers or highways, and as irrefutable. Generations to come, looking back over the years, are bound to find that the best, most solid creative effort of our decades was spent in the movies, and it's time someone came clean and said so.

There is no RKO any longer. The studio on Gower Street is given over to other pursuits. The child who was born that day, when I was struggling with the mystery-thriller with my distinguished collaborator, is now full grown, busy with his own affairs, away from home. In the middle of the night the phone rings and we rouse from sleep. "It's Adele," my wife says to me, carefully covering the mouthpiece with her hand to spare the caller's feelings, and then she removes her hand and they go on talking over the phone. Adele is a once famous star, now inactive, unwanted, the years having flown. We don't know Adele and she doesn't know us. Originally she was looking for some people named Ridgway, a family who used to live in our house. She knows the Ridgways aren't here, my wife tells her; but she likes the sound of my wife's voice, it is a solace, and in the dead hours of the night she continues to phone, prolonging this curious friendship that has formed between us. "Is this Mr. Ridgway's residence?" she begins shyly, and my wife says no, soft and solicitous, and they commune.

How illusory is the nature of desire; how wonderfully strange and various are the strivings of the hidden heart. Long ago, I was assigned (by the same diligent, untiring producer who was involved in the mystery-thriller upset, not that it matters) to help with a story of backstage life which was supposed to be fictitious but was actually based on the true experiences of another star, an actress then at the height of her success, fresh and vibrant, with that incredible shining beauty they have. When she was fourteen years old, she had been tampered with by a passing entertainer. Her aunt, with whom she lived, was an ambitious woman. She immediately took hold of the opportunity; forced the entertainer to marry her niece; left her own husband and latched on; and in this way the two of them, the aunt and the niece, escaped from their depression-ridden New England industrial town and gained a foothold in show business. The entertainer, burdened with a wife he didn't want and with this overbearing aunt in the bargain, ducked and weaved, eventually managed to shake free; he drifted off. The two went on by themselves. The girl scored, going straight to the top in one of those dazzling overnight leaps. The entertainer made a rapid turnabout, clamored after his wife, publicly protested he was being abandoned, slashed his wrists a little. A settlement was arranged; the matter was taken care of.

This was the story behind the star's rise to fame. These were the facts, bedraggled and humanly forlorn, as they were commonly known, as we had them to deal with. We improvised. We glossed. We inserted a few nobilities. The entertainer became a tragic figure, genuinely in love, genuinely bereaved; when he attempted suicide, he succeeded. The fourteen year old—now seventeen—was purely a victim, innocent and unthinking. We changed New England to Oklahoma; we made the aunt a sister, so that she might be more readily cast, sisters being less aged than aunts. We were having enough trouble trying to cast the leading role. For a long time we were stumped, it seemed altogether impossible to find the right actress. Acting on a sudden, desperate brainstorm, we decided to offer the part to the star herself. She read the script—astonishingly, it went straight past her. She never recognized herself in the drama. "You know," she said to us at lunch, as we were wooing her, "this might almost be the story of me and my aunt."

She turned us down, the part disturbing her, and in any case she was much too grand in those days for our modest project; the picture went out with another player. But the years passed by, twelve or fourteen, and it happened that we fell in with one another again, the actress appearing in another picture I was concerned with, amenable now, subdued. She knew by this time the backstage story had been about her—someone had told her or she had come to it herself; I often caught her glance upon my face—rueful, bemused. "Do you want to know what really happened, sonny?" she said to me one day on the set, when there was a lull in the activity, when we all stood by and everything idled.

She was dead game, conceding nothing to time. The legs were muscled, hard and used, the hard, unkind lines showing. That pearly, short-lived radiance was gone. I remembered the stories I knew about her, how when she used to make public appearances in the big movie houses, she would go darting up to the balcony between shows with a companion, to look at the picture, to neck.

There had been no tampering, no seduction. No one had had his way with her. There had been no hasty marriage. It had been all her own idea, on her own initiative. It was odd how the facts were scrambled. The entertainer had been a friend of the family, was going with an older cousin, was engaged. When she was fourteen years old, she had watched the courtship from the distance, had quietly set her cap for him. "I thought he was the handsomest man I had ever seen in my life," she told me that afternoon. "I wanted him. I made up my mind. I went for him. I got him. I knew how. And then, later . . ." She shrugged, her voice fell away; she turned aside, smiling and helpless, dreaming. "You change," she said. "Time passes . . ." She wandered off and left me—someone called her name. It was the time of day on the set when the mood grows gray, when the electricians and grips yawn and the work goes soft, when extras and bit players—out of monotony, to beguile the moments away —face one another and start jiggling on their feet, dancing by themselves in this unspoken, sleepy mockery, the faces of the girls flushed and wicked and tempted, when the air is filled with longing and the promise of better things seems just around the bend.

DREAM CITY,
OR THE DRUGGED LAKE

Alastair and Hilliard, the boy and girl of the original story, work on a radio program. Frank Pulps is the son of their chief advertiser, a dog food called Bandolo. He is a Robert Young type and loves Hilliard, who, however, loves Alastair. That is the springboard.

Pulps Senior is disappointed with advertising results and the boy-girl are fired, leaving Junior feeling bad since he is a Robert Young type. The boy-girl celebrate their discharge — this is a smart comedy — by throwing a party. At the party Alastair gets an advertising idea that is so good that Senior rehires them. Alastair is kidnapped, the work of rival dog-food makers. Junior rescues Alastair, and when he brings him back to the arms of Hilliard, he, a Robert Young type to the end, leaves them gaily but underneath feels that Biarritz, Long Island, and Newport will no longer mean much to him now as an extension of the Princeton campus.

That is the story, and my producer, Mr. Fox, told me it was great. Everybody liked it, only it wasn't so hot, and he asked me to see what I could do with it.

I tried hard in a half-hearted way, and I changed the story around here and there. It made no more, no less sense than before. That was not important. What disturbed me, from the beginning, was the complete pointlessness of the work. It was like a hot day, with the perspiration on your face glazed, a dry taste in your mouth, no ambition, nothing to do, nothing you want. It was like being in a pocket somewhere where nothing existed.

I finished the work and turned it in. Mr. Fox searched honestly in his mind for a moment or two, seeking a reaction to the stuff. He found none, said nonsense to fill in the time, knew he was saying nonsense, suddenly found no hope for himself and collapsed all at once. He just got tired of everything, I suppose. I went back to my office and waited.

Some days later the telephone rang. It was a sort of salesman and he asked me whether I would like to go to some hotel in Mexico. I said maybe. Somehow he understood me and let it go at that, but as an afterthought he left me with the statement that here, at that hotel, was the finest fishing in the world. I told him I was glad to hear it. After him, I read three acts of *King Lear*. The telephone did not ring.

The next day I looked at picture magazines. A man stuck his head into my room about noon and asked if I was Mr. Gordon. I thought about it until I was able to say, no, I wasn't Mr. Gordon. He shook his head in an understanding way. Later in the day I had another such visitor, who stayed about a half hour.

The funny thing for Wednesday was the men's room. I spent most of the day there. The first time I kept soaping my hands for twenty minutes, I think, just working the lather up in a dreamy way. Then I dried my hands and went back to my office. The telephone rang and a girl who talked as though her talking mechanism worked on compressed air asked me to find Mr. Astar or Astarre. I told her all right, all right.

"Don't you forget!" she barked at me. "Yes! Yes! We've been waiting an hour! Find him!"

"Yes! Yes!" I answered back to her. "I certainly will!"

"Don't you make fun of me!" she cracked. "See, I don't want it! Do you realize who you're talking to?"

I began to feel funny. "Yes! Yes!" I cried, mimicking her in a crazy way. I meant nothing, I was just unable to help myself. Then the man outside on the lot started playing his piano and singing probably a great hit that he was composing. It went like this: Oh, I ADORE you, ADORE you, ADORE you—you WONDERFUL thing! Well, I grew mixed up and I tried to assure the girl I would certainly unbend every effort to find Mr. Astar.

"Don't you call me a wonderful thing!" she bit off at me. "Don't you dare get fresh with me! You haven't heard the end of this, and what do you think of *that* for a fact?"

She hung up on me and it was so quiet, so I said "Yes! Yes! Yes!" into the dead receiver. Some people were passing my window and they looked at me. I think I made a good impression on them because I sounded forceful and tired, a good combination, indicating that I knew exactly what I wanted and was just a little impatient with the person on the other end of the telephone, but I wouldn't be giving in.

Then I went up into the men's room again and began hollering for Mr. Astar, but he wasn't there apparently. So there was nothing I could do and I began to soap my hands. I think this lasted at least an hour, although I want to be careful not to exaggerate anything here since it would ruin the whole intention of my report.

I didn't realize I was so long at the basin until my friend George came in. He told me it was funny but he was certain he had just seen me washing my hands. It was an illusion, he said—but it seemed to worry him. He asked me whether that had ever happened with me. I told him very often, especially with type: I'd read something and as I read it I'd begin to feel I had once read the very same words before. Only, the trouble with this, I said, was that actually I *had* read the words before. I grew a little confused about this, and George wasn't comforted by me. He said he would mention the phenomenon to his psychoanalyst. Then we got to talking about reincarnation, and he had to leave. He was waiting for his producer to call him, and I said that reminded me, I had something to do, too. I dried my hands, which smelled very clean by this time, and went back to the telephone. The composer outside was still working on the song about the wonderful thing I adore you, but now he was angry because he was singing everything in capitals, shouting out. I could illustrate this, but I suppose it really isn't necessary.

My wife telephoned. I asked her what was on her mind.

"That's good," she said. "Here you tell me to telephone you and I call you up and now you ask what's on my mind."

"Oh, yes," I said. "I must have been thinking about something else."

"This is sort of silly," she said. "You ask me to telephone you. I telephone you. Now what?"

"Oh, don't worry about it. I mean, it's nothing so terrible that you have to worry about it."

"Listen," she said, "something funny's going on."

"No," I said, hoping she would not get impatient with me. "By the way, what time is it?" She told me the time and I thanked her. Then we talked about what day it was. It was hard to settle, the way things sometimes are, and we fought about it for a little while. This kept up until she became annoyed and asked what difference it made what day it was, we had to stay in Hollywood ten more weeks anyhow.

"Well, anyway," I said, "it was nice to hear your voice. Call me up again, will you?"

"What for?"

"Oh, nothing. Just call me up."

"All right, what time?"

"Oh, about three or four."

"It's almost past four now!"

"Well, O.K. then. In that case just call me up when you feel like it."

The next morning Mr. Fox outlined a new story. It was a wonderful one, he said; the studio had paid twelve thousand dollars for it. It went like this: Harvey (a Robert Montgomery type, serious but funny) wants to study archaeology. That's all he has on his mind. But his father, a self-made businessman, wants him to learn a trade, to go into the plumbing business. They make a bet: If Harvey will prove a satisfactory plumber, go for two weeks without making a single slip, the father will be convinced that the son can take care of himself. Harvey can then go to Greece and explore. Otherwise he goes into the plumbing business. Harvey, now a plumber, meets Rosanna in a rich man's home. He mistakes her for a maid when in reality she is the daughter of the millionaire who owns the house. Their love story proceeds until they discover they are both rich men's children and can get married. Mr. Fox said there was room for many hilarious situations here because the premise, the springboard of the story, was a dandy one. He wanted to know what I thought of it, and whether I would be interested in working on it.

I said the story was terrible, really impossible, there was no use even talking about it. Mr. Fox didn't say anything but hovered, uncertain in his mind, looking at me in the meanwhile. I think he didn't know whether to get angry at me or what. Then suddenly he capitulated and agreed with me. He said I was right, what was the use. For some moments we both just sat in his office, looking sad, listening to some man outside on the lot yelling: "Oh, Charlie Humphries! Oh, Charlie Humphries!"

The silence, gentle as it was, was growing impolite. Mr. Fox slapped his thighs and hummed cheerfully, and I went out to my office. I sat down at my typewriter and began writing:

```
Is money worth everything?

Honesty is the best policy.

Life is too short.

Now is the time, etc. etc. etc.
```

I kept on typing like that, smoking my pipe and giving everyone who passed my window the impression I was a writer busy with my writing. Then I started studying the calendar I had on my desk, jumping the weeks to the time my contract would end. On the calendar that date didn't seem so far at all. It was something of a consolation, and I put on my hat and went home.

A HOLLYWOOD DIARY

April 26—For ten days I have been sitting around in my two-room office, waiting for some producer on the lot to call me up and put me to work on a script. Every morning I walk the distance from my apartment on Orchid Avenue and appear at the studio promptly at nine. The other writers pass my window an hour or so later, see me ready for work in my shirtsleeves and suspenders, and yell jovially "Scab!" But I don't want to miss that phone call.

I sent my secretary back to the stenographic department and told her I'd call her when I needed her. It was embarrassing with the two of us just sitting there and waiting.

Naturally, I can't expect an organization of this size to stop everything until I'm properly placed, but they pay me two hundred dollars a week and I do nothing to earn it. Himmer, my agent, tells me I'm getting "beans" and have no reason to think of the waste of money.

The main thing is not to grow demoralized and cynical.

A letter from home: "Hollywood must be different and exciting. Which actress are you bringing east for a wife?"

In the evening I walk down Hollywood Boulevard with all the other tourists, hoping for a glimpse of Carole Lombard and Adolphe Menjou.

And after I get tired of walking I drop into a drugstore, where, with the lonely ladies from Iowa, I secretly drink a thick strawberry soda.

APRIL 27 — The telephone rang today but it was only the parking-lot attendant across the street. He wanted to know why I hadn't been using the parking space the studio assigned to me. I explained I had no car, which left him bewildered.

The truth is I can't buy one. When I left New York I owned a five-dollar bill and had to borrow six hundred dollars from my agent to pay my debts and get out here respectably.

My agent is collecting his six hundred dollars in weekly installments of fifty dollars. Also taking nips out of my check are his twenty-dollar weekly commission, the California unemployment tax, the federal old-age relief tax, and the Motion Picture Relief Fund, so that what actually comes to me isn't two hundred dollars at all, and it would take some time to get enough money together for a car.

With all these cuts I'm still making more money than I ever earned per week. Just the same, I'm kicking. The trouble is, I suppose, that it's misleading to think of salary in weekly figures when you work for the movies. Hardly anyone works fifty-two weeks a year; my own contract lasts thirteen weeks.

Still no telephone call from any producer.

APRIL 28 — Himmer, my agent, dropped in. He doesn't seem worried by my inactivity. "The check comes every week, doesn't it?" he asks. "It's good money, isn't it?"

APRIL 29 — I was put to work this morning. Mara, a sad-looking man who produces B pictures for the studio, asked me to do a "treatment" of a story called No Bread to Butter. This is an "original" — a twenty-page synopsis of a picture for which the studio paid fifteen hundred dollars. Mara had put some other writers to work on treatments, but hadn't liked what they'd done any better than he liked the original. I didn't under-stand at all. Why had he bought No Bread to Butter if it was no good, I asked him. Mara smoked his cigar patiently for a while. "Listen," he said, "do I ask you personal questions?"

He wouldn't tell me what was wrong with the original or what he wanted. "The whole intention in the matter is to bring on a writer with a fresh approach. If I talk, you'll go to work with preconceived notions in your head. Tell the story as you see it and we'll see what comes out."

I went back to my office. *No Bread to Butter* seems to be a baldly manufactured story, but I'm eager to see what I can do with it. I feel good, a regular writer now, with an assignment. It appears to worry the other writers that I have found something to do at last. They seemed fonder of me when I was just hanging around.

I phoned Himmer to tell him the good news. "See?" he said. "Didn't I tell you I'd take care of it? You let me handle everything and don't worry." He talked with no great enthusiasm.

MAY 5 — The boys tell me I'm a fool to hand in my treatment so soon. Two or three weeks are the minimum time, they say, but I was eager to get the work done to show Mara what I could do. Mara's secretary said I should hear from him in the morning.

MAY 6 — Mara did not phone.

MAY 10 — No phone.

MAY 11 — No phone.

MAY 12 — Mr. Barry phoned. He's assistant to the vice president in charge of production and represents the front office. He called me at my apartment last night, after work. "Listen here, kid," he said, "I've been trying to reach you at your home all day. You've been out on the Coast a month now. Don't you think it's time you showed up at the lot?"

I protested, almost tearfully.

Seems that the administration building checked up on the absences of writers by the report sent in by the parking-lot attendant. Since I had no car, I hadn't been checked in. I explained, but Barry hung up, sounding unconvinced.

MAY 13 — Nothing.

The malted milks in this town are made with three full scoops of ice cream. Opulence.

MAY 14—Mara finally called me in today, rubbed his nose for a few minutes, and then told me my treatment was altogether too good. "You come in with a script," he explained. "It's fine, it's subtle and serious. It's perfect—for Gary Cooper, not for my kind of talent."

I tried to get Mara to make a stab at the script anyhow, but nothing doing. Naturally, I'm not especially depressed.

MAY 17—Barry, front-office man, called me up again, this time at my office. He told me Mara had sent in an enthusiastic report on me. I was a fine writer—"serious"—and fit only for the A producers. Barry, who is taking "personal charge" of me, told me to see St. John, one of the company's best producers.

St. John's secretary made an appointment for me for the morning. She seemed to know who I was.

MAY 18—St. John gave me a cordial welcome and told me he's been wanting to do a historical frontier picture but has been held up because he can't find the right character. He's been hunting for three years now and asked me to get to work on the research.

I told him frankly I didn't imagine I'd be very successful with this, but he brushed my objections aside.

I'm back at the office and don't know exactly what to do. I don't want to spend time on anything as flimsy as this assignment. Nevertheless, I phoned the research department and asked them to send me everything they had on the early West. This turns out to be several very old books on Texas. I go through them with no great interest.

MAY 19—Still Texas. Sometimes, when I stop to see myself sitting in a room and reading books on Texas, I get a weird, dreamlike feeling.

Frank Coleman, one of the writers I've come to know, dropped in and asked me to play a little casino with him, five cents a hand. We played for about a half hour.

MAY 21—Interoffice memo from St. John: "The front office tells me their program for the year is full and they have no room for an expensive frontier picture. Sorry."

I was struck again with the dreamlike quality of my work here.

Frank Coleman, who dropped in for some casino, explained St. John's note. When a writer goes to work for a producer, the writer's salary is immediately attached to the producer's budget. St. John simply didn't want to be responsible for my salary.

At any rate I'm glad to be free of the Texas research.

MAY 24 — Barry, front-office man, sent me to another producer, Marc Wilde, who gave me the full shooting script of *Dark Island*, which was made in 1926 as a silent picture. "My thought," said Wilde, "is to shoot the story in a talking version. However, before I put you to work on it, I want to find out what you think of it, whether you care to work on it, et cetera. So read it."

MAY 25 — I didn't like *Dark Island* at all, but I didn't want to antagonize Wilde by being too outspoken. I asked him what he thought of it. "Me?" Wilde asked. "Why ask me? I haven't read the script."

Coleman and I play casino every afternoon now.

MAY 26 — I've been coming to work at nine-thirty lately and today I walked in at ten. All the boys seem to like me now, and it is well-intentioned friendship, too. They pick me up at twelve for lunch at the commissary, where we all eat at the "round table." That is, the lesser writers ($100–$500) eat at a large round table. The intermediates ($500–$750) eat privately or off the lot. The big shots eat at the executives' table along with topflight stars and producers. They shoot craps with their meals.

We're at lunch from twelve to two. Afterward we tour the lot for an hour or so in the sunshine, just walking around and looking at the sets in the different barns. Then it takes us a half hour to break up at the doorway to the writers' building. When we finally go to our separate offices the boys generally take a nap. I took one, too, today. Coleman comes in at four for a half hour's play at the cards and then we meet the other boys again at the commissary for afternoon tea, which amounts to a carbonated drink called 7-Up. This leaves me a few minutes for these notes; I put on my hat and go home.

MAY 28 — My fingernails seem to grow very rapidly. It may be the climate or simply because I have more time to notice them.

JUNE 1 — Very lazy. I read picture magazines from ten-thirty until twelve. After that the day goes fast enough.

JUNE 3 — The story editor called me up today and said Kolb wants to see me. Kolb is second- or third-ranking producer on the lot; when I mentioned the news to the boys, they all grew silent and ill at ease with me. No casino, no tour, no tea.

Appointment with Kolb in the morning. Himmer, who dropped in, seemed impressed. "Kid," he said, "this is your big chance."

JUNE 4 — Kolb strikes me as a man who knows what he wants and how to get it. He is a short man, conscious of his shortness. He stands on his toes when he talks, for the sake of the height, and punches out his words.

It seems I have to take a special course of instruction with him before he will put me to work. We spent an hour today in friendly conversation, mainly an autobiographical sketch of Kolb, together with lessons drawn therefrom for my own advantage. I'm to return to his office after the weekend.

Coleman passed me and didn't speak.

JUNE 6 — Today Kolb described his system to me. You start off with a premise.

"Just for the sake of example," he said, "you take a girl who always screams when she sees a milkman. See, she's got a grudge against the milkman because a dearly beloved pet dog was once run over by a milk truck. Something like that — good comedy situation. Only, you must first invent a springboard." This is the scene that starts the picture, and Kolb wants it intriguing, even mystifying. "I'm not afraid of any man, big or small," he said, "but I shake in my boots when that skinny little guy in the movie theater begins to reach under his seat for his hat." The function of the springboard is to hold the skinny man in his seat. "For example, purely for example, suppose we show the boy when the picture opens. See, he's walking into the Automat. He goes to the cake slot. He puts in two nickels or three nickels, as the case may be. The slot opens and out comes—the girl! Is that interesting? Will the skinny guy take his hat? No, he wants to know how that girl got there and what's going to happen now."

Kolb started to continue with the complications his springboard made possible, but was still fascinated by the Automat girl. He considered for a while and then said, "What the hell. It's nuts!" Then he seemed to lose interest in the lesson. "Listen," he finally said, "the best way to know what I want is to see the actual products. You go down and see the stuff I've made." He told his secretary to make arrangements.

JUNE 7—Kolb's secretary sent me to a projection room, where I was shown three of his pictures. I understand what Kolb means by springboards. His pictures all begin very well, sometimes with shock, but the rest of the plot is a mess because it has to justify the outrageous beginning.

JUNE 8—Kolb's secretary phoned and told me I was to see three more Kolb *opera*. I sit all by myself in a projection room, thinking of Ludwig of Bavaria in his exclusive theater, and feeling grand too.

What impresses me is the extent to which these pictures duplicate themselves, not only in the essential material but in many details of character, gags, plot, etc.

JUNE 9—Three more pictures today.

JUNE 10—More Kolb masterpieces. He has been in movies for twenty years and must have made a hundred pictures.

JUNE 14—Today I was rescued from the projection room and was put to work. Kolb really shone with enthusiasm for the assignment he was giving me.

His idea was to rewrite a picture he did two years ago called *Dreams at Twilight*. If it pulled them in once, he said, then it would pull them in again. *Dreams at Twilight* involved a dashing, lighthearted hero who was constantly being chased by a flippant-minded girl. The hero deeply loved the girl, but avoided her because he was prejudiced against matrimony. "Sweet premise," Kolb said. "It's got charm, see what I mean?"

In addition to outwitting the heroine, the hero is fully occupied in the course of the picture: He is a detective and has a murder to solve.

"Now," Kolb said, "we remake the picture. *But*—instead of having the dashing boy detective, we make it a dashing girl this time. In other words, we make the picture in reverse. How's that for a new twist?"

He stood back in triumph and regarded my face for shock.

"Know why I'm changing the roles?" He whispered. His whole manner suddenly became wickedly secretive. "This picture is for Francine Waldron!"

I began to tremble gently, not because Waldron was one of the three most important actresses in Hollywood but because Kolb's mood was contagious and I had to respond as a matter of common politeness. When he saw the flush of excitement deepen on my face, he sent me off to work. He told his secretary to put me on his budget.

JUNE 15—I finished a rough outline of the Waldron script, working hard on it—nine to five, and no drifting about the lot. It's a bare sketch but I'd like to get Kolb's reaction to it before going ahead. His secretary, however, told me Mr. Kolb was all tied up at the moment.

I'm going ahead, filling in the outline rather than waste the time.

JUNE 18—Phoned Kolb's secretary, but he's still busy.

That peculiar feeling of dreamy suspension is very strong with me lately.

JUNE 20—*Hollywood Reporter* notes that Kolb has bought a property called *Nothing for a Dime*. It is described as a story in which a girl plays the part of a debonair detective, usually assigned to a man.

What's going on?

JUNE 21—Finished a forty-page treatment of the Waldron script and asked Kolb's secretary to show this to him, since he couldn't see me. She said he would get it immediately, and would let me know very shortly.

JUNE 22—Begins nothing again.

JUNE 23—Nothing.

JUNE 24 — Frank Coleman dropped in for casino — a depressing sign.

JUNE 25 — Barry, of the front office, called me in for a long personal interview. He told me that I was respected as a fine, serious writer, held in high regard. Was everything — office accommodations — suitable in every way? Then he said that the studio was putting me entirely on my own, allowing me to work without restrictions or supervision. The point was, I was an artist and could work without shackles.

At this point I interrupted and told him about the script I had written for Kolb.

"Kolb?" Barry asked. "Who says you're working for Kolb? He hasn't got you listed as one of his writers. You've been marked 'available' for twenty-four days now."

Nevertheless, I insisted that the story editor had sent me to Kolb, I had worked for him, and was waiting to see what he thought of my story. Barry didn't understand it. "Okay," he said uncertainly. "I'll see Kolb at once and clear this all up."

More and more confusing. What impresses me, though, is that I don't feel bewildered or affected in any way. It's as though I'm not the one who's concerned here. Other days, other places, I should have been, to put it mildly, raving. However, I did phone Himmer, my agent. He heard me out and said he would scout around and that I was not to worry.

JUNE 29 — Barry phoned. He had seen Kolb and Kolb didn't like my script. Would I please get to work on my unrestricted, unsupervised assignment?

I didn't know quite how to begin on a thing like that and so I decided to make a beginning after the weekend. Went to the commissary for a soda and bumped into Kolb himself, coming out. He beamed kindly at me. "Kid, I know what it is to wait around," he said. "I'm awfully busy at the moment but sooner or later I'll get around to reading your script." He patted my shoulder and left.

JUNE 30 — Himmer dropped in. "About that Kolb," he said. "I picked up the inside story. See, what it was was this: When Kolb came to put you on his budget he called up to find out what your salary was. That's how he found out you get two hundred."

"So?"

"So. Kolb figures he deserves the best writers on the lot. He told them he wouldn't put up with any two-hundred-dollar trash. It's a natural reaction."

We both sat there a while, passing time and talking about the administration in Washington.

"By the way," Himmer asked, "what kind of story did Kolb have you work on?"

"A business for Francine Waldron."

Himmer laughed genially. "Waldron has no commitments on this lot. She doesn't work here, you know."

We both laughed pleasantly at the strange mind Kolb had and what went on in it.

July 1 — Nothing worth noting.

July 12 — I asked Coleman over casino how the front office told you that you were fired. "They don't tell you," Coleman said. "They're supposed to pick up options two weeks before the contract expires. If they don't, they don't. That's all."

The two-week period with me began some days ago.

July 14 — I keep coming to work, although I understand this isn't really necessary. But it's pleasant to see the boys, who are touching in their solicitude for me.

July 15 — I came to work at ten-thirty this morning and found a genial, eager chap sitting at my desk in his shirtsleeves. "There must be some mistake," he stammered. "I'm new here. They told me to take this office."

I assured him there was no mistake. He seemed to be a fine fellow, sincere and impatient to start work. We sat around and chatted for an hour or so. While I cleaned up my desk, he had the embarrassed tact to leave me alone.

FLORIDA

Tafferty, president of Superb Productions, lay sprawled over the couch in his office and covered his eyes with his arms — limp, exhausted, hopelessly overburdened. Johnny Mantle bit his lip, worried by the performance the boss was putting on for his benefit. He talked fast.

"O.K., you're right," he began. "I admit it. Two rockets is a bust. It won't draw a dime at the box office, but—"

"Oh, don't worry about it, Johnny," Tafferty broke in, his voice soft and low with self-pity. "I know some studios want their producers to turn out money-makers exclusively. Not me. I'm different. I'll go to bat one hundred percent for any one of you young kids who want to make a high-class artistic picture, serious stuff like the French make. Listen, Johnny, is the money everything? Is that the *only* thing we sweat and struggle for out here?"

Talk fast, Johnny told himself, *talk fast*. "No!" he said. "You're being damned decent about it but I won't let you. Let them keep their Academy Awards. We want the box-office smashes, and I've got a sure-fire hit in the works for you right now. I mean this Florida script. A cavalcade of the state's history, from tropical waste to a great winter resort, all told through the ups and downs of one man's story. Wait till you see it.

39

Darryl Zanuck's heart'll break when he finds out we beat him to the punch. It'll be the biggest money-maker Superb ever had."

Tafferty let him talk but wasn't listening. "You got me entirely wrong, Johnny," he mourned. "You talk like I was bringing you up on the carpet or something. You got nothing to defend with me. I'm perfectly willing to take the rap for my producers. I'll be the fall guy. I don't care."

"You won't have to take any rap on my account," Johnny insisted. "I've got George Maderna reading the script. As soon as he takes the lead, we start shooting. With Maderna's name on the picture, it'll be a cinch. It'll net a cool million for the studio—and for *you*, Tafferty. A million!"

Tafferty flapped his hand hopelessly in the air. "Don't give it a second thought, Johnny. The bank back east is sending out a couple of men to look into things on the lot, but do I care? Am I worried? The hell with them. Ideals are sometimes more important than money." He rolled over on his side and showed his back to Johnny. "I'm so weary," he moaned. "I'd love to retire and leave all the headaches forever, but who would there be to take my place?"

Johnny opened his mouth but caught himself. He realized it wouldn't help to keep on talking. He left the boss on the couch and went down swiftly to the studio alley on his way back to his own office. One flop and the skids were readied beneath you. Johnny had left Broadway and the legitimate stage little more than a year ago but he had been out on the Coast long enough to recognize the signs. When the time came to put the knife into you, they always said they were forced to do the dirty work of somebody on top, and as soon as Johnny had heard Tafferty mention the bank people back east, he had gone cold inside.

He walked into his secretary's office.

"Get my wife on the phone," he told the girl. "Three things. I want her to turn in the closed car and order the most expensive custom-built job they have in the place. Tell her to get in touch with my insurance man and raise my endowment policies a hundred thousand dollars. And tell her to see the real-estate agent about a plot in Brentwood. We're building a new house. You have all that straight, Hazel?"

The girl was staring at him, her mouth open.

"What's the matter?" Johnny asked. "Won't that be enough to keep the wise guys from calling me a has-been?"

"My goodness," Hazel said, turning her eyes down tactfully. "I'm sure I don't know exactly what you mean, Mr. Mantle." She looked at her scratchpad. "Mrs. Mantle called this morning. She'd like you to phone back."

"She called up?" He reached for the phone but stopped. "Later," he said. "I'm going to lunch." He had no time. He hurried out to the commissary but it wasn't because he was hungry. He had to see George Maderna.

The top-flight stars, still wearing their heavy tan makeup, sat at the executives' table along with the big men from the Administration Building and with the A-picture producers. They rolled dice busily as they ate, but when Johnny came in, they all paused a moment to look at him. The dice stopped. News certainly traveled fast in Hollywood. They all knew he had been called up to Tafferty's office. Johnny saw the sly, pleased shine in their eyes but he smiled brightly right back at them. Free and easy, with nothing to hide, he went up to Maderna, slapped him on the back and took a chair next to him.

"The pace that kills," Johnny said. "Don't you guys ever stop gambling? You'll wear yourselves out."

"I'm down two hundred and seventy bucks," Maderna said. He knew Johnny wanted to see him about Florida and he looked uncomfortable already. "Did you ever hear of a lunch that cost two hundred and seventy bucks? No wonder I get peculiar sensations all the time. I abuse my digestive system by gambling too much. I'm a physical and nervous wreck."

Johnny gave his order to the waitress. The dice rolled again. He could read their minds as they ate and gambled. *Goodbye, Mantle,* they were saying to themselves. *Great guy, excellent personality, too bad he lost his touch so quick.* Maderna was probably thanking his luck and his agent that very minute because his contract contained an approval clause that permitted him to pass up a script he didn't like. Nobody wanted to work for a producer who was slipping, and Maderna didn't have to go into Florida. Johnny knew, too, that the other producers at the table were silently splitting up among themselves the names, scripts, and budgets he would have drawn, but he didn't take time to grow bitter about it. He wasn't through in Hollywood. One box-office flop might be enough to ruin you in this town but all it took to put you back on top again was one juicy smash hit. He told himself he'd keep after Maderna day and night until the star gave in and joined the cast.

The crap game broke up. Most of the high-priced talent went back to work but there were three or four men left at the table. Johnny stalled over his plate, waiting for them to leave so that be could tackle Maderna alone, but the waiter came up and told him he was wanted on the phone.

"Find out who it is," Johnny said. "Say I'll call right back."

"But it's Mrs. Mantle," the girl said. It was almost a rebuke. "She's waiting on the wire."

"All right," Johnny said and went into the little room where they kept the phone. "Yes, Vivian," he said.

"Oh, Johnny," she began, "about this new house and the car—"

"Yes, I know, Vivian. It sounds crazy but do as I say, will you, dear? I'll explain it all later."

"Well then, couldn't it wait until I see you first? I'd like—"

"I wish you'd go right ahead. It's really important to me."

"It can wait a day, can't it, Johnny? I'd like to see you first."

Time was passing. He'd lose Maderna in another minute. "All right, dear. All right, then, let it wait."

"Listen—don't hang up. Will I see you tonight?"

"Sure, dear. Of course."

"I mean for dinner. I haven't—"

"Yes, dear. Dinner."

"Well, let me finish." Her voice grew sharp. "I haven't had a chance to talk to you in a week. I hardly ever see you."

"Yes, dear. Tonight. I'll make it for dinner."

"*Yes, dear! Yes, dear!*" she cried at him angrily. "Don't be so impatient with me. Don't—"

"Now, Vivian—listen, kid—holy smoke! Don't be unreasonable. Don't let's fight around now."

"Oh, Johnny," she wept over the phone. "I want to hang up on you. I really ought to do it too, but I know I'll only be calling you up again to say I'm sorry. And then you'd have another phone call from me to be annoyed with."

"Honey, listen," he begged. "I'm all balled up here. Things are in a jam but they'll get straightened out soon and then everything will be fine."

"All right, go," she said tearfully. "Hang up. Goodbye."

"Honey, don't feel bad! Don't be mad at me!"

"All right. I'm not mad. I don't feel bad. Hang up."

"Yes, dear," he said helplessly. He put the phone back on the rest and rubbed his eyes for a moment. Then he straightened up, took a deep breath and went back to the executives' table, but Maderna was gone.

Johnny spent the next two or three hours hunting for him. The gateman reported the actor hadn't left the lot, but Johnny couldn't reach him any place by phone. There was nothing else for him to do but set out on foot and run him down. It was almost six o'clock when he finally walked into Maderna in the men's room at the songwriters' building. The actor was looking into the mirror, studying his face with great concentration.

"I don't think my senses are quite coordinated," he said solemnly. "I mean, for example, I touch something hot and I feel cold or neutral. I think I must be all shot to pieces inside."

"Listen, George," Johnny said. "How did you like the script?"

"Stinks."

"Why, George, George!" Johnny said, working up enthusiasm. "Man, you're passing up the dramatic opportunity of a lifetime. You'll be the biggest thing in Hollywood for years and years as a result of this one picture."

Maderna put his hand on Johnny's shoulder, interrupting him. "Another thing about me," he said. "I hear unrelated noises. Sometimes it's an organ playing highbrow music. Or else it's a man speaking in a hall. Oh, boy," the actor sighed, "if it's a neurosis I have, it's certainty exclusive with me. I defy anybody to classify it."

"Listen, just listen," Johnny begged, and then, right there in the men's room, finding the strength somewhere within him, he acted out the choice bits of the script. He talked for fifteen minutes without a stop. "Then you get the great inspiration," he cried, reaching the climax. "Your eyes get noble and dreamy just like Tyrone Power. 'I see a great state springing forth,' you say. 'I see millions flocking from the bitter northern cold to the health-giving rays of Florida.' Can you see it, George? Can you visualize it? It's terrific!" He stopped, covered with perspiration. He was breathing hard but his eyes flashed with hope.

"The worst thing," Maderna said slowly, "is my eyes. When I'm with people, I see their mouths open but I don't hear a thing. I tell you, Johnny, it's getting pretty serious, no fooling."

Johnny collapsed against the wall. Outside in the growing darkness for some time now, a man had been calling: "Johnny Mantle! Johnny Mantle! Johnny Mantle!" He left Maderna to his mirror and weakly made his way down to the alley.

"The boss wants you," the man told him. "He's been waiting ten minutes to see you."

Tafferty was pacing the floor when Johnny came into the office.

"I'll break down under the strain," the boss said promptly. "After all, I'm human just like anybody else, ain't I?"

"Yes," Johnny said. "Yes. What can I do?" It always made him nervous to see the boss put on an act.

"Everything devolves on me. I have to take care of a man called Dolgos tonight just because he owns the biggest chain of movie houses in the Middle West and the studio can't afford to hurt his feelings. We're giving him a stag dinner at the Anatole tonight and I'm just not up to it," he wept. "I give up. I've reached the breaking point at last."

Johnny winced, expecting the worst. "Yes?" he asked. "Yes?"

"Take over," the boss gasped feebly. "You'll have to go in my place. Take care of Dolgos for me."

"I can't," Johnny cried. "Tafferty, listen, I can't make it."

The boss wasn't listening. "I'm heading for a nervous breakdown," he was whimpering. He looked at Johnny. "Don't let me down!" he begged pathetically. "Don't let *Superb* down!"

There was no use arguing.

When he reached his own office, he felt too tired and hopeless even to turn on the light. He kept a suit of evening clothes and a stiff shirt in the place for emergencies like this, and he just lay down in the darkness until it was time to leave for the Anatole.

The nightclub was full of male celebrities, from the Superb lot and from other studios. Dolgos turned out to be a pleasant, mild-mannered man full of wonder at the fuss they were raising over him as well as at the strange ways of Hollwood. This had been his first visit and he couldn't get back to Kansas City fast enough. He was leaving on the morning plane. "My, my," he kept saying. "You boys certainly burn yourselves out to the ash."

Maderna was there too, elegant in tails but looking completely blank-faced. He was probably busy analyzing whatever sensations he was experiencing within him at the moment. Johnny decided to leave him alone tonight. He lay back in his chair, relaxing.

A man, passing by, stopped to say hello. It was William Drice. Drice had been chief at Domino two years ago. He was through now but he had never been able to realize it.

"Confidentially," the old man was telling Johnny, "confidentially I'm pretty tired dickering here and dickering there. Listen, I wouldn't be surprised at myself if I suddenly threw all those deals overboard, bought myself in at United Artists and started producing independently."

"Good idea," Johnny said. "Why don't you?"

"I will," Drice said, wagging a finger wisely. "Someday I will."

He walked on. Whenever you ran into Drice he always had some plan that was going to bring back all his old glories. Every night he came to the different Brown Derbies, the Trocadero or the Anatole, pretending he was still on top, still the big shot, acting out a crazy kind of Eric Von Stroheim role in life. *Look at him*, Johnny said to himself. *That's you too if you don't get a move on pretty soon.* He took his eyes away from the man.

Johnny suddenly grew aware that Maderna had been wrapped in conversation with Dolgos for the last hour. It was odd to see the two of them together but he didn't get suspicious until he saw the actor leave the table.

"Hey, George," Johnny called. "Where are you going?"

"Home," the actor said. "I've got to pack. I'm leaving for Kansas City in the morning."

"Kansas City!" The news shook him up to full awakeness like a shower of cold water. "What for?" he cried.

"Dolgos knows a doctor back there who performs medical miracles daily. I want to give him a whack at me. Maybe he can help."

"But you can't go!" Johnny was thinking fast. "You can't leave now. Listen. The boys are playing a little *chemin de fer*. They were counting you in."

Maderna thought it over. "The plane doesn't leave until eleven," he said. "O.K. I'll play an hour or two." He went back to Dolgos and explained.

Johnny rounded up a dozen men and took them upstairs to a private room. William Drice tagged along, unwilling to let them think he couldn't afford to keep up with them. Then the waiter came in with a shoe of cards and the game began. Johnny wondered how long he could keep it going.

At two o'clock William Drice suddenly doubled up with appendicitis pains. He had been losing steadily to Johnny, who sat right next to him, owing him twenty-eight hundred dollars when he collapsed. The attack of appendicitis was the most graceful, pride-saving way out he could think of.

Near four the proprietor started to hover about them, coughing apologetically until he finally managed to tell them that they would really have to leave. Johnny spoke up quickly.

"We can't stop now," he told the boys. "The game's just getting hot. Listen. I'll take you guys to a place where nobody can disturb us."

"All right," Maderna said. "Just an hour or two longer."

They took the chips and a couple of shoes of cards with them and drove back to the Superb lot. Johnny led them into Stage 4, fixed up a table and some chairs, and the game went on in that great barn. While the others watched the cards, Johnny went outside and found one of the night men.

"I want this stage sealed," he told him. "As soon as the studio cops come to work, put a man at each door. Nobody gets in and nobody gets out, I don't care who he is or what. Understand?" Then he went back to the game.

He must have dozed off in his chair soon after. When he awoke, he saw the knot of men still grouped over the table. They looked weird, sitting in their evening clothes in the big spaces of that empty stage. Johnny suddenly jumped to his feet. Maderna was missing. Cursing his luck, Johnny looked at his watch and saw it wasn't quite ten. There was a telephone in the barn and he swiftly got his secretary on the wire.

"Drive out to the airport right away," he told her. "Watch for Maderna. When you see him, hang on and don't let go until you hear from me." He threw the telephone on the floor and started out for Maderna's house, hoping to head him off there.

As he ran into the broad daylight of the alley, a girl sitting on a pile of flats called out to him.

"Can't take time now," he said over his shoulder. "See me later."

"Johnny!" she called. "You go now and you'll never see me again."

He jerked to a halt. It was his wife. It came back to him with a sobering rush of guilt that he had completely forgotten to phone her last night after he had seen Tafferty. Maderna would have to wait somehow. Worried and unhappy, he led her into an empty projection room just off the alley to talk.

"Look at yourself," she said, her voice hard and cold. "Wearing a crumpled-up evening suit at ten in the morning, staying up all night in a studio stage, playing the Hollywood game of bluff with your new cars and Brentwood houses. . . . This town's no good for you, Johnny."

"I know," he said clumsily. "It is a lunatic merry-go-round but I can't help myself just now. I'll make it all up to you soon, Vivian."

"It's not that. It's not me. I hate to see you chase yourself for nothing. Johnny, let's stop," she said and the anger went out of her voice. "Let's live normally again, among normal people. Johnny, let's go back east now."

"I can't, Vivian. I've got a big picture in the works right now. It means a lot to me. I can't leave it."

"Leave it and come." She was pleading with him. "Everything's no good here. All the fake bluff, the crazy running around, the gambling and the drinks, the freaks and the nuts you see here—all those things make people think Hollywood is a great funny joke but it isn't really funny at all. All that doesn't happen out of nowhere. Everyone here is scared silly all the time. The stars, the writers, the producers, even the big bosses—they're all afraid they'll wake up one morning and find out they've lost their magic touch with the public. It's fear. It spoils everything that's normal and simple. Johnny," she said, "get out of it, now. Come home."

He didn't know what to say. He kept looking down at the floor. "I can't quit, Vivian," he said painfully. "You're right. God knows what you say is right, but honey . . . honey . . ." He stopped. He didn't have to say more. She began to cry softly.

"I hate it," she wept hopelessly. "Everything's no good. I'm sick and tired. Johnny," she sobbed, "I'm going to have a baby."

His head came up with a jerk and he stared blankly at her. "Oh, Vivian!" he said. Then the realization drove home sharp and all at once, how alone she must have felt. "Oh, my poor kid," he said. "My poor baby, what a heel I've been . . ."

Finally he lifted her to her feet and took her outside. As they walked to the gate to drive home, a man came up and told him Tafferty wanted to see him immediately. Johnny didn't even pause to answer him but as they continued to the gate he suddenly halted and then turned to the Administration Building. "Come on," he said to Vivian and they went up to Tafferty's office.

"Hollywood is Hollywood, I realize," the boss began, "but this is no joke." He saw Vivian was there too but he was so swollen with resentment that he couldn't stop. "How would it look for me if the bank people found out you tied up a whole stage just for a card game? It gives me a bad name. It gives Hollywood a bad name. You can't do—"

"Save it," Johnny said. "Keep it for yourself. I don't want to hear it."

"What?" Tafferty cried, staring him in bewilderment.

"That's right. I said *can* it. You don't have to hold the bank people over my head any longer. You don't have to wait until my contract is up. I've finally got some sense into my head. I'm *through!*"

The boss fell back slowly into his chair, actually too perplexed to speak.

"Come on, Vivian," Johnny said. "We've had enough of this madhouse town. We're going back east."

He took her arm and they went down into the alley again.

For the first time perhaps since they had come to Hollywood they had their dinner together quietly and with a sense of pleasure. They talked a great deal of the East and their friends there, and how pleasant it would be to work on Broadway again; they talked with real warmth of the baby and how things would be with the three of them together somewhere in the country back home, living simply and peacefully. And later, when they went to the Hollywood Bowl for the concert, they both grew still, happy enough just to be together, and they listened to the music with her hand in his, the way they did years ago. Time passed so fast that they were both surprised when the lights went on over the amphitheater and the concert was over.

"The night's young," he said as they rose to leave. "Listen, honey, suppose we go somewhere for a bite."

"All right," she said, smiling but looking at him carefully. "What is it, Johnny? Beginning to feel restless?"

"Oh, no," he said quickly. "It's not that at all. It's just that we're leaving Hollywood so soon. It's just that I feel something like saying goodbye to the nutty old town, you know."

They went to the Vine Street Brown Derby. As soon as they sat down at an alcove, William Drice unexpectedly came up to them.

"I've been waiting for you," Drice said. "Before it slips my mind. I owed you twenty-eight hundred dollars when I broke down last night, didn't I?" He took out a check and put it on the table.

Johnny had to admire the old man, even as he felt sorry for him. He wouldn't touch the check. "Sit down," he said. "Have something with us."

"No, thanks. I can't stay. I'm late. I was due at the Domino lot an hour ago. You know how it is yourself."

Deeply touched by the performance the old man was putting on, Johnny suddenly couldn't help himself. "Oh for the love of Pete," he broke out. "Stop it, Drice. Cut it out. I can't keep on seeing a man like you play that cockeyed game."

Drice stared at him for a moment, his mouth loose. "What game, Johnny?" he asked slowly.

"You know what game. You're fooling nobody. Nuts," he said, breaking off. "Forget it. I'm sorry. Who am I to tell you what to do?"

Drice sat down at the table. He picked up a fork and studied it carefully as he spoke. There was a peculiar smile on his face that Johnny didn't understand. "You're not telling me anything I didn't know," the old man said quietly. "Yes, I've bluffed and everybody kidded me along. It's been cheap, stupid, bitter. Don't think I've enjoyed it, but what was I going to do with myself anyhow? Listen. I know pictures, Johnny. I like pictures and I'm going to stay in pictures all my life or nothing else will do for me. We're all like that, aren't we?" He stood up, still wearing that funny smile on his face. "Hollywood might be every screwy, heartbreaking thing they say of it. The whole point is, we like it. We wouldn't know how to live any place else."

He started to leave but Johnny touched his sleeve. "Drice, take the check with you. I don't want it."

The old man laughed outright. "Where were you two kids all day?" he asked. "I thought news traveled fast in Hollywood. Don't worry about that little check. I got my old job back at Domino this afternoon. Yes, they elected me vice president in charge of production again." He saw the surprised look on Johnny's face and felt he had to explain. "That's Hollywood," he said.

For a long time after he left, Johnny could find little to say. Vivian was watching him but he didn't seem to be able to meet her eyes.

"What is it?" she asked. "Drice said it, didn't he? Drice—"

"Said what?" Johnny broke in. "Forget him. He's just a sentimental old bird who likes to talk. What does he know?" He began eating, keeping his head down, but the food had little taste. When he looked up again, he saw his secretary standing before him.

"I've been trying to locate you all night, Mr. Mantle," she said.

"Well, what is it, Hazel?"

"What is it?" She spoke with a fine shade of indignation. "You told me to find George Maderna. I'm exhausted."

"Oh, Maderna," Johnny said, remembering. "What happened to him? Didn't he get to Kansas City?"

"He's at his home resting, Mr. Mantle. He missed the plane. What happened, he ran into a swarm of lady admirers and he couldn't get rid of them for hours. You told me to stay with him until I heard from you, true, but enough was enough, Mr. Mantle. I'm exhausted."

"I'm sorry, Hazel. I guess I just forgot. You see, it doesn't matter about Maderna now."

The girl took a moment to stare at him. Her lips made a straight line. Then she turned sharply on her heel and stalked to the door. Johnny looked after her glumly and started rubbing his cheek with his hand. He didn't speak.

"Johnny," Vivian said at last. Her voice was low. "Listen, don't sit there moping like that. Go after Maderna. Get back into pictures."

"No," he said. "That's out for good. You're swell to say it but we're going east."

"I was wrong, Johnny. Drice showed me how wrong I was. If your heart's set on it, I can't stop you."

"Oh, it's too late," he said dully, "even if I wanted to. I fixed myself for good when I told Tafferty off. It's all settled."

"It's not settled. You've got to try to get your job back. Or else get a new one. I can't fool myself you'll be happy at home. People live in Hollywood and they have babies too. We can be happy here too . . ."

She wanted to go on but just then the waiter came up with the telephone. He plugged in for the connection and then Johnny was listening to Tafferty.

"You're not getting away with it!" the boss barked out at him. "I won't oblige you by breaking your contract for you!"

Johnny was so mystified that all he could do was to gag into the mouthpiece.

"Ha! You can't say a word! You're tongue-tied with shame because we've caught you!" Tafferty was shouting so furiously over the phone that Vivian could hear every word from where she sat. "You're not going over to Domino!"

"Domino?" Johnny cried. "What the—?"

"Now, you were seen! I can put two and two together, you know. Of course! That little act you pulled in my office didn't fool me. I refuse to fire you just so you can be free to go over to Domino. Now, you were seen talking to Drice just a short while ago. You can't deny it. Don't deny it. Don't try!"

Johnny covered the mouthpiece with his hand and turned to Vivian. "Holy smokes!" he chortled. "Crazy? Nuts? Holy smokes!"

"Johnny, my boy, I realize we've been unsympathetic lately." Tafferty was pleading now. "But we really need you at Superb. Forget Domino. We'll make you perfectly happy from now on. Listen, I take it on myself personally to get you a million-dollar appropriation for Florida. Listen, Johnny, I'll make it a million and a quarter!"

Johnny finally hung up in a daze. "A million and a quarter," he breathed dreamily. "Just wait till Maderna hears that. He'll come running." He stopped suddenly and looked at Vivian. "Honey," he faltered. "Honey . . ."

"I meant it," she said quietly. "We're not going east. We're staying. That's what I really want you to do."

He gave her a swift hug. "You won't be sorry," he promised, the words pouring out ardently. "I'll change from day to night. You wait and see. I'll take things slowly, sanely. You can work Hollywood right if you only know where to draw the line. Honey," he said, grabbing his hat from the alcove bench, "would you mind going home alone? I've got to see Maderna right away. I want to start shooting tomorrow. You understand, honey, don't you?"

"Yes," she said, and he went hurrying down the aisle to the door. Her eyes were misty as she looked after him but she was smiling too. "Yes, Johnny," she whispered. "I know."

THE GOLDEN WEST

As everyone knows, the movie business isn't what it used to be. For many of us who used to work at the studios, the pleasant, oversized checks that came every Thursday have stopped. The blow fell softly, mainly because when the crisis developed we couldn't believe or didn't want to believe that it was upon us. Some of us went back to the kind of work we had done before we were brought out to Hollywood. Others, like a certain group of people I had come to know, and saw almost every week, simply stayed on, hanging.

The California sunshine continued to pour down. The streets, the stucco mansions, the lawns and shrubbery sparkled with light. These friends of mine went on visiting one another's homes and giving outdoor dinner parties, the ladies in their lovely frocks scattered over the terrace at the tables, chattering and affectionate, while their husbands stood off by themselves in small clusters, nodding and smiling and smoking; my friends kept on their housekeepers and gardeners and children's nurses; they still sent their children to dancing school, to supervised play groups. "And every month," as a man named Curtis Spogel once remarked sadly to me, "another few Defense Bonds cashed in at the bank and dissipated."

Spogel was a certified public accountant by profession, and he was also in the movie business. He was in the exhibition end, the noncreative side, but he was mixed in with the creative people through his brother-in-law Julie Vencie, a top producer in the industry, now no longer attached to any major studio. "If they would only awaken to the realities. If they would only face the facts and do something," Spogel said. "But what?" he added immediately. His movie houses, eight-hundred-seaters, were upstate in Kern County—in rural communities, far from the cities, from the television stations. His income was relatively unaffected by the debacle, and he didn't want to seem unfeeling.

One Sunday afternoon, I drove over to his home in Beverly Hills, high up on Angelo Drive. As I left my car in the parking space near the garage, I could tell at once I was the first to arrive. The garden lay fresh and still, the water was quiet in the swimming pool, and Mrs. Vencie, Mrs. Spogel's mother, was sitting on the terrace, in the shade, reading a foreign-language newspaper. Mrs. Vencie lived with the Spogels.

I wanted to avoid the old lady. I knew she would fasten on to me and talk, about the bad times, about her son Julie—her golden boy, she used to call him.

A row of large, old oleander bushes separated the garage area from the grounds and the house. I went up the row of oleanders and made my way around the terrace, reached the house, and slipped inside by the front way. Passing through the entrance hall, I saw Edith Spogel standing alone in the living room, leaning against the back of a couch in the dimness there, her eyes shut. She was listening to the New York Philharmonic concert on the radio and was lost in the music. I started to speak to her, but just then I became aware of Spogel creeping up on her. He was wearing a pair of tennis trunks and carrying a box of chocolates. "Boo!" he said.

"Oh, Curtis!" she said, startled.

"Have a sweet!" Spogel said, playful and eager.

"No, thanks," Edith said, and then, as he kept pressing the chocolates on her, she said, "Oh, Curtis, really! How can you, in the middle of the day—Oh, hello, David," she said, seeing me. She smoothed her eyebrows with her fingertips and sighed. "How are you?" she said to me. "How's the family? Come—let's go out on the terrace. Let's listen to the music there." She touched the switches on the little box that controlled the various radio speakers, and went outside.

"Everything these days is like walking on eggshells," Spogel said to me, disappointed, the candy box still in his hands. "We seem to exist in perpetual tension."

Auditing other people's books, working on the inside, Spogel was able to spot good business opportunities. That was how he had wandered into the movie field, buying that chain of theaters upstate; that was how he had met Julie Vencie, and then Julie's sister. Edith was a year or two older than her brother, and getting on. The marriage was one of those arranged, matchmaker's affairs. At the time, Julie was a big producer, under contract, bustling and sprightly, four thousand a week at the majors, and there was a certain atmosphere, a kind of glamour. But now the glamour was gone, and Spogel saddled with the support of his wife's mother, too. He was awed by this whole circle of movie people among whom he had, so to speak, blundered. He admired them. He thought they possessed some quality, some mystery, that he lacked. He always felt inferior and apologetic with them. He was apologetic and self-conscious over everything he did—because he showed Gene Autrys and Randolph Scotts at his movie houses, or sex-and-sands with Yvonne de Carlo, because he ate candy in the daytime and had no personality, because he neglected his reducing exercises. He wanted to reduce, he sincerely meant to do the exercises every day, but they made his stomach muscles hurt, and so he would forget and then, later, feel guilty. "I am a sybarite!" he said one day, daringly, when we came upon him with one of those thirty-cent chocolate bars in his hands. And then, when no one smiled, he said, "I don't smoke, I don't drink—so this is my vice, sweets. Everybody has a vice or two . . ." That was the way he was.

When we went out on the terrace, Mrs. Vencie was chattering at full speed, every word getting on Edith's nerves.

"Rich, rich—famous!" the old lady was saying, meaning her son Julie, of course. "He always wanted to be a big shot. I used to argue patiently with him by the hour. 'Julie,' I would say to him, 'you'll give yourself a breakdown. You'll bust a spring in your head! Julie, what do you want it for, who needs it—the ulcers, the hypertension, the Cadillacs? A trolley car won't get you there just the same?'"

"Ma," Edith said.

"When he was a boy," Mrs. Vencie went on, ignoring the interruption, "when we lived on the East Side, you know what he did? He walked! He couldn't stand the tenements—the babies crying, the dumbwaiters, the garbage. He would walk for miles and miles, making up dreams in his head, having ambitions. He would go and find a dime and ride on the Fifth Avenue bus—he couldn't live if he didn't look at the fancy stores, at the rich people!"

"Ma," Edith said again.

"Dear," Spogel said to his wife. "Why must you aggravate yourself and take everything to heart so? What difference does it make if Mother harmlessly—"

"Curtis, please," Edith said, and he stopped at once, turning aside.

"I know nothing," he murmured to me. "I am a businessman, bour-geois—sex-and-sands."

"Reaching for the stars!" Mrs. Vencie said. "They say if you don't give them affection when they're little, it will have bad aftereffects on them and give them scars. So it was my fault? I didn't give him enough affec-tion? Who had time for affection, I had seven small little children. I had to scrub floors, cook supper, wash the clothes—not like the modern women nowadays, believe me. Everything the children wore, I sewed by myself on the machine—the jumpers, the knee pants, the dresses for the girls. When I gave birth to Edith and had to lay in bed for three whole days, naturally, of course, I couldn't watch out, and so that's how we had the tragedy—that's how we lost Freddie."

"Ma!" Edith cried.

"Ma!" Mrs. Vencie burst out, nettled. "What are you hollering on me 'Ma' for? It ain't the truth? Poor little Freddie didn't go up on the roof to play, and they didn't push him off?"

"Nobody's interested," Edith said. "You told us the whole story a dozen times. It happened a hundred years ago. I'm trying to listen to the Symphony!"

"Symphony!" Mrs. Vencie said. "Fancy lady! What's the matter—I embarrass you? I didn't do enough for you? When the doctor took out your tonsils and I gave you the wrong medicine by mistake, didn't I hurry up quick and drink the whole bottle?"

"Oh, it's hopeless, it's hopeless," Edith said. "Again the story with the tonsils and the medicine, again the whole repertoire!" She turned away and went back into the house.

Mrs. Vencie's shoulders started to shake, and I saw she was laughing. "David, you could make a book!" she said, chortling, and wiping her nose with the back of her hand. "It was a regular Charlie Chaplin! See, innocently, I thought I poisoned her—that's why I hurried up and drank the whole bottle. But in the excitement, in the hoorah I made, Edith vomited it up—excuse me, David—but me, I kept my share down and I still got it in me to this day! I was furious! Poor Papa," she said, her mood suddenly shifting. She was thinking now, it turned out, of Freddie, of the tragedy. Mr. Vencie had worked in fur, but he had caught the furrier's lung disease and had been totally incapacitated. At the time of the accident, he had just been getting on his feet again—he had a small candy stand. "It took ten years off his life, that's why he died so soon," Mrs. Vencie said. "When the police officers came and they informed him, he went running home from the candy store, hitting his head with his hands and hollering in the street, '*Gevalt, gevalt!*'. . . Oh, look, look, look," she said, her face lighting up. Another pair of visitors had emerged from the parking space. "Now we have the newlyweds," Mrs. Vencie said with satisfaction, settling herself.

The newcomers were the Kittershoys, Boris and Daisy. Boris was Julie's partner, the "kay" in Veeankay Pictures, an independent producing company they were trying to get started.

"Curtis! Curtis!" Daisy cried as she came scampering across the garden. "You should feel my thighs—like iron bands!" She was taking ballet and tennis lessons—that was all she meant by the reference to her thighs. She and Boris had recently been married, and although she was by no means in her first youth, she acted like a bride. "Doom, doom," she said as she joined us on the terrace, chiding her husband as well as Spogel. They both had long faces. "Smile!" she said. "Show optimism! The world is not coming to an end."

Boris Kittershoy came to the Spogels' hoping to see Julie, who was unpredictable, with a violent temper, and hard to approach. These meetings at the Spogels' parties were about the only chance Boris had to talk to his partner. I knew all this, so I knew what it meant to Boris when Julie failed to appear and, instead, his wife, Imogene, came, not long after the Kittershoys. She had an overnight bag. She and Julie were fighting again, it developed. She had left him or he had left her or had driven her away.

"He is an *enfant terrible*," Boris said. The Spogels and I were huddled around Imogene in the living room—away from Mrs. Vencie, on the terrace. "We are going under, perishing," Boris said, "and he must pick this time to fight with his wife! He is clinical."

"How irresponsible they are," Spogel whispered to me. "How temperamental and undisciplined." His eyes kept wavering and he glanced constantly at Edith, to see how she was managing under the new strain.

Boris and Julie had gone ahead with their independent picture largely on assurances given to them by an executive at a major studio. He had promised, orally, to furnish them with a release, with the principal financing, with a director, with name stars. The deal had fallen through, as Hollywood deals do. The executive hadn't reneged or double-crossed them; his studio had simply decided at the last moment to withdraw. It was a change of policy, but it left Veeankay with two hundred thousand dollars hard cash, or more, sunk in the venture, and no place to go. "He is a mass of contradictions, and he poses, and nobody can get along with him," Boris said, half rocking there in the dim light, on his upholstered chair.

"It never fails!" Daisy said. "When a man is in the dumps and business is bad, he immediately gets infatuated with his wife all over again. They put you on a pedestal, and think you are the most beautiful woman in the world, and they give you no peace."

"I suppose," Imogene said, listless. "He's crazy."

Whenever they had their fights, she drove straight up the hill to the Spogels, because she was safe there; she knew Julie couldn't suspect her of wrongdoing while she was with Spogel and her in-laws. She was very pretty. She had been in show business, had gone to work in her teens, and you always had the feeling that she was helpless and vulnerable. Julie had been giving her a bad time the last year or so. She had been crying all morning, and her face was blurry and she still had a Frownie—those things women wear when they sleep, to avoid wrinkles—stuck on her forehead between the eyebrows. "I don't know what he wants from me," she said. "Who am I? I'm just a person. I'm not even intelligent, like he always says when he throws it up at me. I'm common and have no background. Well, actually, you know, he's not wrong. I mean, what was I before I met him, what sort of a life did I have? I always had the blues. I was ordinary. You know, he can be awfully nice when he wants to. He's disadjusted."

The quarrel had been going on since early the previous morning. She had made a face at him—that was how it had all started. She and Julie used separate bedrooms. She had gone into his room yesterday morning, looked, and seen he was still asleep, and then—on an impulse, thoughtlessly—she had made a face at him. Only he hadn't been asleep. He had been peeking at her, through his eyelashes.

She went on talking, hopeless, tearful. Time was passing, she said, and what did she do, where did she go? All she ever did was look at the television set, switching the dial all evening from channel to channel, watching the news and the wrestling and "This Is Your Life," and it was depressing. She had a lump under her arm, she said, and everybody talked about hysterectomies and she ought to go and see the doctor, and every time she combed her hair she saw more gray. "I used to sing with a band in Atlantic City," she said. "I got a hundred a week. Only two shows a night and the rest of the time to myself. I used to sunbathe on the beach all day. I ought to have my head examined for giving that all up."

She rose. Julie always came after her at the Spogels'—to fight some more or to make up—and she had to change her clothes and be ready for him. She looked around now for her overnight bag.

"You're too good to him," Daisy said. "You're too loyal. You should have an affair!"

"That's all we need now," Boris said. "That's a fine piece of advice you're giving her. Thank you very much."

"No, I'm right!" Daisy insisted gaily. "She must make herself precious to him. She must teach him a lesson. Have an affair!"

"You think it's so easy?" Imogene said. "Try it sometime yourself and you'll see. What do you think—you can just go up to a man and confront him? Everybody can always tell you exactly what to do. It's not so simple." She saw the little suitcase on the floor and stooped to pick it up. "Once I called up Eversall and I said to him—What could I say? I didn't know what to say. So I asked him did he want to take me out to dinner. And you know Eversall, how tight he is. He refused. You'd be surprised," she said, dabbing at her eyes with her handkerchief. "They know your husband or you know their wives, or you can't stand them in the first place—there are all kinds of things that crop up."

She went off to one of the bedrooms in the back of the house. Everyone remained silent for several moments. Even Daisy.

"What is there to mourn?" she said suddenly.

"There she goes again," Boris said, hitting the arm of his chair.

"No, seriously," she said. "I mean, after all, what is there for us to get so all worked up about? In the last analysis, what do we really possess? We have our naked bodies, just ourselves. That's all that really matters. I mean—" In addition to the ballet and tennis lessons, Daisy took courses at U C L A, and she was also having her teeth straightened, and at parties she would scream out how the Kittershoy wives were spirited, like race-horses—but nothing helped. It was her money Boris had put into the independent company. She had owned a children's-wear factory before their marriage. Boris hadn't had a dime. He had married her; he had taken the earnings of a lifetime in the children's-wear trade and had put every penny of it into the Veeankay disaster, and at night it was an agony for her to fall asleep.

"Yes, yes, we understand—we know what you mean," Spogel said, trying to head her off, but she wouldn't stop. She couldn't stop.

"No, truth," she said. "Ultimately there is only truth. Truth and good-ness and beauty—those are the only basic values!"

"Sweetheart, say nothing!" Boris roared at his wife. "When I am without you, I am without an arm. But when I am *with* you, I am with-out a head—shut up! You don't understand conditions. You don't know what's going on. For God's sakes, do not try to be cheerful and alleviate the situation!"

"Oh, look at her, look at her!" Daisy cried, turning for no reason, to Edith, who had been sitting by quietly all this time. "Isn't she dainty? Isn't she darling?"

"Truth! Truth! Beauty!" Boris shouted. "Life is worth living! She don't want to hear bad news; it don't exist for her. There are lines standing all around the corner—the box office is booming!"

"Oh, I love her, I love her, I love her!" Daisy said. "Curtis, you must always be kind to her. You must never hurt her. She is my very best friend!"

She subsided abruptly. The living room became still again.

The Spogels had a pocket-billiards table in a game room that stood off by itself at the foot of the garden, not far from the garage. We were on the terrace—the Kittershoys, the Spogels, and I—when suddenly we heard the rolling of the balls, the clicks they made as they hit, and we knew it was Julie down there, shooting pool. Edith went to tell Imogene, and in a few minutes Imogene wearily crossed the garden to join her husband. We settled down to wait.

More guests were arriving. They played at the swimming pool or sat in the sun or were waylaid on the terrace by old Mrs. Vencie. Daisy Kittershoy was talking to one of the guests, a doctor, describing her symptoms to him. She had called his office, I heard her say, but then had canceled the appointment because there was really nothing the matter with her. It was just that she couldn't seem to think clearly or energetically. It was just that she couldn't seem to enjoy anything. She was tired and not tired. If she could only do manual labor or something and get herself really exhausted, she said. She kept waiting for that morning when you wake up and feel bright and everything is sharp and fine again. She had a ringing in her ears—no, not a ringing, not a buzzing—more like telephone wires singing in the wind, a humming.

The doctor kept nodding. "It's very clear. Yes, I know," he said. "Those are the typical symptoms of mental fatigue. Do you perspire?"

"Oh, Doctor, you're so wonderful!" Daisy cried. "That's all I wanted to know—that there was nothing physically wrong with me. That's why you're so popular, Doctor—you always tell your patients exactly what they want to hear!"

"Ridiculous situation," Spogel murmured to me unhappily. "The whole thing just on account of a face she made, over a dirty look she gave him."

He took me along for company as he went walking around the grounds. He pretended to be seeing after his guests, but his real purpose was to get near the game room, to find out how Imogene and Julie were doing. "Girls are so peculiar," he mused. "To make a face at a sleeping man! Who knows what goes on in their heads? Once—naturally, long before I knew Edith—I had a lady friend. She cooked for me, we went out together, she came to my place—you know, everything. But she wouldn't marry me. Once I asked her, 'Reba, would you marry me if I asked you serious?' And she said 'No!'"

We had reached the game-room window, and he stepped up to it cautiously. We eavesdropped. "Julie, I'll get a cold," we heard Imogene saying. "Julie, it's damp here. It's chilly." She was barefoot, wearing her shorts and sun top, and she was obviously trying to get him away from the game room, into the house, where she apparently felt she could do more with him. "Julie, you know I'm allergic and always catch colds. Julie, I'm shivering," she said.

"Take an allergy pill, dear," Julie said, cheerful and matter-of-fact, going on with his game. We could hear the balls rolling and mixing.

"Anything transpire?" Boris Kittershoy whispered, coming up to us.

Spogel shook his head. "Patience," he said.

Boris started to moan, under his breath. There were industry people here, contacts, items of trade gossip to be picked up. "We could talk, we could inquire—we could try!" he said. A man named Irving Lissak had telephoned Edith, inviting himself over, and the visit might mean something, Boris said; the visit might be an approach, a feeler. There were two Lissaks, brothers. They were an independent company, actively in production, and it might very well be that they could be interested into taking over the Veeankay white elephant. "Who knows—it's a possibility!" Boris exclaimed softly. "But he is incommunicado, fighting with Imogene! Why does he always do this? It seems he was put into the world only to twist and scheme up ways to make life miserable!"

"He is an enigma," Spogel whispered, nodding.

"He is a pain in the neck!" Boris said.

Boris took himself off—to inquire, to try—and Spogel and I turned back to the game-room window. "Julie, I'm sick," Imogene was saying now. "Julie, my teeth are chattering. I'll have to go back into the house and leave you all alone. Julie, I'm leaving. Julie, I'm going back to the house."

"Yes, dear. Why don't you do that?" Julie said.

He was probably just waking up. Julie followed a peculiar twenty-four-hour cycle. During the early part of the day, he was dead to the world, groggy and glazed. As the afternoon wore on, the color would start filtering into his face. By nighttime, he was rosy and glowing again, the picture of health, full of energy. He downed a bottle of whiskey every night. He smoked thick, expensive cigars. He made people play cards with him and kept them up till all hours of the night. He worked up gags against his partner. Then, suddenly, unaccountably, he would turn cold sober, troubled and groping. "Why do I like you?" he once said to me, in a bewildering rush of affection. He gripped me by the shoulders. "I mean it, David. That's the best thing that's happened to me all year—my meeting you. I mean it. Listen—tell me about your-self," he said, catching himself up abruptly, joking again. "Come on, pappy, you always lay low and play possum. Tell me about your wife. What sort of a girl is she? What do you think of her? What does she think of you?" And in another moment he was throwing himself around the room, drinking and laughing and getting some friend of his at the county morgue to call up Boris, to say that he, Julie, had been killed in an auto accident.

"Tell me you told me," he was saying to Imogene now in the game room. "Tell me you didn't tell me. Tell me *you* lied, *I* lied. Deny every-thing. Admit everything. Dress, undress, take off your clothes—you think I don't know what you're doing?"

"Oh, my goodness, he is on the warpath," Spogel said. Spogel had begun to shuffle on his feet, out of worry. "Here it's half past four already, getting on five, and I'm still in my tennis trunks. I have to shave and take a shower!"

"You poor, pathetic broad," Julie said to Imogene, "you had me— you won out. Only you were too dumb to realize it."

"When? When did I win out?" Imogene asked.

"Yesterday—when I kicked you, when you started out for your hair-dresser's appointment," Julie said. It seemed she had been taking her dress off all day, and all day he had successfully managed to resist the maneuver—up to the hairdresser's appointment, up to the moment when she had started to leave and had turned and he had seen that sweet, little, round whatsis of hers, he said. Then he had caved in. He simply had been unable to hold out any longer—that was why he had kicked her, he said. "You had me in the palm of your hand right then and there," he went on. "Only, you had to go ahead and ruin everything."

"How? Why? What did I do so terrible to spoil everything?" Imogene cried.

"You don't remember?" Julie said. "After I kicked you, you turned around and what did you say? You said, 'Oh, darling, if I could only undo the hurt that I have caused you.' Where do you pick up language like that? Is that the way they talk in the dance-band business? What kind of books do you read?"

"I'm always at fault," Imogene said, sobbing. "No matter what I do, I'm always wrong. I'm responsible for everything."

"Oh, when will be the end?" Spogel said, sighing and jiggling his feet.

Up on the terrace, the extra help had arrived and were setting the tables. The people at the swimming pool had changed back into their clothes, and here and there we could see a guest in a dinner jacket.

Spogel nudged my elbow. "Listen, listen," he said. The game room had turned oddly quiet. Julie had stopped playing pool. We couldn't hear him laughing or talking any longer—just Imogene sobbing—and Spogel thought perhaps this meant they were making up in there at last. "What do you think? David, how does it sound to you?" he said, and then "Now what?" Daisy Kittershoy and Edith were hurrying down to us from the terrace. They appeared to be having some kind of altercation.

"Sh–h–h! He'll hear!" Spogel begged when the two women came up. "Please! Don't make a commotion—he'll think we're peeking!"

It turned out Daisy had heard of the impending visit of Irving Lissak, the active independent producer, and had come hurrying down to ask Spogel what he knew about the visit. Did Spogel think it was business or pleasure? Was Lissak a frequent guest here? Did Spogel know him so very well socially, or was there really something doing? "Daisy, I told you!" Edith cried. "I met him at a party weeks ago, and I told him to drop in any Sunday! You're making a whole hullabaloo over nothing!"

But Daisy wouldn't listen. "No, no!" she said, shaking her head. "I was speaking to Curtis—let Curtis answer!"

"Sh–h–h!" Spogel whispered, gesturing, "He'll hear! You came intruding at the worst possible moment. They're just starting to reconcile!"

"We're not reconciling, don't worry," Imogene said bitterly. She had come out of the game room, her eyes and cheeks smudged with tears. "You can talk all you want—he's not inside to hear."

Daisy and Edith rushed over to her. "He got hungry," Imogene said. "I hate him. He went up to the house to get a snack. He eats and has the time of his life while all the time I'm dying. He enjoys it!"

So that was why the game room had suddenly turned quiet. Spogel was dazed with disappointment. "What will be the outcome?" he said.

He meant when would they ever reconcile now, Imogene here, Julie in the house somewhere, everything up in the air? On the terrace, the tables were all set—the tablecloths gleaming, the candles lit and shining quietly. "Oh, why did you do it?" Spogel said to Imogene.

"Leave her alone!" Edith said to her husband. "Can't you see she's miserable enough?"

"Why did I do what?" Imogene said.

"Go into his bedroom yesterday," Spogel said. "Make the face. Why did you needlessly have to provoke him?"

"What should I do? Love him to death because he's so irresistible and tortures me to pieces?"

"But what good did it do?" Spogel said. "What purpose could it have accomplished? What was the *sense*?"

"I thought he was *asleep!*" Imogene wailed. "Oh, Curtis, do you think people know what they do?"

She ran off into the oleander bushes. Spogel wanted to go after her, but Edith checked him. They stood together, squabbling wretchedly. Spogel wanted to bring Imogene back. They had guests to entertain, a dinner party to live through, and it was ridiculous—all this upset, everybody going around in circles, all over a dirty look, a face. "Let her go!" Edith cried. "Didn't you bother her enough? Don't interfere! Don't make difficulties!"

"I'm making difficulties?" Spogel said.

At this moment, old Mrs. Vencie came up. She was taking a little walk. "Isn't it remarkable?" she said, looking up at the ladies in the garden, the guests. She was marveling at their appearance, at the way they kept themselves, their figures. "Imagine!" the old woman went on, full of wonder. "They get pregnant only when they want to!"

"Ma!" Edith said.

"I give them all the credit in the world," Mrs. Vencie said. "They're smarter than my generation. What, then—they should let themselves go and become sloppy and fat like a horse? Let them make the beauty, let them diet. They're absolutely right!"

"Oh, for heaven's sake, Ma, couldn't you take a day off just once and spare us all your observations and comments?" Edith said, through her teeth.

"Look at her!" Mrs. Vencie said, wiping her nose with the back of her hand. "Somebody would think she's having a miscarriage. What's the matter—I'm killing people?"

"Oh, she comes right out with everything, no inhibitions at all," Edith said.

Just then, Boris Kittershoy came stamping down on us, panting with his news, holding up two fingers in the air. *Both* Lissaks had arrived, not just Irving. The visit definitely had to be a feeler, or else why *both*? Boris couldn't stop talking and pumping. The Lissaks had access to oil money, he said, the Lissaks had a release with U–L, they were in a position where they needed product, and a deal was perfectly feasible!

"Good, good," Mrs. Vencie said, happy for them. "What a fool I was," she said, going on with her own thoughts. "How ignorant we all were in my time. When I had the twins, I would wash out a whole clothesline of diapers every day, and then I would stand by the window and look out and I would feel *good*—I was so simple—because the diapers came out nice and white. I even used to put in bluing!" She went off, resuming her walk, mingling with the guests.

Spogel was in agonies. He wanted to go looking for Julie immediately. He wanted to tell him about the two Lissaks. But Edith was dead set against it. "Curtis, please!" she cried. "Believe me, you don't know what it is. You just don't understand, so do me a favor and stay out of it!"

Boris, in the meanwhile, had just found out from Daisy that Julie was still incommunicado, that the reconciliation had broken down, and he was putting on a big show of despair. "I have done my best," he said. "I have eaten gall and wormwood, and now I am finished with him. This is the end!"

"But I do, I do—I do understand why he always fights with Imogene!" Spogel was saying hoarsely to Edith. "She is the symbol to him of his youth, of his hopes and dreams and aspirations, and naturally, in his downfall, he takes everything out on her. She is his Mona Lisa! You think I don't know. Don't judge a product by its container. I am not nec-essarily an ignoramus without sensitivity!"

Daisy urged Boris to start negotiations with the Lissaks by himself; after all, he was vice president, a partner. But he refused. "I should ini-tiate everything so that he can renege on me and make me out a fool again?" he said. "I had my experience once—no, thank you!" Boris was

referring to something that happened with Ronnie Fitts—another independent, a man whose wife had made a fortune during the war buying
Beverly Hills real estate on margin. Boris had arranged matters with Fitts,
had paved the way for a possible deal, and all that had been left was a final
meeting. Julie had agreed to the meeting; for once, he had appeared on
time; he had promised to behave himself. But when they entered Fitts's
home for the conference and Julie saw the original Impressionist paintings hanging on the walls there, he turned wild with fury. He walked
straight up to Fitts and insulted him right and left; he was a slob, Julie
said, and what right did he have to be owning Cézannes? "He is a mad-
man!" Boris said now, pulling away from Daisy. "He is tactless and antag-
onizes people. He malingers. He makes practical jokes. Suddenly, he
goes flying away on trips and runs up expenses, and let somebody else
have the pleasure—I suffered with him long enough!" Boris kept trying
to escape from his wife, she kept arguing and clinging to him, and now
the two went off together, into the garden.

"Oh, why must you have such a sensitive nature and tremble over
every least little thing?" Spogel cried out at Edith. "What harm would
there be if I went and talked to him?"

"But it is not my nature!" Edith cried back at him. "You don't know
what happened! Believe me, you have no understanding of the situation!"

"But I do! I do!" Spogel said, his eyes shut tight. "I just told you. I do
understand—" He stopped. He listened. Edith was complaining about
her mother again, saying how the old woman always had to open up her
big mouth and talk, talk, talk. "Oh, why do you fix on Mother all the
time?" Spogel said, exasperated. "Why must you pick on her now? Don't
we have more serious problems?"

"But she made the whole trouble!" Edith said. "Julie was here yesterday. He saw her, and that's when it really started! Oh, really, it's too
impossible—it's humiliating!" she said. "I'd rather not talk about it."

But, little by little, the story came out. Julie snored. It was an affliction;
he had a deviated septum. That was the reason he and Imogene used
separate bedrooms. But yesterday, after Imogene made the face at him,
he came to see his mother and asked the old woman if it was really true
that he snored. And Mrs. Vencie had told a white lie. She had said he
didn't snore at all.

Spogel didn't stay to hear any more. He could see the whole picture in a flash. It was the worst possible thing Mrs. Vencie could have said. Julie, of course, had immediately gone off convinced that Imogene had been avoiding him, that the talk about his snoring had been nothing but a pretext all along.

"Wait! Don't go to him!" Edith cried, clutching at her husband, but Spogel wouldn't be held back this time. He fought free and went rushing away—to find Julie, to tell him, to clear up the whole foolish misunderstanding once for all and restore peace.

"Oh, stop him!" Edith said to me, her eyes big with alarm. "David, do something! He'll go blundering in where he doesn't belong, and it will be awful!" And now she blurted out the rest of the story. She hadn't finished. It wasn't the face, the dirty look; it wasn't Mrs. Vencie's white lie. Imogene had been unfaithful to Julie. She had had an affair, and he had found out all about it. The mischief hadn't ended with Mrs. Vencie. One thing had led to another. After Julie talked to his mother, he had gone straight back to his own home. Simmering with suspicions, furious, he had searched Imogene's room, and there had been some letters. Imogene had been at a hotel at Lake Tahoe not long ago, and she had met a man there, one of the players in the band.

"Oh, run!" Edith cried to me now as we saw Spogel weaving in and out among the guests in the garden, hurrying up to the house. "Run, David—run, or it will be too late!"

By the time I came up to the terrace, I had lost Spogel in the press of people. I looked everywhere for him, but there was too much coming and going—new arrivals crossing over to greet their friends, the extra help passing through with trays of drinks and appetizers, the guests constantly shifting as they formed into groups. I saw the Kittershoys. Off to one side, on the flagstones under the lights, Boris was playing Ping-Pong, and Daisy hovered nearby. She was with some people, but she kept anxiously watching the Ping-Pong game. Boris was playing with a Mrs. Ashton, a lady who had an extremely full bosom and wore a low-cut dress. Mrs. Ashton was an intensely serious person, and as she lunged and flung herself about, she clearly had no idea of the violent effect the game was having on her bosom.

"Boris! Boris!" I heard Daisy call out. "Boris, take care—you will overexert!"

A few moments later, making my way through the guests, I stumbled on the Kittershoys again. Daisy had contrived somehow to get her husband away from the Ping-Pong table, and now, standing in a corner in the shadows, she was warning him against Mrs. Ashton. "She is literal-minded. She is intellectual. She will have a heart-to-heart talk with her husband and ask him for a divorce and then come running back to you, and then what? She has been analyzed!"

"But I am only amusing myself!" Boris said. "What do you want from me? I am only doing what you always preach—smile! Enjoy life! The world isn't coming to an end!" He left her and went off into the crowd.

It occurred to me that Spogel might be in the house. I went inside, and found him right away. He was in the library, but I had spent too much time wandering around outside and listening to the Kittershoys. Julie was already in there with him. Spogel had talked, had told him all about the white lie, and the damage was done.

Julie wouldn't talk about Imogene. He passed over the whole business of the snoring and the unfortunate misunderstanding. His color was high, his eyes shone, and he looked bursting with vigor and good health. "You don't say!" he said when Spogel told him that Imogene was only thoughtless and feminine, that he, Julie, was perhaps being unduly harsh with her. Spogel sensed trouble. He knew something had gone terribly awry, but for the life of him he couldn't imagine what was wrong, and he could only go ahead. "Is that so?" Julie said, in his hearty, friendly manner when Spogel told him about the Lissaks, both brothers appearing at the party, all the signs pointing to the clear-cut possibility of a transaction in the offing. "They do, do they?" Julie said when he heard the Lissaks had connections with oil people. Then he went to work on Spogel and took him apart.

Up in Kern County, Julie said, where Spogel had his theaters, the authorities let you pop the popcorn on the premises, and Spogel worked the contraptions in his houses so that the popcorn smell was piped directly out into the auditoriums, overpowering the audiences. "Not only that," Julie said, "you purposely put too much salt into the popcorn, so all during the show the poor farmers have to keep running out into the lobby to buy drinks. You chop the credits off the Westerns and run the same godforsaken pictures all over again with new titles, and nobody knows the difference. You import burlesque dancers for live shows, raise the prices sky-high, and then you short-change the yokels on the bumps and grinds because you're scared to death the P.T.A.'ll kick. And every year you add to your capital. Every month you set aside a nice, tidy sum for another few shares of American Tel. & Tel. What are you yammering to me about the Lissaks for? Who asked you?"

"But they are *here!*" Spogel gasped. "They have financing—they have a release!"

"What do you expect out of the Lissaks? What do you think they're going to do?" Julie said. He wouldn't go near the Lissaks with a ten-foot pole. They were greedy. They were ragpickers, junkmen. They came around shopping for bargains, looking to take advantage of desperation cases. They'd move in and immediately start taking over the whole show. Overnight they'd become experts on script, on casting, on cutting. They'd want to hog it all—a Lissak Brothers Production Produced by Julian Vencie. What are the Lissaks—beginners, children, public bene-factors? Didn't they know the score? Didn't they know he had tried the banks everywhere—downtown in Los Angeles, in New York, in Boston? Didn't the Lissaks know he was two hundred thousand dollars in the hole? "Would *you* give me the money, just like that?" Julie pounded. The notion struck his fancy. "Come on, Spogel!" he cried. "You're a sport. You're a rich man. You got capital. Why don't *you* give me the money?"

"Gladly!" Spogel said. "I would do it like a shot, only what would be the sense?" The fact of the matter was that he himself was getting out of the business, selling his houses, liquidating and how would it be to liq-uidate everything and then jump right back in again, investing in a movie? "Julie, darling, the handwriting is on the wall!" Spogel pleaded.

Julie roared with laughter. He roared because Spogel looked so comical, with his arms extended, his face honest and confounded, and because Spogel was so beautifully right. Spogel had put it perfectly: The handwriting was on the wall. The industry was dead. It was all over—the years of picture-making, the work, the rush, the all-night sessions at the studio, the whole wonderful excitement and rapture.

The library had two doors, one leading to the hall, the other to the back of the house. Now, as Julie stood shaking with his innocent glee,

Edith came running in from the hall. "They're gone! They're gone!" she said to her husband, meaning the Lissaks. "Curtis, they only came in for a cocktail on their way to Malibu. It was purely social!"

Julie was perversely triumphant, enormously delighted to learn that he was so far gone that the Lissaks didn't even want to take advantage of him. Just then, the other door opened. Imogene walked in. She had borrowed one of Edith's dresses, had carefully made up her face, had carefully done her hair, and she came in smiling, and lovely, and hopeful.

"That Bartók baloney!" Julie said to her by way of greeting. "All you have to do is mention Braque and the art of Arnold Schoenberg, and they drop like flies!" Her face fell, under the fresh makeup.

It turned out that Julie was referring to the letters, to things he had read in the correspondence with the hotel-band player.

"Julie, don't—not here, not in front of everybody!" she said, but he wouldn't spare her. He kept quoting from the letters, mentioning the most delicate intimacies, merrily relishing every tender tidbit.

"Oh, Julie, how can you!" Edith said. She went up to Imogene and put her arm around her, and they moved toward the door.

"I didn't know!" Spogel protested fervently, apologizing to Imogene and Edith both. "I didn't know. Believe me, I meant only for the best!"

"You ought to read that fancy stuff!" Julie said. "They weren't going to live to make money; they would make money to live! They had it all figured out—he would play the fiddle only three days a week, and have the rest of the time for life and love. What were they going to do for four days every week—talk about Bartók?"

Imogene and the Spogels had reached the hall. The door closed behind them, and the room grew quiet. Julie paused. He was still wound up, but he had no one now to rail at. He went to the desk. He picked up the phone and dialed a number. Suddenly, he had become altogether transformed. In another moment, I heard him arguing fiercely over the phone. He was talking business now, blustering and wangling, desperately trying to make a deal. He was talking to Ronnie Fitts—the other independent producer, the one he had insulted, the man whose wife's earnings in real estate had bought him the original French paintings. "I'll let you have control!" Julie was saying. "Now wait a minute, pappy, listen. I'll let you cast the picture. You'll do it all! You'll hire and fire, you'll handle the rushes in the projection room. It'll be your name on the card, not mine!" He cajoled. He begged.

I hadn't intended to stay for the party; I was expected home for dinner. As I began walking down the hall, I heard Spogel calling to me in a stage whisper. He was standing at the door of one of the bedrooms. "David! David, quick, please, come here, help . . ." Imogene had gone in there, and Spogel didn't know what she might be doing to herself. He feared the worst. "There are pills on the dressing table—sleeping pills! Oh, I never would forgive myself! Imogene!" he whispered frantically, turning back to the door. "Imogene!" He tried the knob.

The door wasn't locked. It opened easily. Imogene was sitting at the dressing table, facing herself in the mirror. She was softly singing "Some Enchanted Evening" and trying on a sequined hairnet of Edith's. She stared at Spogel. "I'm not committing suicide on his account, don't worry," she said slowly. "What did you think—" She broke off. It happened that our eyes met, Imogene's and mine, and we looked at each other for a second, suspended in silence. I noticed the curve of her cheek, and in that instant I saw her as a little girl, chubby and fresh and clear-eyed, everything yet to come. She looked at me with defiance, and then she turned away.

"Sorry," Spogel said sadly. He gently closed the door and, without a word, walked off to shave and take his shower.

In the entrance hall, I found Daisy Kittershoy—all alone there, oddly hunched over the wraps and topcoats on the table, searching away through the pile. "All the years, all the years, all the years," she was saying to herself, like a chant. "You can't know, David," she said, speaking straight at me but not really seeing me, "you don't know how much I looked forward to retiring from the business world. I thought, you see—I anticipated—What you must understand, you see, is that all my life I have been a businesswoman, my mind always taken up, every morning in the shop—I expected a paradise on earth!"

She turned back to the pile of clothing on the table. She was looking for Boris's topcoat, she told me—for the car keys in his pocket. He had left the party. She didn't know where he'd gone, and now she wanted to go home. She had a headache. Her ears throbbed. She wanted to take a bath. She wanted to lie down and rest and sleep. "Seventy-eight thousand dollars!" she said, anguish welling up in her. "Seventy-eight thousand dollars. Do you know what that means, David? All the years, all the years—fighting in the shop, fighting with the contractors, with the buyers, the returns, the rejections!" She wept. She held her face in her hands. "No," she said, making an effort, taking a grip on herself. She dropped her hands and straightened her shoulders. "I mustn't. I mustn't. That was always my trouble—I was always overpreoccupied with material values. It teaches me a lesson. It serves me right. I never had time for literature, or lectures—gardening!" she said. She found Boris's topcoat and reached into the pocket for the keys.

Out on the terrace, old Mrs. Vencie was sitting in her usual place, still going strong. She caught my arm as I passed. "Look, look!" she said, pointing to the city below us, to the thousands and thousands of lights spreading for miles all the way out to the ocean. "Isn't it remarkable, David? All the lights, all the people, each and every one a living human being, the blood in their veins just as red as you or me." On the road winding above us there were headlights moving—young people, undergraduates at the university, driving to the top of the hill on a weekend night. Edith and Spogel were always careful to tell Mrs. Vencie the youngsters went up there to see the view, to hold romantic conversations, but the old woman wasn't fooled. She knew what they did in the parked cars—they necked. "And why not?" Mrs. Vencie said.

The Spogels' dinner party was well under way. The servants bustled. The ladies in their lovely frocks chattered over the candlelight, their faces animated and affectionate, while their husbands stood by themselves, quietly smoking, quietly discussing the situation of the industry.

Mrs. Vencie was telling me how she met her husband. "So," she said, "they told me, 'Go to the shop, make believe you don't know anything, look on him, see if you like him—what will it hurt?' So I went there, to the fur shop where he worked. But, unbeknownst to me, they told him the same story. They told him to look and see, too, maybe he would be interested—so there we stood, like two big dumbbells, spying on each other, bashful and ashamed!"

"Outdoor living," I heard someone say. On the hillside below, bulldozers had scooped out level sites. Homes now lay before us in descending tiers. Most people on Angelo Drive had buffet dinners on Sunday evenings, and it made a picture—the splashes of light down there, the guests grouped on the lawns, the blue-tiled swimming pools.

"Poor Papa," Mrs. Vencie said, nodding, remembering. "You should have seen him when he was alive, David. He was elegant. He had a Kaiser Wilhelm mustache, with the points—a prince! On Sunday morning, he bought the breakfast, and if you asked him what did the whitefish cost, the carp, he never knew. He was too aristocratic to ask the store-keeper the price—he just paid the whole bill. Once, when I was in the mountains with the children, he sent me a letter—he was giving me a big surprise. I wondered to myself, what could it be? Was it a new gas range, maybe? A new icebox, even? It was a picture of himself! He went to a photographer and took a picture—with the mustache, with his Palm Beach summer suit, blowing me a kiss. Poor Papa!"

She took time out to marvel at the view. "Look! It shimmers before the eyes!" she said, pointing again, meaning the multitude of lights. She was old. She knew that nothing was out of the ordinary, that hopes were betrayed, that you always started out with illusion, and yet everything was a wonder to her. "Isn't it gorgeous?" she said to me. "It's like a fairy-land, David. It's like magic!"

TRIPLICATE

A scatter of guests, overflowing the house, were out on the terrace, the men standing together on the tiles or sitting at the tables along with those women who weren't worried about what the damp air would do to their hair. It was an anomaly that the area, basically a desert, where it was said that every shrub, bush, and tree had originally been brought in and planted by hand, had also once been swampland. The name of one of the main boulevards, La Cienega, the Spanish word for swamp, attested to the fact, and you felt the marshlike nature of the region especially when you came to Los Angeles by plane; very often, when the plane landed and you filed out on the tarmac, the thick, wet heat rose up off the ground like a miasma and enveloped you.

Nearby, in a corner of the terrace, a small disturbance was going on, attracting the attention of the guests who now and then looked up from their talk to observe the fuss. It was the young actress, J—— B——, in the first throes of her romance with the director of the picture in which she had the leading role. He was overdue at the party. He was supposed to have met her here at Garrison's house a good while ago, and she had the phone on its long extension cord, calling him to account for his tardiness and at the same time trying to deal with a friend of hers who kept tagging close by at her shoulder, interfering and advising. The actress was skittish, new to sex. Both her parents were New England professional people with established reputations in academic circles, and she had had a carefully restricted bringing up. Her protected life, as a matter of fact, had made problems when she came to the studio. The electricians and carpenters on her sets were asked to go slow out of consideration for her background, to watch their language, and everyone who had business with her similarly took pains to be guarded. But when she fell in love, the word was, the sexual side took her completely by surprise. It was an unexpected world of sensations. The director, James F———, kept a Packard limousine parked just outside the sound stage, the car huddled by itself against the great wall of the barnlike structure, and in the late afternoons—when everyone was busy indoors and the studio streets and grounds were deserted—during the waits between camera setups, the two would go hurrying off to the limousine for a half hour's stolen pleasure, and then they would reappear on the set, going on with the work, when the lights and camera were ready. The director F——— was enormously successful, hardworking and dedicated, doing one picture after the other; he was at the high point of his popularity, on the crest, famous for his exploits, for his winning recklessness, and he captivated the young star. She thought he was the only man she could ever care for. She lost weight. Her clothes all became too big and stopped fitting her, so that when he tussled with her in the hallways or on parking lots it was a desperate struggle for her to keep herself together and stay covered as she fought to beat him off.

"You are merely prolonging the agony," the actress's friend said to her, pulling at her shoulder. "He is begging and begging. You have him at your mercy and you are taking advantage of him merely to assert your possessiveness and strengthen your hold over him. He has to find his car. Let him go and find the car."

That was the trouble; the director had misplaced his car. He was calling from a restaurant. He had finished his dinner, had been on his way to pick up the actress at Garrison's party, only to discover, when he reached the restaurant parking lot, that his car wasn't to be seen—he couldn't find it.

"Who is jealous? Who is possessive? What are you talking about?

pressed him. He was taken with the company at the party, the well-dressed, vigorous people among whom he found himself. He had watched the women inside the house, all of them without exception handsome, remarkably bland, appraising everyone evenly; they were arranged together on the couches, sitting more or less sideways as they tried to face one another in this strained position, so that when you looked at them you were conscious of their calves, thighs, and hips. The men were equally self-possessed. In the way of these large gatherings, there were few introductions, but whether Rosengarten had been introduced to them or not, they were unvaryingly cordial. They looked up as they passed by, greeted him, their well-scrubbed faces shining—"Good evening, good evening"—and were gone. They were individuals whose origins and backgrounds were altogether foreign to him, unknown territory, and moreover they made a point of never talking about their beginnings, shrewd and hard enough to know it was better for them if no one knew where they came from and how they had lived. Rosengarten's wife, Millicent, said he made too much of a mystery of strangers when he met them, that he wondered about them excessively and gave them credit for more than they were, only to be disenchanted as time went by, and what she said was true. It had happened like that in the past, but the strangers he met and had to do with here had a manner that attracted him even though he realized the manner was worked up deliberately for effect, put on. They were energetic, on the rise, smiling and generous, seeking, it seemed to Rosengarten, a true excitement for themselves, an *elixir vitae*, so there was a bona fide quality behind the impersonations they put up, and he couldn't help thinking about them and being drawn to them. With the people in Brooklyn, in the Brownsville section where he grew up and where, until not very long ago, he had lived, there wasn't much to know. When he was young, he sometimes secretly prided himself that he could tell almost on sight how it was with any one of them, what the man did for a living, what he aspired to, the kind of home he had, what his parents looked like, his uncles. They were limited, held down, moving in swarms over the pavements, on their way to and from their jobs, to and from the subways. Rosengarten knew what they would give to be here, how they yearned for the spaciousness, the ease of the life. It used to puzzle him, when he went to work in the studios and settled in California, that they apparently took a special interest in him in the east. Word would get back to him now and then indicating that they talked about him and about how he was faring, that so many of them seemed to know who he was, that his name appeared in the columns. He didn't know what to make of these reports or whether to take stock in them until someone pointed out to him that they regarded him as one of their own, as a part of them, that to them he had done well and gotten away, and so they followed his career with a lingering personal concern. He had an instance of this possessiveness people felt for him when, earlier in the evening, he met for the first time a New York City critic, also a guest at the party. The critic was contemporaneous with him, came from the same sort of background and circumstances, and it was for this reason, Rosengarten always thought, that the critic had taken special notice of his work, that he had several times cited him in his surveys of the Jewish-American novel. Rosengarten had been standing with a doctor prominent in the movie colony when the critic came up. The doctor had many friends in the industry, actors and producers. He went traveling with them in Europe, was close to retirement, limiting his practice at present to the breast, and spoke with a tinge of regret in his voice. "When I was in obstetrics, in the early years, when they were in labor, they used to cry and beg me, 'Abie, help me, help me.' What could I do?" he said to Rosengarten. "They got themselves pregnant without me and just had to wait out the time. I took care of them, delivered them, cleaned them out, and two weeks later they were on their feet, running around and making trouble as usual." He was obviously fond of the many women patients he had had; the memory was dear to him. "It's different with the young doctors now," he said. "You walk into their office and there's always the framed studio portrait of the wife on the desk. When they get established, they marry some kid from a fancy high-up society family and they think she comes from another world. They're half scared of her. In my time the girl generally put the fellow through medical school. She was a schoolteacher or worked in business. And then when the fellow got started, it wasn't so good. He couldn't wait to get free of her. In the old days a doctor came from very poor people. They couldn't put him through medical school. Nowadays there's more money around." When the New York critic came up, the doctor, sensing the rapport between the critic and Rosengarten, stopped reminiscing and grew silent. He stepped back, deferring to them, so that they could talk together.

"Old friends," he said.

Rosengarten explained that while they had never met or even corresponded, they were practically kinsmen, had the same roots in common, that the critic had mentioned him in his articles, and always favorably.

"It's about time we got together," the critic said to Rosengarten. "Somebody mentioned that you were here and I thought I'd look you up and present myself."

He had strong academic credentials; his field was American literature, early and modern, but he had a hankering to extend his range to the larger scene and sometimes wrote essays on the movies. That was why he had come to California on this brief visit, to acquaint himself with the studios and see something of the life, but the trip wasn't turning out as he expected. He felt out of place at the party in his heavy eastern clothes, in his heavy, thick-soled, scuffed shoes. He resented the women, all of them golden and flawless and remote, never having anything to say, so perfectly turned out that he had trouble telling them apart. It irked him that Rosengarten, with his handful of novels and the stories in the magazines, had been able to wangle himself into the studios, and he saw now with a rush of clarity where he had made his mistake. He should have gone to CCNY, not Columbia. The Pulitzer scholarship he had won at high school took him to the private institution, and there, out of vanity over his achievement and a sophomoric sense of superiority, he had let himself be misguided into putting his faith in the higher life of the mind, in criticism, whereas—had he gone to City—he would have had the brains to know from the outset that the intellect was nothing, that nobody wanted it, and that the big rewards lay in fiction, not in literary criticism.

"Kramer makes *The Defiant Ones*," the critic said. "He puts Poitier and Tony Curtis together, handcuffs them, and the experts immediately come up with their hidden themes—the American obsession with the Negro, the American preoccupation with guilt." He was talking about the new breed of movie fans—he was in the middle of telling Rosengarten and the doctor about the widespread interest in film at the universities, that the elite had taken it up. "The big joke, of course, is that Renoir made the same story in France years ago in *Grand Illusion*. The first thing the moviemaker does when he starts on a new picture, as you know," he said to Rosengarten, "is to sit in the projection room and run four or five of the best pictures in the category he's working in. He takes what he needs. He copies. He doesn't bother with the indigenous national themes and undercurrents. *Room at the Top*, for example, is basically the same story as *An American Tragedy*, if you stop to think about it. When Stevens remade the picture, he dropped the whole first volume of Dreiser's book. He didn't worry about the social documentation and the temper of the times—he just stuck to the story."

The doctor felt a hostility in the air. He held off and didn't interfere, leaving the floor to the two of them. Rosengarten was confused. He didn't know what the critic was getting at. As well as he could remember, those were the methods the critic used in his essays—in fact, if he remembered right, the critic himself had written about the Negro and the American guilt-obsession as recurrent motifs in the movies.

"Aren't you repudiating your own work?" Rosengarten said. "Don't you think these principles are valid and worth looking into?"

"Who cares about principles?" the critic said bitterly, waving the objections aside. "Why should themes and motivations give anyone a heart-on? Who wants them? It's the life, the life, the sex, the ass. That's what it all comes down to—the vicarious experience readers crave and writers stubbornly refuse to give."

Rosengarten's wife wouldn't go to these parties and she didn't approve of Solly Renick, who secured the invitations and was the one through whom Rosengarten got to know people. She said Solly used them as a front, that their home was a convenient, respectable place for him to bring his lady acquaintances in the evening and that it gave him status to have a screenwriter like Rosengarten as a close friend. Millicent stayed away from the parties, not because of moral considerations. She said it was all right for Solly and Rosengarten to go to these affairs if they liked, two men on the loose walking in, but that it would be wrong for her to tag along, that it would be unseemly, and the truth was she liked Solly, even though she thought he was underhanded, and really enjoyed meeting the different women he brought to the house—she sat and probed and talked to them by the hour. Solly was small, dark, and intense. He was socially active, busy and ingratiating, with a wide circle of friends, and he had a special, important relationship with Paul Devaney, a top performer, whom he idolized and who was expected at the party later in the evening. Solly served him as a retainer. He waited on the star, went ahead of him in restaurants, cleared the way, handled headwaiters. When Devaney made his appearance at the party tonight, there would be a cluster immediately forming around him, and Solly would then stand by, near at hand, to catch signals and do what was required. "If I only had your talent," he once said to Rosengarten ruefully, meaning how much more he could do for himself, how much easier it would be for him; he worked in the casting department of one of the studios on a week-to-week basis. Rosengarten once spent an hour with Paul Devaney at his home. Rosengarten was at the house on a Sunday afternoon, going along with Solly who had some errand to do there, and the actor kept them, making a visit of it. He brought out some splits of champagne and they sat at the bar, the three of them, and passed the time. Devaney had the advantages of his good looks; he had a suppleness to him, a wonderful ease and lack of strain, which, along with his looks, made it pleasant to be with him and no doubt was a large part of the reason for his success with the public; although here again Rosengarten had to have in mind Millicent's caution, that he tended to glamorize people he didn't know well and make them more than they were. Devaney was in casual clothes that Sunday afternoon, relaxed, unshaven, and at one point Rosengarten — out of awkwardness, speaking when he didn't need to speak — said how strange it was to see him with a day's beard. "Why? What makes you say that?" Devaney said, smiling. "How much older than you do you think I am?"

He seemed amused by the younger man. He started to talk about Bushwick and Borough Park, two residential sections of Brooklyn. He went on to name some of the streets Rosengarten came from, Stagg Street, Maujer, Humboldt, to tease him and show his familiarity with those out-of-the-way, unlikely places. A maid came in and whispered something to him. "Yes, I know what she likes," he said, nodding and getting up. He went behind the bar, mixed a drink, and gave it to the maid, who took it away upstairs, and it was only after a moment or two that Rosengarten realized the drink was for Devaney's wife, that she was in the house somewhere.

Rosengarten had been alone in the library or game room of Garrison's house when the host walked in and they met. Rosengarten had arrived too early at the party — he had been asked as an after-dinner guest — and the company was still at the table in the dining room deep in the house, their voices carrying over. The large living room lay deserted, just a maid straightening up, and, to keep out of the way, he had drifted over to a second, smaller living room, the library or game room with its bar and card tables, which extended off the other side of the entrance hall. It was while he was examining the books on the shelves that Garrison came in through a back passageway and found him. Garrison was a bachelor, divorced, and there was no lady of the house to help him. He was hurrying, heading for the bar to get things ready there before the guests finished up in the dining room. "Bob Rosengarten," Rosengarten said, holding out his hand.

"Oh, you didn't have to say that. I know who you are," Garrison said. He took Rosengarten with him to the bar, warm and friendly from the outset. He made the scotch and soda Rosengarten said he wanted, put the glass in his hand, and then busied himself systematically behind the bar, pulling out bottles of club soda and opening up the wrapped square bundles of ice cubes.

"I was at my parents' all day and things get neglected," he said as he worked. "They're reaching an age now and I want to be as close to them as I can. That's why I relocated. That's why I bought the house. My parents used to come out to California every winter to escape the cold and they finally decided to make it permanent. About my buying this fancy big house," he went on, "the size of it and the alterations, I suppose you might call it a reaction to living in hotels, which is what I've been doing for the past number of years, which is what I did when I used to come out here to see my parents and keep an eye on them. I was in a position to manage it, so I indulged myself. Living in a hotel gets you down after a while. You feel confined, always in the one room, the four walls, and, also, over a lifetime you accumulate a clutter of possessions. This way at least I have a place to put them instead of keeping them in storage."

Garrison came from extremely wealthy people. His mother was a member of a Manhattan family distinguished for its philanthropies and public service, and his father, while his fortune never came near his wife's, was a personage in his own right—there was a museum donated to the city back east bearing the family name, which Rosengarten had passed many times long before he had any idea he would ever get to know Stanley Garrison and be a guest at his home. It was as though his family's prominence had nothing to do with Garrison. The philanthropies, the great wealth, the museum didn't weigh on him. He was pudgy, a man in his late forties, wearing loose-fitting clothes designed to make the best of his plump figure, and he shuffled and ambled as he walked. He seemed absorbed in his duties as host, sincerely enjoying the conviviality going on around him in his house. Rosengarten watched him when he tended the bar for the company. He worked hard at it, offering the guests exotic drinks, concoctions that he obviously had spent a good deal of time discovering and learning how to mix—he would stand back and wait and then laugh with pleasure when the drinks proved a success and the guests complimented him. He had a similar interest in small games, those gimcracky hand-held commercial jokes and puzzles people like to acquire to edify their friends with. He had an assortment of them, some lying on the bar and some which he had on him in his pockets, and Rosengarten saw the real satisfaction it gave him as he showed off his acquisitions to the guests, as the puzzles mystified them and held their attention. There were two magic and joke stores in town—Rosengarten had noticed them on his walks in Hollywood—both of them on the poorer part of Hollywood Boulevard, where the street straggled off into used-car lots with their overhead strings of cheap colored-paper pennants —and it was odd to think of Garrison so bitten by his preoccupation with the gadgets and novelties that he went all the way from his home in West Los Angeles, in Holmby Hills, to these obscure, grimy stores to purchase them.

He took an immediate liking to Rosengarten. They hit it off. Garrison seemed to feel almost as strange and diffident with the guests here as Rosengarten did, almost as much of an outsider even though it was his house, and so the two fell in naturally with each other. Garrison took him by the arm and they walked together, Rosengarten accompanying him on his rounds as host. Rosengarten had assumed without thinking about it that Garrison was another of Solly Renick's surprisingly varied collection of acquaintances and that was how he had come to be asked here tonight, through Solly, but that wasn't the case. Solly didn't know Garrison. It was Louisa Lissak, a young woman Solly had met some months ago, whom he had become good friends with and taken under his wing. She knew the host through longtime family connections in the east, and Rosengarten was soon made aware that he and Solly both were at the party really because of her. The way this came about was that Garrison, as they went walking together, soon started to play a game with Rosengarten, confusing him and throwing him off-balance—he seemed to know a great deal about him, where he lived, that his wife was pretty, a brunette, her name Millicent, that they had a son, and it baffled Rosengarten until the answer came out and Garrison told him about Louisa Lissak.

"Is that how you knew?" Rosengarten said.

"Yes!" Garrison said, pleased with his little deception.

She had been to the Rosengartens' several times, brought there by Solly for an evening's visit. She was attractive, not very young, unattached; she had lived and traveled in Europe for a period of years, had received part of her education there, and had settled recently in California, intending apparently to make her home here for good. She was quiet, self-contained. She wore tasteful, well-made dresses, always in high heels and stockings—Rosengarten never saw her in slacks or in the Levi's the women were wearing here before they were commonly seen elsewhere in the country. She would arrive with an armful of records to be played, Solly standing by and looking on, taking pride in her good manners, her amiability; or else she brought a two-pound box of Allen Wertz chocolates. On one visit she had a beaded bag with her. It had been damaged, the rows of beads breaking and becoming unstrung. This was the year when those very expensive beaded bags were in style, and instead of taking it to a repair shop, she worked away at the job herself, sitting on the couch in the light of the table lamp and threading the tiny beads back into place. It came out after they knew her for a good while that her father was the head and principal owner of a nationally known jewelry store, a century-old institution with branches in a half dozen of the rich East Coast communities—Millicent drew the admission from her one evening when they were having coffee and cake and talking. ("Would you have believed me?" Solly said with a touch of hauteur when Rosengarten asked him why he had kept this piece of news about her to himself, why he hadn't told them who she was and what her father did.) Her father and the elder Garrisons mixed in the same charities and social functions, the families knew each other well, and so Louisa and Stanley Garrison got together when they found themselves both living in California. She had told him all about them, Garrison explained, and he said—on the walk, when he played the game—that now that he had met Rosengarten in person, he hoped to see more of him; he wanted Rosengarten to make it for dinner the next time, no more of this after-dinner nonsense, he said, and of course Mrs. Rosengarten too, Millicent; he wanted them both at the next dinner party he gave at the house.

When he finished with the actress at the phone and came back and rejoined Rosengarten, waiting for him there on the terrace, he was excited; although he spoke to Rosengarten, his eyes weren't on him and he was really thinking aloud. He left the actress and her confidante carrying on at the phone, the actress locked in her heart-and-soul quarrel with the director, but he had the information he was after and knew what he wanted to do.

"Ramsey," he said. That was the name of the maître d' at the restaurant where F—— was stranded. "I know him well. I know the manager too. I'll call the restaurant and have it all taken care of in no time." He meant the problem with the director's missing car. What he intended to do was to have the restaurant send F—— out in a car of their own. "There's always somebody in the office," Garrison said to Rosengarten, "the bookkeeper or one of the cashier's assistants or a relative, so it's no big inconvenience, they can spare an employee for a half hour, and they'll be glad to do it for me if I ask them."

He was exhilarated because he saw a chance of adding F—— to the list of party guests. The director was legendary, a nonpareil, hard to get ahold of. When he appeared in a room, there was a quickening. People looked up and glowed, entranced by the aura of success—it was as though they believed that by being in his presence they might absorb something of his personality and aura, that he would do something for them—and through this stratagem with the restaurant people, by having F—— driven over and dropped off at the house, Garrison thought the director might well be induced to stay on at the party since he would have no car and would be unable to pick up the actress and take her off to wherever they were going, as they had originally planned. It would be a coup, Garrison felt—the party would be talked about and become memorable.

"What generally happens in these cases when they can't find their cars," he said, "is that they come in one vehicle which they borrow from a friend or the studio lets them have the use of, and then they forget and go looking all over the parking lot for their own car, which of course isn't there. I'll bet you anything that's what happened to F———. Just for fun, later on, when he gets here, let's remember to check and see if I wasn't right."

He kept moving on past the tables on the terrace and into the dining room, now darkened and still, the room having been put back in order by the maids. Rosengarten didn't know where Garrison was going and he was further confused, not sure if he was still supposed to accompany him. The actress was on the phone, tying up the line, and he didn't know how Garrison expected to get through to the restaurant, but when he brought up the point Garrison explained there was more than one phone in the house, that there were three of them installed. He was going to his daughter's apartment, to use the phone there. They were building a whole separate unit for her—Garrison had told Rosengarten about it when he was showing him around the house and discussing the renovations they were making. There was a daughter, an only child. She was a young lady, sixteen, away at school in the East, and when she came to stay with him on vacations, he wanted her to have her own special place so that she could feel free to come and go with her friends as she pleased and be her own person. Garrison had been heading for the kitchen, to reach the daughter's apartment by the back stairs, and there was an awkward tangle for a moment or two as he halted in the dining room, not wanting to hurt Rosengarten's feelings yet trying to disengage himself, and Rosengarten for his part realizing clearly now that he was in the way and holding him up.

"You're welcome to come along but there's nothing to see, just lumber," Garrison said. "They're still working on the apartment and you'll get yourself dusty."

"Oh, no, please. I just misunderstood," Rosengarten said, urging him on, and the host, breaking free, went padding into the kitchen to put his scheme into operation.

Rosengarten stayed on by himself in the dining room, savoring the glossy quiet as the commotion over the famous director died away. He took in the flower arrangements, the antiqued mirrors over the sideboard, the panels of antiqued mirror that ran along the sides of the raised centerpiece on the table; he could imagine the faces of the diners, reflected in the mirrors, as they ate and talked in the warm lighting of the room. His wife, Millicent, had no interest in his preoccupations with the life here. She didn't care to see him spend his time with Solly Renick, and Rosengarten himself tried to temper his enthusiasm and not show it too plainly, but she didn't understand what it meant to him to have doors opened, to be able to get into these places he had never seen before and be with the energetic, smiling individuals he met here. Millicent felt Solly was on the shady side, and a case could be made out for her objections. There was the time Solly came to him with a letter he had just received from a wife, a woman he didn't know, had never met or seen, whose husband he had on occasion accommodated with a phone number. The woman, in the letter, accused him of leading her husband astray, of supplying him with girls, of being a pimp. "And it's true!" Solly had said, the dark brown eyes going deep with bewilderment and shock. "It's what I do!" When Rosengarten was at Paul Devaney's house, on that Sunday afternoon visit with Solly, the sips of champagne he had had became too much for him and he was brought home in disgrace, one of the few times he had been drunk in his life; it was the heat of the day, the pressure and novelty of the studio work, the idea of visiting with the star and being in his home. Sitting in the actor's bar with the glass in his hand and sipping from it, he hadn't been aware there was anything wrong with him, but Devaney, looking him over, concerned, when it was time for them to leave, told Solly to drive him home. "Let Bob leave his car here. He can come back for it some other time," he said to Solly —Rosengarten and Solly had arrived separately, each in his own car. Solly had a four-door, dark green convertible, and they went driving off in the open air with the top down, Rosengarten talking away, animated, recounting his impressions of the visit and the star, when Solly at one point, seeing that all was going well, asked if he could stop off and make a call—he was due to take one of his girls somewhere that evening and had to collect her (the reason they had arrived at Devaney's in their own cars). Solly went inside, and while he was gone, while the girl was getting herself together, during the protracted wait, the champagne rose up suddenly and struck Rosengarten, a nausea taking hold and blinding him. When they got Rosengarten home, the girl, Solly's acquaintance, had to lend a hand. Solly, undersized and slight, couldn't manage Rosengarten's weight—he went staggering with him over the lawn—and the girl, who was much larger than Solly, got out of the convertible and, between the two of them, holding him up, half carrying, half walking him, they steered him into the house. "If you want people to see strange women dragging you home across the lawn, I don't mind," Millicent said to him the next morning. On the surface, what Solly did was distasteful or worse, but there was a curious difference between the appearance of something reprehensible and what happened when you were on close terms with the perpetrator, when you were on the ground and saw the man as he was. It wasn't the way Millicent thought it was. When Solly came out of the apartment house with the girl, for example, Rosengarten had been lying stretched out flat on the back seat of the convertible, out of view. Solly couldn't see him and immediately started wandering up and down the street, looking for him and fretting. "Baby, where are you? Baby, where are you?" he called, and anyone who had seen him then, hopping on his toes and crying out in distress, couldn't have judged him harshly or disliked him.

Rosengarten had caught glimpses of F—— now and then—at some movie-industry charity affair, passing through a studio commissary, on the stage in a blaze of light, speaking at a writers and directors' conference held at Royce Hall on the UCLA campus; he had heard the talk, the stories of the different exploits and the legends. The director had a southern courtliness of manner, a way of immersing himself in his attention to the person he was with, and the attention wasn't bogus—it was a genuine politeness, a conscientious considerateness and interest. He worked without a stop. While he was finishing up on one picture, overseeing the editing, the scoring, he was already busy with the screenwriters on the script of his next, and no matter how hard pressed he was, he was always patient, always courtly, good to the people who worked with him, handing out largesse and jobs. He expended himself with a headlong intensity, falling off horses, getting into fistfights, pursuing women and sex, as he did, with a dead-set tenacity; someone saw him falling off his horse at the beach one day, hitting the hard wet sand like a sack of cement, getting up, remounting, falling off again and slamming into the ground. There was a story, certainly true—about a woman going off to meet F—— for a weekend at a desert resort hideaway, when a friend unexpectedly called on her as she was leaving. Her suitcase happened at this time to fall open, and among the articles and garments she was taking with her to the resort was a full-sized monkey outfit, a costume, which, it turned out, the woman had to put on and wear to please

F—— while they were making love. Rosengarten knew that in these things you could only go by yourself, but the monkey costume was an eroticism he couldn't share or feel, beyond his imagining, and it stumped him. Rosengarten was unable to pinpoint a certain element in F——'s work. The director had a remarkable list of smash-hit pictures —and this in a field where it would be found on a close look that the strongest moviemakers, those with the top reputations, very often had no more than two or three solid successes to their credit—but even when his pictures failed and went badly awry, there was always something that held interest and stirred respect. It was a quirk, a tension, a forthrightness, a stamp of character and authority. Rosengarten, starting out in the business and trying to learn for himself what was required, couldn't tell what it was—the director himself seemed to be in the dark; in an interview he once said, "All I can do is hope that if I find something interesting and like it, other people will find it interesting and like it too"—and he wondered if it wasn't some mysterious inborn quality or conglomeration of inherited traits in F—— that accounted for the character and tone in the work he produced.

For Rosengarten, coming out to California was like making a trip to some far-off place, fresh and full of promise, waiting to be explored. It was all new to him; it had the allure of first impressions. He was stimulated by the vitality of these people he had fallen in with and about whom he was eager to learn more; he was excited by their escapades and high spirits, their good looks, their shining good health, their open generosity and bravura style, although he was aware of the disillusion that could come with the passing of time and familiarity. When he first started to write, casting about for material, he found himself going further and further away from the life around him. It was bedraggled, tired. In those days it didn't even occur to him to model characters on real people. He made them up, using his wits and such artifices as he had to make them seem real; the main thing was for the material to be edifying, lively, and effective. Rosengarten understood it didn't matter that a story was untrue —that was, after all, the meaning of the word "fiction"—and yet at the same time it troubled him that there was a disparity between what he was attempting to do and reality, that the experience he was offering was contrived. How many times, while he was struggling with a piece of fiction, did the thought come into his mind that he was committed to the

understanding, if something came up he didn't want to bother with, and was off again on whatever it was that absorbed him at the moment.

He had built up a brilliant record, scoring with his first ventures, his work marked from the beginning by his own strong, independent taste. They were productions still remembered by theatergoers for their artistry, for the mellow sets by Dreyfus and Mielziner; he cast and dressed his productions so expensively that in at least one instance it actually happened that the house playing to full capacity, eight times a week, couldn't pay back the costs or realize a profit. He brought over plays from London, a city he, like many New Yorkers, adored; he put on three and four productions a season, relying on his instinct with an unswerving, defiant conviction. The bulk of his shows was American, and in these outspoken, hard-paced comedies and melodramas, working closely with the playwrights on the revisions, often infuriating them, he evolved a style of his own, new for its time. Other managements were led by the force of his example and success to try for the same clarity, the same hard intelligence and control in their productions, and so, together with his followers and imitators, he had a clear influence on the New York stage and helped give it its distinctive character. It was surprising how many producers and directors could be found who had started out with him. They didn't like to admit the connection and seldom mentioned it—out of old hurts and animosities—but it would turn out that they had once been messenger boys or publicity agents for him, that they had shuttled through the narrow passageways in the back of the Taylor Theatre until they picked up the feel of the work for themselves and felt they were ready to go out on their own. There was a similarly surprising list of actors and actresses, in Hollywood, London, and New York, who had been started or advanced by him and who were also reluctant to have it known that they were indebted to him. Hammet was sallow; he had wide-spaced, small teeth, a bony jaw, and in repose his features lapsed into a glum, homely blankness, but when he was aroused, when he was off on one of his nonstop disquisitions, the intensity of his remarks brought everything to life, the blood went coursing through him, and his face took on a radiance and became transformed. "They don't know," he would say to a writer he was for one reason or another favoring with his attentions, allying himself with the writer against the *nudniks*, the naysayers, the *kvetches*, the *creschers* (groaners), as he called them.

What he objected to in the critics was their presumption and that they acted without responsibility of any sort. "It never occurs to them they're free riders. It never occurs to them that it's possible they don't know they don't know. The worst thing you could do to yourself is to fall into the trap of thinking they have a competence because they nag and hit people over the head. They can't help you. They have no understanding of what makes a story go or how it takes its shape. When they have an original idea, it so upsets them they rush into print with it, not realizing the idea could be a bad idea and that it was most likely considered and discarded long before they had their inspiration." In the same way that he dismissed the critics out of hand, he totally disregarded the personal attacks against him and the animosities. "You must never, never mind them," he said, clipping the words out through his sharp, small teeth. He had a Jermyn Street fastidiousness, the London manner he admired so warmly and which no doubt was part of the image he had in his mind of himself when he was at his best and took pains to foster. "How long did it take you to write that story?" he would say to the writer whom he was in the process of courting, referring to some story he knew the writer prized, and when the writer said a month, six weeks, he would turn away, wincing with envy, pretending that he could never work with such speed so well, and the writer, devastated, would have the heart go out of him with the compliment.

A group of men at a table at the edge of the terrace, the table closest to the dining room, which was where Hammet found Rosengarten, looked on; the sight of Hammet, turning up at the party as he did, brought back the old stories, and, sitting in the darkness, watching him as he held on to Rosengarten and kept talking to him, they gossiped about the producer, remembering his foibles, his egotism. They were studio people who had had dealings with him in the past, directly or indirectly, or knew people who had had dealings with him. "It's not the deafness," a man at the table said. "He just likes to do the talking. It wouldn't make any difference whether he could hear or not. When you're with him, while you're saying something to him, he doesn't listen. You can see his mind working, thinking on ahead to what he's going to say next. I guarantee you in fifteen minutes he'll take over and run the show here. He must. He has to be the main attraction. Two years ago I was in Lichtman's office in the executive building when the girl in the outer office announced Hammet. 'Just watch,' Lichtman told me. 'Wait and see what he does when he gets in here.' He had holes in his shoes. He wore a turtleneck sweater, he needed a shave, and he was up there to see what he could get out of Lichtman. In no time at all, before we knew it, he had somehow exchanged places with Lichtman—Lichtman was sitting there on the couch and he was in the swivel chair with his feet up on the desk, holding forth. We could see the big fat circles on the soles of his shoes with the holes in the middle where the leather was worn through." Someone else spoke up. This was a producer long prominent in the community. He was related to the head of the studio where he worked and had been a fixture for years—his mother and the wife of the head of the studio were sisters—and in the dark he now recalled an encounter he had had with Hammet when Hammet had come into his office to try to sell him a story, and he hadn't liked it and turned it down. "Boy, did I get a bawling out," the nephew said, rueful with the memory of it. "He gave me a lecture, told me I didn't know my ass from my elbow, and had no right to exist. The story was no good. He was just trying to hit the studio for a fast fifty thousand dollars."

Hammet was here on this trip to work with a husband-and-wife screenwriter team on a play they had written. The New York man who had the play under option had sent him out to see what he could do to help with the revisions, to more or less guide or supervise the changes, but the writers wouldn't cooperate and the project was blocked from the start. Hammet had never stayed in Los Angeles for any length of time or worked in pictures. He came and went, making sudden forays when he needed money, in the old days, negotiating with Hughes, Goldwyn, and Selznick. The husband and wife, in the present case, were demoralized. They were successful movie writers but they were dissatisfied with their status in the studios and had hoped to improve themselves with the prestige of a Broadway play. They were sick with disappointment. To them, Hammet was a has-been. They had no faith in him, didn't think the changes would come to anything, and were worn out with the wrangles and months of toil. They knew Hammet had a contempt for the kind of writing they did and had taken the job only for the five-hundred-dollar fee the New York management was paying him and the fare to the coast, so they shut him out. They wouldn't come to the phone when he called, kept out of reach, and it seemed there wouldn't be much for him to do while he was out here.

Hammet had Rosengarten by the arm, taking charge, his eyes shifting about as he talked, to see who was at the party that he knew or could recognize. "I always love to watch what happens when the studios bring people out on contract from the east and they settle down here to live," he said with enthusiasm. "They come from Washington Heights, West Bronx, Philadelphia, and Chicago, and it's a wonder to see how they open their hearts to the greenery. They're enchanted with the lawns, the Japanese gardeners, the plants and flowers, the bougainvillea blossoms, the hibiscus and oleander." He was exhilarated by his presence in California again, by the change of scene, and by the party. He didn't stop for amenities. He wouldn't let Rosengarten intervene. If Rosengarten had asked him how he was, what he was doing in California, how things were going for him, he would have waved the inquiries aside as of no interest to him; he would have resented the intrusion into his affairs. He had Rosengarten explain to him what was going on with the actress and her companion at the phone, and the story of the fuss the actress was having with the director F—— set him off—he was intrigued by the love-play, the frolic. "What people don't understand about this place is that the whole idea is not to make great pictures but to enjoy life in the sun. They keep asking for works of art, but the picture-making from the beginning was secondary, starting with the Fairbanks–Pickford days when they entertained visiting royalty and statesmen. That's why the pictures had their worldwide success. They were made without strain by happy, unneurotic people who were busy having a good time and who worked naturally out of their instincts, and audiences everywhere were intelligent enough to perceive this and treasure it. It's the climate, the desert. It comes with the locality. You'll notice the further west you go, the more polite people become, the more relaxed. People who complain that Los Angeles is sprawling and without roots and has no character are uninformed. It just means they haven't been here long enough. They're not familiar with Santa Anas. They don't know about heat, its crispness, and what the sun does. You sense this best as you come off the canyon roads —Benedict Canyon, Coldwater—and the big houses lie spread out on the flat before you, in the middle of the day, with the streets empty, with no one on the sidewalks, and you see the red-tiled roofs, the lawns and flowers, everything sparkling in the sun."

He was in form, rattling off his pronouncements on California and the movies with that high-handed, aggressive sureness that grated on people and set them against him, pronouncements which—Rosengarten knew—he was just as likely to reverse and repudiate the next time out ("Did I say that? I have no recollection of it. . . ."). Rosengarten was in an awkward position. He himself was something of an interloper, an after-dinner guest, there at the party invited at second or third hand—through Solly who was there through Louisa Lissak who was the one who knew Garrison—and it was an embarrassment now to have Hammet suddenly turn up and barge in on them. Rosengarten didn't know what Garrison would make of it or what the host would think of him. He was distressed for Hammet. In his student days, when he bought those cut-rate tickets at Leblang's in the basement of Gray's Drug Store, at a time when Hammet was only a name to him, remote, he would sit up in the balcony and marvel at the gemlike quality of the plays the producer was responsible for. They had values Rosengarten had never seen before nor had been able to envision. He absorbed the effects with the ardor of youth, with the young man's open wonder of discovery. The memory of these golden plays and the impact they had on him stayed with him, coloring his feelings for the producer, and it hurt to see him now in his decline, derided and in disgrace. Rosengarten wished his wife had been more discreet and hadn't told Hammet where he was. He didn't know why she had had to do this—she must have known Hammet could very well take it into his head to come after him at the party. For himself, Rosengarten didn't mind the producer's overbearing manner. He shrugged it off, he made allowances, but he knew Hammet—how self-centered he was, how grossly rude he could be, how his total indifference to the feelings of others acted on people—and he couldn't expect anyone else to feel about him as he did.

"*Must talk. Must talk,*" Hammet said. "I had this dream where I was with a group of people at a dinner party. In my dream, I dozed off, forgot myself. There was a lull in the conversation, nothing going on, and suddenly I roused in a panic of excitement—*Must talk! Must talk!* I told myself in my dream and went back to work." He told the story on himself, still holding on to Rosengarten, still looking off and taking in the scene, watching whoever passed by, and continued, talking now about Solly Renick. "He saw me as I came in and bolted. He tried to lose himself in the crowd and thinks I didn't see him, but I did," Hammet said. He asked Rosengarten questions about Solly—what was Solly's connection at the party, was he still doing a big business, did Rosengarten see a great deal of him—and ran on, not halting long enough to hear out such answers as Rosengarten could think to tell him. Hammet had spotted Solly in the entrance hall; Solly had stationed himself there, at the door, to pick up Paul Devaney when the star entered. Solly had once worked for Hammet. He had been one of the messenger boys or assistants at the Taylor Theatre—that was where Rosengarten met him; they used to talk in the long narrow corridors while Rosengarten was waiting to get in to see Hammet, and became friends—and now he avoided his former employer on his trips to the coast. Hammet chaffed him badly when they ran into each other, and so Solly made a point of staying out of his way.

Hammet was wound up from the plane trip, from the difference in time and his prolonged day. He was unsettled, at a standstill and blocked. With his active, restless brain, he was constantly seeking diversion—all he had had to hear from Millicent was that there was a party and he came flying. When he took an exaggerated interest in the actress and her running quarrel with F——, what struck his fancy was how famous they were, that F—— with all his renown and record of hard work could still lose himself in innocent antics. It was as if by putting up a show of elation Hammet thought he could attach himself to their youth and high spirits and renew himself. He had lost desire. That was at the bottom of his trouble. He, who had driven himself, whose scrawny overheated body used to burn up energy, couldn't get started. If he took on a project, he soon lost confidence in it. A lethargy took over and it was almost impossible for him to persevere with it to a finish, and so he bantered and threw up a screen of talk, in this respect resembling certain of the homosexual dress designers at the studios. "Wasn't it terrible—did you ever see such dreadful hats?" they would say if asked their opinion of Gone With the Wind. "What is it—it's just a dark hollow triangle, isn't it?" they would say, speaking of cleavage, pretending be mystified by it and the fuss made over it, queening. They knew what cleavage was. It was in the line of their work. They wore a different mien when they were by themselves working among the garment racks in the studio wardrobe departments, when the old Jewish tailors, in the heavy odor of camphor, looked on, wondering about them, what it was they did, what good they got out of it.

"It was the clearest case of love at first sight I know of," Hammet said, going on about Solly. Solly, originally from Manhattan's Lower East Side, was enamored of Broadway from the day he went the few miles uptown and left the tenement streets, and Hammet was now recalling the event and the change it made in Solly's life. "The little martinet. He couldn't stand the toilets in the kitchens, the janitors collecting the garbage on the hall landings. The instant he saw the stage lights and the bright fancy people, he knew this was what he had to have. It burst on him with the force of revelation. To get there and hang on, he's willing to lie, steal, commit felonies and do anything that's required."

In New York, when Rosengarten first knew him, Solly had a top-floor cold-water flat, but he fitted it out as a kind of studio and was even in those days managing to set himself up in the style he yearned for. The walls were painted midnight blue. He had an easel standing ready under the skylight. There were his young actress friends who were always in the place, contentedly knitting. Solly handled himself with an air, imitating the elegant theater people he admired—he would stand in a drizzle with his topcoat thrown over his shoulders, his dark brown eyes flashing imperiously, the raindrops glistening on his hair. He imitated, in fact, most of all the fastidious manner of Hammet for whom he worked, and thinking of those days when Solly idolized the producer and modeled himself on him, Rosengarten felt guilty. He winced inwardly and was uncomfortable because he had gone over to Solly and made friends with him, because it would seem that he was siding with Solly and that he too was running out on Hammet now that his fortunes had turned— that was what Hammet meant, Rosengarten felt sure, when he asked if he was seeing a good deal of Solly these days. But while Rosengarten was reproaching himself and taken up with these feelings of guilt, Hammet suddenly switched away from Solly and was now going after him. The rancor that he had suppressed so far, which as a matter of taste and pride he normally would not allow himself to show, now spilled out. He chivvied Rosengarten, as he usually did when he came to California, holding him to account for his movie work, but never before in such earnest. It was a surprisingly bitter personal assault.

"How do you do it?" Hammet asked. "What do they do, do they just call you up and hire you?" He made himself an outsider, pretending he had no knowledge of the studio procedure. "Do they have a supply of story properties that they hand out to different writers according to a system of rotation, and you then proceed to write a screenplay for them? Doesn't it disturb you to write on order? Can you do your best under such conditions? Do you really feel at this particular moment like writing a cops-and-robbers gangster story for Sidney Margulies?" He had found out from Millicent, when he spoke to her on the phone and badgered her with his questions, what Rosengarten was doing, so he knew the name of the producer and what the assignment was.

"You don't write for hire," Rosengarten said. The script he was doing for the studio—a police story, not a gangster picture—centered on the life in a day of a police station in a large city. He had gone out on patrols with the squad cars, had spent a number of evenings at the Los Angeles Police Department headquarters downtown in the City Hall, and was sincerely impressed with the material he had picked up and the possibilities. It wasn't a case of having an assignment forced on him, and he tried to say so to Hammet and explain how he felt. "It can be as good as you want to make it. There's no reason why you can't do good work on a movie."

"Is it the same kind of writing you do when you're writing for yourself? Would you write this way for —————?" He stood before Rosengarten with his dead, famished Rasputin eyes, with his bony jaw and wide-spaced teeth, dealing out his gibes with the smoldering contempt that made him repellent and gave him the reputation he had. The stories Rosengarten had done for ————— were brief pieces, a few thousand words. They were carefully worked over, really vaudeville turns, depending on mimicry, and they had little relation to the writing he did for the movies.

"In a sense you're writing to order for them too," Rosengarten said. "They have their own conventions and you meet them whether you know it or not."

"Nothing you do for Sidney Margulies has the ghost of a chance of being any good," Hammet said. "You weren't honest when you took on the assignment. You weren't excited by the possibilities. You just talked yourself into it, which is something no high-class *cuver* ever does. Do you know what a *cuver* [whore] is? That's what you are, a *cuver*. If you were on a deserted island with three months to live, you wouldn't be writing a story for Margulies," he declared. "There's nothing more satisfying for an artist than to work to the limits of his strength. You don't know what happens when you break through. You become important to yourself. Your spirits soar. No one can touch you. What you've done is there, irrefutable. There's nothing for anyone to say. Instead of bothering with made-up plots and concocted dramas, you should go for the actual thing, for the bone, the substance, the inside unexplained and unexplainable essence of the phenomenon. You don't make it up or invent it. You find it—and when you do, if you catch it right, when you get it down on paper it surprises even you who wrote it."

He was bored with what he had done in the past. He set no store on those fine London plays with their Dreyfus and Mielziner sets, which theatergoers still talked about. To him, strangely, they were transparent. The dramatic form palled. He was irked by the reliance on dialogue, by the tedium of dialogue; he was irked by the manufactured excitements, the studied staging, the actresses ascending staircases. He had used up his interest in the games of fiction, in the foolishnesses of fiction. He shied at going into production with a new play. He knew the enormous expenditure of energy that would be demanded and he knew he didn't have it in him, that he no longer could beat himself up and maintain the necessary lunatic frenzy to carry him through a production; or if he was trapped, if he had somehow committed himself and was already in production, he would soon begin to shift and shirk until in the end he managed to close the show down on the road, in Wilmington or Philadelphia or wherever they were, and broke free. He detested every part of the business, down to the soggy Rialto typescripts. It was a bore to him, a weight on his mind, a never-ending irritation and affliction, and it was the only thing he wanted to do. "X———— [a leading playwright] wears me out," he declared in an interview. "M———— [another leading playwright] has told me everything he has to say and there's no need for me to go on listening to him." He ticked them off, one after the other, explaining why he wasn't attracted to the theater and had become inactive, and in the process alienating the best of the established playwrights as well as the new ones coming up. "There isn't a dramatist at present that can startle or delight me," he said in the interview. "When

I go to the theater, I have an idea of what I'm likely to see, and it never fails, that's what I get."

He fought the Dramatists Guild, having differences with them over the rules that gave the playwright control of the script and the revisions. He fought the stagehands over their regulations and featherbedding. With his fierce self-esteem, his awareness of his eminence in the theater and the deference due him, with his special brand of nastiness and disdain, he flared out in vicious, periodic rages, dressing down the critics, investors, other managements, and the public, until it was reckoned at one time that he had affronted every segment of the Broadway establishment. He was so far behind in his taxes that he could never catch up through straight income earnings; only the more favorably taxed capital gains could pull him out but he had shut the door on most of the people who could have been of help to him. He had dealings with lawyers and other intermediaries, trying to get them to flush out businessmen backers for him. He would light on some story property and try to work it up into a movie project; or he would collaborate with a writer, on the writer's idea or his own idea, and then take the treatment out to California to see if he could dazzle a movie producer with it and make the sale and killing. He was debt-ridden, haggard, alone, his wives long gone and out of mind; to avoid the mortifications that he knew would invariably ensue—because he would misbehave, because there would be squabbles—he made a practice of turning aside acquaintances and kept to himself, and so became something of a loner or recluse. There was a story told about him that he was in an agent's office one day, trying to knock down the price of a paperback novel he wanted. In the heat of the goings-on, as he argued and maneuvered, putting pressure on the author of the novel who was also present, suddenly something possessed him. He stopped. He changed tactics. "Give me a break," he said, harsh, fixing them with his eyes—so that the author there wasn't clear whether Hammet was begging or meant to be sardonic and mocking.

When Rosengarten and his wife were still new to California, they found themselves one evening, almost by accident, in the company of a group of illustrious personages, people who to Rosengarten were illustrious—what happened was that the couple he and Millicent were supposed to be with that evening were unexpectedly called to greet some arrivals just in from New York, and the couple insisted on having the

Rosengartens come along with them and join the group. As Rosengarten, at this impromptu gathering, sat quietly listening to the visiting notables and their friends, whose faces and names were in most cases familiar to him but whom he had never met, he suddenly realized the conversation had taken a turn and that they were all talking about Hammet. They were New York theater personalities—important actors with their fine women, a Pulitzer Prize–winning playwright, people a good generation or so ahead of Rosengarten and Millicent—and it impressed him to see with what unanimity and vindictiveness they ran Hammet down. They were rollicking along, telling their stories, and as they went on, there was a feeling in the air of unseemliness, that the proceedings were one-sided and that something ought to be said to balance the malice, and soon a man there—not one of the visiting party but a screenwriter who worked at Rosengarten's studio and who had lunch with him at the writers' table in the commissary—looked around, saw Rosengarten, and, meaning well, on the impulse, urged him to speak out and defend Hammet. The terrible part of it was that the screenwriter, having noticed that Rosengarten had been silent all evening, seized the opportunity really only because he wanted to draw him into the conversation and please him. "You know Hammet. You like him. Why don't you tell us what you think?" the screenwriter said. "Rosengarten here is the only man in the country who adores Rogers Hammet," he explained to the group.

Rosengarten was flustered, suddenly conspicuous. He had no idea he had talked so much about Hammet or that what he said had been absorbed and remembered. He was sitting on a couch, placed between two of the extremely attractive, imposing New York ladies, and they stared at him in silence at close quarters, waiting to hear what he had to say. He knew he didn't measure up to the company, that he was unknown, out of his class, and when Lee Oelrichs, the tall, slender New York stage-veteran leading man, who was among the visiting personages there, approached him, smiling and quizzical, inviting him to begin—"Yes, yes, we'll be glad to be enlightened," he said in the high, thin gasp of a voice this actor had—Rosengarten set forth, determined not to be abashed.

He said—as he often recalled during the many years the memory of that mortifying incident remained with him—that you could after all only judge a person according to your experience with him, and in his dealings with Hammet he had found him agreeable and interesting. Rosengarten said that he invariably heard Hammet attacked, that wherever he went people spoke unkindly about him, as they had here this evening, but the remarkable thing was that he could seldom pinpoint the specific basis for the complaint. People didn't substantiate their charges; they just made them and let it go at that. As a matter of fact, in the case of his own dealings with Hammet, he wasn't sure he hadn't received more than he had given. He wasn't sure that in any encounter with Hammet you weren't rewarded in one way or another.

"How can you say that?" Oelrichs said, still smiling his weary, benign smile. "How about that?" he said to the others. "Here we are, fighting over Rogers Hammet and Hammet doesn't even have to take the trouble to be present and extend himself. It just shows the power of the man. Did anything come of your project, your venture with Hammet, whatever it was?" he asked Rosengarten, turning back to him. "Did he go through with it?"

"No," Rosengarten said. What he had in mind was the fund of ill feeling in people, that when an acting part fell through or a project collapsed, the natural tendency was to strike out and blame whoever could be blamed. Rosengarten was thinking of the time they had to give up on his own project, when the dramatization of his novel failed to come off and had to be abandoned. "Now you'll go around like everyone else and say what a terrible person Rogers Hammet is," Hammet had said to him. Rosengarten wanted to say that with ambitious people in the theater, a certain amount of bitterness was predictable and had to be discounted, but he was rushed, not at his best, he spoke out more strongly than he intended, and his choice of words was unlucky—he was squashed down there on the couch, wedged in the cushions, with Oelrichs at his full height towering above him. "Nobody has to go to Hammet," Rosengarten said boldly. "We're warned enough. We know what we're getting. The trouble is people want certain things from him and when they're disappointed, they become enraged and the gossip starts making the rounds. They want to use him. It works both ways. He just takes them before they take him."

A shudder went through Oelrichs, a flash of irritation. The smile left. That leading-man's way of holding himself, the easy poise and authority strangely fell apart. He was years older than he made himself appear, not at all really slender any longer.

"If you were ever closed on the road by Hammet, you'd know what we were talking about," the actor said. "This isn't a game of bridge we're playing. These are people who have their livelihoods to earn, whose careers are on the line. No one can be more of a spellbinder than Rogers Hammet when he wants to be and then after you've committed yourself for the season and passed up other managements, he just walks away without a by-your-leave and leaves you hanging out to dry. And you never know if that wasn't the idea from the start, that it was all to cross the other managements and he never had the slightest intention of going ahead with you in the first place. This is a man who takes pleasure in seeing how treacherous he can be. You say you want proof, you want charges substantiated. I can give you times and places—the broken promises, the incredible things he's done to people . . ." He stopped, chagrined, annoyed with himself for his outburst, for his loss of self-possession. He tried to cross back and joke and recover himself, but couldn't carry it off. "Everyone knows he's a double-dealing scoundrel, no one likes him, no one trusts him, and if he walked through that door right this minute and offered me the best part in the world, I'd get down on my knees and take it. Oh, come on," he said, "let's get out of here. Let's get some air. Let's go out and listen to some music."

The rhythm of the evening was broken, the whole welcoming reception ruined. This was a rented California hillside house, and in the dim, raw lighting of the place there was a flurry of movement, people shifting, getting past the furniture, preparing to leave. It was a rout. Rosengarten foundered in the soft cushions of the couch, unable to get to his feet, wanting only to find Millicent and escape, jostled by the big Junoesque ladies around him as they gathered their wraps and glanced back at him with disapproval. In the maelstrom and bad light, a face suddenly loomed before him. It was the Pulitzer Prize–winning playwright, seeking him out. "There may very well be a good deal of truth in what you say," he assured Rosengarten, solemn and kind. "You may be absolutely right for all we know, and we in the wrong."

Oelrichs tried to make it up to Rosengarten just a few days later. Oelrichs was sitting on a bench outside one of the huge stucco sound stages at Metro, the studio where Rosengarten was employed, chatting with a small group around him while he waited for the after-lunch shooting to resume. Rosengarten, who liked to walk through the rows of the big barns after he had his lunch, made a turn around the corner of one of the stages, and as he did, came flush upon Oelrichs and the group with him; it was the first Rosengarten knew that the actor was making a picture on the lot, that it was in fact the picture here that had brought him out. "Oh, Rosengarten," Oelrichs called in that unusual feathery voice of his, beckoning to him to come over, to join them, to talk, but Rosengarten, in his perverse obstinacy, even before he was aware of what he was doing, refused to acknowledge the greeting. He didn't turn, kept walking straight ahead, and then a month and a half later, while Oelrichs's company was still in production with the picture, it happened that the actor died. The company had gone to the Orient to pick up some location shots, and it was on that trip that Oelrichs had his fatal heart attack.

For Rosengarten, when he first got to know Hammet, there was the glow of excitement of being with someone celebrated and admired from the distance, and then, by some wonderful piece of luck, suddenly made accessible. The telephone call, coming late at night, out of the blue, had the impact of an electrical charge. Rosengarten was teaching grade school, living with Millicent in a one-room Brooklyn apartment, with the Murphy bed swinging out of a closet; the apartment building in Flatbush, on Ocean Avenue not far from the park, Prospect Park, was a step or two up from Brownsville but nothing like the trip over the bridge into Manhattan—and the call from Hammet, the summons to the Taylor Theatre, and the long drawn-out sessions and conversations that followed had the effect of a release, opening up to Rosengarten the prospect of those places and allurements he had aspired to and which so far were closed to him. It was a beginning. "Mr. Rosengarten? This is Rogers Hammet," the voice came over the phone that night, and Rosengarten, caught off guard, half-asleep, replied, "Mr. Fishzohn? This is Theodore Dreiser. Yes, Louis, what is it?" He never dreamed it could be Hammet calling him.

"Who is Louis? Who is Fishzohn—someone you know?" Hammet had asked and gone on, not waiting for the answer, as he wouldn't. "No, no, this is Rogers Hammet. I want to talk to you about your novel, which I like. . . ." And then the electrical charge, Rosengarten coming fully awake, as he realized it was actually Hammet. Louis Fishzohn was a friend who taught at Rosengarten's school with him and liked to play these practical jokes over the phone.

Hammet had a way, when Rosengarten came to see him at the theater, of keeping him with him or making him stand by and wait out in
the corridor while he did what he had to do during the course of the
day, and so Rosengarten spent hours at a stretch with him, whole afternoons going into the evenings. He would accompany Hammet in and
out of the theater, they would have dinner together in the plain businessmen's restaurants in the garment district just below the theatrical
section of the city, and once, after they had eaten, Hammet took him to
the place where he was living, a three-story red-brick private house on a
street just off lower Fifth Avenue. It was one of the few luxurious homes
Rosengarten had ever been in. The long living rooms were furnished in
a spread of warm colors; a uniformed maid, while they were there,
opened a door in the rear of the house somewhere and three amazingly
beautiful standard-size black poodles came bounding in joyously to greet
Hammet and frolic with him. At the theater, he was then preparing *The
Almond Trees*, the play by the Pulitzer Prize–winning Clarence Kelley
(another Pulitzer Prize winner, not the one Rosengarten was to meet
some years later in Hollywood). The outer office would be filled with
actresses, some of them in riding clothes or other costumes, waiting to
read for the play, and there were other people Hammet had to see, but
he would put the work off and talk to Rosengarten by the hour, about
racehorses, dolphins, or living in London. He seemed to like to have
Rosengarten there to talk to, Rosengarten could never figure out why
and often thought about it, but of course he couldn't very well ask him.

Rosengarten one afternoon truthfully told him that in starting to
write his novels, what he had done to get himself going was to model
his work on Huxley's books, on *Point Counter Point*.

"Why did you do that?" Hammet wanted to know. "Because of the
novelist character in the book, because of Quarles? Did his theories on
the novel attract you?"

"No, it wasn't the diaries, the theories, or any of the other ideas in the
books." The truth was Rosengarten always had trouble with the larger
intellectual statements and abstractions in novels; he had trouble understanding them—they had no body, there was no development or form—
and he secretly believed other readers didn't really understand them
either. "I used to skip those parts," he told Hammet. "It was the people,
the characters."

"Is that what you wanted to do, to copy the people in Huxley—in *Point Counter Point*, in *Antic Hay?*"

"I thought they were wonderful," Rosengarten said. "The way they talked, their attitudes, that they bothered with intellectual matters and had their personal problems. I wanted to get the same kind of liveliness and commotion in my own writing." Hammet was amused by the notion of patterning Brownsville, Brooklyn, life on Bloomsbury and Belgravia, and understood it. He came from the same neighborhood streets and he knew all about the tenement backyards, the constant reading that went on at those windows where the light was good, the constant reaching out and obsession with other ways and places. The subject bored him, something far in the past for him, along with his aunts and uncles. It was all behind him. Hammet came from Passaic, New Jersey. He had changed his name on an impulse that meant nothing to him now and that he wouldn't think about or discuss. As a youngster, graduating from high school in New Jersey, he had actually gotten himself enrolled in one of the Ivy League colleges and had attended classes there for two and a half semesters—an outlandish venture, in those years, for a person in Hammet's circumstances, a Jew, and this too was something he wouldn't talk about; he would shrug off the inquiry if it came up, making use of his deafness and not answering. He teased Rosengarten about the old-time homemade crystal radio sets. He recalled the New York *Sun*, the hookups that newspaper published, the coils and shellac. He recalled to Rosengarten the hours spent at night with the earphones clamped in place, listening to the name bands of those days and the sounds coming from the grand hotels they played at—the McAlpin Roof, the Hotel Bossert Roof Garden, B. A. Rolfe, The Pennsylvanians. The poor-boy ardor to get out in the world was an old story to him and a banality, and yet when Rosengarten—in speaking of the skimpy indifferent reviews his first novel got ("The horrors of life in a Brooklyn slum," one notice read)—mentioned that Sean O'Casey, almost alone, from across the water, had taken the pains to search out the book and praise it, the reaction from Hammet was startling in the intensity of his feeling. "Did he do that? I'm so glad you told me. I'm so glad it was O'Casey." It sent a genuine thrill of pleasure through him, Rosengarten could tell, to think of the Irish rebel reaching out to join with his young counterpart in the Brooklyn tenements. The reference stirred up old remembrances, old bitternesses and mortifications. "What you must do," he told Rosengarten, "is go out to Floyd Bennett Field. That's at the end of Flatbush Avenue in Brooklyn. Get up in one of the skywriting planes they have there, and in letters fifty feet high, all over the center of Manhattan, write FUCK YOU. That's the only way you'll ever amount to anything as an artist and a man."

He had seen a Sunday family outing at the museum in the park, the point about this particular family being that there was a dwarf among them, and he sketched out the scene one day, putting it on the stage for Rosengarten, as they idled in the office, as the young actresses waited outside. Hammet described the ugliness of the midget, a girl or young woman, and spoke of her fierce determination to surmount her disabilities, to keep up with the others in the group, her shoes jutting out like claws, he said, as she skimmed over the marble floors; he described the young normal-sized, good-looking brother gamely staying close by, gamely smiling. Another time Hammet spoke of an item in a magazine about a colleague who had left Broadway, who had disappeared from sight and subsequently turned up working in Hollywood in the movies. "————— didn't die, he just went west," was the way the magazine article began. Hammet took a special delight in noting the basic human frailties, the petty disguised jealousies and acts of malice. "They must have busted their balls thinking that one up," he said, meaning the wisecrack. "The only thing to do when they print some crap about you is to ignore it," he said to Rosengarten. "They're of no importance. They shouldn't be allowed to touch you. I was in a restaurant once with some people after a play of mine had opened. I was depressed, the reviews had been bad, every one of us was gloomy, and suddenly, as we were sitting there eating in the gloom, I started to gag and whoosh. My friends thought I had finally gone out of my head with grief and was breaking down, but I wasn't deranged. I was choking on my food and literally laughing myself to death because it suddenly occurred to me—who, who were these critics? What were they to me? What did they know? You see their names over the reviews," Hammet said, "and the print has a certain impact, but the illusion vanishes the instant you meet them in person. Without the by-line they're nothing, and sooner or later they're gone, someone else coming along to take their place." He cited the examples of Harold Rexford and Agatha Dampf, not a great many years ago flour-

ishing and rambunctious, now barely remembered, the critics compa-
rable, he said, to the present —————— and —————— . "There's
nothing more woebegone than a reviewer who's lost his job and is on
the beach," Hammet said.

He talked about his enthusiasms, about horses and horseracing, in
which Rosengarten also had an interest. Hammet would go on about
Coucci's riding style, the view from the roof of the grandstand at Bel-
mont Park, the sight of horses flying down the homestretch. He and
Rosengarten would spend time over the *Morning Telegraph*, handicap-
ping a Saturday-afternoon stakes race together, matching horses. "The
whole point about being at the races is that when you're there you're not
in some dreary hospital, waiting to see how the surgery came out. Intelligent people understand that," Hammet said. During the time Rosengarten was involved with him on the stage adaptation of his novel, it
happened that a popular young Broadway singer, a boy still in his early
twenties, extremely successful but suffering from a congestive heart condition, was suddenly stricken, was labored and struggled over, and, after a
time, died—and the waste, the harsh interruption, got to Hammet. The
singer had been so young, so successful, the whole banquet lying spread
out before him.

"Now you used up your whole Easter vacation," Hammet said to
Rosengarten one day, the cloudy Rasputin eyes hovering on him. This
was when Rosengarten had finished typing up the dramatization and
had turned it in. He had done the actual writing job during the school
spring holidays, working nonstop through the ten free days he had—
Rosengarten, in those days, could work from the time he got up in the
morning until he went to sleep. Hammet held the script in his hands.
He hadn't read it. He probably hadn't even riffed through the pages—he
talked, joking, about a producer around town who was known never to
read anything but who, according to the story, was able to choose the
plays he wanted to do from the feel of the manuscript in his hands.
Hammet had given up on the project for some time now. The fancy that
had taken him to Rosengarten's novel had soon languished and evapo-
rated. "Now you'll go around like everyone else and say what a terrible
heel Rogers Hammet is," he said, the dead eyes still on him.

"Oh, no," Rosengarten said. For him the whole experience had been
a boon. He wasn't seriously disappointed. He knew from the start he

wasn't going to have a play produced on Broadway so fast and hadn't banked on it; coming from where he grew up, he didn't expect miracles, he knew how it was with people, how they backed down and vacillated. For him it was enough just to have been with Hammet, that Hammet had given him the time. What a thrill it was for Rosengarten to go from his classes each afternoon and make the subway trip into Manhattan to the Taylor Theatre, to be accepted there and be able to move freely in this unfamiliar, splendid world. Hammet, with his perpetual monologues, which offended so many people, with his peculiar compulsion to speak out, to assert himself and lecture and perform, was for Rosengarten a treat, and, whether he was aware of what he was doing and specifically intended it or not, was responsible for a turning point in Rosengarten's life.

"I'm telling you you have talent. That should put an end to it, you can stop worrying about it from now on," he said late one afternoon, annoyed that day by Rosengarten's general ineptitude, by his lack of savvy—Hammet couldn't get over what he considered a hopelessly clumsy title Rosengarten had given one of his novels and repeatedly chided him for it. It annoyed him that afternoon that Rosengarten was poor, that he earned six dollars a day as a permanent-substitute teacher at his elementary school, and he undertook right then and there to instruct him and set him on the high road to fortune. "Do something with yourself. Spread yourself out. Get out of the *shtetl*. Never write about people who can't fiddle with their destinies." ("Did I say that?" he said some years later, in California, when Rosengarten reminded him of the occasion and brought up this piece of advice. "I have no recollection of it. . . .")

Not long after he had been with Hammet, Rosengarten took it upon himself to write a story aimed at one of the large-circulation national magazines. He gave it to his agent and ten days later *The Saturday Evening Post* sent them a check for six hundred dollars. The summer vacation came on; Rosengarten never went back to teaching school. All through that summer and into the fall he wrote story after story. They all sold. The agent was able to place most of them with the *Post* or *Collier's*, the few that failed going to one of the lesser markets. The guidelines were easy once Rosengarten hit on them—to sustain a pervasive tone, the hero sorrowing and heavy-laden with the cares of the world but enduring, or else tight-lipped, brave, shunning self-pity. The trick was to arrange some tantalizing, seemingly insoluble dilemma. It was a matter of aligning the sympathies of the reader according to a calculated continuity or plot. The ingredients were not only artificially put together, they weren't even interesting to Rosengarten, especially after the fourth or fifth time around. He wrote the stories with no real feeling, but he turned them out skillfully, making them each full-bodied, having no trouble duplicating the effects in a succession of contexts—a prizefighter, a wrestler, a trainer at the track, a jockey, a trapeze artist, an entertainer. The variations seemed endless. It was an exciting time for Rosengarten. He became a different person, the transformation taking him by surprise and delighting him—it was a great thing to be affluent, to have pockets full of spending money, to be young, to have the feeling that anything he put his hand to couldn't miss.

With Hammet it was all on the other side of the hill. The reason he spoke out in these compulsive bursts and monopolized the conversation was that most of the time, having no intimates, he was by himself and the long speeches were a reaction to the stretches of time spent in silence. He led a kind of underground life, always balked, surly and grasping, griped by his disgusting inability to work. The fine red-brick townhouse on lower Fifth Avenue, which had so impressed Rosengarten, wasn't Hammet's. It belonged to a famous movie actress, along with the beautiful show dogs; she was letting him use the place while she was away. When Rosengarten started out on his story-writing spree, one of the first of them, as might be expected, was based on Hammet, and even though Hammet in those early days was a figure of power and glamour to him, the story nevertheless turned into an account of a man at the bottom, fighting to redeem himself, to recoup his position (of course Rosengarten lightened the characterization, dressing it up, omitting the grubbiness); even then, with all his admiration, Rosengarten sensed the seaminess and breakdown. The play Hammet was working on when Rosengarten met him—the one the young girls in the anteroom were waiting to try out for, *The Almond Trees*—came to nothing. Instead of closing it on the road, he this time went along with the pressures and momentum and let it open, disastrously, in New York. ("Rogers Hammet was off on an ocean voyage, let's leave it at that," the Pulitzer Prizewinning author said, after the debacle.)

What he was looking for was the magic secret that made a story take off, that would give him the play in his mind. The actuality he talked about, the event as event, wasn't enough. More was required. It was the thing that lived in the material, the spirit, the driving force, indistinct and amorphous as this might be—it could be something in a person, something in a desire, in an offense or injury—but without it the story fell apart, it couldn't be recognized for what it was, it had no form, no existence. Certain stories, defective and grossly handled, mysteriously soared, while other stories, unblemished, floundered. There were instances of people who had had their great success, or two grand successes, and were thereafter left groping and besieged, unable to score again, in the dark, never having understood in the first place what it was in their successful work that had caused it to succeed.... It was, for Hammet, a never-ending pursuit, a wretched giving over of himself to his obsession to the exclusion of all other interests and responsibilities, a hard-riding anxiety that gave him no rest, and then there was the worst terror, that this all-consuming passion, which was always with him, which sickened him and which he was sick of, would suddenly leave him, that one morning he would wake up and the rage would be out of him.

A good part of the reason for his present trip to California and the main reason for the jumpy, disagreeable state of mind he was in had to do, in both cases, with Rosengarten—although Rosengarten himself was quite unaware of what he had done and knew nothing of what had happened. Hammet had been through a long, bitterly trying day, and Rosengarten, who hadn't been with him or seen anything of him until late this evening, was the cause of it. Rosengarten, some months ago, four or five months ago, had come across one of those collections of American literature, an anthology that contained an edited-down version of *Life on the Mississippi*. It was the first time he had really read the work, so the material was all more or less new to him. He was carried away with it, with the fresh clean air and innocence, but it was the condensation, the lucky intelligent editing and stripping of the account to its bones, that gave him the idea of how easily it could be managed as a movie. He saw the line of action, the steady forward movement of the piece; he could feel the echoes and remembrances that would be left in the minds of the viewers long after they had seen the picture. Hammet happened to be in town just then, and Rosengarten, with the excitement of the discovery at the moment—an excitement which by now he had long forgotten

—spoke freely to him, saying how eager he would be for the assignment, how much he would give for the chance to write the screenplay. Hammet, who took away with him Rosengarten's copy of the anthology and failed to return it, also saw what could be done with the material, and when the five-hundred-dollar doctoring job on the play by the husband-and-wife screenwriting team got him out to the coast again, he brought the book along with him and immediately went to work to drum up a deal and see what good he could do for himself.

He had spent the entire day at a studio, selling an executive, one of the few still accessible to him, persevering and not letting up until the executive agreed to take the proposition upstairs to the head of the studio for a decision. Hammet never left the place. He rattled around the studio, putting in the hours, until the word finally came down that they would go for the story, giving Hammet pretty much the production setup he wanted, with the distinct provision, however, that Rosengarten had to be part of the arrangement. The studios in these things banked heavily on the enthusiasm of the writer, if the writer had standing and they believed his enthusiasm was genuine. The reports on Rosengarten were good. Hammet knew that, he knew his own position wasn't of the best; to clinch the deal he had given assurances he could deliver Rosengarten, that Rosengarten was heart and soul for the project; and so it was a blow, everything ruined, when he called Millicent, kept after her and found out that Rosengarten was tied up on the assignment with Sidney Margulies. At loose ends, for want of anything better to do, he went after Rosengarten at the party, walking in uninvited, hating Margulies and all the rest of them, in his desperate, roiling mood.

Garrison came back from his daughter's apartment, the unit they were fixing up for her upstairs. His whole manner was changed. When he started out, he honestly thought he could help. He was sure he had the answer, that F——, as had happened with others, had forgotten the car he had come in and was simply looking for the wrong one in the restaurant parking lot. But as Garrison went upstairs, to use the phone they had installed for his daughter, he remembered Paul Devaney was expected and the misgivings set in. Garrison wanted his party to be a success and so there had been that happy rush of eagerness when he thought he could get F—— to join them and add to the luster of the evening, but now he realized it was a risky business to have two top celebrities at the same affair. They couldn't both hold the center of the stage and there was bound to be friction and unpleasantness. Garrison became alarmed and his misgivings deepened when he got the restaurant manager on the phone. As he started to explain why he thought F—— couldn't find his car, that he had probably driven up in a borrowed vehicle, it came to him with a shock that the director hadn't driven up anywhere, that the story he had been telling the actress was an obvious stall from the start. F—— didn't drive. Everyone knew that. His driver's license had been taken away. He had had a series of run-ins with the Department of Motor Vehicles. He didn't handle a car well, there had been accidents, the last one serious, and whether it was part of the arrangement the studio made with the DMV to get him off or his own idea, to spare himself and keep from injuring more people, the fact was he hadn't driven a car for years. Garrison wondered how soon it would occur to the actress as it had to him, that F—— didn't have the license, and he certainly meant for his part to keep what he knew to himself and not upset her more than she already was, but when he went up to her on the terrace and started to talk to her, he almost immediately gave himself away and there was a wrangle, the actress falling on him with questions and Garrison protesting, lying, and trying to calm her.

Hammet noticed the new commotion at the phone. Garrison— coming back from the apartment, again using the kitchen back stairs— had passed through the dining room where Hammet, standing with Rosengarten, had picked him up. Hammet had followed him with his eyes to the actress, saw the outbreak, and went over, busy and gleaming, to find out what was going on. He swiftly pieced the details together. He saw the fuss they were making over F——, the extent of the disruption the great man was causing, and that was all he needed. "That hambone!" he said. He took the floor. He couldn't restrain himself. He was charged up, overwound, overtired. He and F—— had had something to do with each other from time to time over the years. F—— had once brought him a play script—this was on Broadway, when F—— was getting started—which Hammet had considered and rejected, and there had been other encounters, on the coast, when they had discussed possible picture deals or met socially. "People think it's part of his Deep South flimflam when he shows an interest and asks you how you are, where have you been, what did you think of Rio and Peru"—Hammet here imi-

tated the director's rich courtliness—"but it's not. He really wants to
know. When he asks you about your wife, what you think of her, what
she thinks of you; when he looks you over and marvels how you've filled
in and put on weight and muscle; when he asks about the human body,
the changes that come with age, the changes in the circulatory system,
he's not being polite. These are things he wants to know about. It's his
way of educating himself. He's the most ignorant talented person I know.
He makes it a rule never to turn down an assignment, as they say here,
and does picture after picture because he's always in a panic. He hopes,
he imagines that if three or four miss, the fifth will pull him out."

There had been, to begin with, the bystanders watching Garrison and
the actress and enjoying the lovers' tempest. They turned to Hammet
when he came up, and listened respectfully from the outset, a perfect
audience, not interfering—they knew his reputation and waited atten-
tively to see what kind of show he would put on for them and whether
he would live up to his reputation. Others came by. Word passed. There
was a stir of movement, people on the terrace wanting to know what was
happening, intrigued by Hammet, leaving their friends and walking over
to share in the event, so that Hammet was having a sizable group gathering around him, the group constantly growing larger, and it was becoming a scene. Garrison was dismayed. It was the scene he had wanted to
avoid, the sudden unseemly disturbance that marred parties, that guests
relished and that perversely became the highlight of the evening and
was talked about for a long time afterward. Garrison had been caught
by surprise. He didn't know Hammet, had had trouble realizing who he
was, wouldn't have invited him to his party, and didn't know how to get
him to leave without raising a greater disturbance and making more disorder. While Garrison watched and fretted, a man not far from him
had spoken up, interjecting a joke, that is, asking why he was plugging
(praising) F——, and Hammet, with his hearing problem, unable to
make out what the man had said, went after him. "What? What? What
did he say?" Hammet asked, turning to the other guests because the
speaker—having by now knocked himself out over his witticism and
becoming suddenly abashed or fearful—was quickly edging away, taking flight. "It was nothing. He said nothing. It was a joke," Garrison said.

"When I think of F——, I see him working away for dear life, the
hair hanging over his eyes, boosting up some poor girl's rump, strug-

gling to get her pants off," Hammet said. "He has the instincts of a rural snake-oil salesman, which is basically what he is and the key to his success. In Palo Alto, in a motel bedroom, he came near to losing his life—this is not an exaggeration—and was saved only because at the critical moment the pistol jammed. Before the husband could get it firing again, F—— went to work on him. The lady in the bedroom was an actress and he convinced the husband she was only pursuing her career and advancing herself, that it was business and not a matter of honor, and the two walked out of the room together arm in arm, like brothers, and went to dinner." He let himself go, out of control, carried away by a wicked, senseless merriment, a kind of lunatic clowning that sometimes overcame and possessed him. He took ridiculous pains with his gibes, making sure his listeners got the full benefit of each of the thrusts, too far gone and engrossed in his shenanigans to worry about the amenities, the spectacle he was making of himself, and what he was doing to Garrison's party. He couldn't stand the movie director's preeminence, the entourage, the applause, his easy, unthinking way of accepting his fame and popularity and the adulation as if it all came to him naturally and by right. "At the Plaza, in New York, Tony Altschuler was moaning and groaning, going through one of his fits of depression, and F——, to make the grandstand play and impress the people, agreed to jump off the window ledge and commit suicide with him. 'You jump first,' Altschuler said. 'I'll jump and you'll be still standing there on the window ledge.'"

Louisa Lissak came up, the young woman through whom Rosengarten and Solly Renick had been invited to the party, whose family were old friends of the Garrisons back East—and Hammet, when he saw her, immediately welcomed her, greeting her with open arms. He reached out through the group and drew her over to him, so that he had her standing beside him in front of everyone. He couldn't stop. He knew who she was. It amazed him that anyone as well brought up as Louisa Lissak, with her background and advantages, could have anything to do with Solly Renick and become one of his girls; it always angered him that Solly—by being on the spot, by knowing some doctors and dentists, by turning up a semi-retired ladies' custom tailor on the 100 block south of Wilshire—was able to acquire his astounding following and make an important personage of himself.

Hammet had witnessed an incident some time ago involving Louisa, where she had been talked about, and the story now was more than he could bear to pass up.

"——————— was in town," he said to the group, naming a well-publicized bachelor, a stylish financier active in a number or enterprises. "This was in Mike Larrabee's office. Solly Renick was there, it was after work, and they were trying to accommodate the visitor with a dinner companion for the evening." Larrabee was the investment counselor in the Beverly Hills business triangle, someone Hammet knew. Hammet had walked into the private office, unannounced, had been unnoticed in the talk and conferring going on, and caught Solly in action.

The men had been sitting in the gloom of the place, the drapes drawn to keep out the sun, the work of the day done, casting about to fix up the financier with a date. Larrabee, a genial, expansive party-giver, had his book out, but it was short notice, so late in the afternoon, no one suitable was available, and so Solly finally came up with Louisa's name. That was when Hammet walked in, unobserved. What had actually happened was that Solly, in offering Louisa's name, stipulated that the financier had to treat her gently, and Larrabee had chimed in, also cautioning that this was a lady, of a different class, and there was to be no sex on the first date, but on a second meeting; Hammet, however, hadn't any intention of telling the incident exactly as it had happened.

"Solly brought out Louisa's telephone number and said it was all right to call her and ask her to dinner. But he made it crystal clear it was for dinner and dinner only, he wanted there to be no misunderstandings . . ." He held her tight by the arm beside him. He kept her in suspense. He ran on, sly and jubilant, not facing her, omitting the rest of it. "You should have been there," he chortled to the group. "You should have seen little Solly, laying down the law, kicking the big shots around." He made the necessary elisions. He turned the story around so that it was complimentary to Louisa—the whole idea ostensibly was to show the high regard she was held in, that she wasn't to be trifled with; the whole idea was to show how cunningly perverse he could be—but even as he spoke, before he spoke, he realized the elisions did no good, that it was damage enough just to have it known that she was offered about in the back rooms of business offices late in the day after work. He saw the hurt and embarrassment he was causing her in front of these people, but he went on ahead, adamant, not worrying over the boorishness of his behavior, refusing to think of the mortification or remorse that would come, and what people would say about him.

She stood by, smiling and pleasant, appearing untouched by the story, as if its meaning went straight past her—there was after all nothing she could do. But when he let her go and she finally slipped away, her composure broke and she was left in a turmoil of fear. Her heart beat fast. He had opened up a mass of doubts. She had had an affair with F—— a little more than a year ago, a relationship which, so far as she knew, she had successfully kept quiet. She believed it was forgotten, over with. When she walked up to the group around Hammet, she had heard him going on about F——, and since he then immediately, on the sight of her, switched over to her, she wondered if in some way he had found out about her and the old affair with the movie director, if that was the connection in his mind and the reason he was so familiar with her and went on to tease and torment her as he did.

The affair had been intensive but short-lived. F—— was too wild for her. He grabbed her when she went by, put her on his lap, rumpled her clothes. In the bedroom, he was demanding, dressing her up in lingerie and experimenting. He was hard-ridden with his movie work, always on the move and distracted, and in her circumstances she needed someone less in the public eye. The word had a way of getting out. Someone walked into a room at an unlucky moment, something was overheard, or for that matter she herself could give the show away—there was the incident with the monkey suit, when she was meeting the director for the weekend at the desert hotel-resort, when the suitcase fell open and the friend who was with her when it happened wanted to know why she was taking the monkey costume with her, what she wanted it for; she had had to tell the friend something.

She had prudently broken off the affair and now it came back to beset her at the most awkward time possible, when she was unsettled and trying to make up her mind. Garrison was asking her to marry him. That was what the housewarming was for, why he had bought the place and was remodeling it. It was as an inducement to her. He thought that by setting up this new home, by entertaining and surrounding himself with lively people and celebrities, he would create an atmosphere around himself that would please her and make up for the differences in their ages and his other deficiencies. He took her in the afternoon to the

County Art Museum in Exposition Park, courting her, and they walked together past the big dark paintings of unknown Angelenos, or paintings donated by them, while he waited for her decision. He had been over-shadowed all his life by his prominent, wealthy parents. They were very old now, and Garrison—who had never been able to fit into any of the family businesses and couldn't be said to have had an occupation—devoted himself to them, seeing them every day. Things hadn't gone well for him. His wife had divorced him and then after she divorced him, she died, leaving him with a young daughter to bring up by himself. He wanted to make a new start, and Louisa didn't know what it would mean to him, how he would feel, if this old affair turned up again and he heard stories about her.

She didn't know what she wanted to do. He was short and plump, much older than she was. She was tired of being exposed to men like Hammet, of having to wonder what they knew and always being on her guard. She knew it wasn't good for a woman to be alone. The man she had been seeing recently, up to a few months ago, a lawyer with a title insurance company, to whom she had explained everything, didn't argue with her and stayed neutral, but he reminded her how it was with her, that discreet as she was and keeping to the background, she neverthe-less led a full life, men attracted to her and seeking her out and she lik-ing to be with them, that it was bound to bring on trouble. "I won't do it anymore," she said.

The family name and importance would give her standing. She would have a base, position. It was a consideration. And the time was passing. "And I haven't even been married once," she said to herself or aloud to someone, when she saw her friends, almost everyone she knew, getting divorced, remarrying, and then getting divorced again. People were always startled and unbelieving when she told them the reason she had never married, that no one had ever asked her.

Inside the house, with the evening wearing on, the party had settled into its pattern. The bloom of the party was over—it was the other side of the party, the other side of the evening. There were empty patches of space in the living room; the tables there were littered with glasses and ashtrays. The large green-silk couches which Garrison had had custom-built and took great pride in were left unused, the guests having shifted off according to a mood of their own into a different arrangement. They were clustered in the front part of the living room near the entrance hall, and in the entrance hall itself, and then in the second, smaller living room at the other side of the entrance hall, the library or game room, in which the bar was located. That was the area the guests chose to favor. There was a constant current of movement to and from the bar, people threading through; people stood together in the press of the crowd, holding drinks and talking above the music from the hi-fi phonograph; and at the edges of the crowd, where there was some open space, couples danced.

Behind the two living rooms and the entrance hall, deep in the house, was an interior hall, the passageway that connected the dining room with the pantries and kitchen and ran on, around the back, reaching the game room through another, rear door. Here in this interior corridor, secluded and out of view, a young man and a woman were embraced in an intense, private spate of grief and affection. "My sweet angel," the woman said, eyes brimming with tears, the teardrops falling. She clung close to the young man as he held and comforted her. "You are my sweet angel," she said. Mom, he called her. He was slim, slight, very carefully gotten up and groomed, with rich black wavy hair like flat-curl karakul, Hebraic. She was extremely beautiful, blond, in show business once, of that caliber. His fingers were trembling. "Mom," he said. "Mom . . ."

Rosengarten, who had learned about the back hall when Garrison took him around and showed him the house, was heading for the game room, going this way in order to avoid the crush at the front of the house. He was dispirited and perplexed, his mind taken up. Solly Renick had brought along a pair of girls to the party. He had slipped them in with him, two sisters from the southeastern part of the country whom he was trying to help get started, and he had asked Rosengarten to find them now at the bar in the game room and tell them for him that he had been called away, that they would have to see about getting home by themselves— Solly had previously told the sisters to station themselves at the bar, the best place to be seen and get to meet people. Solly was on the run, looking out for himself. He didn't want to stay at the party while Hammet was there. Hammet was impossible, he said; there was no telling what he would take it into his head to do when Paul Devaney arrived, and Solly wasn't going to be there to be insulted and have his relationship with the star put in jeopardy.

"That's the end of that. I'll never see her again," Solly had said, confusing Rosengarten even further. It had taken a few moments before he realized Solly was referring to Louisa Lissak, and then he didn't know what Solly had done to her and why she wouldn't want to see him any more. Rosengarten felt tired and knocked about, his throat hurting from having to talk to Hammet, from trying to get through his deafness, and he hadn't understood why Hammet had been so bitter, calling him a prostitute, attacking the producer Margulies and the work he was doing at the studio. "It's too complicated to go into now. I'll explain it later," Solly had said, disgruntled, still talking about Louisa, and had hurried off.

Rosengarten was weighed down by a nagging dissatisfaction and worry. It was his old problem—the everlasting difference between the expectation, the allurements that he was seeking, the allurements and excitements that he wanted to get into his writings, and what happened when those expectations and hopes came up against reality. For Rosengarten, what was of most importance in a piece of writing was a certain exhilaration, a life, a liveliness, a sense of well-being arising from the scene and the people, hard for him to describe or even to understand clearly, and yet the thing that gave him a sinking terror when it was missing, when he knew it wasn't there. It was this craving for experience, this obsession, that had led him to the English novels of his youth, to his visions of the life in Belgravia and other far-off places. When he was in high school in Brooklyn, back in those days, his friend and the teacher in his English classes, Jerry Pargot, had told him, "You can write. The trouble is you don't know what you want to write about. When you find what you want, you'll be all right"—and started him off on his way, to see what he could discover of the variations of humankind, to see what he could make out of them, to shirk and dodge, to use the subterfuges of comedy and mimicry, to win, to fail. "Make something," Rosengarten said to himself in the narrow inside passageway of Garrison's home. He hadn't the slightest idea why he wanted to write and be a writer—if someone had asked him, he wouldn't have known what to tell him. He longed only for those moments when he would be impelled to write, easily and without doubts, out of instinct. "Make something that didn't exist before," he said to himself, "a thing, a fact, your own, absolute, unassailable. Do something with it. Don't let it just stand there. Make something happen—an elation, a joy."

The irony was that F———, so in command of himself and resplendent in everyone's eyes, whose celebrity had galled Hammet and who was responsible for the whole eruption, was himself unsteady and not what he was thought to be. For all his grand manner and generosity, he was ridden with uncertainties. Rosengarten worked with him on a picture a number of years after Garrison's party, going off with him on that occasion on a two-week trip across the country, ostensibly to look for locations while they worked up the script, ostensibly to be free of the studio executives and the producer, but actually because F——— was restless and unhappy and wanted to get away for a spell—and Rosengarten worked again with him, on another turn of the wheel, on a subsequent writing assignment some years after the first one. The director was genuinely humble, genuinely insecure. Rosengarten used to watch him flogging his brains to get himself into the run of his story. He would stand in the room intoning in his strong dramatic voice, his hair falling over his eyes, as he strove to lose himself in the mood of the fiction and search out its life. He didn't know about his talent, what it was, if such a thing existed. "I can only hope that if I like something, the public will like it too—that's all I can go on," he said in interviews and believed, but what was wrong with that was that he could never be sure of what he liked; he couldn't tell if the story invention he admired so ardently was something he had talked himself into admiring, if it was there only in his mind, if it hadn't been realized and didn't come off and was dead in the film. They were talking one day about a picture of his, perhaps his single most famous success, and when Rosengarten, curious about these things, asked if he knew while he was making the picture that he had a great one, F——— confessed frankly that he never knew in advance, not on the set, not in the projection room—that it was only when the picture was out and proved to be a hit, when everyone came and told him, that he knew it was good; he could then go back, he said, and say with conviction exactly what had gone into the picture and why it had been bound from the start to score. He was driven. He feared sloth. He went off on extended, punishing sprees that he didn't understand himself, and was involved in miserable struggles to extricate himself from the messes he got himself into. He was one of those who thought other people had the answers. When he met someone new, he applied himself with his courtly politeness and became engaged in long, sober conversations, thinking the new acquaintance might well have a superior knowledge. It surprised Rosengarten that F———, who was so much more widely experienced in the world than he was and famous, looked up to him and wanted his advice; he asked Rosengarten questions about vasectomies, sex, vitamins, the deterioration that came with time and what if anything could be done to forestall it. On that trip Rosengarten took with the director when they were supposed to be looking for location sites, parties sprang up in their hotel rooms wherever they went— old connections of F———'s coming by, young girls trying for movie work, whoever heard he was in the city. At one these parties, a handsome airline pilot was having a sort of muted, running feud with his wife, who was in the early months of her pregnancy. She was drinking, and chipped and punched at him every time they brushed past each other in the crowded room. When the party halted for dinner, the pilot, slipping away with a new partner he had found, vanished. F——— went down with his guests to the hotel dining room, but after a while, during a wait between courses, he excused himself and left the table, returning, it developed, to the room. What happened there, happened—hours later, when the party was breaking up and the visitors prepared to leave, the pile of overcoats that had been thrown on one of the beds suddenly started to heave and shift. It was the pilot's wife under the coats, coming awake. She hadn't left. She had been in the room all evening, and for some time afterward she was on F———'s mind. He worried about her, he thought he might have laid up trouble for her—he astounded Rosengarten, as they traveled on to the next city, by asking if it was possible to knock up, to impregnate, a woman who was already pregnant. He talked to Rosengarten about an early marriage when he had been very young. The marriage had gone wrong long ago, but the thought of it still came back to him and he brooded about it. "I made excessive sexual demands. I was too much for her and simply didn't understand. I thought she was rejecting me and didn't love me," he explained to Rosengarten.

A number of doctors, and dentists too, in the Beverly Hills triangle took to the unusual procedure of opening their offices very early in the morning—to suit patients who wanted to make their visits before going to work or wanted to avoid the crowded streets later in the day, the traffic and parking problems. And so there was a curious furtive life astir during those early hours, the janitors hosing down the sidewalks, the flat sparkling rays of sunshine glancing off the buildings, while well-dressed men, the patients, moved about in the quiet to get to their appointments, the patients arriving sometimes even before the stock-market investors appeared on the scene on their way to the various brokerage houses to catch—with the difference in the time zones—the opening New York prices. In that compact, relatively small area, extremely well-known personalities could often be encountered—an old-time actor, strangely frail, waiting for his driver or crossing the street to look for a public phone booth; the stalwarts themselves, the famous leading men, still in their prime and handsome, disconsolate as they walked in the halls past the proctologists, the cardiovascular internists, as they unexpectedly ran into one another and sat together in the waiting rooms. F—— was also seen now and then entering the medical buildings. He had been away, one of the movie contingent that had left the country to live in Europe, generally in London, to make pictures there or on the Continent or elsewhere in the world. They would come home at intervals on flying visits to have their dental work done, going through grueling, all-day sessions in the dentist's chair. Or they came back when they were ailing, counting on the crack doctors here with their diagnostic techniques and high-powered programs of treatment. As the time went on, the expatriate moviemakers tended more and more—once they came back—to stay on. They did this because they had used up their time in Europe, the attractiveness wore off, or they wanted to be close to the doctors, and in the end they almost all returned, F—— along with the others. They frequented the old restaurants, or the ones that had supplanted them, and began working again out of the local studios.

He had become sly, diffident, pawky, difficult to reach. He would smoke the big Romeo and Juliet cigars he cadged from his producer, and instead of going into the studio, instead of having story meetings and working on the script, he would cajole the writer with him into playing gin; they would sit in the sunken rumpus room, the den, in the producer's house and go through game after game by the hour. "Staying indoors and outside the sun shines," the producer would murmur, scolding F——. The producer would sit alongside him and *kibitz*, telling him which cards to throw out. It was hard to say if F—— had his mind on the game and was really interested in it; it was hard to say if he really liked the people he was associated with—the writer, the producer—or was putting up with them through the force of circumstances. On one occasion he had won a fairly sizable sum from the writer, and he wavered, irresolute, while the writer filled out the check. The producer also looked on in silence, not knowing what to make of these goings-on. From his point of view, F——'s behavior was a mystery, unaccountable and frivolous, but he kept the peace and said nothing. He wanted good pictures and was at the mercy of F——, and besides, apart from business considerations, he was fond of him—he liked to be linked with the director, to share in his aura, in the bursts of activity, the rowdiness, the surprises—and was happy to indulge him. A studio F—— worked at and went into from time to time was located near one of those large telephone buildings. In some peculiar way he became involved with the girls employed there and soon had himself installed in a flat three of them rented together. He lived there with them. It started out as an overnight stay during a weekend and the weekend stretched itself out. The girls knew who he was but grew used to the idea of having him with them, and so for a while he did his studio business out of that close, airless place, with its clutter of furniture, with the narrow, single bird's-eye maple beds and sagging mattresses, with the girls moving about, changing and primping, getting in and out of their clothes.

The people who drove him around and gave him lifts—since he didn't drive—wondered about him and what he was up to, but they liked him, they never could be sure whether he liked them or not, they were disinclined to intrude or do anything to displease him, and so they kept silent and asked him no questions. There was a group of women, four or five, who, as it happened, for one reason or another, had become unattached at the same time. They lived in the same small, posh apartment-hotel above the Sunset Strip, and, together with some friends who came to call on them, formed a kind of band or club—in the late afternoons the cars could be seen drawing up the hill to the macadam parking lot of the apartment building. They were lively women, beautiful and intelligent, not all of them actresses, edging forty or past it, good companions, and they were all intimates of F——'s, but he didn't go there. Coming up, say, from a studio in Culver City, he would sit next to the driver, slumped and limp, letting himself be jostled by the motion of the car in traffic, not complaining; he would flash that warm princely smile of friendship, as if to establish a communion between them, to ask for forbearance, for understanding of the essential human folly and weakness. "No, no, go straight ahead. You're making the wrong turn," he would say. There would begin an intricate tic-tac-toe rigmarole. The driver— an assistant director, a favored member of the crew, the writer who was working with F —— on the assignment—would stare at him, befuddled. "I would know better than anyone where I'm staying," F —— would say "You mixed up the two hotels in your head. I'm at the Beverly Hills, not the Beverly Wilshire."

"But I picked you up this morning at the Beverly Wilshire."

"Yes, of course. I know. I moved. There was a quarrel. I got out. I had my things sent over."

At the Beverly Hills Hotel, a mile or so to the north, when they got there, there would be another colloquy, more disagreement, F —— insisting the diagonal driveway leading up to the hotel entrance was a false turn-off, instructing the driver to bear right. This put them in Coldwater Canyon, on the road going over the mountain into the San Fernando Valley. "Just keep on driving, go straight on ahead—it's going to be pefectly all right," F —— would say, coaxing the driver along stretch by stretch, and wouldn't stop until they got to the other side and reached the sun-battered, paint-flaked cheap motel that had been his destination from the start. He sought out these decaying hideaways, located near railroad sidings, among warehouses, in industrial areas. The barrenness had an attraction for him. The slovenly young girls he arranged to meet him here were what he wanted. He would lock himself away in the room, lost in the stifling heat, the stillness, the lubricity. At a house party late one Sunday evening, there was an awkward, brittle occur- rence, a piece of tomfoolery that got out of hand and miscarried. In the waning minutes, with half the company gone home, a woman, to upset and bait her husband, had moved around the room, offering to have sex with any man there for a cash payment. F ——, who was among the remaining guests, took her on and went off with her, no one could tell for sure whether it was antic play and harmless fun or what would be likely to happen. Time passed—twenty minutes, a half hour. They had gone out into the garden, and now finally she was seen hurrying up the slope back to the house, disheveled, white with fright, repentant, plead- ing with her husband as she ran up to him, "Nothing happened. Noth- ing happened. He couldn't do anything."

He began to adopt poses, making use of an actor's way of working up a part, assuming that deep deadpan intensity and immersion in the impersonation. In restaurants and offices, when he was with people, he maintained a guise; he would become the elder statesman — grave, formal, magisterial, benign. "How grand for you. But surely that must be an unprecedented compliment!" he would say, speaking to the new desperados, the Frankenheimers, the Peckinpahs, careful to hide his jealousy as they appeared in their turn, careful not to show he was irked by their exuberance, their glee in picture-making, their feats of derring-do and excesses. "They must think the world of you in the executive offices. But it must be a tremendous burden to have the entire responsibility on your shoulders, the studio giving you carte blanche, you say, the final cut? Call on me when you're in doubt or have problems. I'll help you. I'll lighten the load." The rich, assured voice was now grainy, forced. He fell into the habit of sketching faces, a sketchpad almost always near him, and so he was on the slant, not facing the person he was with, looking at him as he sketched and not looking at him. ("Never trust a man who sketches" — this in his magisterial, Whistlerian phase.) There was a late marriage, entered into by F—— on some misbegotten notion, that lasted a matter of months, and in the throes of the breakup he lived temporarily in one of the out of the way unit houses at the bottom edge of Beverly Hills, a complex of low-level apartment cottages. In the mornings, while he lived there, the rooms became filled with a miasma of cosmetic smells. A former showgirl, once statuesque, now obese, had the downstairs flat. She had been in a highly successful landmark revue years ago, a show designed for the tourists who came to the movie capital, made up of animal acts, midgets, comedians, busty women — and it was the bubble baths this woman took each morning that sent up the overpowering reek. F—— spied her one day, very early in the morning, as she slipped out of her ground-floor flat, still in her nightgown, a baby-doll outfit, and stole across the backyard or garden to cut some flowers for her living room. She applied herself to her task at the flowerbed, reaching out among the zinnias and marigolds in the bright sunshine, engrossed in what she was doing and unaware she was being watched, incongruous in the baby-doll costume with her great, battered thighs. The sight of her in the sun brought back memories of the revue, of the master of ceremonies of the show with his trained troupe of little birds — the face of the master of ceremonies appeared out of the past, enlarged and imperturbable in the close-up, as he worked away at his high counter, sending up billows of smoke, running on with his patter, putting his tiny charges through their paces in front of the miniature wicker cages—and with these recollections of the old Hollywood show and those days came a depression, a recognition of the basic human flaw, the basic mediocrity, that the high hopes and excitements of youth were bound with time to fail and fall away.

A listlessness fell over F———. The hambone was dispensed with. He no longer troubled to put on a show for the sightseers. Peculiar reports came from the people who worked with him on the set, that he sat by himself and didn't stir, that he had no interest in the work—they said he let the cameraman, the assistants, shoot anything they liked. It was hard to think of him, so alive and gifted, with his collection of foibles, his royal good nature, the spasms of doubts and guilts, now shaken and unnerved. There had been a glimpse of him some years back on little Santa Monica Boulevard in Beverly Hills—caught from the window of a car driving through—as he went loping down the middle of the street. He had a girl with him. They were racing together from a restaurant to their car, getting on with their evening, F———'s face shining and alert, the larceny in his eyes, as he devoted himself to the girl, wooing her and getting her rosy.

"No more, no more," Rogers Hammet said when he was spreading himself out for his hearer's benefit one day—this was in California, on another one of his expeditions to the studios. He was jeering at the disabilities of the old, the falling off of desire and the way the life went, the regret—"Regret is the name of the only filly to win the Kentucky Derby. Brevity was a crack two-year-old, a winner the first time out." It was the midday lull, the middle of the afternoon, everyone, it seemed, but Hammet and the man he was walking with busy somewhere at work and off the streets. The sunshine poured down on the red-tiled roofs, on the lawns, the rows of fuchsia, the masses of bougainvillea blossoms, the stands of hibiscus and oleander, all of it brilliant in the light. "The hardest words there are, the saddest words: 'I used to do that'—when a project turns up you'd like to do, when an attractive piece goes by. 'Of cuss, of cuss—but he dunt appil to me, doctor,'" he clowned, making use of the stand-up comedians' jokes he heard on the late-night television shows and professed to admire. "'How can you be so promiscuous, four abortions in eighteen months and now coming for the fifth?' 'I'm not promiscuous. It's the same man.' 'The same man—then why don't you get married?' 'Because he dunt appil to me,' the lady said."

He had come out to the coast to break the monotony, to divert himself, to see if he could pick up some money. He had just been turned down on a loan he had half counted on. He had staged the affair carefully, arranging a discreet, formal meeting in the darkened bar of a class hotel; but the man with him, the one selected for the loan—no beginner, seasoned, who had been around for a number of years—saw no point in being set up, in handing over the five thousand dollars Hammet wanted, and had said no. Hammet had laughed at the rejection, had launched into a story about how someone had once asked him for a loan, how he had turned the man down, and how, the man saying he saw no hope for himself and would put an end to his life, Hammet had told him, "Go ahead. Do that. The river's eight blocks away. I'll lend you taxi fare."

"Sometimes as you move along in a crowd, a woman's face will suddenly flash out at you, a resemblance to someone who died a long time ago, someone you haven't even thought about in years, and it comes to you with a pang—the life going on, everything as usual, and your friend not there. That's the rub, the shiver. The most vivid idea I have of what death is like is when I'm here, in California or New York, and think of London, the theaters, the parks, the greenery, the normal life of the city going on as it always goes on, except that you're not there, without you. No more, no more," he said, the bony jaw jutting out, malevolent and harsh. "What did Mrs. Ponce de León say to Ponce de León—'You're going to Miami without me?' The horses getting away from the gate at the track, and you not there," Hammet said. "The life going on in Knightsbridge, and you not there. The young girls in the late fall afternoons, the smell of snow in the air, the feel of winter coming on, the people getting out of cabs, bringing home packages, going to restaurants, the streetlamps lighting up, the bustle, the life—no more, no more, no more."

THE AFTERSHOCK:
A LETTER FROM
HOLLYWOOD, 1971

A visitor comes out to see me in California—a colleague, a writer. We have never met; there's only been correspondence, an introduction of one sort or another. He is a man smiling, eager, modest—a man very much like myself, to look at us both now as we greet each other.

There is the film of disappointment. The visitor's eyes shift. His spirits fall. Is that all there is? We are on the wrong side of Santa Monica Boulevard here in Beverly Hills. There are no spacious grounds, no swimming pool, no stars. ("What was the powerful Hollywood seduction— Money? Women? Fame?"—this, from a big-city newspaper.)

And then the true malaise takes hold, the aftershock. The room is large, the ceiling beamed and high. The carpet is thick. He sees the patio through the French doors—the hibiscus blossoms, the oleanders, the lawn, the colors live and warm in the peaceful California sun. Everything is tidy, calm. The dinner has been easily managed. There is room in this house for the children; they are nowhere underfoot, they are out of sight and hearing. There is clearly in this house no sign of the strain that comes from the lack of money. The wretchedness settles in deep.

He is no less talented than his host, no less energetic, no more homely, from the same hard background, or from better, or worse—why can't it be for him, too, why can't he also have it? And, of course, he is right. ("You were always lucky, Daniel.")

The party to which I have taken the visitor—the same visitor or another one, it doesn't matter—swings along. People dance. We sit in the comfortable chairs and look at the assemblage, the crystal chandeliers, the pleasant commotion. "How much did they pay you for *Love Me or Leave Me?*" the visitor asks me.

I demur, tip the conversation, and we talk about something else. Why do we never like to tell what we get paid? Because it's seldom as much as they think it is, and they will be disappointed. Because it's too much, lavish beyond anything they earn in two years or three, and they will only be sick again.

I walk out of the school building, P.S. 225 in Brighton Beach, in the middle of the day, into the dingy quiet of the deserted neighborhood street during school hours. I have been teaching for seven years as what is known as a permanent-substitute—that is, we are permanently assigned, have the same duties as permanent teachers, but are paid by the day, each day we work, six dollars per day. Yom Kippurs we fast, and Christmases, and all through the summer vacation months.

"Hey, Fuchs, just a minute," the cop on the corner comes over and stops me, "what are you doing out in the middle of the day, where do you think you're going?"

"I'm going to Hollywood, Frank."

"Cut it out. What's the trouble?"

"No, on the level." I murmur and explain—have been writing all the years, fortune favors, screenwriter, Hollywood contract.

"You mean it?"

I nod. His eyes glaze. He stands there for a moment, alone on his feet. "Well, bring me back a remembrance from Carole Lombard, goodbye."

The principal calls me up, rattled and on fire, as we pack at home. "What are you doing to me? What did you tell them? Hurry, talk to Mrs. G., here!" I've told my class that I won't be seeing them again, that I'm leaving for Hollywood, and they've told their parents, but the parents don't believe a word of it. They think I've been fired and they're out in force to back me up. The mob of them are at Branower's home.

I speak to Mrs. G. over the phone. "Oh, no, dear madam. Not fired at all. It's true — Hollywood, thirteen-week contract . . ."

It drifts in. "You're not just covering up for him?" And then hard and jumbled, coming at me: "Do you think it's morally right to leave the children in the middle of the term?"

I parley, reason — permanent-substitute, no tenure, seven years . . .

"Then all right," she says, relenting, seeing it from my point of view. "Then we'll all come to the station to see you off, the mothers and the children. What's the track number? What time does the train go?"

Thirty years later I'm on the Brighton Beach Express again. The stops have been all changed, everything is different and alien, I am lost and ask the young lady passenger sitting beside me for directions. It turns out she attended P.S. 225, and I tell her I once taught at the school. Who is still there — Miss Raices? Mrs. Susselman? Did she ever have Mr. Rhine, Mr. Spevack, Mr. Frank? She frowns — one or two of the names seem faintly familiar to her, she doesn't know. Do they remember the principal, Mr. Branower, at the school? "Did you ever hear of me — Mr. Fuchs?" "No . . ." she says.

When I come out to southern California in 1937, the area is still undeveloped, so I am granted the boon of being in a new place fresh and brimming and unawakened, at the beginning. There are masses of bougainvillea, Joshua trees and yucca on the hills, a light shining at the door, the scent of orange blossoms in the evening air, honeysuckle and jasmine. I work in those days at Warner Brothers in the San Fernando Valley, and coming home out of the thick valley heat, cutting through the Cahuenga Pass, I suddenly go speeding into the cool air from the ocean, and there is a buoyancy, a lift at the heart. As I reach Beverly Hills, on Sunset Boulevard, a half-field of poinsettias lies spread out before me. I drive, on my free days, through the Santa Susana Pass into the Simi Valley, or to the ranges of the San Gabriels and the deserts beyond them, or over great, open spaces to the harbors of Wilmington and San Pedro — everything in this new land wonderfully solitary, burning, and kind.

People work in the citrus groves and in the oil fields, but this activity is slight, and by far the largest part of the preoccupation of the city is with the seven or eight motion-picture studios. It is amazing how they

the studios here, how the studios dominate all their minds and
studios exude an excitement, a sense of life, a reach and
extent hard to describe.

The first picture is O.K. The second one scores, is something of a hit.
My children play on the sidewalk in their spotless playsuits, in their white
piqué sun hats, and when they get off the pavement to come indoors,
there is miraculously not a smidgen of dirt on their hands and legs or on
their playsuits. Their faces are brown, the rosiness showing through the
year-round tan; they pass me by, aloof. The bones in their bodies are dear
to me. On sunny afternoons, by myself, I roam the studio back lots—the
Western streets, the piers, the empty railroad depots, the somnolent New
Bedford fishing villages of a hundred-fifty years ago. I watch the studio
bravos in their costumes at their perpetual play, folk coming from backgrounds unknown to me, people with a smiling, generous style.

We go careening between assignments, my friend and I, driving up
north, to San Francisco—wherever the highway opens up a likely view.
The last day of the expedition I insist on going to Golden Gate. "That
was the understanding between us. We said I'd get one day at least at the
races."

We come too late for the first race. We lose the second. We win the
third race. We win the fourth, the fifth, the sixth. We win the seventh at
twenty-two to one—five races in a row. "Well, I can see why you're interested in the races. I suppose there's something to it," Phil says, pocket-
ing the cash, looking out to the road, eager to get going again.

Four months later he dies—senselessly, inexplicably. I can't go to the
races any longer. I can't bear to win—I shiver and tremble and am bothered by forebodings.

"A screenwriter," says Isherwood in his lovely movie novel *Prater
Violet*, "is a man who is being tortured to confess and has nothing to
confess." I've been by this time through the traumas at Huntington Park
and Long Beach, those sneak previews where the audience goes flat,
where the picture fails, where the mortification writhes within you and
you sweat the miserable hundred minutes through; I've had those, too.
I sit in my room at the studio, searching for clues, for omens, willing to
believe anything anyone wants to tell me. "The long despair of never

getting anything right—that *cafard*, that lousiness, that hangs around a writer's life," says Graham Greene, who surely doesn't have to.

An old-timer in the business, a sweet soul of other days, drops into my room. "Don't be so upset," he says, seeing my face. "They're not shooting the picture tomorrow. Something will turn up. You'll revise." I ask him what in his opinion there is to write, what does he think will make a good picture. He casts back in his mind to ancient successes, on Broadway and on film, and tries to help me out. "Well, to me, for an example—now this might sometimes come in handy—it's when a person is trying to do something to another person, and the second fellow all the time is trying to do it to him, and they both of them don't know." Another man has once told me the secret of motion-picture construction: "A good story, for the houses, it's when the ticket buyer, if he should walk into the theater in the middle of the picture—he shouldn't get confused but know pretty soon what's going on." "The highest form of art is a man and a woman dancing together," still a third man has told me.

I drive to my office at the studio and have no recollection of the trip; I don't remember getting there. The quarter-mile road to the main building on the Fox lot, if you enter through the Santa Monica Boulevard gate, is made up of a succession of sharp dips and rises, you drive up hill and down dale, and I go over the roller coaster this morning, wracking my brains to see if I can think up some way of committing suicide without dying. I'm on my fourteenth week with this assignment, and my producer and I can come to no understanding. I am oppressed by the terrible passage of time; the mountain of checks looms before me—fourteen weeks and I haven't begun the screenplay, I haven't written *Fade In*. I long to be taken off the assignment, but they don't let you run out on them. I offer seriously to go off salary for a while, simply to relieve the pressure on me, and they stare at me: "How can we let you work for nothing?" And then suddenly it comes to me. I almost lose control of the car and go piling into the ditch. I see the answer in a dazzling rush of clarity that scares me: All I have to do to commit suicide without dying is to murder the producer.

We are whores working in a brothel, a journal says of us, a journal noted generally for its civility and enlightened wit. We are regularly assailed, censured, pestered. "Did the Pope tell Michelangelo how to paint?" a big-city newspaper asks, and they read out the roll of names:

Fitzgerald and West and . . . and . . . and . . . who? I can rely on old friends to remind and reprove me; the correspondence doesn't slacken: What happened to you? Why have you fallen into silence? Why have you stopped writing? I write, in collaboration or alone, from my own original material or from other source material, in the morning and in the night, on studio time and on my own time, until I fill shelves and prize Reticence as the rarest of all jewels. But they don't mean movie writing. What they mean—they don't know what they mean, and the truth is they don't know as much about Hollywood as they believe they know. What they mean is that I am extravagantly paid, and in this, of course, they are right.

Marcellus, my gifted director friend, is tangling with the head of the studio, the two of them going round and round in the way they do, savaging and testing each other. And then I see my friend suddenly falter, distracted, something gnawing at him. He blurts out, asking for advice. "What do you do when they print some crap about you? Is it worthwhile getting after them? The only thing to do is always to ignore them, isn't that right?"

The boss holds up, doesn't answer. He's been at it fifty years, the head of the company for the last twenty, is one of the three or four best-hated men in the community, and has had his share of the vilification.

Over the years I wonder at times at the quality that exists in the main-eventers—whatever it is they have in them that makes them stars, whether they know they have it in them or whether they consciously work at it and build it up, whether they have anything in them at all. I'm hired to do a script for X—and get driven up to his house in the hills to meet him. The gates are posted: THESE GROUNDS PATROLLED— TAKE CARE—STAY OUT. But we know the password, announce ourselves, and are admitted; the gates silently draw open by themselves. He stands before me, carefully dressed, a reserve in him, a dignity, cool and as if unawares. As far as I can tell, he makes no effort to put himself out for my benefit, and yet it is there—something inborn, his own. Months later I am to have bitter differences with others in the company, disgraceful quarrels; I finish the first draft, turn it in, will have nothing more to do with them, walk away, and the studio lays down a barrage of writs on me—claims for damages, injunctions, show-causes. I send a note to X: "Is this the language of artists?" And the legal proceedings stop.

The afternoon wears on, and he talks of a new performer on the scene, of the startling effects she is able to offer. "And she still doesn't know how to use the microphone," he points out to me, as if this is some special lore, as indeed it may well be. He speaks of a friend of his, a performer who deliberately seeks out difficulties, who—out of vanity or pride—insists on opening his evening's act with a reckless disregard of pacing. "He starts out high, where anyone else in his senses would hope to finish—and then he carries it through all the way from there."

He touches on matters foreign to me. I see there is a substance, a competence, I know nothing about. I get glimpses of people impelled to work to the limits of their strength, at the top of their form. I remember those inside, professional shows where actors perform solely for other actors, out of pride or vanity; I think of one team I've seen at such an occasion whose work has a complexity, grace, and surprise that astound me. I think they are champions, goaded, endowed with the gifts that make it possible for a man to leap twenty-seven feet or run a mile in well under four minutes. I think they have to do with those splashes of light that come to us in the night, which we know we will lose hopelessly by morning, but which they in some remarkable fashion are able to sustain, and that it is as hard to determine what it is they have in them as it is to define the thing in melody, a child or cat.

At the door, as I start to leave, he detains me, and at first I have trouble understanding what he's trying to tell me. There's been some minor incident in town, some talk about a personality, and he goes around the subject, idle and cursory. He thinks it's just as well not to say anything about people we know, whether it's for good or bad. "We don't talk about people, don't you agree?" he says, looking at me.

The executive is widely known as a thug, perhaps the roughest of the breed, ruthless and thoroughly hated in life, still reviled a little now that he is dead. I watch him from the distance. He courses the studio with his chest slung low to the ground, hunting for lights that should have been turned off and are left burning, looking for employees to harass. I have the notion one day of titling a picture A *Figure and a Face*, and mention the suggestion to him. "Would you really want to call a picture that? Oh, Daniel, I'm surprised," he chides me.

They are hassling before us in the executives' private dining room, the executive and a famous Broadway producer, putting on their show, chopping away at each other in that furious, hand-to-hand combat they love here to engage in. The advantage in this bout is all with the executive. He has the producer at his mercy—the producer has just failed on Broadway, is out of funds and in disgrace; that's why he's at the studio now, to get his breath back and recoup—and the executive doesn't let up for an instant: "You just had a terrible flop. You had to close. You couldn't last three days."

"Why?" the producer says, meaning why did the play close, what was the alchemy that was missing; and the executive immediately checks himself, knows that he's been trumped, holds a finger to the side of his nose, ruefully conceding defeat. The executive knows that this is the blood, that anyone can cavil; he knows, from old, old campaigns, the head-breaking torment it takes to find those secret elixirs, hideously slippery and intangible, that make a work of the imagination go. In that single flickering admission of defeat, he wins me over and gains a respect that I hold on to while he lives and when he's dead.

On his way home from the airport, driving past, he spots my wife and me walking on Bedford Drive, and the next day at the studio dining room he puts me through the hoops, teasing. It's the dress my wife was wearing, pale blue, a linen.

"You were carrying a bunch of flowers."

"That's true."

"And a box of candy."

The box of candy is too much. We were having some friends to dinner and it's true I had the candy as well as the flowers, but they're all looking at me at the table, and so I say he was mistaken, that there was no candy. But he insists. I repeat my denial, we go back and forth, and I am now caught up in my ridiculous lie. He keeps at me. He won't give up, and it strikes me how this thug, harsh and ruthless, must have it that the crazy sums his company pays me go for chocolates and blue dresses.

"No, Mr. Cohn," I persist, "just the flowers—and a bottle of gin..."

The child, who—when they moved in across the street some twenty years ago—was so shy that she turned her back and hid her face to avoid being seen, is now full grown, a young lady, charming, more distinguished and accomplished than any of us could ever be; I watch her gratefully through the thick spread of leaves of the sycamore trees that line our street. From the window of the room I work in at home, I look out at the fine patterns of light and shade the brickwork of the chimneys makes in the sparkling sunshine. I look down at the flowerbed, the stock and asters. (When I tell the gardener some years ago that we'll be leaving again, this time for Switzerland, he cries out at me, "No!" and for this, Suto, I won't forget you.)

My next-door neighbor re-landscapes his side of the driveway, a strip of ground that, because of the layout of his house, it is impossible for him to see from his windows. I ask him why he's done this. "Well, Thelma and I said, if you put in stock and asters for us to enjoy, the least we can do is dress up the driveway for you." From another window of my workroom I see the tall buildings now going up in Century City, a city that once was the Fox back lot where, on Saturday afternoons gone by, I used to bring my children to play in the courtyards of castles, along the canals stemming from Lake Erie.

The earth staggers and rolls. Power lines go down; the sky flares up. There is an incredible tumult of noise—doors and windows slamming in their frames, books tumbling to the floor, the bricks of the chimneys smashing to the pavement of the driveway. It goes on and on and doesn't stop. All we can do, this morning of February the ninth, is to stand there huddling in a helpless fright—and then I suddenly understand, stark and plain and unalterable. Mystery is explained: *Nothing is given freely, payment is exacted.*

For the boon of work; for the joy of leisure, the happy, lazy days; for the castles and drowsy back lots; for the stalwarts I've come to know, John and Bob and Sam; for the parties at Barney's, the times at Phil's, the flowers, the sycamores, the blessings of the sun.

WEST OF THE ROCKIES

Burt Claris was a grifter. He worked for a top-flight talent agency on Wilshire Boulevard, but the job was secured for him through the influence of his wife's relations, and people acquainted with his circumstances understood it was window dressing; although, for that matter, how many instances are there where parents, quietly and behind the scenes, make this sort of accommodation for their sons-in-law. He was an ex-pro football player, one of those sports celebrities to be seen at the clubs and gatherings around town, the nature of the community being what it was. He had courted the young daughter of an extremely wealthy family, had married her, and the family found the place for him at the agency so that he would have something to do and keep occupied.

The agency used him as a leg man in the field—because he was personable and a former athlete and so had something to trade on, and because he wasn't much good to them in any other capacity. His job essentially was to move around with the stars on the list and in this way give them the feeling they were being worried about; but in the case of Adele Hogue it had gone further than that. He had taken up with her, had gotten into her good graces, slept with her. Claris was no better than most. She was accessible. She was on the rebound, just back from

England, the latest of her marriages having collapsed on her. She was a big name, one of the handful who really brought people into the movie house. Claris had been with the agency long enough to know what a personality like Hogue meant in the business; he wasn't unaffected by her standing and importance, knew how useful a connection with her could be; and so, with the opportunity presenting itself, he had gone ahead. Now she was creating a major disturbance. In a fit or fury, she had run away from the picture she was shooting in, had driven out to this hotel-resort in the desert, leaving everything at a standstill, the production schedule completely disrupted—and Claris was trapped in the heart of the upset. Dick Prescott, the senior man on the assignment and the one properly in charge, called him straight out to the hotel as soon as the crisis broke, and was turning the whole responsibility over to him. When Claris caught up with his associate, it was down at the hotel parking lot. Prescott was already on his way to his car, hurrying to duck out.

"That's what you get for *schtuppin* with the talent, you're stuck," Prescott said. He was a slick, easy-rolling individual, a bachelor at the present time, his mind on motels and the after-hours rat race, and he was in this testy, distracted mood not so much on account of Hogue and the commotion but because he was having trouble with the chippies lately, a standup just the night before. "Ever since television," he said. "They can all get some kind of a jerk job, dancing, or else just standing around, acting, and I tell you it's rough."

Claris didn't like the idea of having the whole load thrust on his shoulders. He was out of his depth. It was too much for him. The actress was tying up an expensive production. Hard losses could result. She was an intense, unstable bundle of a woman, with a long record of excesses behind her, periodically in the papers with her marriages and tantrums, and there was no telling to what extremes she might go or what could happen.

"True, true," Prescott said, as Claris stood parleying with him in the sun. "But what could I do with her? What could anybody in the office do? You're the logical choice. You're in solid with her and I'm only getting out of the way so you can have a free hand." That was what he would tell them at the agency if they came at him later on with a beef. He wanted to stay as far away from the mess as he could get.

"Nice for you. You've got it all worked out," Claris said.

"That's right," Prescott said.

"If anything goes wrong, I'm the heavy."

"Why should I jeopardize myself? You knew what you were doing when you started up with her, now take the consequences. Do it, do it. Ride it out," Prescott said, brushing him off and moving around the front of the car. "Nothing'll happen. Sooner or later they get sick of it. She'll simmer down. She'll go back to the studio and that'll be the end of it." He got the car into gear, backed out, and Claris was left alone, fretting and uncertain in the heavy heat.

He was in an awkward position. He had to tread carefully. He couldn't afford to take chances with his in-laws, his wife's parents, her uncles and brothers, the whole clan, and get mixed up in a scandal, and considering the relationship he had fallen into with the actress, he was wide open. He didn't know what to do, how to proceed. Adele Hogue had one of the outside bungalows that were spaced around the main building; she wasn't in the hotel itself. Claris had looked up a Filipino steward he knew on the place, had had the bungalow pointed out to him when he had arrived, so he knew which one she was in, and he started out now, thinking he would go up and see her.

The hotel-resort lay in the Palm Springs area, that is to say, for the sake of those not familiar with this section of the country, in that heavily promoted desert real-estate development a hundred miles southeast of Los Angeles on the freeways. It was patronized, naturally, by rich people, not necessarily in the movie business—all kinds, from all over. They were people getting on in years, shunning the limelight and seasoned, the women the second and third wives of men who made big money in meat, oil, or textiles. The men had their offices in Saint Louis, in Chicago, in cities in Texas, and since they or their wives insisted on living on the West Coast, they were constantly obliged to be in transit, commuting from point to point. The husbands, those who were coming out this morning, were still on the freeways, driving in from the airports in Los Angeles, and when Claris emerged from the parking lot, there were few couples about, just a scattering of guests, mainly women, lolling in the sun and chatting.

The grounds stretched hushed, everything spick-and-span and burning, so early in the morning. Claris didn't feel at home with these people. He knew he didn't belong with them and that he was on his own. He kept away from them, taking a circuitous route to the actress's cottage, sticking to the edges of the grounds, and as he went on, he suddenly came around a bend in the path and saw a couple straight ahead, the woman very well cared for and beautiful, the husband so-so. Claris held up. The couple weren't aware they were being observed. "Sexy figure, Sid," the wife said, nudging her husband, indicating a guest not far off in a playsuit. It was as though she was appraising the guest for his benefit, and Sid, the husband, dourly inspected the guest and chomped his cigar.

"You ought to see her in the morning when she gets out of bed in her nightgown," he said.

Claris didn't stir, lingering in the shade to give the couple time to move on. He was on the grift and had been on the grift practically since his college days, but, remarkably, his way of life hadn't hardened him. He remembered the plane trips after the game, when he was still playing ball; he remembered how he used to sit in the gloom on those homeward trips, whether they had won or lost, hurting from the beatings he had to take, wondering what would happen to him after he was through and they didn't want him around any more. He had worked his luck, had gotten himself into the favored clubs and dining rooms, had listened to the smart money talk to be heard in those glossy, comfortable places: "The rich get wrinkles only from smiling." "I've been poor, I've been rich—believe me, being rich is better." It hadn't turned out for him as he thought it would. Everything stayed remote. The smart money talk didn't apply to him. His wife's folks had all kinds of money—a West Coast chain of supermarkets, together with the real estate and financing that went with such an operation, the subsidiary interests by this time easily accounting for the larger share of their wealth. But the money had nothing to do with him. Very little of it came his way. The family bought Claris and his wife a home; they provided servants, a nurse for the baby when the child came along; they fixed him up with the job. Claris trooped to the different studios with his agent's black book, working at his bogus, makeshift job. He was consistently unfaithful to his young, inexperienced wife. He didn't know why he did these things, why he seemed compelled to do them, or why he seemed determined to get himself into the hot, sticky impasses his infidelities invariably led to. "Maybe everything would be all right if only she wasn't so rich," he

mused aloud, killing a half hour in some office as he made his rounds
at the studios. He tried to put the blame on that, on the heavy money
standing there all the time in the background behind her. "She's sweet.
She's simple. I could love her. We should be happy. Of course," he said,
frowning and shifting, "if it wasn't for the money, if it wasn't for the
supermarkets and the holding companies, I wouldn't be there, would I?"
His mother came visiting at his lavish home on Sundays and sat at the
poolside with the baby in her lap, her eyes silently pleading—she needed
money. The man she had married didn't work, and Claris seesawed with
her painfully, giving her most of the three hundred a week he earned at
the agency. He was bothered by his debasement. He was mortified by
his mother's halfhearted visits, by his wrangles with her, by the incredible
way in which he openly talked about his troubles to people he met in
studio offices. And wherever he went, at the back of his neck he waited
for the cry to ring out: "Stop thief!"

When he got into the room with her at the cottage, she was in a
black slip, fighting with her daughter Melanie, a lumpish child of ten,
with thick-lensed glasses, who was sitting in a corner waiting for the
harangue to be over with so that she could get on with the book she was
reading. The actress had two other children besides Melanie, a set of
twins by a later, also unsuccessful marriage. As she stood in her slip
berating the child, she held an armful of combs and brushes that she
was evidently in the process of cleaning at this time. She looked up at
Claris, over the heap of combs and brushes, and shot him a hard, angry
glance, either because she resented his intrusion or else because she had
been waiting for him and he had been slow in coming, Claris didn't
know which.

"What did they do, send you down to chastise me?" she asked.
"What do you think you're going to be able to accomplish?"

Claris gave her to understand he wasn't acting as an agent, that he
hadn't made the trip solely for business purposes. "I don't know what
you get by running away and driving people crazy," he said. "Are you
planning to stay cooped up for the rest of your life? You're going to have
to come out some day." The bolt had caught him by surprise. He hadn't
known anything about the disturbance until he heard from Prescott.
"Why didn't you at least call me before you took off?"

"Because I didn't want to do it that way," she said. "Because I wanted you to come flying to me of your own volition. Don't you know, we crave attention. They say when you're with one of us, you have to stop living and do nothing but worry about our problems."

The drapes were pulled together at the windows, but the lights were turned on and there was a hothouse, unnatural glare in the room—the lights all burning at ten o'clock in the morning. Claris saw there was no point in tackling her head on, so he settled himself in the hot bath of light, waiting on her and letting her give forth—which was probably what she wanted him there for, he supposed—and it became an arduous, drawn-out vigil, the child sitting in the room with them, keeping her nose buried in the book but not missing a trick.

The times he and the actress had been together had been mean, furtive sessions, afternoons snatched on the run and under pressure— they were times when she should have been on the set, when he had gone after her, ostensibly to argue with her and wheedle her down to the sound stages; and in the heat of those stealthy sessions together, Claris— who was on edge and flustered enough as it was with his own misgivings, not quite sure of what he was taking on—had never known how to contend with the nutty-putty ball of despair that he had with her. He didn't know what to make of her. She was a main-eventer, a true box-office money star—Claris knew you could walk into any studio with just her name on a contract and make your own deal, and it was this consideration, no doubt, in the back of his mind somewhere, that had led him to start up with her in the first place and ingratiate himself with her. She had lived through big things—the many marriages, children by different husbands, this last marriage in England to a marquis or lord, the son of a famous, highly publicized sporting duke—but when he was in the room with her, it was startling how little there was to her. She was ordinary, immature, smaller and slighter, as they all seemed off screen, altogether incapable of surmounting the difficulties that were besetting her. She couldn't get on with the picture. She couldn't make it to the set. It was one of those pictures with the crickets chirping all the way through on the soundtrack. She had to walk around in flat-heeled shoes in the part, and she didn't know what to do with herself, she didn't know what was expected of her. She couldn't stand the gray mourning doves outside her hotel in Beverly Hills, the way they groaned and gurgled. She couldn't stand the commercial planes rattling overhead one after the other these days like freight cars in the sky. People's faces suddenly seemed strange to her; there was something about the eyes, the eyes were speckled—even the faces she saw on television. She was worried about the vertical ridges on her fingernails; she read Dr. Alvarez in the morning paper, and Dr. Alvarez, or somebody like him, said the vertical ridges meant the root ends of your nerves inside you were fraying and giving out. Together with her hallucinations and caprices, she was filled with that raw, unmanageable grievance they had, that wholesale complaint and rebellion. They were in demand, always fiddled with, diddled, sweet-talked, misused, and betrayed, and when they had something troubling them, this festering, senseless belligerence was the only way they seemed to know of fending for themselves. She was eaten up with the fiasco of her English marriage. That was at the bottom of the emotional turmoil she was going through, of the outcries and wild fights; but there had been other upheavals, other fiascos, other causes. She had sailed off in style a year and a half ago, starting out on her grand new life—and now it was eighteen months later and everything was a savage comedown for her, a humiliating torment.

"People are so persnickety. They all think they have dibs on you," she said. She was taking out in her misery after the sightseers and hangers-on, those wealthy women guests at the hotel who preferred the life on the West Coast and hovered on the fringes of the movie scene. "Everybody around here is so broad-beamed and phlegmatic. They lay there with their aplomb, getting their perfect, even suntans. They think they've got it all solved. It seems the only enjoyment people can get out of life is to look down on you and be superior. Why don't you go out of doors and play for five minutes?" she said, turning on Melanie, afflicted now by the child's unfortunate appearance, by the thick glasses and the roly-poly awkwardness. "Why don't you take care of the twins?" The twins were boys, four or five years younger than Melanie.

"But I don't know where they are," Melanie said, stolid, holding fast.

"Find them, look for them. That's the whole idea. It wouldn't do you harm to be active and lose some weight. Sticks to me like glue," she said, breaking off. "She sits like a bump on a log, reading and ruining her eyesight, and I can't get her off my head. I don't even have ammonia," she said, embittered. She needed the ammonia for the combs and brushes.

Ammonia was the only thing. "It just goes to show," she said, "the lousy, unsatisfactory way I live—I don't even have the most common, ordinary, everyday household articles when I need them."

Claris didn't know why she was chipping away at the fashionable women guests outside or why she had to come here if these strangers annoyed her so. He didn't know what was beating up in her, why she was so agitated. Prescott had said she would simmer down, that sooner or later they got sick of the commotions they raised, but there was no sign of a letup in her. The slip hiked up on her legs as she carried on, as she came flaring at Claris with her complaints about the bottle of ammonia that she needed and didn't have, and he saw the flash of the flesh at her thighs, he saw the breasts pulling and quivering there at the top of the slip, and he wondered at the stark force and energy of the turbulence in her. Generally they had a bosom companion with them to tide them over a bad spell—a favorite hairdresser, somebody from casting—but she was all alone, nobody with her but the child, nobody to turn to but Claris himself, and suddenly it struck him—he was the bosom companion. That was why she wanted him near her. That was why she had succumbed and fallen into his arms. He was the one who was getting taken, not the other way around.

She was sitting on the edge of the washbasin in the bathroom, the water running over the combs and brushes in the basin, while in the meantime she worked carefully at the medicine-chest mirror on her eye makeup, penciling in the dark smeary stuff under the lids. She was running water over the combs and brushes instead of soaking them in the ammonia she needed because she wouldn't call the desk for ammonia —because it was too much trouble, because she didn't want to ask, because she had no patience. The shopping she had to do brought on a similar convulsion of feeling, a similar flurry, and it was ultimately the clue that took Claris to the heart of the difficulty. That was why she was in the black slip—she was preparing, in her own time, to get dressed and go out to the shops. She needed clothes; she had nothing to wear; she didn't know anybody at the shops in Palm Springs or where to go; but again she backed and fussed. Again she wouldn't bestir herself. She didn't want the hotel to set up appointments for her. She didn't want to make a hullabaloo. She wasn't going to call on Fannie Case and let her do favors for her, and then it came to Claris—with the mention of

Fannie Case's name, the pieces fell into place in his mind. It wasn't the stylish ladies at the resort who were upsetting the actress. It was Harry Case, Fannie Case's former husband. Fannie Case owned the hotel; she was the proprietor and manager of the place. It was an old story, an excitement in the papers at the time and still a recurring blind item now and then in the columns. Harry Case was, or had been, an operator in the gambling rackets—slot machines, horse-betting syndicates, Eastern connections, as Claris recalled. It had all happened in the days not long after the war, when the people came flocking out to California, when the boom began. Adele Hogue had gone a furious, fast few rounds with him. The romance hadn't lasted—Adele had soon left him high and dry—but it was enough to break up the Cases' marriage, and, in the peculiar, illogical way of these things, it ended—as Claris should have remembered— with the three of them knit together on a continuing, more or less permanent basis, Fannie becoming friends with the star and Harry hankering after her. He carried the torch. He kept interfering in her doings, taking an interest in her welfare and never letting go—and with the crisis she had made for herself by bolting the picture and coming to the hotel, he now had a royal, heaven-sent chance to move in on her again.

She had balked at the production calls morning after morning. It was a kind of paralysis that immobilized her—they still had the first foot of film on her to photograph. "You lose interest. Nobody likes to do anything all of the time," she had once told Claris, tossing and resisting and defending herself. "You stand in front of them—the electricians, the cameramen, the director. You don't know what to do. There is nothing there. You are nothing. You feel guilty. You feel like the worst criminal in the world." Out of the blue, in some spasm of determination or contrition, she had abruptly decided to make peace with the company; she had given assurances that she was ready to work, that she had herself under control and would appear on the set positively and without fail. And then when the deadline came on and the paralysis seized hold again, when she physically couldn't get herself to the set, she couldn't just sit there in her shame at the hotel in Beverly Hills. She had to do something, so she had grabbed the children and gone running to Fannie. That was how it had happened. But from her point of view, it was the worst possible thing she could have done. Claris stared at her, befuddled. It was as though she had deliberately gone looking for trouble.

havoc and ruin going on within, but here at the main building of the hotel, thirty or forty yards away, the life of the resort was following its usual course. There was the swirl of action, the rise of voices, the women sitting at the different tables in their friendly clusters, passing the time among themselves, and as Claris came by, he could hear fragments of the conversation, bits of the patter and gossip. The women guests knew what was happening with Hogue—the news was all over the place—but these cataclysms, these runaways and panics, weren't infrequent in the business, and the women took them, when they came along, with a decent restraint. Claris didn't particularly care to be with the crowd, but he hadn't much choice. There was no other place for him to go. He couldn't leave the premises; the agency wanted at least one man there all the time. It was almost confounding how strung up and imprisoned he was by the realities of his predicament. He hadn't been able to stay locked in forever with the actress while she stewed and fussed and end-lessly prepared to go shopping, so he had slipped out of the bungalow some time ago, had wandered over the grounds, and now found himself on the terrace, like an impostor or sneak thief on the prowl, part of the social hubbub and the company, whether he wanted or didn't want to be with them. He paused at the edge of the tables, taking up a position between the terrace and the hotel lobby from which it extended so that he could look out on both areas, and as he loitered at this position the voices of the women at the adjoining table reached him. They were talking about garter fasteners, garter clasps, the difficulties they had in finding the right kind. "It's such a nuisance, always having the old fas-teners to sew on," a woman in the group was saying; she preferred the flat buckles, not the ones with the little knobs that showed through the dress, and every time she bought a new girdle, she said, she had to go through the inconvenience of transferring the fasteners. "Strange to say, the salesgirls all tell me that flat buckles aren't popular, no one wants them," the woman said.

Bearing down in Claris's direction, making her way through the guests and calling out greetings to them, surrounded by a covey of her assis-tants, was the proprietor of the hotel, Fannie Case. Claris had stopped off a few moments on his wanderings to check with Louis, the Filipino steward he knew on the place. Louis had mentioned the hotel owner would be there—that was probably one of the reasons that had led Claris

to the terrace. She was an old-timer; her fingers were covered with diamond rings, large stones, and her white hair was blued. This was her
busy time of day. By rights she should have been down in the kitchen—
she had the ordering to supervise, the cooks to talk to—but instead she
was out on the floor, doing her work in this makeshift manner with her
assistants, because she wanted to be close to the desk in the lobby and
on hand when her former husband arrived. As nearly as Claris could
make out, Harry Case was being held up by a tie-up on the freeway.
Louis had heard the radio Sigalert, the police call advising motorists—
those, that is, who still hadn't entered the freeway—to choose alternate
routes to their destination where possible. They had these great jams on
the freeways. Normally the traffic drummed ahead in its furor, the cars
careening at sixty-five miles an hour or more over the four-lane sweep
of the freeway; but when an accident occurred, a collision or breakdown, the cars piled up in a fearful chain reaction, slamming into one
another and hurtling themselves all over the hard, concrete roadbed,
blocking the four lanes, and then the traffic backed up for miles and the
whole roaring maelstrom came to a halt. It took a long time to clear the
wreckage after one of these crashes, to send the miles of stalled cars
speeding again, and so Mrs. Case was now on the terrace, bustling and
hooting to the guests, attending to her work on the move, while she
waited for her ex-husband to show up.

Claris didn't want to draw attention to himself. His idea was to keep
under cover, to do everything he could to avoid being publicly associated
with the case. His wife was out of town, as it happened, on a visit with
Eastern relatives, with her grandparents, and he had a certain leeway as
far as she was concerned, at least for the time being; but there were his
in-laws to think of, the brothers and the uncles, and he didn't know who
there might be in this crowd who could give him away and make trouble
for him if anything broke. Everybody knew everybody, people liked to
talk, and you could always count on the word getting through where it
would do the most damage. Claris hoped the hotel owner would sweep
by with her entourage and not notice him; but also on the terrace, roving
through the guests, was the producer of the picture, Robert Wigler. The
producer had a heavy weight on him, his sets standing idle in Culver
City, the overhead mounting, and the actress here in Palm Springs, in-
transigent. He was ensconced at the hotel, waiting on events, without

too much to do, and when he spied Claris, he walked over—to discuss the situation, to confer. Mrs. Case saw him, and promptly came surging forward, the assistants bobbing along after her. She set herself up on the spot with Wigler and Claris, speaking out and unburdening herself, riffling through the invoices from the supply houses, and they became a threesome, a social cluster of their own, in full, open view of everyone. "Not so glamorous," she said, harsh and oblivious, referring to the star.

She was wound up, all excited by the emergency. It was a long-standing relationship between her and Adele, dating back, as Claris knew, to the scandal. According to the stories, Fannie had never had anything against the actress from the beginning. She was too hardheaded and practical to be able to blame the breakup of her marriage on the younger woman. So they had fallen in together in the unusual aftermath. Fannie became the confidante, the guide. An attachment grew up over the years. Adele Hogue invariably went straight to Fannie's when she was in trouble, and now Fannie had the whole upset deposited in her lap, the ménage with the three small children, the strife, and her ex-husband coming up in a rush too. "Every time you see the twins, they're running around the lobby like two little rats, peeking into the ladies' room," Fannie said. Claris didn't know how well she knew Wigler, but she was a direct individual, with no nonsense to her, and she let go freely with whatever was on her mind. "She is all girl, always looking for love—'At last, at last, I have found the one man who can interest me romantically.'" She was mimicking the actress's words, referring to all the liaisons, to the many marriages, to this last one which was responsible for the turmoil now. "She goes shooting off, seeking the bluebird of happiness, and then I'm the one who has to pick up the pieces. I'm the patsy." Mrs. Case knew about the shopping the actress intended to do. "She lays there in the dumps, all tuckered out and exhausted, neglects the children and diets, and then suddenly her clothes don't fit and she starts hollering she needs a whole new wardrobe." Hogue had a driver with her at the hotel—the driver was on call for the trip into Palm Springs—and it was comparatively easy for Mrs. Case to know what the actress was up to by checking with the chauffeur.

Not far from where they were standing, in the dimness of the lobby, a man—one of the husbands who commuted to the resort and who had just pulled in—was having a heated, deeply felt argument with his wife.

The husband had beaten the pack, scrambling over the alternate routes, and in his haste and anxiety, frazzled by the traffic delay, by the hard ride over the country side roads, he had pitched into his wife right then and there, his voice coming over in a steady, muted cataract. The diversion nettled Mrs. Case.

"Too damned inconsiderate and carried away to go upstairs to the room and fight in private like they should," she said, thrown off stride and crowded by the marital quarrel. "I wouldn't give you five cents for all them big-hit, rich-guy marriages put together. What do you expect, they're no dummies." She was referring to the husbands. "Deep down they know the wife's got nothing but contempt for them, and it's a Donnybrook, cat and dog from the word go." She looked up, saw Claris watching her, and took a moment for him. "You the feller from the agency? It's a dilly—make yourself at home." She meant the whole eruption with Hogue, the crisis, and that they wouldn't be getting through with it so fast.

The women at the adjoining tables stirred in the chairs, glancing over their shoulders at the couple in the hall. The women commented on the fracas.

"What is it, she has a fetish—a hundred and eight dollars for stockings?" That was what the husband was clamoring at his wife about, among other things, that she was spending too much, that she was heedless and uncaring.

"No, no. Not at one time. Over the year, over the year."

"He adds it up?"

"Well, he's dipping into capital," the second woman said, the one who had corrected the first speaker. "He's having troubles, I don't know —business, taxes."

Her voice trailed, and in the lull the voice of the husband came over, sharp and maddened. "You got an idea the kind of money it costs nowadays to send a person through medical college?" He was meeting the bills for her younger brother's education, it appeared. "And what about your mother," he went on, "blackmailing us, threatening to take us into court for non-support, the three hundred a month I give her not enough to suit her?"

"Good, good," Mrs. Case said, taking a vicious delight in the husband's outburst, in his discomfiture. She was the first wife, so to speak, and Claris could well understand the rancor in her. He could see why she was so aroused or enlivened, and what the present situation meant to her. "These old fools with the pots," she said, scribbling on the invoices, "the minute they accumulate a lousy few hundred thousand dollars, right away they're off to the races. They can't wait, it burns in them, they got to get themselves a jazzy looker, and then boom, doubts, recriminations—the wife don't reciprocate enough." She had had the bad years in New York with Case, when he was bruising his way up to the top, full of power and muscle in those days, mixing with the rough element in the gambling rackets. She had had the grief and worry, as Claris had heard, hunting for Case at the Turkish baths, at the hotels in the Catskills, when he had disappeared from sight; and then when they had finally made it, when they came out to California to live, he had gone dancing off without a by-your-leave, putting on the big show, monkeying with movie stars, and it hurt, for all her broadmindedness and tolerance and toughness. She wasn't made of stone, and it was a kind of victory, a tingling retribution, everything coming home to roost with her—after all, it was her hotel. She owned the place. "Good!" she trumpeted, finishing with her work, shoving the papers over to her assistants. "They wanted a showgirl for a wife, then let them suffer. Let them see the belly doctors. Let them go to Cedars with nervous exhaustion." She turned to a guest sunning herself there some steps away on a chaise. "Hey, Debbie," she hallooed, invigorated, "the gams are holding out great—who gives you shots?"

She shooed the kitchen help away, sending them back to their jobs, and then made her excuses to Wigler and Claris—she had to talk a little Turkish to the Mexican chambermaids, she said. "See you later." She wheeled about, went marching off into the lobby, soon dwindled in the distance, in the screen of passersby, and Claris was left alone with the producer. Cedars of Lebanon, of course, was the big hospital in Hollywood.

In the lobby, the husband broke away from his wife; the cataract ceased. Claris could see the face of the man as he went tearing past, ravaged and grim. The woman on the chaise, the one Mrs. Case had addressed, was getting ready to go in—somebody was calling her name. She sat up on the chaise, hovered a moment, and looked at her legs. "Another two years, three at the most, and then goodbye," she said, more to herself than to anyone near her. "Coming, coming," she called. She got to her feet, straightened her blouse, her shorts, and started sliding between the tables. Claris was pinned down; as a matter of courtesy, nodding and agreeing, at the same time his eyes constantly veered to the lobby. He was searching for Fannie Case. He had lost track of her. He was puzzled, uneasy—she was obviously bent on meeting her former husband as he arrived, and yet she had gone marching clear off the floor to talk to the chambermaids somewhere. Claris didn't know how he was going to be able to recognize Case when he appeared. Louis had promised to tip him off as soon as Case drove in, but Louis was badly rushed with the guests today, receiving them and settling them down, the arrivals disorganized because of the freeway tie-up, and Claris doubted that the steward would be able to get away.

The producer was gone, no longer standing alongside. He had finished with his observations, or had tired and lost interest, and had drawn off without notice or ceremony. Claris could see him pushing out among the guests, and just at that moment, as he cast about to pick up Wigler in the swirl, out of the corner of his eye he glimpsed Mrs. Case in the lobby again. She had turned up out of nowhere and was moving fast toward the desk, toward a man there, a single arrival, Case.

Claris waited a moment, letting Wigler get out of range, and then gingerly maneuvered himself down to the desk. People were coming and going. Claris had to take pains to make it not seem that he was eavesdropping, and as he dawdled in the area, keeping aloof and pretending he was waiting for someone to come down and join him, the interchange between the Cases carried across to him in hot, disjointed bursts and snatches. The two of them were rattling away, lost and embroiled, standing together under an arch to the side of the reception desk. "Shopping? Shopping?" Case said, hard-ridden, perplexed, and then Claris heard Fannie singing out: "How should I know what goes on in her head?" Case had apparently asked about Hogue, wanting to know what she was doing, and Fannie apparently had told him. Case was low-slung, pugnacious, with a prizefighter's stance and truculence, the hurry and stress of the moment putting a homely crimp to his features, and Claris could hear Fannie chipping at him, looking him over. "What's new in Vegas?" she said, mocking, giving him none of the best of it. "The faces go lopsided and start falling apart. He's got a mirror in his apartment there that shows him he has a full head of hair and still looks good."

"Boy, you step out of line with them and they got it on you for the rest of your life," Case said. He had reached the place some minutes ago and had evidently been kept waiting by the desk clerk until Fannie could get to him and go to work on him. He was used up, out of temper from the hours in the desert heat, from the tie-up. He wanted a room. He wanted a shower. "She's burned out," he said, grating, meaning Adele. "Them cookies go good so long as it's unconscious. The minute they get on to themselves, they're through. The flop sweat comes crawling out on her and she starts shaking in her boots."

"What are you yammering at me for?" Fannie said, indignant. "What am I got to do with it?"

"She got down on her hands and knees, apologizing to beat the band, making a first-class sap out of herself, and then when the showdown came, nothing—the same as before." Claris winced as the image came back to him. Case was referring to the scene Hogue had made, to the impulsive, deluded act of contrition that had misfired and sent her driving out to the resort. What she had done, in her derangement, was to go out to the set. She had faced the whole company, the cast and crew, on that bare, hushed sound stage—demeaning herself without stint, saying how unprofessional her conduct was. She had promised with all her heart that she would make amends, that she would be the first one on the set the following morning and that henceforth all would go well.

Their voices fell low. They were huddled in tight, going round and round now, and Claris had to steal up closer in order to catch the drift of what they were saying. Fannie was driving away in earnest. She was trying to head Case off, to keep him away from Adele, telling him his presence on the scene would only aggravate the problem. Case fought back, shunting aside her arguments, not wanting to hear them, and it impressed Claris, even as they intently bickered and belabored each other, that there was still a peculiar bond between them, an old-time intimacy and rapport.

"You want to let her go straight down the drain?" Case demanded. Somebody had to take hold, he said. Somebody had to put her back on the rails. "This ain't the old days. They'll throw her right out on her keister. There's the kids to be protected. You think of that? What about the kids in the middle?"

"You'll be the one who'll save the situation? You're the champion? Tell the truth, Harry," she said, blunt and unsparing, "every time she got a divorce, didn't you get a sense of satisfaction out of it? Didn't you go running Johnnie-on-the-Spot?"

"What's that got to do with it?" Case asked. "What are you bringing that up for? Who wants her? It's the kids."

"Who are you trying to fool?" Fannie said. "Don't I know you from the old days? Don't I know you better than you know yourself? You were star crazy then and you're still star crazy. You saw your chance and you came busting all over yourself. You can't wait to get your fingers on her."

"For my part she can go walking out into the ocean until her hat floats," Case said, crashing down, bringing the argument to a finish once and for all, and from where Claris was standing at the wall, remembering to remain hidden, he could feel the hard force in the man, the anger and exasperation. "Fannie, don't stand me on my head. You don't know anything about it. Whatever she has to do, she'll do. Just let me handle it. Lords and dukes," he seethed. "The phonies we got here weren't flashy enough for her. She had to go for that international jet-set bull and marry this English foul ball with the racing stables."

"The language is very nice," Fannie said, seeing it was a lost cause. Case wasn't turning around and going back. "That's all we need, a few refined expressions out of your vocabulary."

"Am I making it up? It's not the truth? She heard about them pansies all going over there and she had to get a whiff of it too—Monte Carlo and all them ritzy foreign places with the lousy plumbing." He had gone after her, wanting her, carrying the torch, as the saying went, whatever carrying the torch meant with these people, and she had steadfastly kept knocking him down. She had gotten away from him altogether—eighteen months out of the country with the European crowd—and now that she was on the skids and he had her back again, wild horses weren't going to stop him. "Bunch of no-good parasites and freeloaders, the whole crummy bunch of them," he said. "Who are they? Have they got a pot or a window to throw it out of, any single one of them?"

"For crying out loud, have a heart, Harry—there's people passing!"

"What did I say?" He caught himself. He saw what he had said. "If they never heard it before, then they won't know what I'm talking about. If they know what it means, then what have they got to be so chintzy about? What do you have to do around here to get a room?" he said. "You going to let me stay in the lobby all day?"

"Give him the room," Fannie said to the desk clerk. The boy was rattled, fumbled the job at the keyboard, and it ended with Fannie going around the counter herself. "That puts the lid on it," she said, fed up, disgusted. "She'll take one look at you and goodbye Charlie. Now we got it. She comes here, a woman at the end of her rope with three small children on her hands, always impractical, too goddam big to bother with alimony—not like these prostitutes here."

"I should tip my hat to her?" Case said.

"Big shot!" Fannie said. "She insulted his ego and committed the crime of the century!"

"She's in no bed of roses." Case had himself in control again and was standing at the desk while Fannie went through the business of booking him into the hotel. He'd get at Adele as soon as he cleaned up, he said, shopping or no shopping—she could change her mind and go shopping some other time. "One thing about these kewpie dolls, they always boomerang on themselves. Cripes, they never know how to win."

"The room's not ready. You'll have to wait until they make it up," Fannie said to him. "Don't even know how to buy." She was back on Adele again. "In New York one time she stayed petrified in the hotel suite, too scared of her shadow to go out. 'For Chrissake,' I told her, 'call Ceil Chapman, call Bonwit's. They'll send up a raft of dresses—you'll pick and choose.' But no, she couldn't budge herself—no moxie in her, no energy."

But she was talking to herself. It was over. Case had taken the key off the desk, had picked up his bag, and was waddling down to the room —he knew the way and didn't require a bellboy to carry his bag for him. Fannie busied herself behind the desk for a while, bossing the clerk around. Then her heels went tapping on the floor tiles, the tapping faded away, and Claris was released.

The hotel was built on a rise of ground, the kitchen lying on a lower level, to the back of and under the structure. Claris was going around the side of the hotel, getting away from the lobby, when he was unexpectedly brought to a stop by Louis, the steward. There was a kind of hollow leading down to the kitchen entrance, and Louis, standing at the kitchen door, called to him. Louis assumed that by this time Claris was aware of Case's presence on the grounds; what he was waiting to tell Claris about was the news of a man they knew, a singer or actor named

Pepi Straeger, who had just been killed in a car crash. Dealing with the guests as they came in off the freeway, Louis had been able to get word of the accident. Pepi Straeger was a hanger-on, a fixture at the social gatherings at homes and tennis clubs, a Viennese singer who had once been fairly successful in operettas, in revues, but who had fallen on bad days, his style of singing having years ago gone out of favor. Claris had seen him around, pushing his luck—jockeying cars for people, making himself handy, hunting up bit acting parts—and it was a disagreeable shock to hear now of his sudden death. Louis couldn't say whether it was actually this accident that had caused the freeway jam, but if it wasn't this accident, then Straeger had met his death in another accident, occurring down the line on some other stretch of the road, at another time; or else, as sometimes happened, there were two accidents, separate and yet related, both of them contributing to and causing the traffic pileup.

Louis was taking a break, having a smoke outside the kitchen entrance between errands, and Claris stayed with him there, lost in a train of thought about the singer and his passing. Straeger had lately been in the foreground. He had some months ago linked himself to a woman with a really substantial fortune, a patent medicine company whose product was a household name. It was a big coup, a stroke on the grand scale, but Straeger had managed it—the wedding was announced —and Claris didn't know whether the accident, coming just then, was a portent, an admonition, or whether it came with no meaning at all. Louis lingered alongside, with his reticence, with his way of making a little stunt out of smoking a cigarette, exhaling in fine, discreet slants. He was slight of build, a Filipino, his hair thinning evenly over his scalp, and he held himself with a stiff reserve. He had a deep, respectful regard for Claris, admiring him for his physique, for his athletic prowess, for the celebrity of his marriage—an admiration that Claris could do without. Claris didn't want his solicitude or respectful regard. Louis understood all about Hogue and the awkward position Claris was in right now with the actress, and he wondered whether the accident of Straeger's would bring on more complications. "Will they want you to go down and take care of things?" Louis said, murmuring, keeping his distance. He meant the agency. He mistakenly thought Straeger was a client of the agency.

"No, he's not one of ours," Claris said. "We don't really have anything to do with him."

Claris had caught Straeger in a show or two, this in earlier days, in New York, long before Claris had any inkling that he would wind up in California, and so it had been something to get to know the performer and watch him close at hand. Straeger used to go bumbling along, light-hearted and devil-may-care, putting on a happy face, singing tunes to himself—"The Night Was Made for Love." He put on a happy face because he knew they couldn't stand you if you griped, if you were in the dumps and discontented. "She gives him fifty dollars a week spending money and he has to genuflect to her like she's a female Buddha," Claris had once heard him saying, the envy burning in him, speaking of an acquaintance, a member of the fraternity, who had already scored with a marriage. Claris had happened to be in a studio casting office when they were trying to fill some minor, unimportant part, and, on the impulse, thinking of Straeger as he had seen him on the stage in New York, had mentioned his name, getting the part for him—that was why Louis had the impression Straeger was represented by the agency and that Claris was associated with him. Straeger found out Claris had mentioned his name, and came to him, brimming and shy, genuinely pleased: "You did this for me—why?" Straeger, as soon as he had connected solidly with his lady, had had his teeth capped, that expert theatrical job they did for the top stars, and Claris thought of the caps, the vacuum-fired porcelain jacket crowns, strewn now somewhere on the concrete pavement of the highway; but what persisted most steadily in his mind as he gazed out at the hot, bright sunshine was the vision of Straeger's face, suddenly young and fresh, as he must have seemed when a boy, as he came forward that time and said, "You did this for me—why?"

Claris, on leaving Louis, worked back to the public side of the hotel —the terrace, the lawns, the walks. He stood some distance away from the building, keeping close to a row of oleander bushes that lined the path. Everyone had gone in. It was the afternoon hiatus, the siesta. The grounds were empty; the terrace was heaped with chairs and tables. Down at the cottage, the hired chauffeur had the limousine ready for Hogue, and Claris knew the limousine had been parked there for the last forty minutes or so. A good many of the actresses liked to go shopping in the late-afternoon off hours, when the business was light and there weren't too many people around, and Claris supposed that Hogue

—with the fears and constraints riding her—had most likely been stalling
all day with this specific purpose in mind. But the constraints still had
her fast; she still dallied and couldn't get herself out of the bungalow.
Claris looked over to the hotel, to the different entrances from which
Case might appear. Case should have been coming out any minute now
—he must have easily finished changing and showering by this time—
and Claris wished the actress would bestir herself, that she would hurry
and get away. In the end they had to come to their senses. Eventually,
they shook out of their troubles and went back to the studio—after all,
the pictures always got made. But if she collided with Case now, there
would be an uproar, a continuing diversion, something for her to seize
upon and brood on and busy herself with, and she would be put that
much further back on the road. It suddenly began to worry Claris, as he
wavered there in the baking desert heat, that perhaps Case had gotten
by him in some way, that perhaps he was already inside the cottage with
her, battling with her. Claris didn't know. Case could have come out by
some other, hidden door. He could have left earlier, while Claris was still
talking to Louis at the kitchen door, and in his uncertainty, restless and
perspiring, he decided to go down to the cottage, to look in on Hogue
and see what was happening.

He started out, following the row of oleanders. He went past the terrace and was moving on toward a portico, toward an open flight of stairs
they had there, in back of the terrace, when he heard the quick, hasty
slidings of footsteps over the tiles, the sounds of some kind of scuffle
going on. It was the producer, Robert Wigler, making a pass at a woman,
attempting to fondle her—in spite of the production standstill, in spite
of his crucial problems with the moneymen—and Claris had to hold up,
compelled to witness this incongruous encounter. "Oh, for God's sakes,
Wigler, amn't I in trouble enough?" the woman said. She was the one
who had been having the hard time with her husband, the woman in
the lobby. She was extremely attractive, as they all were, shapely and soft
and tempting, but she wasn't as young as she looked, and she was suffering from arthritis. Her left shoulder and elbow were killing her. That
was what she was doing on the portico stairs when Wigler fell on her—
she had run out of aspirin and was going down for a new supply.

Wigler let her go. He stood back, his arms at his sides. Claris dug into
the oleanders and waited. "You take your life in your hands the minute

you walk out of the room," the woman said. She patted her hair in place, adjusted her dress, and walked on. Wigler turned around and plodded away.

Case wasn't with the actress. She was on the way out as Claris came into the cottage, but that didn't mean she was leaving immediately— Claris didn't know how long she had been on her way out. She wandered around the room, struggling to get herself in order so that she could leave. The rebelliousness and belligerence were gone. She was changed, worn down from the hours in the bungalow, from this unneeded shopping business with which she had saddled herself all day. Melanie waited at the door, bent on accompanying her mother to the stores, but Adele was too low in spirit, too spent, to resist the child or find fault with her. The thought of the chauffeur outside with the car weighed on the actress. She had the chauffeur's feelings to consider now on top of her other distractions. She didn't want to go on holding the man up—"The next thing you know he'll spread it around I'm a nut," she said. But every time she started for the door, there was something to bring her back, something more to be done and delay her. Her scalp burned. She suddenly halted in her wanderings and held her hand to her head. This scalp-burning was a peculiar, mysterious ailment that always threw her into a depression. The burning came out in patches on her scalp. The sensation came and went. It was a neuritis, a misdirected neuralgia, a punishment sent down to plague her. In addition to her other vagaries and hallucinations, she thought she was being systematically persecuted. She hated comedians, was racked by old phantoms, believed that every time you turned a light out someone somewhere died. She was in a flutter. She couldn't control the fluttering. Claris knew it was no pose, no imaginary symptom to win her sympathy, or if it was, the discomfort to her was no less real. When she got busy, when she had some task to apply herself to, an appointment to meet, a breathlessness took hold of her. There was a racing, an agitation. Her heart palpitated. Sometimes she had a wild, unbelievably penetrating, wicked pain in her left arm, always the left arm, and during the fright of those moments, the only thing she could do was to hang motionless and hope and pray for the deep, bone-piercing pain to leave. She wouldn't talk to Claris. When he tried to say something to steady her, she just brushed past him and left him standing there. She didn't want to open herself up to him any more than she had to. She had exposed herself enough.

"You have to keep it to yourself. What should I do, bore people stiff with my miseries? You become anathema. They stay away from you in droves. The poor kids," she said, thinking of the twins, "the minute they see me, they run for the hills—you can't blame them." She understood how repugnant she made herself with her constant complaints, with her everlasting, self-centered concerns and excitements, and so her agony was doubled and redoubled. She was worried about the twins. Out of some instinct or deviltry, the little boys made it a point to steer clear of her and the bungalow, and she hadn't seen them since early morning. She didn't know what they were doing, if they had had anything to eat. She hoped somebody was looking after them, that they wouldn't come to harm.

She finally got herself to the door. Claris thought it was over, that she would surely make it this time—she was halfway out of the door—but then, at the last minute, she turned back and flung herself into a new fit of despair. "Oh, look at me—just look at what I'm doing!" She was wearing that thin cotton wrapper they use when they're doing their hair, their makeup. Claris had wondered what she was doing, walking out of the bungalow in the wrapper. She had forgotten her dress. She had forgotten she was still in the wrapper. She had nothing on underneath but a slip, and this small mental lapse on her part upset and depressed her out of all proportion. "They'll take one look at me traipsing in with nothing on and they'll really think I'm crazy!"

She tore the wrapper off, went to one of the suitcases lying on the floor, stooped down and started rummaging for a dress she could wear. "Mother, everyone forgets," Melanie said, reasoning with her. "It's nothing. We all make absent-minded mistakes." And while Melanie coaxed and reasoned, while Adele kept bringing garments out of the suitcase, the door opened and Case was with them.

He had taken pains with his appearance, had shaved and smartened himself according to a certain style, and for an instant Claris glimpsed the image of the man as he once was, years back, light on his feet and resilient, like some Irish welterweight boxer just out of the barber shop, the world on a string; but the sparkle, the illusion, the whole witch-hazel

air of well-being and style went glimmering before the violence of the
reception Adele gave him. Claris didn't know where she had the energy
in her. She drew herself up and came alive, a charge jolting through her
body at the first sight of Case. It would have done no good if Claris had
offered to leave, if he had tried to walk out. She wanted him there. She
would have insisted on his presence—to defy Case, to show him she had
allies, the agency behind her, and didn't need outsiders. "The sightseers
and autograph hunters have broken into the place," she said, almost
glad, it seemed to Claris, to have Case in the room with her, almost eager
to take him on even though she must have known she could only get
hurt and come out second best in any tangle with him. Case ignored
her. He stared at Claris, swiftly put him down for one of the college-
educated nobodies they had on the staffs of the agencies, one of the family connections that had to be taken care of, and—so far as Claris could
tell—paid him no further notice. "How are you, Melanie?" he said, fore-
stalling Adele, keeping his back to her. He made conversation with the
child—did she like it here? Was she having a good time? This was no
place for her, he remarked, dry, looking around the room. No, she didn't
mind it at the hotel, Melanie said, calm, steady, standing up for her
mother. It was agreeable. It was quiet.

"What do you have to do here?" Case asked her.

"What do you have to do anywhere?" Melanie said. "And everything
is air-conditioned."

Fannie came clattering in. She had evidently been on the lookout for
Case too. She had no intention of letting her ex-husband rap into Adele
unless she was on the spot to get between them. She waded in and started
tidying up the room, grumbling—the twins had just been in the sprin-
klers, were sopping wet, needed a change from top to bottom, and were
turning the hotel into a public playground. "What are you going to do
now," she said to Case, "move mountains? Go ahead, convince her."

It always impressed Claris how these thugs, so wary and practical, so
ready in their dealings to search through to the essential unworthiness
of people, could, when it came to a woman, drop their guard and give
themselves over with a complete, headlong abandon. Melanie trudged
off into one of the bedrooms to find dry clothing for the twins, to get
herself out of the way. Claris could hear her through the partition, put-
tering and pulling out drawers, while the contest went on between Case

and her mother. It was a straight standoff affair, Case settling himself for the duration, acting as though it was foregone, open and shut, just a matter of time until she came to her senses and started back for the studio. He loomed above her, overbearing and peremptory, full of himself, so that it came as a shock to realize that he was actually short in stature, unprepossessing, squat. It was amazing how the pugnacity in him transformed him physically; without it he would be insignificant, would shrink back to size. This was their first meeting since she had returned from England. They hadn't seen each other for eighteen months, but the long separation didn't seem to trouble either one of them. They fell in stride, taking up apparently from where they had left off, and Claris, who was in there on a pass, so to speak, standing at the wall and overlooked, was able to get the inside flavor of their peculiar attachment, the way of them in the past, as they tugged and hauled and wouldn't leave each other alone. "He's got to have her," Fannie said from the sidelines, grinding at Case, not liking the way the tussle was going, seeing no good to it, no outcome, but helpless to stop it. "He has a pigeon to pick on and he can't hold himself in. She don't want, so he wants. It's a must. The knocks he took from her, the insults, the rejections," Fannie said, working on the pillows on the couch, fluffing them up, wrenching the couch itself around into place. "If it was a man, he would throw him straight through the nearest window—there would be murder. But when it's Adele, everything is smiles."

"Did you drop in to feast your eyes?" Adele baited him. "Does it do your heart good to have the advantage over me, to see me right back where I started from?" She dressed him down. She might have known he'd be along. She could imagine how he saw himself—being the big man, spreading himself out.

"Famous lady," Case said. "International beauty." There had been all kinds of publicity—about the homecoming, the breakdown of her celebrated English marriage, the tantrums and irregularities with the picture now—and he wasn't going to let her smear herself up for good just to give the chiselers and column writers a field day. "When that ceiling turns to platinum," he said. He wasn't backing down. He wasn't taking no for an answer. He was still bitten by the freeway tie-up; it griped him that he had had to beat out the traffic for three and a half hours. "You read this stuff they write about you in the papers and you think you have to live up to it. Watch out, you'll talk yourself into it and then you'll really be in trouble."

"You'd think he'd have some scruples and not go where he's not wanted, but he does, he does," Adele said. Case had all the details on the production. He had taken a hand, had moved in on the proceedings. He had made it his business to see the backers or the potential backers, and had given assurances that he would have her straightened out and would deliver her, and it infuriated her—that he had made himself free with her, that he had given people to think that he had authority over her. She combated him with a blazing intensity, dancing on her feet as she confronted him, half coming out of the slip, not caring how it climbed up on her. "He walks in here like the cat that swallowed the canary and starts issuing pronouncements. Who gave you the right to speak for me? Who made you the mastermind?"

"Leave it to her," Fannie said. "She knows what she's doing, every time." Fannie meant the slip, the bare shoulders and arms, the whole shuddering show of flesh. Fannie thought it was a ploy, that Adele had consciously or subconsciously contrived to be waiting for Case in the slip in order to give him ideas and topple him. "They're no dumbbells. They got it in them from the day they're born—that's why they pay them fortunes. Fool!" she said to Adele, defending her, taking her part, at the same time slamming into her too. "If you didn't want him, then why did you come here? You know you did it for the express purpose of leading him on and giving him the needles, so what are you kicking about? You got your wish—clap hands!"

Apparently there had been reconciliations or near-reconciliations, Claris gathered, times when Adele and Case had gotten on, when they hadn't gotten on, when they had bickered and feuded and done who knew what things to each other—and the overlay of the past, of the stinging intimacies and self-betrayals, was more than she could keep out of her mind or bear. Case had the goods on her. That was the burn. That was why she sputtered and fizzled and fought him with such a vehement recklessness. In one way or another he had been with her through the years. He knew her tricks, her foibles, the marriages and romances, the wonderful beginnings of them and then the bitter crash-landing endings; and in facing him, she had to face the messes and mistakes that were convulsing her and making it impossible now for her to work or breathe. To hit back at him, she taunted him on his own early failings. She threw it up to him how, when he first came to California, he had gone chasing to the class restaurants in town, to see and be seen with the movie elite. She rubbed it in—how in those days he used to sneak out to the big movie premières at the Carthay Circle Theatre, how he used to huddle in the crowd on the sidewalk, so that he could gawk and goggle at the stars. She threw it up to him that the management had once had to speak to him at the racetrack because he hopscotched over the boxes and socialized too much with the nabobs and celebrities. "Stupid, dumb broad," he said to her. "You know and I know and the lamppost knows sooner or later you're going to fold, so what are you raising an unnecessary holler for? Nobody expects you to be the great superstar you think people think you have to be. Just go out there and wiggle your butt, that's all they want from you. You don't have to lose your nerve. You don't have to kill yourself. Just do what they tell you to do and you'll be all right." He had her in his bones—the tops of stockings, the pushed-up dress, the rolling on floors, on beds, the whole irrational sexual phantasmagoria that grabbed and goaded them. "Did I come anywhere near you?" he reminded her. "You wanted me to stay away, so I stayed away." He would have been perfectly happy to have nothing to do with her this time around, he said, but she was pulling the roof down on her head and he had to step in before it was too late. "Did I phone or try to contact you in other ways, through second parties?"

But she had him there too. She was back at him like a shot. He hadn't stayed away at all. He had had her watched all the time. He had bribed people on the set, the chief electrician, the unit manager, tipping them a fifty apiece to bring back reports on her, and it was surprising to see the sharp thrill of pleasure this tactical victory gave her. "Do you think I didn't know? Did you think I wouldn't find out?" She had had informants of her own.

"Tell the truth, Harry," Fannie said, "isn't it embarrassing? Don't it go against the grain—to make yourself small and spy on her?"

The fright went shooting through Claris. Of course that was how Case had known the exact details about the scene on the set when Adele had made her speech to the company and had crucified herself. Claris saw the danger he was in, the danger he had been running all along. He had assumed he was relatively safe—a flunky, one of the paid help that came and went around the actresses—but with Case hanging fast and bird-dogging her, Claris could see he was bound to be found out sooner or later. He thought back to the people on the set, the ones he knew and the ones who might know about him. He thought of Prescott, shooting his mouth off, spreading the good news around at the office and in all the other places too, Claris could bet, and he cursed himself for his laxness, for his chronic need to talk and let everyone know what he was doing.

Case was pounding hard. He had taken a good deal of punishment, was getting nowhere, and in the collision and infighting, in the sexual exacerbation, his patience was going fast. He was trying to get her to understand the position Wigler was in, to explain the nature of the financial arrangements. The banks supplied 60 to 70 percent of the financing, leaving it to the end-money investors to bring up the rest, to start the picture and to finish it, in this way guaranteeing the production. The end-money people were caught in a dilemma of their own. On the one hand, they were anxious to get in on a Hogue feature, her first since her return, a sure moneymaker with all the to-do in the papers and the acclaim; but on the other hand, they were nervous about the delays. They were small folk, concerned about what they called the point of no return—that switchover when they were locked in and could only plunge on ahead. They were slow to put their signatures to a contract, and if they jumped and decided not to participate, there would be no bank loan, there would be no financing, Wigler would be left hung out to dry, with the considerable cash outlay already committed and spent, and the whole deal would collapse like a house of cards. Case was struggling to get this all in. "Bust Wigler, and I give you my word you'll never work again," he said, but she was too far gone, too swept up in her loathing and the remembrance of all that had gone on between them, to hear him out, to take time to worry about the financing, the end money and the point of no return.

"What you really want to do is have the say-so over me," she said. "That's why you walked in and tried to be the mastermind. You want to be the man in charge, telling everybody what to do."

"Would you be any the worse for it?" he said to her, lowering his voice, probably more in earnest than he knew. "Would it do you any harm, Adele, to have somebody in your corner to look out for your interests?"

"And then you'd be all over me like a ten-ton truck. That's what you're pushing for all the time. I'd be beholden to you. You'd like it. I'd be at your beck and call."

He let it all out. "Was it bad? At the time, did you suffer from it— the hyenas coming at you, the fights, the studio suspensions? Didn't it help to have a little muscle behind you when you needed it the most?" He went in close, bringing back old mortifications—the old unedifying, protracted bouts and sieges, the dependence on him, the ineptitude in her, the lack of will and courage. "Who are you? You got no strength, no stamina. Without the cameras, you wouldn't know what to do with yourself. You'd dry up and die. You'd wither away. The moves you made all your life," he went on, maddened and deadly, "going overboard for the first guy that comes along with a good line of bull—putting your faith in them, marrying them for good and forever, and then waking up four days later screaming you want out, your whole life is in ruins."

Fannie lunged at him. She wedged herself between them, beating him off. "What's the matter with you? What do you want from her?"

"Going down for the third time, hiding from people," Case said, walking away, annoyed with himself. He saw that he had said more than he had meant to say, that he had blown it and would have to come back to her at another time.

"Get him out of here," Adele said, trembling, sick.

"Knows just the right things to say to her, goes back to machine-gun tactics," Fannie said. "You see she's got the heebie-jeebies, she can't work, and you can only make it worse. What good did it do? Did you honestly think it would help?"

"She'll come off her high horse," Case said. "She just needs somebody to hate at the present time, so let her hate me. That's what I'm here for." The urgencies remained. He was thinking of the headaches, of the reporters now sifting in—he had seen some of them in the freeway tie-up, stranded there along with everybody else, and he didn't know how the publicity would go and what it might do to the production. "Boy, she hates my guts. Her whole body started to shake the minute I walked into the room. I touched her hand, it was wet with sweat." He looked up, saw Claris there before him, remembered who he was, and felt obliged to make some sort of statement to him. "She'll come around," he said to Claris. Claris held still. "Everybody loses their self-confidence and goes into a slump now and then. You get your second wind, only she don't know that yet."

"Get him out of here," Adele said. She couldn't wait for him to leave. "So long as he's on the grounds of the hotel, I'm not budging. I don't need him to lay the law down and tell me the story of my life."

"Can't fall asleep unless the light is shining straight into her eyes and the radio is going full blast," Fannie said to her, still overheated and angry. "What did you think was going to happen? You knew he was no Albert Schweitzer. You knew what you would get. Love's sweet song," she said, advancing on Case, starting him to the door. "The gifts he showered on her, the attentions, the jewelry from Brock's—gone with the wind, water under the bridge."

"Why do you take care of the twins and do everything for her?" Case said, carping with her now over the neglect, the children living out of suitcases and everything let go.

"What should I do, throw her out?"

"If you didn't watch out for the twins, then she would have to do it herself and it would give her a sense of responsibility. Too broken down even to get a nursemaid for the kids," Case said, but Fannie had him arguing at the door, was holding it open, nudged and pushed, and they were gone.

Melanie came out of the bedroom, carrying a pile of clothing—underwear, sweaters. She obviously had not wanted to leave while Case was still in the room, while the dust-up was in progress, and it was clear she was reluctant to leave the bungalow even now. But the evening desert chill was coming on, and she had to get the twins into dry clothes; she had to see to it that they had their dinner. She trundled past Claris, hiding whatever she was feeling behind the thick glasses, as she customarily did, keeping steady, acting as though everything was in order, normal, and went out the door. Claris was left alone with the actress. She didn't keep it to herself this time. She spoke out without reserve, using him, trusting him, not trusting him. She knew there was nothing much she could expect from him. She had been around, was under no illusions, knew exactly what she had in this fast pickup shuffle in the sack with him, but in the mood she was in she didn't care what she said or who heard it. She had to have someone. She was on the skids, as far back as they could get, tied in knots, blocked, tortured by the passing of the years.

"How fast they come out with the once-over—'She still looks good.' It's the battle cry around here. You hear it all over," she said, harsh and unhappy. She had little children to take care of, was unable to sleep, was ridden with hypochondria, with the mass of her neuroses and afflictions, the scalp-burning and palpitations—and yet she had this fierce, perverse streak in her to resist with all her strength and stand them all off. "You want things from people. You make demands," she said. "You hold bitter grudges in your mind and brood because you think they're running out on you and are false and ungrateful—when all the time of course the truth is they're up to their ears in troubles themselves and probably have their own private grudges, thinking people are letting them down and are self-seeking and rotten. So you don't know what you're doing. You hit out and screw everything up, and then you not only have your original miseries still to contend with but you've antagonized everyone who might come near you in the bargain." Claris supposed this was her way of chopping up on herself because she had come this far along and had no friends, no group to belong to; or else it was a backhanded slap at him, letting him know that she was reduced to people like him, people who worked for her.

It had been a sore point between them, a recurring irritation, although they had never spoken of it, that he had had to go slogging off in the evenings, that he had a wife there, a home. Fortunately his wife was away now, so he had room to move around in and could give the actress all the time she wanted, and he told her he was staying at the hotel, that he wasn't driving back, although he didn't think he needed to mention the reason to her. "What's the use of burning yourself up?" he said to her. "What difference does it make what Case has to say to you or what you have to say to him? You're only getting in a state over him because it's easier to do that than buckle down to the work." But she waved him off and made him stop.

"I know I'm not making sense. I don't have to have you to tell me I'm being illogical."

The hired chauffeur had long ago left; Fannie must have sent him away, or the chauffeur must have realized the time was passing and that the trip into town was off. They had the cottage all to themselves. Claris had heard of cases of other performers who had their problems and went through a similar commotion, but he had never witnessed the phenomenon at first hand. He couldn't understand the stark, fanatical violence of their feelings and he didn't know if this violence was assumed, exaggerated, or whether there was some special validity to it. He wouldn't have known how to deal with these other performers and he didn't know what to do with Adele now. She sat in the chair, not looking at him, lost in herself. She felt as though her teeth ached, she said. It reminded her, she said, of a time, years back, when she was a girl, when she had seared the roof of her mouth on a pizza pie. "You know, the melted cheese, it sticks, it clings," she started to explain and then languished and quit explaining. She was redheaded, or what was known as strawberry blond, more reddish than blond, with the thin, clear skin and coloring that went with her hair; Claris could see the freckles still on her face—and the freckles, the high, insistent coloring, together with the dark shooting splotches of her eyes, gave a jarring urgency to the charge of her protest. She sat loosely in the slip, regarding the body in the slip with a kind of angry, detached impatience—the body perpetually pummeled, massaged, costumed, rigged out, and displayed. She had had operations, a hysterectomy, and she spoke up against the hysterectomy too, against the glib, inside trade term the movie doctors used among themselves in connection with the surgical procedure—the Joe E. Brown, the doctors called it, because of the wide line of the abdominal incision. Nothing about her gave her peace; she had reached that point where, if it had anything to do with her, she was at once displeased and wearied. She railed at the dieting and reducing she had to do. She had fits of nibbling, could eat the whole day through, she said. "Putting it on, hacking it off— suddenly you swell out like a balloon," she said. Claris supposed it was this persistence, this force of will, the sheer wanting and refusal to subside, that accounted for the difference in them, that caused certain actresses to project, as the saying was, and come across and draw the attention from the audience. He was disconcerted by the living fact of the person here. He was alarmed by the clamor in her, by the shameless, uncontrolled outpouring, and, in the awkwardness of the moment, worrying about the actress and taken up with her, he juggled his own fears. He saw the hopelessness of the position he was in, and he wondered what he thought he was doing, standing by idly, waiting on the actress— waiting for what, he asked himself.

She had gone back in her mind to Harry Case. She was talking about an incident that had occurred in his office—this was a number of years ago, when the Las Vegas strip was first going up, when they were starting to build the row of gambling hotels. Case had taken a spread of fancy offices in Los Angeles, mainly for the sake of the movie crowd whom he followed so ardently in those days and wanted to impress and be part of. She had gone up to see the place, and she told now—whether to demean Case or score him off, for whatever good it did her—how he had gone after her in the office, bawdy and abashed, still sitting in the desk swivel chair, wriggling after her in the chair, on its casters, pressing her into the corner with his knees. She told of another occasion, when Case had come calling on her at her house, when she had still been in the bedroom, dressing. The maid had told him he would have to wait, but he had pushed past the maid, gone to the bedroom, and poked his head inside the door. "You've got a nerve, walking in here," she had begun, but then he had dangled the present he had brought her, diamond ear-clips from Brock's, and she had invited him in—to the lacy stuff, the garter straps, the high-heeled mules, the whole undressed business they yammered for. "What a fool I was," she said, speaking to Claris, remembering. " 'Come in! Come in!' I told him." She wasn't scoring off Case or running herself down; what she was really doing was trying to get back the feeling of those days—the assurance, the easy spirits. She was still fighting, holding on, talking to herself, striving for that morning when you wake up and everything is miraculously lifted, the depression vanished, and you go speeding off again. She talked of old escapades, times when she had eluded Case and infuriated him, when she had gone stealing off with a weekend companion, some good-looking leading man from the studio, her partner as rash and eager for the spree as she was. She was a star, immediately recognizable wherever they might go, so they had this extra hazard to play with and counter—they had had to seek out obscure desert resorts, Soboba Hot Springs, Murrieta, places at that time still off the beaten path and remote. She spoke of the little old Jews, blinking in the sun and musing, who clustered at those out-of-the-way hotels for the mineral baths, for their health. She told how, sitting on the passenger's side of the car, she had had to duck her head down at the dashboard when they came driving up to some bellboys or young people who would have known who she was. And as she brought out these remembrances, confidences that she would no doubt later on regret and reproach herself

siesta. The married couple, the one engaged the day before in the heated dispute in the lobby, had made up their differences. Claris and Wigler had seen them together on the terrace earlier in the day, the husband smooth-shaven and replenished, all trace of anguish mysteriously disappeared, as if it had never existed. The wife had quieted him, in the ways they had; and now, as the long afternoon siesta began, as Claris and Wigler came up to the portico—the portico with the open staircase, where the married couple had their room—they inadvertently heard the woman's voice, infinitely serene and kind, softly reprimanding, "Oh, you are naughty." The woman's voice, the wayward fragment, in the sunny stillness, had an effect on Wigler.

"They're all secret agents," he murmured to Claris, as they moved along, as they headed on to the office. "Well, it's a lot of fun," he said, distracted, with his broad understanding. "You think it's nothing, to put your hand under a woman's dress?"

He himself had been unlucky straight down the line with women, he said; he didn't have the knack. He had a spoiled marriage behind him, had been through all kinds of vicissitudes, had once attempted suicide— Claris believed he had once seen something about it in the papers— and the woman's tenderness, coming at this time when everything was tense and precarious for him, set him off, leading him to reveries which ordinarily, no doubt, he would have held back from his closest friends, but which—under the circumstances, drifting and idling, groping for something to say—he didn't mind sharing with Claris, an almost total stranger to him. He used to live at the beach, he said. They had had a house, he and his wife—he was talking about his marriage, its dissolution and how it had come to pass. "Up the coast, Malibu, past Malibu, farther, not far from Point Mugu, Port Hueneme—you know, the naval stations. There were these exceptionally big grocery bills," he continued, going to the heart of his account, "and not that I wanted to be picayune about it, you understand, but it was genuinely puzzling to me—after all, we were just two people, my wife and me. So I looked into it, out of curiosity. Well, it's a peculiar thing, but it so happens that I have never been a beer drinker. I don't care for it, and the big grocery bills—they were for beer. The sailors, the sailors," he said, looking away. It was this entirely accidental curiosity about the grocery bills that had awakened him, that had opened up a whole Pandora's box of revelations. He told

Claris all about the attempted suicide, speaking freely. The strain was getting to Wigler. He carried himself with a certain presence, with the courtly authority and calm of the seasoned producer, and bore his losses bravely, but the truth was he was actually without resources in the emergency. For him there was no point of no return. He had long ago gone past it. "All my life, I signed my name to papers which, even while I was signing them, nobody in their right mind would ever dream they would actually be able to hold me to account," he had said to Claris in an earlier, equally wry, offhand admission. He had signed notes, had mortgaged his house, had given guarantees that he couldn't possibly fulfill, and everything for him hinged on the actress. That was why he treated her with such fearful delicacy and wouldn't go near the bungalow. That was why he flitted about in the background. The attempted suicide had occurred in a moment of deep dejection, in a disgraceful, deluded fit of self-pity, he said to Claris. He had checked into a motel, swallowed the handful of sleeping tablets. "The whole schmear, stretched out on the bed, waiting for the end, then seized with panic, calling the Fire Department—'Hurry up, send the ambulance, pump me out!'"

They had reached the office. Some people from the studio had driven out and were waiting for Wigler—the unit manager, office personnel, bringing in the daily cost sheets and other reports that had to be signed.

"I don't know," Wigler said, vacant, musing, staring at his assistants. He couldn't carry a tune, he said. He couldn't whistle and it somehow worried him. "That is, I have it in my head, the song, but when I try to get it out, when I want to sing it—I can't." He couldn't seem to daydream anymore, and this, too disturbed him. This business of being unable to daydream had something to do with television, he thought. You could daydream with the radio on, but not with television—watching the tube took up too much of the mind, didn't leave room for daydreaming. He walked away.

Harry Case was inside the office with Fannie. The door was left standing open, and Claris could see them close together, communing, waiting, Fannie busy with her work at the desk while Case sat alongside in the visitor's chair.

"What are you so sore about?" Fannie said to him.

"Ah, that she makes such an obvious mark of herself, always the fall guy."

"Hello. He first wakes up. What else is new?"

Their voices were subdued; they had settled down with each other. They were aware Claris was loitering in the hall outside the door, but they were used to the sight of him, considered him as part of the family, and went on conversing. Case was talking about the bust-up of his big romance with Adele, about the first parting of the ways—in the lull, passing the time, he was letting his thoughts run backwards. As Claris got it, from what Case was saying, there had been a proposal of marriage; Adele at the last minute had reneged, had wept and begged off; and, apparently, from that point on nothing had ever been the same again. Case was going back over the years, to the events that had finished off his marriage and brought on the divorce, and it struck Claris, as he listened on—this man, so battle-hardened, fighting the bloat and the passage of time, dwelling now on the past, while his ex-wife worked away on her bookkeeping at the desk alongside and heard it all without a flicker. Claris had a mental picture of Adele in those days, on the loose, going with gangsters, or people she thought were gangsters, for the thrill, and then getting scared and scurrying for cover as the situation turned serious on her and became too much to handle.

"Boy, she cried—she cried her eyes out," Case said. "She knew right then and there she was making the mistake of a lifetime. 'Don't cry,' I told her. 'I'm going, I'm going.'"

"You hung one on her," Fannie said. "She told you to take a walk, and you came out the hero."

Case wasn't concerned about the producer. He knew Wigler had no choice—Wigler could go only with Adele and he would hang on, scramble, stall, and do everything he could to keep the project afloat. Case was counting on Adele to exhaust herself. He expected her to get fed up, to act on impulse again and pack and go back and get through with it— that was why he was now staying clear of the bungalow, to give her time to reflect. In the end, when you got right down to it, after all the tantrums and temperament, you went where the money told you to go, he said, and she was strapped. Case, who had taken it on himself to know everything about the actress, evidently knew all about the state of her finances, too. It was a long time between pictures for her. She had to work. Case and Fannie both were keeping an eye on the hired chauffeur. The driver would be the tip-off—they apparently had an arrangement with him,

Claris gathered, to let them know as soon as Adele made her move. "What'll she do with herself in the bungalow all day? Who has she got to talk to—the kid, Melanie? She'll get bored," Case said, thinking aloud, and Claris, standing at the door, felt the flush go through him. He saw the place he had in the setup. He saw what Adele wanted him around for, to be on hand and divert her, while she went on with her antics and kept them all in a ferment.

"What does she want?" Case said.

"What she wants—she wants the moon," Fannie said. "She remembers when she was the belle of the ball, the center of all eyes. She was four times box-office champion—you got an idea what that does to a person? It's the breath of life to them. It gives them confidence and moral support. They feel they're anointed and can do no wrong, and when it blows over, naturally it's a shock and they go to pieces and can't stand themselves. You can understand it. She wants everything to be the way it used to be."

"When she went running up to the balcony between shows at the Paramount and necked?" Case said, slanting the shot in. The studios used to send the young stars out to the big movie houses on personal appearances in those days; Claris knew the story—how Adele had gone up to the balcony between her stage appearances, during the matinees, to look at the feature in the dark with a companion, to cuddle. Case was waiting for the actress to get tired of her shenanigans and go back to the studio, but the afternoon lengthened and there was no sign of movement at the bungalow. The driver didn't send word, and so Case's voice grew testy and impatient, and he slanted the digs in. "When she went sporting weekends with the boys to Soboba Hot Springs and Carlsbad?"

"Yes," Fannie said. "Yes." She stood up at the desk and started stowing the ledgers away. "A lot she knows what she's doing. She comes out of nothing, her mother working there in the beauty shop on Highland Avenue, the two of them fighting over the one good dress, eating out of cans, eating hamburgers. They found her in the malt shop, playing hooky —for God's sakes, she was still going to high school." Fannie was talking about the beginning. The casting people had needed a young sexy girl to be assaulted, to get the picture's story off. They had walked Adele in front of the cameras for four or five hundred feet of film—that was all it had been; she hadn't even had a line—and the walk, the four hundred feet of film had been enough. "They put her in a tight skirt and boom, the people started throwing themselves on the floor—overnight she was a star. 'Fannie, I got to have a husband,' she told me, thunder and lightning, when I pleaded with her, when I tried to talk her out of marrying the piano player that time, the one who later went nuts and wound up at Camarillo. And what about the Army flyer, the colonel? Two weeks after the wedding, she had to meet him in Pittsburgh and she went right past him in the lobby of the hotel without recognizing him—she didn't even know who he was."

"They'll marry anyone," Case said.

Claris felt he ought to be getting away from the door—he had been standing at the one spot long enough. The floor of the lobby lay cool in the dimness. Wigler was still talking to his people a short distance up the hall. They made a group. And Claris, as he started to step away from the office door, glancing over in the direction of Wigler's group as he did so, saw, or for an instant thought he saw, Dick Prescott, his associate at the agency. But it wasn't Prescott. It was a production employee who resembled him to an extent. But just then—as so often happens in these cases for no reason we can ascertain—seconds after Claris mistakenly believed he had seen Prescott and after he realized it wasn't Prescott, Prescott himself came bounding into view, swinging along to Wigler and his group, and joining them. Claris was joggled off balance by this coincidence, by this seeming double vision, and he was also ruffled by the jaunty manner of Prescott, bouncing on his feet and hustling along as he did—when he turned and found Harry Case confronting him. Fannie in the meanwhile had left the office to go off on some other duty, and Case, with time on his hands, had come by to chat. Case tested him, pried, tried to draw him out. It was an uneasy, jittery interview, innocently enough meant by Case but peculiarly taxing for Claris. Case saw Claris as a person in another class—college-educated, new-style, with a good twenty years or more on him. Case had probably been told about Claris's wife, a wealthy girl, non-pro, not in the arena—someone invariably brought up the subject of Claris's marriage; it was his great claim to distinction —and this stratum, so far removed from Case's experience and novel to him, intrigued or amused him, so he probed now, with all his practicality and down-to-earth thug's realism, thinking maybe they had the answers, maybe these folks knew a way. He asked Claris questions about his job—did he like it, did it keep him busy? It was different from his

time, Case commented, running liquor and selling it, bootlegging, back
in the old Prohibition days. He purposefully steered the conversation
around to the circle of Claris's friends, sincerely interested in getting
some notion of how it was with them, how they acted and thought. "You
talk to people today that were *born* in nineteen hundred forty and something. They don't even remember Prohibition. Listen, these new chicks
nowadays—these young kids padding barefoot in the unit apartments,
preparing dinner for their hubbies, humming the hit tunes from the big
Broadway shows—are they on the con?" he asked Claris. "Do they work
their hubbies for dough to give to their families? Do they cheat?"

Claris kept wooden. He stood up to Case, demurring, saying enough
to get by, as Case went on with this gritty, idle third-degree, Case sleepy-
eyed and sly, no doubt spreading himself out a little for Claris's benefit,
letting him see a mellower, unsuspected side to his nature, it never once
entering his head that Claris all the while was carrying on a business
with the actress. Case wrote him off as some lightweight laid away in a
sinecure cooked up for him by his in-laws, laid away in a cushy marriage
he wasn't going to do anything to upset. Claris felt a spasm of anger at
Prescott, his colleague. He knew exactly what Prescott was up to—putting
in a five-minute appearance at the hotel-resort so that he would be covered, so that he could truthfully tell the bosses at the agency, Skip Meyerson, Herbie Cottrell, that he had been on the grounds every day. Claris
was surprised that Prescott had driven the hundred miles to show up at
the hotel at all. He knew Prescott had long ago shunted the whole responsibility over to him, telling Meyerson and Cottrell the inside scoop, giving them the full, juicy details, and Claris bitterly wondered how long
it would take for the word to go traveling around until it got to Case.

There was a harsh, abrupt flurry of movement up the lobby. Wigler
had been going over the daily budget sheets with his assistants, checking
the production costs as they accrued each scheduled day. These statements, which the assistants brought out for him to sign and for which he
was personally liable, were the official forms that were to be filed with the
auditors, and the figures, in black and white, had taken a certain toll. It
was—as was soon evident—a remark from Prescott that provided the final
abrasion and set off the outburst. But essentially, at bottom, what provoked Wigler, what was responsible for the breakdown, was the lowness
of spirit, the waiting and seepage, the constant aura of misfortune that

clung to him. Claris looked up at the first harsh shifting sounds. The cluster around Wigler appeared to be opening up, the men retreating as if on a signal. Wigler's voice was heard speaking to Prescott. "Don't go off! What is this going off! What is so much more important elsewhere that you must go off to attend to it?" And then it broke—inchoate, crazed. It was an astonishing exhibition. "All right, so it's a joke—I am over the barrel and can do nothing. But what is the joke, what will the celebration be if the backers go out on me, the banks to follow, and I am faced with catastrophe?" His eyes were shut tight. The stout body, hitherto so rigorously poised, so stately, heaved up and down with a sickening abandon. It all spilled out—the disappointments, the production delays, the broken marriage, and the six-packs of beer. "What am I here, goddammit, a booby, that I should be fobbed off with second-class help and office boys? What am I, a clod to be ridiculed and tortured to death? I want service! I want Skip Meyerson! I want top priority!" He was booming. The panic rode him. He had given way. He was terrified by the specter of the end-money investors, by their cold-blooded aloofness and iron will, by the remorseless ever-building publicity—through it all, the newspaper reporters had been sending in their bulletins; the wire services had come on and were now adding their mite to the sensation. In the grip of his hysteria, Wigler saw the debacle with a great white blinding clarity.

"You will see, I will be forced to suspend, the project will go to hell, and we will all watch the money running straight down the sewer!"

Case went up the hall, moving like a prizefighter. He took hold of the producer, steadied him, kept talking to him. The paroxysm was halted; and while Case was still busying himself with Wigler, while the others looked on and Claris knew he wouldn't be noticed, he backed off and slipped out of the lobby, leaving by the main entrance—he had spotted Prescott, at the height of the confusion, ducking out through a side door, as he would, and Claris wanted to intercept him before he got to the parking lot and disappeared.

Prescott had a girl stashed away. She was waiting in the car—that was the reason he had driven out to the resort, to use the trip as an excuse to get clear of the office and make a day of it. He had put in his time, had shown himself on the scene, and now was on the run, nothing on his mind but the girl and the workout ahead of him, and so it was a jolt, a rupture in the mood, when Claris caught up with him in the parking lot and started talking to him about the problems with the actress. Prescott had a thief's brain, with a thief's readymade collection of guide-lines and maxims. "That's right, why should I jeopardize myself?" he had told Claris the morning before, flat, without a quiver, when he had turned the whole mess over and had gone skipping off. "If the man says he didn't say it, then the man says he didn't say it," Prescott would say, smug and shiny, to the man's face—this when there was some question over the facts in the case, when Prescott already had the advantage over the fel-low. Claris remembered they had once been in a tight spot with a client —they had given their word to the actor on some matter, had then found out they couldn't keep it, and Claris had wondered what they could do. "No contest. I'll tell him we didn't tell him. I'll tell him we lied," Prescott had said, pat, solving the dilemma. Claris knew you had to be grateful to people like Prescott in this world because you never had to feel sorry for them. But it was a different story when you had to go to them and deal with them. Claris pressed hard. The time was going; it was all closing in. Wigler had blown, asking for the head men, and the least Claris and Prescott could do to appease him was to make sure they were both of them there. Claris explained what he was up against, that Hogue was around the bend, that he had no influence on her.

"I know, laddie, sure. Listen. Let me think about it. Let me see what I can do. I'll get back to you."

"You don't understand," Claris said. "I'm not discussing it with you or asking for your opinion. I'm telling you straight out—I want you on the place. Don't you see, with you around, I won't be so exposed." Claris didn't want to be isolated. They all knew he meant nothing at the agency. They would soon start getting suspicious, asking themselves how it hap-pened that he alone was left with the actress, asking themselves what he was doing there. Claris didn't want any of them asking questions about him. "You know my situation," he said to Prescott. "I can't take a rap. I need a hand. With the two of us here together, I can still work out of it and not get hurt."

"Listen," Prescott said, "let's not make a pest out of ourself. I told you I'd think about—"

"I'll slam you!" It went shooting out of him. He was ready to tear into Prescott. "You son of a bitch! You're not fading out and laying it all on me. You're getting paid. This is your job too!"

"You don't own me. I don't have to take it from you," Prescott said, startled, the breath out of him. His voice broke. He reasoned with Claris, wheedling, placating. "What do you want, to have it on a platter? You got no complaint with me. If you want to take her, then go ahead, all right. You got qualifications, the athletic prestige—you can make it. But why should I do the work for you? Where do I come in?" Claris stared at him. The anger ran out of him. He saw what Prescott meant. There were people who cashed in on actresses. Claris could think immediately of three or four names—men who had latched on, marrying them or living with them, who had set themselves up as producers, as figures to be reckoned with. If you controlled a top motion-picture personality, you counted, you could be solidly established—and Claris didn't know if that had been the plan, if he had been on the make all the while, or what it was exactly that had been in his head when he had gone after the actress and taken up with her. He saw the loose skin on Prescott's face, the crude fear sweating out.

"What did you have to make me look bad in front of the broad for?" Prescott said. "You can't have it both ways. If you want to make it, then you have to work for it. They're not giving anything away for nothing."

He hurried over to the car, to his date there, wrenched and harassed, the chesty arrogance shaken out of him for once, the edge of his afternoon's pleasure rubbed off and tarnished.

For all Claris knew, Wigler was already raising a row with the agency toppers, starting in motion there was no telling what inquiries and rumors; Case was waiting nearby to hear from the hired chauffeur, expecting the inactivity and tedium to pall on Adele; and Claris, aware of the risks to himself, that he was crossing Case and playing it fine, nevertheless went ahead with the actress. He had her in Louis's room, using the steward's quarters over the kitchen as a hiding place where they could be by themselves for an hour or two. There was a small delivery area behind the kitchen for the supply trucks, well away from the public side of the hotel, the area circling around the dusty, begrimed pepper tree they usually had in those places. "You could drive to the door," Louis had said in his clipped, reserved undertones when he had willingly put the room at Claris's disposal, if Claris wanted it, such as it was, he had said; when they had set it up between them beforehand, in the way these things were done. Two or three cars were generally parked in the delivery area, and Louis had said there was no reason why Claris's car would be noticed among them. "Leave the key. I'll take it down to the parking lot and then get it back to you later," Louis had quietly assured him, promising his help, that all would go well. So, while the siesta was still on, Claris had driven her in broad daylight to the kitchen area. They had silently filed into the doorway and gone up the flight of wooden stairs together, hoping they wouldn't run into anyone, trusting it all to the luck of the moment—that brazen chance—taking that was part of the character of these outings. The room was makeshift—the bare boards of the floor showing, the sun coming through the worn, yellowed window shades. Claris stood back and had to wonder at the self-possession of the actress. The battered room didn't faze her. She made herself at home, not minding the bare boards, the old iron bed, the torpor in the room. Claris wasn't sure the squalor of the place didn't in some way give her an added gust of gratification. When they had been together on those other sessions, when he had gone up to see her, ostensibly to talk her into coming down to the set and the cameras, they had used her dressing-room suite for the purpose—those bleached, uninhabited, sun-baked furnished apartments the studio had on the lot for the convenience of the stars; outside, on those occasions, while the time went by, the life of the studio rumbled on around them—and Claris now had the same guilty feeling of seclusion, of secret wrongdoing, which he supposed was also part of the package, the lubricity and lure.

The room had an L-shaped extension or alcove at one end. Adele was busying herself in this cubbyhole, combing her hair and undressing. She naturally assumed she was out of view for the moment, and she would have been except for the mirror on the wall. From where Claris was standing, at the bed, he had a straight line of vision to her reflection, and so for a time, while she stirred and stooped, wrapped up in her private rancors and resolves, whatever they were, not thinking she was being observed, he held still and watched her in this odd, surreptitious way. He saw her face, fleeting and stern in the mirror, the face which gave her trouble, which she couldn't relate to herself and found alien or unfamiliar, which she said didn't go with her. He had been in binds before, of his own doing, binds that it seemed he had almost deliberately sought out; but he had never had this foreboding, this sense of guilt. He wasn't close to the borderline or over it. They didn't know what they had, what it was in them that accounted for their great good fortune. They didn't know how to present it, manipulate it, embellish it, portion it out—since they didn't know what it was or whether in fact they had anything at all. "Star quality," the executives in the front offices called it, using this term as a definition, a term which of course didn't explain anything. So-and-so had it; if the picture went badly at the box office, then he didn't have it, had had it, had lost it—it was gone. "Who? How can you say that? Is that so? You don't say!" the man Claris was thinking of would say, registering an engaging humility, an entreating helplessness, in response to almost any chance remark. He was hamming it, putting on an act. That was his act. They adopted guises, sometimes using a set of them interchangeably, understanding it was a guise, that they were hamming it and putting up a front—but not knowing any other way of getting by, not knowing what was expected of them or what they were supposed to have. Sometimes the front collapsed on them. They would dispense with impersonations and mimicry, would come out in their true selves, what there was to their true selves, and then there would be shattering scenes of violence. Claris had heard stories of the most outlandish excesses, savage bouts of self-destructiveness, breakdowns, scandals. The mind became jumbled, turned in on itself, balked; became vacuous, spent. Adele herself was hung up on some theory that she had evolved on her own. She believed her special effectiveness with the audience was spontaneous, something organic, beyond control. She believed it was the product of the nervous system you were endowed with, and she was convinced her nerves were used up, that you were given just so much. That was why she fretted over the vertical ridges on her fingernails and took to heart the smatterings she read in the medical columns in the morning newspaper—she thought her nerve fibers lay wasted and shriveled and squiggly in their grooves there in the tissue, and were failing her.

"It's a funny thing, no matter how far gone you are, you always know what you're doing," she had commented to Claris in the bungalow, just before they had left for the steward's room. She was thinking of past performances, of previous alarms and crises in which she had figured. "There's always something inside of you, watching you—you know perfectly well you're being impossible and making outrageous demands. But you don't stop. You just go right ahead. You do it." She had delivered the words with a perverse, almost vindictive relish—she clearly realized the size of the difficulties she was causing and that she was behaving badly and would most likely regret it, and yet she was ruthlessly determined to carry through. Claris hadn't tried to argue with her or sway her in the bungalow. He was conscious of the unsavory, impersonal nature of their relationship—that it was all accident, that he was an expedient, that they had fallen in together only because he was the agent and happened to be there and because she was marooned and had no one else. She had pushed behind her the hallucinations, the scalp-burning, the neuroses and palpitations. She no longer let herself be ridden with mortifications. "The biddies with their high couture and dead behinds," she had said contemptuously, referring to the stylish women guests at the hotel, to the expensive, well-fitting girdles they wore. She didn't care what the stylish ladies thought, those second and third wives who had it made and whose hazy, indolent calm she noted so bitterly and wished she could emulate. "They probably go around saying how I ought to be willing to do anything to find a niche for myself and that my whole life is coming apart." Claris had told her something of what was taking place down at Fannie's office in the lobby, and his report filled her with a senseless, disproportionate spread of elation. She gloated. She forgot about the women guests. She saw that she had the upper hand, that they all had to come to her and dance to her tune, that without her there was no picture, and it sent a rush of hope and exultation through her, although Claris couldn't imagine what she was hoping for or thought she could win with her crazy show of defiance. "They're frightened to death of the hullabaloo," she had chortled, meaning the businessmen, the cautious end-money investors, "but at the same time they're dying to get the good of the publicity. They want the hullabaloo. They know it's money in the bank and they can't let go." Melanie had been in the bungalow with them all the while, steeped in her book at her post in the corner, poker-faced and unperturbed and vigilant. There had been the last-minute awkwardness of getting around the child. But the time was passing; the siesta would be ending, the hotel would be coming alive again, and if they were leaving, they had to be leaving soon. So they had gone drifting out in the sunlight; they had driven the three or four hundred yards across the deserted grounds to the rear of the main building, had left the car at the tree for Louis to pick up, and slipped furtively into the hall.

She moved freely in front of him. She had finished undressing and combing her hair, and was going to a closet, looking for a hanger for her dress. She made no fuss over her nakedness before him, either because she considered him of no account or because she was too careworn or because it was her way. In the film, filling the screen, she and most other actresses seemed large-sized and compelling, so that it invariably was a letdown and a surprise when you saw them close up in person; but the hot light from the blinds now, acting on her coloring, on the vivid red hair, gave her a flamboyance and she was larger than life and compelling again. Claris kept at a distance, continuing his surveillance. He struggled with his apprehensions, with his doubts and guilt and the basic pusillanimity in him, and so, as he studied her and dealt with his misgivings, there was a constraint, a resistance between them, nothing going on in the heavy torpor of the room and yet a tension existing, a shimmying encounter, a contest.

"You don't talk very much. You must be one of the silent ones," she said. "Some people talk, some people don't. Why is that?"

"I guess the people who don't talk just don't have anything to say," Claris said.

She held her shoulders straight, carrying her body with that clear-striding, forthright sexual quality they had and which they knew they had. It was the way they were put together; it was the bones in them. It was a readiness or acquiescence to use the body for all the pleasure it could give, a readiness they picked up from their mothers, in the Hollywood malt shops, out of the air. She had had a special upbringing. "I didn't come in on a wagonload of apples, you know," she had said to Claris in one of her bristling, unexpected declarations. Growing up in the Hollywood of her day, she had been exposed to the contagion from the studios. From all Claris had heard, it had been another time, everything closer to the studios in those days, the Los Angeles area still spread thin and relatively undeveloped, a third of what it was to become. The driving ambition among the youngsters, those who were pretty and spirited, was to wangle themselves into the studios somehow, to make the grade. They made the rounds while they were still at school, trying the different side entrances to the business—the small agents, small clubs, advertising conventions—and the sexual instinct was in play from the beginning, a commodity, something accepted as a matter of course. Claris thought of the fervor in the high-school sweetshops, the beginning experimentings and first sallies; and thinking of those early times, he thought of the havoc in her now. When he had stayed on with her last evening in the bungalow after the fracas, when he had tried to console her and she had shut him off, he had seen the despair in her, the stubborn refusal to subside and come to terms with her misery. "Do I appall you? Is it too much?" she had said to him. "People get impatient with you for your woes and grief, but they insist on the right to their own sorrows—their personal hard luck is different and holy."

"For these shenanigans, to carry on a full-scale war with Case, for this you've got the strength," he had said to her. "For the work, no."

"If he thinks he's going to hold it over my head like a club, if he thinks he's going to lord it over me, he's got another think coming." She had meant the disgrace of her homecoming from England, the fiasco of the English marriage and all the other fiascos and debacles that Case had on her. His very appearance set her off. Claris remembered the jolt that had gone through her, how she had quivered the instant Case had stepped through the door and how she hadn't stopped trembling the whole time he had been in the bungalow with her. She couldn't bear the stance on him; it galled her to be reminded that she had been once led to rely on his bullyboy power for protection. She couldn't bear his harsh, swift gutter shots. He went straight to the point, with his thug's crudeness, making it impossible for her to twist away and hide, making her feel like nothing, she had said. Claris was puzzled by the persistence with which she kept herself bound to Case, hating him as she did, trembling with revulsion in his presence and yet needing him and wanting him at hand. She needed and had to have him because he was hers. He had been with her over the years, had witnessed the succession of her follies and failures, was part of the shambles, all she had left, and he belonged to her and she wouldn't let him go. Case hadn't told it all when Claris had overheard him talking to Fannie about the early days, about the marriage proposal. Case had thrown it off—"She cried. 'Don't cry. I'm going.' She knew right then and there she was making a mistake of a lifetime"—but what he had omitted was the rapture, the subservience. "I think of you the first thing in the morning, the last thing at night when I fall asleep," Adele had quoted Case last evening when she was busy running him down and mocking him; and as Claris now followed her with his eyes, contending with her and with himself in this silent one-sided mental jujitsu he was going through, the thought wavered in his mind—the gift-giving, the head-over-heels courting and being in love, now all of it turned into detestation and venom.

She got on the bed, shifting her weight to one knee and then lying back, bringing up the other leg. The walls were thin, partitions—they could hear one or the other of the kitchen help walking about below; a voice rose up to them. The door was locked. Louis was sure to do what he could to steer the traffic away from the room, but in any case Claris didn't think the kitchen help presented much of a problem. They were a different breed, stolid, foreign born, unimpressionable, and even if they had noticed Claris's car in the delivery area, even if they discovered the room was being put to use and that it was Hogue, they would probably just pass it off. "Don't worry about the kitchen help," he said to Adele. "It doesn't mean anything to them. It wouldn't matter to them one way or the other." He finished placing his clothes on the chair. He sat on the bed and turned to her. She opened her arms to him, embraced and clasped him to her, taking him on, somebody on the road, whatever turned up, until the next full-blown, official romance came along. In the stickiness and travail, in the continuing tangle with Case, they took time out for themselves, letting go, as if this was a solution and a help. Claris responded to the pressure, winding through the ritual, the kisses, the fondling, the contriving of an illusion of love—that knavish, coward's thing people relentlessly do with one another. In the times with his wife, there were also kisses and endearments, as mystifying as these. There was the same mindless slippage, and then, later, the dead-and-gone sick hollowness, those cold moments of the night when you are alone and lost and the brute fear rears up before you and envelops you, when you perspire and don't know what you will ever do.

They were on the freeway, miles out of the hotel-resort, speeding along through the open desert countryside, when they were caught in one of those periodic freeway traffic jams and knew they would be held up for at least a half hour. Instead of working back to the bungalow when they left the steward's room, because she didn't want to go back to the bungalow, because the motor was running, he had taken her for a drive. She had sat perched beside him all through the ride, not speaking, con-

didn't know the newcomer in the car with her was Claris, her agent; as for the reporters, they were having a hard time of it keeping the weeks-old story on Hogue going. They were looking around for leads and developments, and so, when the tip came in, they leaped at the chance and were now avidly at work, beating up the new romance, the mysterious and unidentified stranger, for all the yardage and excitement they could get out of it. Claris had often watched the way the rumors seeped through the trade—people understood the gossip was hit and miss, concocted to fill up the columns, for the sake of the general commotion; and yet, by some peculiar aberration, perhaps because the business itself was flighty and laden with imponderables, these same individuals seized on the rumors, brooded on them, believed them and acted on them. That was why publicity agents assiduously invented and planted the items. "The fact that you see it in the papers doesn't necessarily mean it's untrue," the men in the industry reasoned. And so this new excitement —improvised on the spot, without responsibility or scruple, and yet, of course, not wide of the mark, coming at a time when Wigler was stretched out to the limit—was enough to bring on the final blow and send the whole project careening. The end-money investors stampeded. If Hogue was busy with a new romance, if she was off on another fling, then that explained the production delays, that meant she might very well take off for London or Paris and go out of sight again, and they wanted no part of the venture. Claris wasn't particularly worried as they rolled over the hotel grounds on their return from the drive—if they were seen together now, it would only appear that he had driven her somewhere on business, on an errand, as agents did with their clients—but when they reached the cottage, Case and Fannie were waiting inside as a reception committee, and the upheaval was on. Adele had darted on ahead into the bungalow, and when Claris came around the car and followed after her, not thinking anything was amiss, he walked straight into the thick of the scuffle, Case and Adele already at it. Melanie was there. The twins were underfoot. Fannie had fed them and was trying now, with Melanie's help, to herd them off to bed and out of the way, and Claris weaved through the disorder, taking up his place at the wall and listening. Wigler had left for the city earlier in the day. He had been called to a bankers' meeting and had been fiddling with the loan executives, pleading, placating, getting out from under, giving his heart-felt assurances, those guarantees which he could never hope to fulfill, when the blow had fallen on him. He was lunging after the end-money people at this moment, and everything now depended on what Case could do with Adele.

Claris held back, again on the sidelines, again trying not to draw attention to himself, the fright pulsing through him—the old, dismal quickening of all the other near misses, escapes, reprieves—and as he watched and waited, he wondered if he would scrape through this time again, if there would be another reprieve. He wouldn't have known how to face Case and was grateful that he didn't have to. He stared at Adele. He had been with her a while ago in the steward's room. The remembrance of what had gone on there between them was still with him, in the front of his mind. He thought the signs must be written all over his face, but she didn't show a trace of awareness, and he wondered how they did it. For them, the sexual act, once done, was over, forgotten. You saw this bland, cool acceptance in young girls as they sat in restaurants, looking at menus—a certain instinctive reliance, a kind of birthright, which they acknowledged and made use of and on which they seemed to set no great store. She was in the same yellow sleeveless dress, the same stockings, which Claris had seen her take off and put on again. She repulsed Case with a total intensity, her face shiny and perspired, not caring how she looked, not troubled now by that heightened susceptibility to perspiration which distressed and burdened women of her florid coloring. Case rasped at her. He wanted to get off word to Wigler as soon as possible. He wanted her to start back for the studio immediately, to stop the rumors and save Wigler before it was altogether too late, if it wasn't altogether too late already. "There is no time! There is no time!" He was baffled by the obstinacy in her. He was exasperated from the long wait at the hotel—"I laid around all day like a fool, watching the chauffeur, while you go off on a drive!" The expedition over the desert brought back memories of the other jaunts and forays, and he pitched into her recklessly, upbraiding her now for her shiftlessness, for those old, wanton, impulsive one-time engagements. She hit back promptly, reminding him how he used to spy on her. She drew savage pictures of him at the phone, calling up people, asking anxiously who was with her, who had gone into her trailer dressing rooms on the set, if she had left the set and with whom and for how long. She turned and walked away from him.

"If it's not one thing it's the other, always a crisis," Fannie said, coming out of the bedroom, some of the children's clothing in her hands. She was in a wretched mood. She had been in and out all along, had been undressing the twins and had more work to do with them, but she had heard enough to know that things were going badly, that Adele wasn't packing and leaving for the studio. "If you held a pistol to her head, if you turned yourself inside out," Fannie said. Adele had the bathroom door open, and while the actress stood there at the medicine-chest mirror, washing the dust of the drive off her face and running a comb through her hair, Fannie and her ex-husband jawed away at each other, talking at cross purposes, not seeing each other.

"Later on she'll complain and have it against us that we didn't insist and let her do what she wanted to do," Case said.

"So what? What's the tragedy?" Fannie shouted. "Let her do nothing and look at television all day like everybody else." Fannie knew how critical the moment was, was sick about the ruin Adele was bringing down on herself, and it hurt her as much as it did Case, but she saw no way out of the impasse. "He's got a yen for her," she said. "If you want to make it with them, you have to call them up in the middle of the night. You have to give them trouble left and right and then they're happy."

"Were you the guy?" Case asked, switching to Claris. He meant was Claris the man who had been seen in the car with her, the reason for the present speculations and flare-up. Case quickly put it together and saw for himself how the misunderstanding had happened; he realized Adele didn't have another man somewhere, that there hadn't been time for a new romance. "Why did you do that?" he asked Claris, blunt and harassed. "Why did you encourage her? Didn't you have better sense than that? You're supposed to help around here, not make it worse."

He swerved off. Adele had come out of the bathroom, and he went crashing back to her, set on convincing her and making her do his bidding by the force of his will, because he was telling her. He was tied to her. She was warm to him, supple, necessary. Claris had watched the old-timers in the projection rooms at the studios, men grizzled and heavy-eyed, quietly appraising some new girl on film in a screen test. "She's soft, not like these tough babes you see around, everything on the line," a man would say, searching out that indefinable, essentially feminine appeal that worked in the movie houses, that drew these men in their personal lives, too. Adele had this softness for Case, knew she had it, recognized his need for her, counted on it, and took advantage of it to spite and bedevil him in every way she could think of. He was arguing with her now that she had to work whether she was up to it or not up to it, that she had no choice, that this was no time for temperamental fireworks—she couldn't afford to be temperamental. It developed that she had had hard commitments on her when she had flown off and made her international marriage. Claris had heard about the commitments at the office, but he hadn't known too much about them, and no one had ever told him of the big sums that had been advanced on the promise of these pictures in the future—money which she was liable for and had to make good on and which apparently had been squandered in the year and a half she had lived abroad. Case bore away at her. Yes, he had spied on her. He knew all about the winter skiing trips, the high-toned places, Monaco, the yachts, the being in the right places at the right time with the right collection of snobs—as if it mattered, as if anybody cared. "What do you think, they were standing three deep on the sidewalk, waiting to hear all about you?" He knew the hopes she had put on the splurge, on the plush life and the traveling around; he knew how much it had meant to her to have them all back home impressed with her and envious. "If you stopped the first ten people that came walking down the street and asked them, would they know what you were talking about?" He talked about the life-and-death struggle that went on at the mooring basin in Monte Carlo, how they killed themselves there to get the favored mooring posts, to get their yachts anchored up close to the yachts of the reigning muck-a-mucks, so that they could all be one big, important mob.

"How he's got it all down pat," Adele said. "How he knows every little detail. He can't get over it."

"Come on, don't be like that," he said, trying to shake her up, to hurry her over the hard feelings of the past. "Have a little understanding. It's not as much as you think it is. You don't have to hold every last little thing against me." He explained that Wigler was on the ropes, that she was in no position to take a bust-up, that the conditions in the industry weren't what she thought they were, that there were the children. He went charging at her, out of exasperation and anxiety falling more and more into that overbearing, pugnacious manner of his, that gross bully-boy show of muscle, which she couldn't stand and which only reinforced her determination to resist him. Claris could see her nerving herself up against him, how she fired herself to sustain her fury. It was probably one of those spasms when, carried away as she was, she nevertheless knew what she was doing and could stop herself at any point, but deliberately chose not to and forged on ahead. She had been through the mill, had been brought along, and knew now what she once didn't know; she understood the publicity had gone awry, that the picture was being shot out from under her, that she would be isolated, blacklisted by the trade. And yet the old injuries, the remembered ugly scenes and humiliations still stood between them, keeping her alive and blinding her to every practical consideration. Claris could see why she had had to have the procession of husbands—so that she could assert herself over Case and keep him off, so that he wouldn't be able to tear her down.

"Don't look at me like that. Don't give me those faces," Case said to her. "You know the things you got against me are the things you did. It's not me. It's you." He started again, trying to reason with her. "You don't have to be afraid. No one's against you." And then it swept over him. He broke loose. "You got a mania in you, a poison—whatever's no good for you you got to have. You're so racked up and worked over you don't know the day of the week. The only time you know what's happening to you is when you're facing the cameras, and that's the one thing you have to run away from. You don't know how to handle yourself or live, and nobody can straighten you out, nobody can tell you what to do." It was all up with Wigler. The picture was doomed. Case could see he had been laboring for nothing. She wasn't driving back to Culver City. She wasn't going to do a sudden about-face and fall in line with him and his wishes at this late stage. But what stuck in his throat, what had been gnawing in him all along and had started him off, was the bringing back of those desert weekend afternoons, the times on the phone and the hurt, and all that had gone on since.

"Do you call it a life, does it make sense—marrying them and then throwing them out, every year a turnover? You come dragging back, more dead than alive, forced to face the music, and you have to start patching yourself up all over again." He cast up at her the squalls, the wretched, drawn-out contests, each one like a campaign, which she had taken on in her time, wallowed in, and had never seemed able to avoid; he touched on one hideous, thoroughly publicized botch of a marriage, to a man far too old for her, a man who had passed on while she was still married to him. "How many times? Go over the list—the divorces, the battles, fighting them tooth and nail, fighting them to a finish and then having them die on you, this too to worry about, this too to have on your head and carry around with you. Wasn't it always the same, all your life— running out whenever the brainstorm hit you, always wanting, always scared to death you weren't getting your full share? You went shooting off on one foot, chasing the rainbows, dumping everything no matter who got hurt in the process." He rammed home the devastating indict- ments, recalling people dead and buried, people jettisoned on the way; he recalled that mass of ignominies, the blunders, the biting acts of stu- pidity, the chances failed and ruined—that dreary clutter that assails the mind as we lie abed in the dark, never to be redeemed or assuaged, so that we sleep every other night. "You don't care what you do to yourself, how you use yourself up. You don't stop to think what you can stand. And it all goes on in a goldfish bowl—the courts in Santa Monica, the reporters standing around, everything in the open." He reached back to the beginnings, to the rattrap backstage dressing-room areas, to the cheap club dates, when, in her eagerness to break in, she had mixed with the low life of the business, the hangers-on, the felons, the spoilers.

He stopped short. He wrenched out of his tirade. "Who needs it? She's old. Who wants her? She was a hula girl when radio was big." He sud- denly saw himself, raging and excited over something that was past and meant nothing to him. It was out of him. He was through with her. If she wanted to wreck herself, then let her—what was it to him? "It was my fault. It was her fault. Who knows who started what, how it began. I didn't do enough for her. I was a mug. I didn't talk right." He pulled away and started for the door.

"Hello and goodbye!" Fannie said. She was out of the children's bedroom. She had been standing there for some time, listening to the outburst, too embittered to interfere. She knew it would do no good to interfere, that the picture was gone and the damage done, and it also went roiling in her to see the passion in Case, how he took on. "No fool like an old fool, still going for girls," she said, grinding out the words. "He pecks his jaw out and holds his head high in the air to kill the double chin. His fingers are all stuck together from the arthritis and he can't open his hand but he's still got young ideas." Case's left hand was crippled, the fingers remarkably shriveled and wedged in at the palm, a deformity Claris hadn't been aware of until Fannie now referred to it.

"What's going to happen to her?" Case blurted at her, cutting in, and for a while they hacked back and forth at the door, Case wrangling with his ex-wife, talking about the fix Adele was in, the debts, the children. She was broke, he said. The parade was passing her by. If she managed to live down the mess, if it ever did blow over, how many more cracks out of the box did she have in her, how many more pictures was she good for? Four, five? "She's all dried out from the dieting. Who's going to want to see her? There's a whole flock of them coming up, new ones with names nobody ever heard of."

"It was a different story when she first came down the pike, snapping her garters," Fannie said, giving up, seeing the end of it. She knew everything Case said was true, that the outlook was black, and there was nothing to be gained by standing at the door and arguing. "The god-dammed coronaries, the heart attacks and cancer—they're dropping like flies, everywhere you look, and he's still in contention. The showplace house there with the private driveway," she said, going back to the early days, when they had come to California, when he had been enthralled with the movie elite and had gone running after them. "When they came to the house, he couldn't do enough to entertain them. Whatever they wanted—chicken, chicken; steak, steak—he ran a restaurant!" Case was gone. He had slammed out, leaving to place his call to Wigler, to do whatever could be done in the debacle. Fannie was gathering up some laundry—she still had the children's clothes in her hands when she had come out of the bedroom—and Claris waited while she roamed around the room, picking up a pair of socks, a white piqué hat, whatever needed washing, and prepared to follow out after her former husband.

If he could have helped her or comforted her, he would have spoken up, but anything he could think to say would be fatuously out of keeping and would only aggravate the misery in her, so he kept silent. Back at the agency, when they had a hard case on their hands, some actress who was giving trouble, he had watched the men ducking for cover, shuffling the actress from one to the other—"You take her. I had her all day yesterday. You sit with her. You take her to dinner." But here, the way it had worked out, the way he had unwittingly fallen into this morass, the responsibility was all his. He was bound. He couldn't fob her off even if there was anyone to fob her off on, and he could see no way of extricating himself. There wasn't a sound from the back of the cottage. The twins, played out and exhausted after the day's helling around, were sleeping regally on the big, oversized double bed—they had the master bedroom, while Adele and Melanie shared the twin beds in the other room. Melanie didn't come out, sparing them this once, probably too frightened and desolate in there to be able to maintain that poise of hers, that persevering, resolute deadpan calm. "You make it a practice never to look back," Adele said. "You can't go around thinking of all the horrible damn things you did all your life or that you got yourself into, so the result is in the end you lose touch with reality. You become a zombie. You don't know if the thing you're hitting yourself over the head with actually ever happened to you or if you imagined it or dreamed it or if it happened to somebody else and you just heard about it or read it in the paper." She was on a tear; it would be one of those grainy vigils that had become the pattern of his visits with her—at the sun-baked studio dressing-room apartment, at the hotel in Beverly Hills, now here in the bungalow at the resort—when he stood by, saying nothing, not supposed to speak, while she came on with her hard, self-despoiling knock, delivering those flaunting, wild statements and admissions as though he wasn't in the room or didn't count. She was rapping up, for a change, on the fashionable women-guests, the second and third wives with their bored, intelligent eyes. "You can bet they never have to second-guess themselves or have regrets. They play it close, keep it all to themselves, never tell you a dream. The first thing they do, the minute they get out of bed in the morning, is to step on the scales and weigh themselves, like a religious rite." When she was thirteen and fourteen, she had once told Claris, she used to read the women's magazines as they appeared each month. In order to make more of herself and get beyond the local neighborhood improvisations—the homemade tricks, the butterfly kisses, that is, the young girls flicking their eyelashes against the cheeks of their companions—in order to go beyond these attainments and get the jump on the other girls in her group, she would faithfully study the pages of the large-circulation magazines to learn what was done, what was not done, what was worn, to pick up clues, to absorb the explicit sexual information these publications offered. And thinking of her at those glossy pages, he could understand why she compulsively chipped away at the

"Why do you want to make yourself unhappier than you have to be?" Claris said to her. He tried to restrain her, to break the rhythm of her hysteria. "It's not as bad as you think it is. Take my word for it. You'll sleep on it. You'll wake up in the morning and you'll wonder what it was all about, why you let yourself get so upset."

She shook him off. "What do you know about it? What are you pushing yourself into this for? What are you trying to tell me, that you really care, that you're crazy in love with me? Why should people love me— because of my lousy self-centered misery and perpetual troubles? I've been there before, people latching on, with all the good words, fattening off me, getting themselves contracts."

She drove at him. She let him know exactly how desperate her situation was. She told him everything now. The dazzling high life, the fascinating social swirl hadn't been as it appeared. She told him about her husband and the speedy, good-looking crowd he had run with. She told Claris of their sport, their games and antics, the way they had systematically wheedled the money out of her, using one excuse or the other. Claris floundered. Harry Case had talked about the commitments and the money she had squandered, but now Claris began to see why the man had been so angered and bitten with vexation. The racing stables, the plush traveling around, the trips to Monte Carlo, the splurge and show on which she had set such high hopes and which were to make everyone impressed with her and envious—it had all been her money. Her fine aristocrat of a husband had had no money. He was completely dependent on his father for support, and his father, the famous English sporting duke, with his estates and great renown, was the tightwad of the country. Everyone knew it. He wouldn't give up a penny. She had footed the bills, had underwritten the parties. The eighteen months' sojourn, from start to finish, had cost her four hundred thousand dollars.

Claris was staggered by the vastness of the sum, by the hopeless, useless waste. "How could you let them do that? Didn't you know what was going on?"

"Because I didn't know better! Because I was a fool! What was I going to do—come back here where I had all this waiting for me? I had to stick it out," she explained to him, imploring. "I had to make a go of it. I sat there—half the time I didn't know what they were talking about. I was afraid to open my mouth. I'm crazy, don't you understand—looking-in-the-looking-glass crazy. Go ahead—you have all the advice to give. Tell me what to do. Tell me everything is hunky-dory."

She pushed past him and went out of the room. The first hard jolt of dismay had subsided, and a kind of panic now took its place. The lights were all on, as they always were in that place, and he stood in the glare, his mind working and grasping, trying to scrounge out an escape for himself, going over the field, knowing he would do what he wanted to do, what it was in him to do. For a moment, he marveled at the tenacity in her these last weeks, fighting and standing them off, all the time knowing the ground was cut out from under her and that she hadn't a chance. She was blown. She couldn't work. It was all shutting down on her and there was no telling what she might do. They killed themselves, putting matches to their nightgowns, taking the tablets and huddling in some dingy, Godforsaken closet, going there to hide and die as for some reason they did—and all he knew was that he didn't want to be on the scene any longer, that he had to get away. He had gone as far as he had been able to go; he had done the best that it had been in his nature to do.

He loitered in the stiff, gray living room of his home. The sun hadn't burned through the morning mist, the morning damp—the maritime breezes, they called it here. The help—the cook, the baby's nurse—were up and about; Claris could hear them somewhere in the house. He was dressed, shaved and showered, all rigged out for the day's work at the office, except that he had no proper day's work and he didn't know what lay ahead. It was hours too early to start for the office. He had had no clear notion of what he was doing or going to do when he had bolted the resort and driven the hundred miles back to town the night before. He had decided that he would have to play it as it came, riding his luck, seeing how it broke. He was on the run. When the office opened this morning, they would be dealing with the overnight developments; there would be meetings, Meyerson and Cottrell would be having Prescott on the carpet; and Claris wanted to be in the room there when Prescott started double-talking his way out of the jam and reported to the bosses. With the papers making a business out of the brand-new romance, with the columnists' legmen shooting around to hunt up the identity of the mysterious newcomer—that is, in short, looking for him—he was much better off here on the spot in town, looking out for his interests, than he would have been at the resort.

To fill in the time, to get a breathing spell and steady himself, because there was the three hours' difference in time and it wouldn't be too early for her, he called his wife in New York. He got her at her grandparents' house. They talked, Claris speaking in that flat, idle tone that it always astonished him he was able to assume with her at will. "What are you doing there, Barbara?" he chided her as they went along. She had been gone a little longer than it seemed to him they had either of them antici- pated, and, in the natural way, because it was more or less indicated, he felt obliged to put up a protest, reproaching her for the delay in return- ing. There was a pause. She was slow in replying. The exchange became uneven, and in another instant, without warning, the respite, the breath- ing spell, came to an end. "Don't you think you ought to be thinking about getting back? Don't you think the baby needs you?" he asked her.

"I want to think things out," she said, faraway, in her child's voice.

His first instinct was to shy off. "What do you mean, you want to think things out? What's there to think out about?" he said, hustling it, acting as though he hadn't quite heard her, as though he couldn't pos- sibly understand what she meant. He changed the subject, talked about the house, the baby, and brought the conversation to a finish. He hung up. He sat on the couch, wondering what she could have heard or knew, or, as was more likely the case, what some member of that tight-packed, protective family of hers had heard. So far as he could tell, everything had been at peace with him and his wife when she had left on the trip and when he had talked to her the times on the phone, so whatever hap- pened surely had to do with Adele and it had to have happened recently, in the last day or two. He went over the people at the studio, the people at the resort, the steward Louis—he couldn't see how any of them could have given him away. For a moment he wondered if anything could have broken through last night, if that was it—if in some way the reporters had got to Prescott and Prescott had already spilled.

The baby's nurse came passing through—the nurse who had worked in a number of houses in the area and was battle-wise, who had a pretty good idea of how it was with Claris in that household; whenever she spoke to Claris about his wife, she had always referred to her as Missus Claris, hitting the missus. She had a jumpy, resentful nature, was constitutionally dissatisfied, and Claris normally avoided her as much as he could, but in his quandary he turned to her—after all, she had been on the phone with his wife throughout the visit back east. He told her frankly about the phone call. He asked her what she knew, if his wife had said anything to her.

"Why didn't you ask her? If the remark puzzled you, you should have asked her what she meant and had it out," the nurse said, fussing, all at once unstrung and combative.

"Do you know anything?" Claris said.

"No, you should have asked her. I don't see why I should be in the middle. Go to the spare room," the nurse said, suddenly getting the words out. "Try the spare room. Maybe you'll be enlightened." Claris looked at her, dumbfounded, not understanding what the spare room had to do with it. "The mattress, the mattress, under the mattress," the nurse said, and left.

He found the packet of letters. He knew he was being mocked, but he didn't know what to make of this mockery. A moment ago he had been on the run, twisting and calculating, worrying about Prescott and the gossip columnists, and suddenly he was in the clear. The shoe was on the other foot. His wife didn't have the goods on him; he had the goods on her. He undid the packet, untying the candy-box ribbon with which she had carefully kept the letters bound and secure in their hiding place under the mattress. The letters went back over a period of months. She had had them addressed to a friend of hers—that was how she had managed the correspondence. Claris knew the man, the maître d', one of the partners, of a mid-Manhattan restaurant—Claris and his wife had always gone to the place when they were in New York, and had been made welcome. Claris had consistently deceived his wife, phoning in he'd be late, that he was called away, dodging and going through the stratagems, and it now appeared his wife had been busy with undertakings of her own. In the first flush of the discovery, while he was trying to absorb the impact and was still off balance, a mean, eager spurt of relief actually went through him—that he had gotten off and not been caught. And then the full sickening force of the mockery overtook him. He saw what a disaster he had made of himself. Amazingly, at that moment, his wife became dear to him. He longed for her. A homesickness seized him, now that he had come to an ending, that the time with his wife was over and completed. He saw his wife on her back. He wanted to hit out and take revenge. It infuriated him to think of the maître d' having his hands on her, having his chance now at the fortune that went with her—the supermarkets, the real-estate holdings. Claris told himself that it wasn't right, not after what he had gone through, not after what he had done to himself. He thought of his in-laws, those stout-built men, so smug and indulgent and circumspect. He could hear them making up the package when his wife first brought home the news that she wanted to marry him. "You want it, baby? All right, you got it," they must have said. And then they had proceeded with the apparatus, tying up the money, keeping everything separate and at arms' length, figuring that she would tire of him in a few years and that nothing would be lost. They hadn't even considered him for the family business, disposing of him, instead, in a five-minute telephone call to someone they knew at the agency.

He spent the next half hour or so packing two large suitcases, cleaning out his suits, his shirts, his shoes, and the rest of it. He wanted the shelves and closets to be bare, to look bare and stripped and strewn. The cook and nurse probably knew, or at any rate would soon know, what he was doing. He didn't care how it appeared to them or what they would say to his wife when she called. He put the packet of letters into his pocket. He wasn't letting them go. He carried the two bulky suitcases out to the car in the garage, and then drove from the house, in the western part of Los Angeles, through the curves of Sunset Boulevard as it wound around the base of the Hollywood Hills, deep into the Hollywood area until he reached the Athletic Club. He checked into the club-hotel and had himself an address, a place of his own. The club building was drenched in the California sun, that persistent downpour of heat that soaked through the brick of the building, into the room, into the drapes and upholstery. Claris didn't take time to open a window. In the still dead air, he fixed on the name of a lawyer, got the number out of the book, and stood at the phone, insisting on an immediate, early morning appointment. It was important for him not to stop; it was as though he knew that whatever was to be done had to be done without a halt. He could remember, or thought he could easily remember once he tried, other instances where families, similarly placed in a predicament of this sort, quickly came to a settlement, without going through the scandal of a courtroom trial, and he didn't want any indecisiveness or temporizing to weaken his resolve.

He drove to the lawyer's and was led into the private office. There were abominations not to be acknowledged by the mind, but the astounding thing was that you went right ahead and did them. He wasn't a monster. He loved his child. He stood in the office, well groomed, presentable, with his clean, athletic lines, nominally there to ask for advice, to explain the circumstances he found himself in and to see what legal redress he had. But he knew and the lawyer knew that what he was after was to use the child—the custody of the child, the threat of a courtroom fight—to wheedle or blackmail a lump cash settlement out of the family. The lawyer never changed expression. He heard Claris out, unsurprised, unflustered. Claris had often observed these people, so fond and benign in the bosom of their families—good husbands, good fathers and uncles, respectable, mild—and yet, in the business way, when the pinch was on, capable of criminalities and devices of which Claris and his kind knew nothing. In his idiocy, Claris had gone to a lawyer who was one of theirs—where else could Claris have gone, what other lawyers did he know about? Later on, when at odd moments the events of that feverish morning flickered back to him, he would wonder what he had thought he was doing. He would be honestly at a loss to understand the mania that had possessed him. In the heat and impetus of his bungling wrath, there might have been a logic to his behavior, but he hadn't a hope of getting by with his feckless, far-out scheme, and even in his derangement he must have known it. He knew how ruthless his in-laws could be. He knew they handled these holdups and worse every month, that they didn't take alarm, were geared for them, had the required resources and connections. He wasn't in the same league with these people and should never have begun. The lawyer—Claris didn't know how or when it had come about—had shifted from his desk during the interview and was standing now at the door, holding it open.

"All right, all right, go along," the lawyer said, not wanting to enter into a discussion or extend himself, anxious to get Claris moving. "They'll cover you with it until you won't see daylight. They'll take everything away from you and leave you flat as a pancake," he told Claris, and got him out the door.

He went straight to his office from the lawyer's—possibly because he had been heading for the agency before he had been interrupted, because he was panicked and didn't know where else to go. Most of the staff were out in the field, at the different studios, at this time of day. The floor was empty, the halls dim and cool, and he walked past the reception girl at the switchboard and was able to get to his room without being stopped. He sat in the cubicle, routed and demeaned, the ceiling pressing down on his head. He wondered what would become of him. He knew you were lost in this town if you didn't belong, if they didn't want you around, and in one senseless sweep, for reasons that were beyond him and would always be beyond him, he had kicked out every support from under him. In his agitation, he thought of his mother—he didn't know what he would say to her, how he would explain it. He didn't know what she and her husband would do without the weekly check he gave them. The phone rang. He was chopped. Claris couldn't believe it—he had been gone from the lawyer's no more than twenty minutes in all, and already the machinery was grinding. There was no formal notification. They had left it to the switchboard girl to tell him he was through, that his close-out check would be in the mail. "Sorry," the girl said. She ran on, "First they wanted you, tracking you all over, high and low, and then suddenly—forget it, hands off him." Claris was muddled—he didn't know why they had had to track him high and low, what the great rush had been—but when he tried to query the girl, she turned hostile and aloof, as they did when they knew you were down and the knock was in.

Prescott walked into the cubicle, tipped off, no doubt, by the switchboard girl. Working with the bosses all morning as he had, he knew that Claris had been dropped and was no longer with the agency, but that didn't deter him. He came at Claris, complaining and spoiling—Claris had let him down; he was on the spot; he had the whole mess to clean up now by himself; they were all on him and he could lose his job—where was she? What had Claris done with her? Where had he taken her?

Claris didn't know what he wanted or was talking about. He half rose from the chair to shove him out of the room. And then it came to him. Prescott explained what had happened. Adele wasn't at the resort. She had disappeared. With everything at the last failing her, she had done the only thing she knew how to do and had run off again, except that this time no one knew where she was. Claris saw why the bosses had been tracking him down. They thought he had her. That was what Prescott had told them. Prescott, with his thief's brain, had taken it for granted that Claris would be still latching on, that he would never willingly let her go or walk away from him. Prescott realized by now that Claris had nothing to do with the disappearance.

"If she's not with you, then where is she?" Prescott jabbered. The hired chauffeur she had brought up to the resort with her was still on the place. If the chauffeur hadn't driven her, then how did she get away? Who had driven her? Where had she gone?

"You want I should help you find her, Dick?" Claris said, straight-faced, leaden.

"What kind of a crack do you call that?" Prescott said. "That's no contribution. You had the responsibility."

"You think I ought to make amends?" Claris continued. "You want me to make a contribution?"

Prescott started to answer, saw the look on Claris's face, thought better of what he was doing, and suddenly began backing out of the room. Claris let the lunatic gargoyle look fade from his face. He sat at the desk. The heat and tumult were gone. The megrims had him—the rale, the ancient basic horror. When he had gone to the lawyers, yes, it was mania, a compulsive fury to break loose and bring everything down, anything he cared to tell himself—at bottom, and he knew it, he wanted the money. When he had slipped out on the actress, he hadn't admired himself; now that he was going back, the offense was all the greater. He was going back to her because she was alone; because he had no excuses, since it made no difference now whether anyone knew he was mixed up with her or didn't know; because he was destitute and adrift and had nothing going for him; because Prescott, with his thief's brain and scurrilous assumptions, was right.

The hotel-resort, when he reached it, lay still, curiously unchanged and as he had left it, the great 117-degree afternoon desert heat sifting down and holding everything fast. There was no outward sign of disturbance to be detected, whatever was going on with Case and Fannie, however they were searching for Adele and worrying over her disappearance. She was in the steward's quarters over the kitchen. Claris knew where she was. He had put it together and guessed where she had gone the minute he had heard the hired chauffeur hadn't disappeared from the hotel along with her. She had run out of hiding places and retreats; she simply had nowhere she could have told the chauffeur to drive her.

Claris understood the compulsion in her to remove herself from sight and withdraw from contact with the world. That was at the center of her malady. That was the reason why at periodic intervals one star or the other, without warning or explanation, would suddenly scuttle a picture in mid-production and go hurtling off. Overloaded and beyond themselves, appalled by their inability to do what they thought they were expected to do, they craved to pull the shutters down, to give up, to stick themselves in some out-of-the-way corner and let it all go by without them. It wasn't temperament or a taste for sensation, the motives commonly ascribed. Now that she had come to the end of her gyrations, with the reporters ready to flock in on her because of the so-called new romance, she needed a refuge more desperately than before, and so Claris had this tricky, onerous arrangement on his hands, the actress stashed away in Louis's room right there in the midst of them on the premises, while they hunted far and wide for her. Wigler was sunk. That remarkable resilience that carried him from crisis to crisis, that was his stock in trade, wouldn't serve him any longer. His backers had dispersed and he would never group them together again, with all his enduring reliance and tenacity. But for Adele the outlook wasn't necessarily hopeless. It was the unforgivable sin in the industry to bankrupt a production, but Claris had seen cases where actresses, in a similar situation, had nevertheless managed to extricate themselves and come back. It was a matter of time, of waiting for the scandal to die down, as in some miraculous way it often did, of counting on the indefatigable resilience and optimism that were the stock in trade of other producers as well as of Wigler. That was why the stars probably allowed themselves these tantrums in the first place, Claris thought, because they knew they could survive their excesses and be forgiven. The commitments she had for future pictures were all to the good; in order to recoup on their investments and on the advances paid out to her, the producers would be lured in spite of themselves to go on with their projects, so she already had one foot in the door. Claris knew enough of the business to handle the studio details, to make deals and front for her. He could provide a genuine support and service, he told himself, and as he tooled the car over the grounds, he kept testing these reflections in his mind, putting them into an order, really to fortify himself, so that when he saw her, he would come prepared, would have a realistic, plausible program of

She was badly worn, as he might have imagined she would be after the long hours spent by herself. She had left the door unlocked and had obviously been waiting for him to come to her—who else would have known where she was? She had to have him, or somebody, with her all the time, because without a man or husband to dance attendance on them they became woebegone and frantic, but now that he was with her and she had him, he could see from the outset that it was impossible to do anything for her. He stood away, letting her rip at herself. He wondered what she would have done if he hadn't come by. He thought of the other scrapes he had been in, the preposterous backstairs maneuverings, the harum-scarum last-minute escapes. "Take a chance. Are you afraid?" a woman had once said to him in a bar, leading him on, baiting him, and he knew he was through with infidelities and hairbreadth escapes for a good time to come. He couldn't talk to Adele. This was no time to trot out his long-range plans for the future, to show her how they could make it famously as a team together, Claris zealously safeguarding her interests and running interference for her. "One of those," she said. She was referring to herself, to the way she looked and the impression she knew she must be making on him. "You see them—these overwrought ladies with hyperthyroid eyes, going from pillar to post, the lipstick smeared on their mouths. People throw themselves around and don't know what to do with themselves." She looked about her, seeing herself in the Filipino steward's quarters, buried in this unlikely setting while the hunt was on for her. "Nobody knows they're crazy until somebody officially comes and tells them," she said. She was frazzled by the break with Case. She hadn't expected it. Whatever she thought of him and in spite of the venomous, disgraceful jibes she threw out at him when they quarreled, he had been someone to fall back on, to return to, to blame for the errors she had made and the way things had gone. So long as she had him, she could still feel desired somewhere, that she was worth desiring, and now that this familiar support, which she had thought would always be there, was taken away from her, she was bereft, forced to deal by herself with the miseries that plagued her.

She fidgeted, her face freckled and pinkish and perspiring in the strong light that came off the walls, the ceiling, the bare boards of the floor, and suffused the room with its solid heat. She half lay in the chair, her legs bent at the knees and jutting out before her, the body let go, the body that she treated with such an impatient contempt and which she felt had betrayed her. Claris saw the roundness at the upper arms and shoulders, the weight taking hold there, packing in; he saw the slack, plump roll of the belly, the widening at the waist—that thickening which, it had been surveyed and studied in the business, the young people in the movie houses spotted and resented, perhaps without even knowing what they resented, which from their vantage point and youth they found repellent and wouldn't accept. What affected Claris particularly was a certain undercurrent running in her—a life and death anxiety to beat off the dread or desolation fast closing in on her. It was as though she was determined not to let this dread get the better of her or even to concede that it could touch her; as though she knew that if she gave in to it she would be finally swamped and pulled down forever. "If I forgot anything, he reminded me. I didn't believe he had such a thorough knowledge of my transgressions. He must have a special notebook where he writes it all down." She spoke in harsh, abrupt bursts, lingering now on the harangue by Case, when he had presented his list of indictments and had exposed her.

"Is this the best you can do, to stay shut up in the closeness and heat?" Claris said. "Does it make sense?"

"I wasn't sure I'd see you again. I thought we had lost you. I thought you have given up on me. I suppose that ruins my stock with you." She was back on the harangue again, on the sharp dressing-down by Case. "He didn't leave much to the imagination. That makes two of you. They like a woman who has something in reserve and can fight back on even terms. It's no good to them unless there's a certain amount of resistance to build up the excitement and make it interesting."

He didn't answer. She had it against him that he didn't speak, that he was one of the silent ones and kept controlled—if you had to go gingerly and be two-faced and watch what you said, you didn't talk. The door was still unlocked—he hadn't thought to turn the bolt over when he had come into the room—and for a moment he wondered what would happen, how it would seem, if someone by accident wandered in on them. She was ridden out with doubts and shame, the mortifications which she had gone away to England hoping to put behind her once for all and which Case—in his fervor, not meaning to batter her or cause her harm, as Claris had seen—had rammed home again and fully revived. Claris thought of the stories he had heard told about her—a fight in a taxicab, a notorious brawl in a Madrid hotel suite when a marriage had just begun, when it had foundered during the honeymoon—and he could see how these stories and the others, which she knew everyone must know, since they were, after all, part of the gossip around town, must weigh on her, how they must incapacitate her, making her shrink back and feel marked and conspicuous, making every meeting and occasion an agonizing ordeal for her. He could see why she everlastingly castigated herself for a mélange of missteps and gaffes, occurrences which, if he could only speak to her and explain, she would realize weren't gaffes at all, which, if they came from anyone else, would be negligible and be unnoticed, but which, coming from her, became blown up in her mind and distorted and a needless, continuing torment. But he couldn't speak to her; it was too late to start untangling the fears and apprehensions in which she was lost. She was devastated because she couldn't work. In the past, she had had the bustle at the studio, the day-to-day shooting schedules and demands on her, to keep her going, and so it was a double misfortune for her that she was bogged down and blocked, a paralysis that came about because she was distraught, because she didn't know what she could offer, because every idea she had withered and fell away from her. She had been out of action for the year and a half. She didn't know anything about acting, never had, would be the first to say so, and, in addition, she knew that what was required went beyond acting, that technical competence and training really had little to do with it. She was looking for those intangible values, hideously slippery and indefinable, coming out of nowhere, that made a job of work hit; that gave a roundness, an excitement, a constant promise of good things to come, a surprise; that made it possible for the performer to take to the stage. She wanted to find again those inner resources, some mystery of personality that she had or thought she had when she was young and that she felt had been suddenly taken away from her. Nothing was good enough. She saw no reason why anything she might do on the stages should be spunky and alive and compel interest, and so she faltered in a steady anxiety and couldn't get to a start. She was overwhelmed by the magnitude of the financial ruin she had brought on Wigler, now that she had finally managed to kill off the production for him; and as Claris saw her glancing at him and then glancing away, not caring to take her troubles to him because she plainly had no trust in him and knew no great comfort was forthcoming from him, as he saw the panic churning in her to the point where she felt like someone plunging headlong from the top of an eighty-story skyscraper, the guilt and discontent went rankling through him. He looked to himself. He was still used up from the morning he had put in, from the grotesque events already indistinct and seeming unreal to him and which he grimly reminded himself he would make sure became even more shadowy and unreal as time went by, sideslipping and palming his disabilities in the stylish way he had learned all his lifetime so that he could maintain presence and go on. The image of the cold, unfriendly rented rooms he had lived in came back to him. He saw himself on the move, attaching himself to groups, always on the fringes. He faced the sloth, the waste and inertia, the shameful seepage of the will and lack of belief in himself that he had let take away his strength and send him scurrying after disreputable schemes and easy ways out.

He told her about the reporters, that they were on to him and had discovered he was the new man in her life. He talked to her about these things to fill up the silence, to help bring her out of herself, because the reporters would be catching up with them sooner or later, would come clamoring at them with their barrage of questions, and because he and Adele had this grimy little chore also to look forward to. Claris could see the reporters smacking their lips over the new-found tidbit—the supermarkets, the prominent California family, his connection with them—and he knew the columnists would now be able to run a full extra day's enjoyment out of this vital complication. He didn't know when she had eaten last, and thought he ought to get some food in her. "We could go to a drive-in. We could manage it," he urged her. She wouldn't be seen or it would be only a carhop. They'd be in and out before anyone knew it. "You have to have something," he said. But she didn't hear him, just as she probably hadn't heard a word when he had talked to her about the movie reporters, and the ploy failed. He couldn't get her to start thinking of walking out of the room if that had been his intention and the real reason he wanted her to have something to eat.

"I have a headache," she said. "I don't feel well. I know. You told me. These things take care of themselves. The morning comes. You wake up and everything is fine. The moral is never to cut your throat." Claris

she was still the same person now that everything was against her. She wouldn't accept her condition, refused to accept it, fought it steadily and head on, and since there was no solution or palliation, no way of resolving the fright and unhappiness that festered in her, the result was a merciless, minute-by-minute, non-stop abrasion, too much to be borne and yet clinging on, never diminishing. "You made a bad selection," she said. "You never know what you're getting when you go in with a lady friend on a spree. That's one of the hazards. Look at him—how daintily he treats me, standing still there, afraid to say anything that might upset me and start me off." She chipped at him, taking him to task because he humored her, taking it out on him because she had been besmirched and had besmirched herself in the run-in with Case the evening before and he had been there to witness it. "You had yourself a front-row seat to the whole production," she said. Claris didn't respond, holding her down, retreating before her, so to speak, hoping that she would expend herself and eventually get the jitters out of her system by taking it out on him, and as he persevered with her, telling himself it was a disagreeable stretch, an interval of time to be lived through, that it had to be this way or else how could he move in on her and take her, a wave of exasperation, of helplessness, rose in him. He was looking on ahead to what still had to be done and what lay before him—the business of tipping her around, of getting her to go in with him on his plan, the falsity and deception that would ensue, she knowing and he knowing and both of them proceeding in the pretense of decency and good heart. He resented the need to feel sorry for her. He resented her for the woes she ceaselessly insisted on inflicting on herself. Anyone who went near her was drawn in and enslaved, forced to be concerned solely with her activities and derangements, and the worst of it, as Claris knew, was that the enslavement did her no good—the brunt of the grief remained with her. She went right on sopping up the punishment, and in the end, after all the trouble she gave, after making herself objectionable and a burden, she wound up with just another mortification to add to her collection and belabor herself with. She had once been married—early in the game, during the first flush of her success—to a man now widely known for his interest in the amenities, for the elegance of his home, for his standing in that busy social interchange which occupied certain segments of the community and on which they prided themselves. It was a pairing so

in them. He had watched her these last weeks, driving herself without stint, rushing willfully into catastrophe, fighting to the limits of her strength and then pushing herself on to find new strength so that she could fight some more. Even now when she was beaten and it was over, she wouldn't give up. Claris thought of this thing she had just done—breaking in on Louis, making the flight in the dark to bury herself, out of a desperate wish to be no longer seen or heard of, and also, since nothing with her could be uncluttered, causing this newest sensation in a last-ditch bid for attention, to keep them all coming at her and worrying about her, Case included. To the public the behavior of people like Hogue was incomprehensible, a show of temperament indulged in by the actresses because they were spoiled, foolhardy, overly impressed with their importance. But Claris had been in the room with her, in the electric light. He had seen her sick, the stomach turning over in her, the body going suddenly unstrung, that uncontrollable fluttering or racing taking possession of her. He tried to drive these meanderings and misgivings from his mind. She had no choice, he told himself—as a matter of hard practicality, she would have to go in with him, so in the end he would have the working partnership he wanted. Whatever compunctions he might have he would get over, he told himself, just as in the past, when he had had to squirm through some unholy mess or other, he had always managed to find it in him to comfort himself and survive. Nor in the welter, as he stayed with her, silently countering and giving ground, according to his tactic, did he miss the joke on himself, the incongruity, that he should be bothering himself with remorse and fine shadings of sensibility, he who had lived by small larcenies all his life and was yet so constituted that this morning, when he was busy trying to use his child to get a cash settlement out of his in-laws, he could be startled, genuinely amazed that he was in fact doing this. She lay back in the chair —lackluster, loose, indifferent. She had been revealed to Claris. One by one the details of her life had been brought out to the light before him, a stripping away which she more than anyone must find grating, but she brushed aside all restraint and let him stare—because they were in the room together and she had no one else, because it was just another crudity along with the rest of the crudities and defeats she could do nothing about and had to live with. She dispensed with the guise, that artificial personality we put out for the sake of appearances, to get us through a meeting, when for one reason or another the heart is out of us, so that it often happens that we are two or three persons, depending on the sets of people we are with and the throw of the circumstances that have brought us to these different groups. He saw her as she had always been —improvident, ill equipped, precipitate. She had never had the quality of the women-guests at the hotel, those soft-spoken women who not only had little to say but seldom even listened, who, in their relationships with men, offered an ardor overwhelmingly tender and solicitous and at the same time impersonal, a kindness that they could discontinue seemingly without an instant's feeling or trace of remembrance.

She roused, pulling herself to her feet in an odd, abrupt surge of movement that puzzled Claris until he realized that she was gasping, that she was fighting to get her breath. The mass of nervous ailments that harrowed her never let her alone for long. If it wasn't the scalp-burning, the stitches in the side of her head, the angina, the overbreathing, then it was the eyes going out on her, refusing to focus and producing those gauzy, bluish spots, so that other people in turn became speckle-eyed and shifty before her. The neurotic manifestation this time took the form of suffocation. She simply didn't breathe, a failure due to an involuntary constriction of the throat or diaphragm, or else it was that she just forgot to take the trouble to breathe. The seizure crept up on her— suddenly, as she lay there, she felt herself sinking away; suddenly she was swallowing for air. "You have to get up and start walking around or else you'll strangle to death," she said. "You have to start learning how to breathe all over again." She ran on, going off now on some theory she had evidently figured out for herself, one of the superstitious fancies with which she encumbered herself as if she hadn't enough to muddle herself with. She was blocked, she said; there was nothing she could do to help herself. God or something of the kind was hammering down on her, meting out a prearranged, astrological ordering of events which neither she nor anyone else could alter. She believed that payment had to be made, that she was now paying for the good things, the dazzling successes, that had been given to her, that it always worked out in this way, according to a sinister, unknowable pact. She claimed that everyone who had risen to the top and was in the public eye was blighted somewhere in the background in this manner, that they all carried with them a secret sorrow, a taint that affected them or a child or whoever was close to them.

He broke out at her. It got to him—the two of them perspiring in the heat, huddled in the room over the kitchen. "Why do you talk such nonsense?" He couldn't make things right for her. He couldn't bring back the years. He was tired of struggling with her neurotic afflictions, her hallucinations, the endless string of her troubles, miseries that were real and incontrovertible and that he wished he didn't have to know, that he had really tried to run away from when he had driven off the place in his rush the night before. He lashed out at her—she had just blown a fortune of money. She was in debt. She hadn't stopped until she had smashed the picture and brought everything down on her. She had the whole town against her. She was alone, she who couldn't fend for herself when the going was good, who always had to have someone to cry to and hold her up. "Who have you got to go to? Who can help you? Can you carry it by yourself? Don't you see what you're forcing me to do?" Whether he wanted to take her or didn't want to take her had nothing to do with it. It wasn't up to him. He had to move in on her. There was no one else. They would go hand in hand now, doting on each other, loving. He would be in business, one of the smooth operators, prospering and living off her, and as he bore down on her in this wild, irrational charge, blaming her for the injury he was doing to her, he heard the whine in his ears, the ever-present mediocrity that he had never been able to beat.

She came apart, every guard down, every license permitted. Who was he to hold forth over her? What did he think she was going to do, stand there and listen to his strictures? If he thought he knew so much about her, then she wanted him to know the rest—the reasons why she had come to be as she was, the offenses committed against her, worse, the offenses she herself had committed, not meaning to do them, meaning to do them, acting out of fear, out of greediness, out of ignorance, because she had been new and raw and hadn't known what was expected of her or how she was supposed to behave. What poured out was the black devastation, when you sit in a room and silently hope to draw strength and an anchoring just from being with people; what poured out was that feeling of dissolution, impossible to express or make clear to another, normally held tight and secret, but which she was now determined to get out of her and share. She told him of one remembered abomination, of a drive home from the racetrack with one of her husbands—the mismatch, the husband who was too old for her, when they all said she was

on. "If I saw him again, I wouldn't spit in his eye," she said, but the vitu-
peration wasn't meant for this far-distant partner—it was meant for herself, that she had been so abject, so impoverished and unequipped. She
spoke of the seedy business district in the daylight, the vacant room over
the store in Santa Monica, the doctor saying to her, "If you scream I'll
throw you right out into the street." She jumped the years. She was talking about her mother, the way she had died, the emergency call and the
things that had happened then. Her mother had been living in the Bay
Area, in one of the cities outside of San Francisco, and Adele had had to
pull herself together in the haste, forgetting the studio alarms and involve-
ments, going up there alone, as it fell out, without a companion or friend.
She had taken a room at the hotel nearest to the hospital, so that she
would be close at hand, so that she could settle in for the siege, the business of hospital visiting, of going to and fro, and as she sped on, rigorously giving the full, lacerating account, he saw that what she was really
trying to do with him was reach out for a dispensation and release. She
told how it had all recoiled on her—the way she had lived, the bicker-
ing and struggling to maintain status, the fretting, the going to the top-
line directors of the moment, begging them, "Tell me what to do. Tell
me what to do." It had all fallen away from her, and, since Claris had
been in these straits himself, he understood from his own experience
how she had felt and what she was trying to explain to him. It was a time
for summing up, for self-recriminations—the omissions crowding in,
the instances of neglect, of ingratitude, the persons cold-shouldered and
failed, the pitiless, incessant, well-founded demands made on her when
she herself was beyond her strength and it was all she could do to keep
her head above water. She told of the stealth, the unreality she had moved
in, people starting to stare at her, spotting her, muttering to themselves,
"Who was that? Wasn't that. . . ?" She hadn't had the courage or presence
of mind to go out for her meals—it had been a fourth-rate hotel, one of
the older, leftover structures, without dining-room facilities; she hadn't
had the wit to send someone out for the food she needed, and so had
found herself in the blaze of the all-night supermarket, haunting the
shelves, looking for tomato juice, for tuna fish. She spoke of the hours
at the bedside, her mother there inhuman and far away in the great, in-
conceivable, searing pain, and the woman neighbor, her mother's friend,
sitting alongside, mourning and moaning softly, "Why didn't you help

her, Adele?" "It was cancer," she cried out to Claris. "What could I have done? You can't fight cancer. I couldn't have saved her life and made her well again. Why was the blame on me?" But it was true, what the neighbor woman had said was true, and Adele knew it. She had flung out of the hospital, she told Claris, not even going back to the hotel, leaving them there with something more to wonder about, mystifying them completely, and the memory of this final default remained to burn in her too. "I used to believe people committed suicide because they were sick or hopeless or trying to make someone feel sorry for them. It's not that," she said. "You lose connection. Something happens to you. People who are close to you, whom you've known for years, suddenly become strangers and you don't know who they are or what they have to do with you. You don't feel anything. You can't love anything or anyone. You can't work. That's why they kill themselves."

He left her alone. The barriers were down. Everything was said, so they had reached that wry understanding from which they could now go on, and he knew she would soon be ready to leave with him, that he would have her out of the room. In the distress between them, he considered all that had gone before with her, the scale of her doings, the force and commotion. It came back to him how she had had it in her from the beginning—in those easy high school days, when the seven or eight motion-picture companies dominated the life of the city—to take on the big risks, to strike out boldly for the top scores, looking even then for the enhancement and importance she knew she had to have. He only had to think of her conglomeration of neurotic symptoms to realize the fanatic energy she had put in, the energy which was more than people were willing to exert or could exert and which was what, after all, made the difference. He saw her in the concourse at the high school, the skirt hitched up at the waist, because it didn't fit, because it was her mother's; he saw her in the first enterprising venturings—caught in lies, waiting for the maid to leave, the blush, the wickedness and temptation. Fannie had pleaded with her, others had taken a hand—at the agency, at the studio—but there had been nothing anyone could do to keep her from the succession of husbands. She had been up against the good-looking boys, those idlers and ne'er-do-wells who, for all their idleness, worked industriously on their manner, everything calculated to provide that limber amiability which caused people to want to be with them. They could be wonderfully persuasive in private, with their playmaker's sincerity, that actor's game of illusion that went on among them apart from the acting on the stages. They had about them an airiness, a promise of vivacity and pleasure, as fraudulent and short-lived as it was enticing; and even though she had just been through one disaster of a marriage and had learned her lesson, even though she had been through the aftermaths, the vindictiveness, the eviction notices and lawsuits, she would plunge straight into the next mess, aware of what she was doing and of the probable consequences but actively following out her misfortune, contrary and perverse, as if believing she had a right to her folly. She had gone repeatedly back to Case, caught up in this erratic relationship that had tortured itself out over the years and was also part of the commotion of her life. She had gone after Case—Claris had seen how she hadn't rested until she had contrived to bring him out to the hotel-resort. She had made the overtures, had been the one to weep and carry on in those steamy eruptions behind locked doors; and Case, for reasons of his own, in the obstinate way of these arrangements, had chosen to keep on with her, however his attachment appeared to outsiders and whatever he let them make of it. She had stayed close to him in a wary, hostile proximity, accepting the abuse and grudges that accrued with the years, knowing he had the full record on her, which was what she meant when she said he made her feel like nothing—she had stayed close to him because she at least knew what she had in him, because she had had to have his devotion and need. She had had no allegiance to him or affection, had felt free to go to other men, to marry, and yet if he wasn't there to spy on her she would become instantly stricken and contrite and would go into a decline. Because she had this problem with her clothes, everything at the moment either too big for her or too small, she had resorted—in the weeks Claris had been with her—mainly to wraparound dresses; and in his mind's eye, in thinking about her and how it must have been for her in the years past, even though she was in the room before him now, he had the vision of her in one of the wraparound dresses, agitated and provoked, moving in stride, as he had seen her so often, the lace yoke of her slip showing, the breasts there bobbing and heaving. Without the razzle-dazzle, the achievement and attention, she would be nothing, somebody on a parking lot, a passer-by in the street, and he saw her constantly embattled, fighting off the whittlers and belittlers and whoever would bring her down, fighting off the dinginess of heart, the ogre, which she had abhorred from the outset and had been determined to best. She had known she wasn't the strongest person, or if she hadn't known, then Case and Fannie had made it sufficiently clear when they argued with her that she exhausted herself and had no stamina, but she had driven herself on with her flamboyant, unsparing tenacity, and Claris wondered now at her illnesses, at the mauling she had absorbed in her time—the curettages, the operations, the bad operation, the babies before that, the brutal intensive reducing regimens, when, to meet a shooting schedule and get herself in shape, she installed herself in the hospital and they systematically sloughed the weight off her, so that she herself came to view her body with a sick distaste. It was all of a piece, the patches and pictures all coming together—musing on her in this way, he could still see her bustling down the high school paths, rapt in the glow of that time, in the butterfly kisses, the women's magazines, the competition and the thrill of expectation, all things then being possible and seeming just around the turn for the having, and it occurred to him, if these impressions were so bright and immediate in his mind, how much more recent they must be to her, and he could understand the fury in her, the rage of disbelief and bewilderment, now that all this which she had fought for so desperately was so soon being taken away from her. He understood the loathsome brevity of time, the rapidity with which it goes —the flabbiness of thighs, the changes coming on one after the other, the face transforming itself into somebody else's, the catch at the heart when you suddenly one day realize how old you are. She had told him a story about herself, this in one of the countless confessions and effusions when they had been together and the time had gone by—a story of an encounter with a salesman in a used-car lot in the auto row at Culver City. She had told the story on herself, going back to the days when she was unknown and hard-pressed, as so many of them liked to do, the contrast appealing to them, no doubt, because it gave them an inner confidence, a continuing renewal of courage. She had managed to be invited that afternoon to a gathering at one of the glittering West Los Angeles homes, and she had wanted this certain car on display, whether she could make the full down payment on it or not, because she was young, because she had the image of herself arriving at the party on her own. The feeling of the Culver City area of the period came to Claris—the empty lots,

the same as the other times when Adele had started a new romance and he had gone crazy, and Fannie knew it. He was interested in wrapping it up, in getting back to Las Vegas. He talked about Adele, still concerned, wondering how it would be with her now, if the new man could do anything for her. She wasn't getting any younger, he told Fannie.

"What do you think, you got older and she got younger? It don't go like that. What did you expect?" The trouble was, to him, in his eyes, she had never changed—she was always the Wampas Baby Star. Fannie had noticed the look on Case's face last night when he had finally seen Adele without the rose-colored glasses, as she was, a woman getting on, the same as everyone else, and it had been a pang; Fannie didn't know why and it still annoyed her. She had been the homely one, left out and taken for granted, in another department, and still she had genuinely felt for him and for Adele too, because the great passion, which was theirs, not hers, had worn itself out and was gone.

"Who is he?" Case said.

"A man. What the hell. Another husband, another marriage—marriage two hundred and twelve." She had been in the bungalow and had talked to them, but that didn't mean she knew any more than Case did and she couldn't help him out. She walked away from him in the lobby, going on straight to the office, leaving him to pack and start preparing for the trip to Las Vegas. Her heels went rapping over the tiles. She walked away without a backward glance, pushing out the memories, trying to think of the work she had waiting for her, telling herself that if she had it to do all over again, knowing what she knew now, would she be any the wiser; would it be any different; would she be able to steer it along a different course; would she be able to influence him in the least and tell him what to do? She had known better than anyone else what it had meant to him; even in those days when she was the one getting hurt and knew she figured to lose in the long run, even while it was happening, she had imagined it as he imagined it, as it all took hold in him—the cars, the luxury, the homes, the Santa Anas blowing in through the canyons and passes, the women they had here, the movie stars. She had known what he had done in order to make it out to the coast—when he was mixed up with the slot machines, the cherries, apricots, and pears, when he was trying to get in and the parties in control rejected him and wouldn't even let him talk to them. She had lived through the showdown fight with the muscle men, that time when she had been in fear and trembling for his life. "Look out below!" he had yelled the eight times from the roofs. They had broken up eight of his machines for a sign, and he hadn't been able to eat, he hadn't been able to sleep, the fire burning in him. She had warned him they would maim him, but there had been no way of tying him down and holding him in the house. He had gone to eight of their candy-store locations, had carried the heavy slot machines up to the roof one after the other, smashed them down on the pavement three and five stories below, and then they had been finally willing to see him. They had called him in. "I wanted to give but nobody would take," he had said to them and the remark had amused them. They had looked him over a second time and decided they could use him. And the doors had opened wide.

She had gone along with the show, not knowing what they needed it for or what she was doing, but doing it, every morning getting up and starting out again, making herself over and adjusting herself to fit in with the high-class company and not shame anyone, and it had come hard for her—she would start out in those days for I. Magnin's or Harry Cooper's to spend the money and find herself at Ohrbach's. She had been at the hairdresser's at Saks, talking to Mr. Don and Mr. George and the lady receptionist at the desk, ingratiating herself so that she would be known and greeted by name and be also in the swim, when she had heard the news, learning about Adele and the full-blown affair in the beauty salon, which was where they always heard it, over the partitions, except that at Saks they hadn't had partitions, and it had been a blow.

"Fannie, it's true. I love her and she loves me," he had announced to her, very formal and civilized, when she had presented him with the story, and it had bitten deep, the anger going through her, not for herself and all she had endured with him, but for him—that he could have deluded himself to such an extent, living big, taking himself seriously. "You love her and she loves you—over my dead body," Fannie had told him, getting herself together, going to work. "You fool," she had said to him, "don't you know to them you're a freak? Don't you know they go with you because they think you're a gangster and it gives them a kick?" "Fannie, I'm sorry. That's the way it is and that's the way it's going to be," he had said to her, and then had gone back to Adele to find out that at the last minute she wanted to beg off, that she was busy at the time with the other fellow, with another fiancé. "Here," Fannie had said to him, seeing him pine and what the disappointment was doing to him, "you wanted the goddam divorce, take it." But she had seen to it that she didn't suffer in the meantime; she had gotten everything that was coming to her.

There had been the hot, rambunctious flurries of the first years, when he had tracked Adele on the desert rambles, when he had put friends on her, gotten reports on the phone. It had shaken down into this hard and fast pattern, the two of them unable to let go of each other over the interruptions, the marriages, and absences. He had had her in mind, one of those men tough in business or whatever they spent their time on, with the chopped-up faces, with their down to earth big-league savvy and smart catch-phrases, a corner reserved in them, a soft spot. They hung on and took the knocks, because they liked it that way, because it gave them something to think about and filled out their lives. He had been on the sidelines when she had gone ahead with the Canadian fellow, the man who had retired and come down to California to live and who had been a good twenty-five years older than she was. The wedding had been the gala of the year—the whole hotel ballroom redecorated, a hundred and twenty-five dollars a place setting, the table napery and the gowns of the bridesmaids matching. There had been a kind of reception line, the new husband proudly introducing Adele to the guests at the wedding, and they had stood there like two wooden statues facing each other: "How do you do, Mrs. Whatever-the-name-was," he had said to her, and she had said to him, "How do you do, Mr. Case."

He had been around at the beginnings, and then at the deadfalls. When she had hurried away from the hospital that time, somebody had had to go back to attend to the arrangements—the death certificate, the funeral, the closing up of the place her mother had lived in—and so, for this reason and all the other reasons, she had found herself with him again in that series of departures and returnings. He had still had the house on La Brea Avenue, the secondhand paradise, and they had been together on the grounds, he on one side of the pool, she on the other side, walking by herself in the dark glasses, a figure in a dress, something still there, the body still having it for him—the shiver, the attraction. The nerve had been fading fast; she had had the feeling—the downhill drift, the scare, the need for prayers. For the others who had traveled over to

Europe, because that was where the pictures were being made, it had been the old partying again, but she hadn't belonged in that clique, just as she had never been one of them when they were all back in Hollywood. She had understood what she was doing when she had taken on the titled Englishman. There had been the acclaim and respect tendered to her, the deference that went with being a movie star, and in this world of celebrity, of fast movement and shiny living, she had thought there might very well be a place for her too, that it could just possibly be a way. She hadn't expected wonders. She had set out this time to be sensible, to make the best of it, as people did. She had held on to the last, putting up with her husband and his friends, with their savage, hard-running play, using up the money she had had, doing everything in her power to stay with the marriage and keep from coming home where she hadn't anyone or anything she wanted to come back to.

The women-guests were grouped at the tables on the terrace, providing a background for the press conference Adele was holding to announce her engagement. "Again the catering to them, again the fixing their coffee, putting in the sugar and cream, stirring it for them," a woman at one of the tables said, referring—it wasn't clear—either to the new liaison coming into being, or to the married couple who had had the open altercation and had reconciled, who were also there, or to herself. They had all been in the business at one time or another, as stand-ins or stock girls, understood the exigencies, had made their own adjustments, and they looked on in the evening quiet, happy to lend a hand, not approving and not disapproving. The two little boys, the twins, were running wild, tripping over the television cables, bumping into the news cameramen, having themselves a time. Fannie was going after them, struggling to hold onto them, one kid tearing free as she grabbed out for the other, and Case hurried over to help, boxing them in. "The little rats know they can get away with murder, so they take advantage," Fannie said, breathing hard. Somebody had given the twins Good Humors on a stick and now Case complained, "Why did they do that? Didn't they know it would make a mess and look lousy?" He and Fannie both were anxious for the press meeting to go off well. It was the best thing that could have happened under the circumstances. If the reporters wanted to blow up the romance, then it would be a readymade cover, accounting for the turmoil of the last weeks, throwing a new light on the whole affair from the publicity standpoint. Adele had the debts, the lawsuits and back taxes, and needed the pictures as fast as she could get them. That was why she had had to go through with the announcement whether she was in the mood for it or not, and that was why Fannie and Case were fussing on the floor of the terrace with the twins, restraining them and keeping up appearances. Adele herself was over to the side, surrounded by a cluster of reporters. She handled the gaff, cool and in control, letting the press see for themselves that she was up to the mark, that she still looked good and could go on. Did she miss Europe, did she like it in Palm Springs, was she enjoying her visit? "Yes, so far so good," she said, not knowing what to answer, giving them anything for an answer. "Do you think this marriage will last?" "What?" "I mean, considering the track record—" She cut him off. She knew what he meant. "You'll be the first to know. When we come to the parting of the ways, we won't do a thing without getting in touch with you. Just leave us your name and the name of your newspaper and you'll have the exclusive," she said.

Claris came walking off the grounds toward the steps of the terrace, bringing Melanie with him. At the other end of the terrace, where it merged with the lobby of the hotel, Case and Fannie were still busy with the twins, delivering them to some of the Mexican chambermaids there for safekeeping. The reporters, seeing Claris approach, stepped back, clearing a path so that he and Melanie could get up to Adele and join her. The reporters followed Claris with their eyes, frankly admiring —because by sweet talk, by the luck of his physique, and by who knew what special wiles he had, he had won this still highly valuable partnership with Hogue and had pulled it off. Claris had gone back for Melanie. She had remained in the bungalow and had been almost overlooked. He knew how she felt and what she thought of him, and by going back for her, by showing he remembered her and wanted her to be with them, he had meant to attest to her that her fears would be proven groundless. He wanted to reassure her. He wanted to make it up to her, for her homeliness, for the terrible thick glasses and the pain that lay in wait for her, and as he went with her through the aisle of reporters, disregarding their stares, he vowed in his heart that whatever one person could do for another he would do for her.

Adele smiled as he came up, and made room for him beside her. They stood together, arm in arm. Transcending the ignominies that had passed between them, falling into the guise they would now assiduously practice with each other, they presented themselves to the onlookers, brazening it out, challenging them and uncaring. The press photographers darted about, getting their still pictures from all the different angles they seemed to require. The television people threaded in and out, tending to their equipment. In the activity going on around her, suddenly confused and oppressed by the activity, she turned her face up to Claris, forgetting her resolution, forgetting the crush or even where she was. She knew from her experience on the stages that anything she said would be picked up on the soundtracks, and whether it was for this reason or because of some other mental quirk, she formed the words to him, not speaking them or even whispering, just the lips moving soundlessly: I love you, I love you, I love you. The women sat at the tables. The reporters, the technicians surged about, all this in a time already gone by, the events recounted here having taken place some twelve years ago, when television was comparatively new and the big picture studios still throbbed, the collapse yet to come, the people enmeshed in their concerns, those pursuits, dreams, and diversions which occupy us so that we are each of us precious to ourselves and wouldn't exchange ourselves, the being in us, with any other, those wonderful moments which as they happen go by almost unnoticed but which return again and again in our thoughts to bemuse and warm us, the stir of smoking mountain panoramas, the ache of sweet summer days, of trees in leaf, of being in love, this prize, this treasure, this phantom life.

STRICTLY MOVIE:
A LETTER FROM
HOLLYWOOD, 1989

Dear Editors:

One day a while ago I was back in Beverly Hills, where I had lived for more than thirty years, and on an impulse, since I was in the area, I decided to drop in on my old agent. His office was on South Beverly Drive, a few doors down the street, below Wilshire Boulevard, at the bottom of what is known here as the business triangle. But when I faced his building I was altogether puzzled. It wasn't his building at all. I had walked to his office I don't know how many times over the years—my home was all of five blocks away—but now everything was changed and different. I went into the Union Bank on the corner and asked them for their Beverly Hills telephone book, so that I could check the address at least and see what sense I could make of the mystery. (The Union Bank building now occupied a good part of the streetfront of the block, which, as I remembered it, used to consist of a sleepy low-lying row of one-story structures—a small neighborhood bank, a Bank of America branch, a florist, the Old Vienna Chocolate store, the Mayfair Riding Shop, and, I believe, one or two other stores.)

I quickly saw my mistake and wondered how I could have made it. I still don't understand it. Lazar, my agent, had his office on the 200 block, as I well knew, on the second block, a few doors down the street from Charleville Boulevard, not Wilshire Boulevard; I had simply gone around the wrong corner. But when I finally reached the true familiar building, I was in for another surprise. The whole interior street floor of the building was stripped. They were making a total rearrangement of the floor space—all the old offices had been cleared away, the partitions knocked down, leaving only the bare building walls. A young woman, a girl, was sitting alone in the desolation, perched on a high stool. She told me that Lazar was still in the building, that he was now renting a single, one-room office on the floor above, and was able to give me the room number. (The girl, perched on the stool, wore a bulky, cumbersome crucifix and was eating a roasted half-chicken.)

Lazar wasn't in. I stayed in the office with his secretary for a few minutes and we chatted. She remarked that by an odd coincidence Lazar just recently had been on the verge of paying me a visit. What happened, it seemed, was that Lazar, in the mood for a walk that afternoon, to give himself a destination for his walk, had said, as he started out, that he would go by my house ("Dan's house") and drop in on me. "Mr. Lazar, he doesn't live there anymore. They moved years ago," she said she told him.

When I lived in Beverly Hills I had the habit of getting out very early in the morning, to take care of something I had to do in the business triangle and many times just for the enjoyment of it. In the stillness of the streets there was a subdued, almost stealthy, undercurrent of activity going on. Men could be glimpsed here and there threading their way to the brokerage houses to catch the opening market prices; there was, of course, the time difference of the coasts and so they had to be in their chairs by seven. I think the high movie folk preferred the before-hours doctor and dental appointments for the sake of privacy, to keep their maladies and problems to themselves; I once saw an important star at the head of a flight of stairs in a Bedford Drive medical building, pausing for a moment, regal and poised, larger than he appeared on the screen, as he prepared to descend the steps. Very early one Sunday morning, a woman, who obviously hadn't slept all night, went past me crying

to herself, racked in some deep emotional tangle; I knew who she was—
I had seen her and her husband at various social gatherings—and I have
an idea that she had recognized me, too, as she went by me. On another
early Sunday, I saw a star (Jack Lemmon) wheeling a baby carriage on
the sidewalk, quietly taking a stroll with his child in the carriage down
the street.

One day I was moving along to the triangle, for what reason I can't
remember—a dental appointment, I imagine. I was approaching the
corner of the Beverly-Wilshire Hotel drugstore, which was also a coffee
shop, where I would be making the turn into Wilshire Boulevard and
then on to the dentist's, if that was what it was. The entrance to the
drugstore was on the corner, opening on a slant between the two streets,
Wilshire and Rodeo Drive, and as I went barreling around I all but collided with a group of women—there were four or five of them, tourists,
visitors—emerging from the drugstore. I stared at them. They were old
colleagues of mine, people I had taught school with in Brooklyn. The
teachers stared back at me—standing powdered and straight, middle-aged
women, with their hats and gloves and the purses hanging over their
arms. We didn't know what to say to each other, chastened by the realization, I think, of the time gone by, of the passing time.

A man sits in a room, writing novels. Nothing happens. They don't
sell—four hundred copies apiece, the last one a few more. The reviews
are scattered. Twenty-five, thirty years later they are resurrected and
brought out again. I am rediscovered. The books are republished in hardcover, in paperback, in paperback again, then collected and presented
as *The Williamsburg Trilogy* (although one is set in Brighton Beach,
Brooklyn, not Williamsburg, Brooklyn, but no matter) and it turns out
I am a cult with a respectable following somewhere in the country—
and none of this through any doing on my part or with my knowledge
beforehand. How does it feel to be a cult? It's flattering. I like it. I don't
know what to make of it. At bottom I know the books are not first class
and I privately wonder at the acclaim. The books are fine. I wrote about
the restless Americanized sons of their immigrant fathers, and the novels have a good tenement-house yeastiness and sense of life in them, but
I won't reread them (I have never reread them) because the flat print of
the pages will only sicken and disappoint me. It's always like that. It is

the usual author's lamentation, the author's perpetual dissatisfaction with what he's written. Critics and bystanders who concern themselves with the plight of the Hollywood screenwriter don't know the real grief that goes with the job. The worst is the dreariness in the dead sunny afternoons when you consider the misses, the scripts you've labored on and had high hopes for and that wind up on the shelf, when you think of the mountains of failed screenplays on the shelf at the different movie companies; in all my time at the studios, I managed to get my name on a little more than a dozen pictures, most unmemorable, one a major success. It's the same when you write for publication, on your own. You have the same record of misses, the bouts of wretchedness, the typed sheets of paper going flat in your hands—"The *cafard*," Graham Greene has called it. "The despair of never getting anything right." Of course, the difference is that in the movies you get paid when you fail and there is that to carry you over. I must say, in my case, there was never a rebuke.

I liked it in Hollywood and stayed on. I found the life in the studios most agreeable. You're not closed up in a room by yourself. You're always with people, and there are advantages in working company hours. Mordecai Richler went out of his way in a book review to say I bragged about the money I made in Hollywood. Actually, I never made a great deal of money in the movies; sixty thousand a year was about the best I could do, if Richler doesn't mind my saying so. In fact, I went nearly broke, had to sell my house, and then an amazing thing happened. A benefactor, a Hungarian, a character out of a Molnar play—I can't say his name; he once asked me never to cause him bother and intrude— stepped forward. He's been watching out for us over the years and we're quite comfortable. I guess I mention all this to get a rise out of Richler. Hollywood strikes a nerve in some people.*

---

* PS: A visitor to Hollywood—in a personal essay I wrote—asks me how much I was paid for a screenplay I had worked on. This is what started off Richler in his remark about me in his book review. I wrote, in my essay, that we never like to say what we are paid—"Because it's seldom as much as they think it is, and they will be disappointed. Because it's too much, lavish beyond anything they earn in two years or three, and they will only be sick again." I had no awareness that, in writing these lines, I was boasting. I myself was in the low screenwriter-

I used to read everything. There wasn't much else in those days — no television, no radio. There was, in the beginning, the simple homemade crystal set. Do people know about them — the wire coil shellacked around a ten-inch cardboard cylinder, the cat's whisker? You got the hookup out of the New York *Sun*; you made your own crystal set, and at night listened to the society bands playing at the Manhattan hotel roof gardens. When I was still in high school, I read probably all of Chekhov's short stories, those gray, sad sketches. I wrote a whole bunch of them, in imitation. At City College, I came across *The Menorah Journal*, a handsome magazine printed on strong, thick paper, and it was there that I first heard about Isaac Babel and read one or two of his stories, in a wonderful translation, never again approached, by somebody whose name I can't remember. Babel bowled me over. Before I knew it, I had written a story very much like his Odessa tales. It was published, one of my first, in *Story*. I imitated Joyce — the story "A Little Cloud," in *Dubliners*; mine was called "A Clean, Quiet House." You copy, whether you know it or not. When I wrote for *Collier's* and *The Saturday Evening Post*, I generally followed Hemingway. That's permissible. The only outright plagiarism I'm aware of ever having committed was of a line in a short story by Ralph Manheim. I couldn't resist it. I stole the line, turned it upside down, and made it mine. It was a wonderful story. I read it sixty years ago, in *transition*, and I still remember it clearly; Ralph Manheim must be the same now-famous translator. But what really worked on me was vaudeville. Back in the old Williamsburg days, there was a theater, the Republic, within walking distance of my home, on Grand Street Extension. It played five vaudeville acts and the feature picture. I got over

---

salary brackets, certainly not in the first or second echelons, and it would not have occurred to me consciously to brag about the money I made. Of course, this may be the worst kind of bragging.

Richler was on the Dick Cavett television show a short time after his review appeared. He tried to make amends for his ungracious remark about me. He meant well. He found a way of injecting my name in the course of the interview with Cavett, and was going on to say I was a good writer, but stumbled over my name, and then, instead of moving on, stopped to correct himself, only to mispronounce the name again, and — some viewers told me — for a third time and a fourth, thus unwittingly plagiarizing the invention in Edmund Wilson's *Hecate County* story of Spike Milholland, who underwent a similar convulsion on television.

there every chance I had. It was all new to me and enchanted me, a last-ing effect. The stories of mine that appeared in *The New Yorker* are vaudeville-virtuoso mimicries and performed entertainments. I'm a vaudeville fan to this day. That's why I think that Blake Edwards, for one, is an authentic, idiosyncratic talent unrecognized for what he is—those artful Peter Sellers–Clouseau fandangos of his, many of the other comedies, on television and in the movie houses. I don't know Blake Edwards; I admire his work. In 1947, a year earlier than that or a year later, I saw George Burns and Jack Benny on the stage in a benefit. Benny was dressed in women's clothes, playing Gracie, and they were doing a Burns and Allen takeoff. It was special, a rare thing—the shadings, such delicacy, the beautiful flow between them, back and forth, two figures stationary and yet engaged in a kind of dance. The house was absolutely still. They were all insiders, show people. The performance was for them; it wasn't Burns and Benny's usual, public work. You could hear a pin.

You are what the occasion seems to require you to be. You're differ-ent people, depending on the people you're confronted with and what you think is expected of you—if there's somebody in you to begin with. When I first came to Hollywood, for one reason or another, they thought I was the bookish type, inexperienced in the ways of the world, and that was the part I played for them—the wide-eyed newcomer. I kept it up, off and on, and for a long time after I had been there. They heard I had been a schoolteacher and that must have made an impression on them, and we were young, my wife looking even younger, which she was. At Warner Brothers, Mark Hellinger turned me over to Mushy Callahan to smarten me up and show me the world. Hellinger was a whimsical man; he pulled all kinds of stunts. Callahan was an ex-welterweight champion; I think I have the division right. He was technical adviser on the fight pictures and ran the studio gym room. Mushy turned out to be a whole lot more inexperienced than I ever was. He was a saint, spic-and-span and shining, always with a happy smile on his scrubbed face. He took me down to the Hollywood fight-club backrooms, where the fighters dressed and got ready, and to other dungeons, but most of the time we just racketed around, stayed off the lot, and enjoyed ourselves. His real name was Morris Abramowitz, something like that, although I think that was it exactly. He got hit in the face by a horse when he was a newsboy on the Los Angeles streets. His nose was flattened. He looked like a prizefighter, everybody thought he was a prizefighter, so eventually he had to go in for it, and he became very good at it, the champ. Harry Cohn over at Columbia—who at one time had also been very good with his fists—was similarly amused by me. "What's good time for a six-furlong workout?" he said to me, testing me. "One-twelve, one-eleven," I said, and he beamed at the entourage around him as if to say, How about that? Sam Spiegel once said to my wife, regretfully, that I had no elbows. I genuinely liked these men and admired them as doers, and now that I think of them and am recalling the times, I see the answer: the warm feeling I had for them piqued their interest and touched them, and they went easy on me. The producers have lately been in the public eye, through A. Scott Berg's biography of Samuel Goldwyn and the book by Neal Gabler on the immigrant Jews who built Hollywood. Both books, I believe, judging from the reviews, make much of the point that the producers—in their ardor to make themselves welcomed in the country, to disguise their origins, and with their limited experience of Anglo-Saxon culture (the reviewer John Gregory Dunne's phrase)— invented an imaginary Hollywood America of their own, an America they wished existed. I always thought they consciously promoted these wholesome Norman Rockwell magazine-cover values as a public responsibility, just as, in fact, the editors of *The Saturday Evening Post* most likely did. To help create the national myths. Of course, what was basically the case was that this was the kind of movie the public wanted and would go to the movie houses to see—just as the readers of the mass-circulation magazines insisted on Clarence Budington Kelland and the idealized American West invented by Harold Bell Wright and Zane Grey. It was box office, solely that, the cash coming in, the sea of tabulating machines in the company counting rooms—I've seen them. The producers were revelers, extreme characters, great gamblers, willing to go a few rounds with anybody, as Cohn used to say. But their main concern was the studio. They allowed nothing to stand in the way. They were doers, managers. It was their life and passion.

Goldwyn had his own sense of humor. They say, of course, that he often knew what he was doing when he came out with those Goldwyn-isms, that they weren't all accidental. He was, I thought, a handsome man, fairly tall, beautifully dressed—such suits, shoes, and ties. He had, at times, a pixie charm. "Do you know what day it is today?" he said to us at lunch—we used to sit with him in his studio's dining room while he talked to us and held forth. We didn't know. "It's George Bernard Shaw's birthday today," he said. He wanted us, after lunch, to go back to our rooms, to stop whatever we were doing and read Shaw, each of us to pick out a separate play, in homage. Goldwyn talked on Shaw that day —his fame, his industriousness, his plays a hit all over the world, commercially and artistically. Goldwyn had gone to England and sought out the playwright at his home in the country, pursuing him for the rights to one of his plays—with no success at all. This was long before *My Fair Lady*, the sensation it made, an all-time smash, under other management.

"Never trust a vegetarian," Goldwyn told us. "Not one of them is honest. In the middle of the night when nobody is looking and everybody is sleeping, they go down to the kitchen and take out a piece of chicken or steak from the refrigerator and eat. They do this all the time."

Sy Bartlett, a seasoned, well-known Hollywood figure, a screenwriter, took me one night to the small private club that Preston Sturges maintained. The club, whose existence most people didn't know about, was on a rise, on one of the tiny side streets above Sunset Boulevard. It was a walk-up, hidden away, the outside staircase covered with bougainvillea, and was modeled after a New York City speakeasy of the period, the setting of Sturges's Broadway hit play *Strictly Dishonorable*. There was a dark entry hall, a peephole in the door. The lighting was dim; no more than four or five men were in the place, gambling at baccarat. The night Bartlett and I were there, a young woman, flawlessly turned out, with the professional showgirl's stunning presence and composure, was sitting at a side table close by her husband, who was one of the group gambling. She was five-foot-seven, seven-and-a-half. I still remember her. She wore a gray tailored suit, without a blouse. "I'm not *com*-fitabil," she said at intervals, but her husband didn't take his eyes off the cards coming out of the shoe, and ignored her without a flicker. Sturges wasn't on the premises. I didn't see him, but the place itself was enough to give me a notion of the nature of this fastidious man, that he should think up such a quaint testimonial to himself, a speakeasy in honor of his play, and keep it going, even though hardly anyone knew where it was or heard of it. It was a compulsion in him, an oddity of style, the act they all put on and elaborated, just as, for that matter, Sy Bartlett, who had brought me to the club, felt it was incumbent on him, as one of the grand men of the community, to take me around and show me the high spots. People were drawn to Hollywood from all parts of the country, from foreign countries. They were starting out afresh, with their own customs, their own ideas of personality. They had the need or chance to set themselves up and stand out, and they worked so faithfully on the impersonation they had chosen for themselves that the impersonation became the actuality and all they were; there was nothing else. Bartlett himself had an Old World courtliness to him, a studied formality. His background was unclear— White Russian, Chicago, gangsters. He wore tab-collar shirts with the tie pulled tight at the throat, was glassy-eyed, his face pitted or scarred and florid in coloring; his coarse, exceedingly wavy, bushy hair was plastered down. At lunch in the commissary, he commanded the room; eyes turned to him. He impressed us with his grooming, the jewelry he wore, the sterling silver apple-corer he carried with him for the apple he ate each day to keep regular. He made a big thing of the shops and establishments he patronized—the barbering, his haberdasher (Oviatt's), his tailor (Eddie Schmidt), the sweatbox at the Athletic Club (I went with him once, just to see the place—a private, businessman's facility on a floor high up in an office building), the sessions with his masseur. At Warner Brothers, Mark Hellinger had the studio carpenters build him a cubicle behind his private office for a hideaway, a lair, and set himself up as a remote, behind-the-scenes character. Like the romantic British author early in the century who traveled with his personal case of anthracite coal (to make sure he'd be kept warm), Hellinger, when he went out for the evening, took along with him a satchel with his own personal supply of brandy. He had a puckish, sly smile on his lips, a Broadway-style savvy and flash; he always wore a New York City midnight-blue shirt and pearly tie, and, when he went out, a hat, an article nobody in Los Angeles used. In the lair behind his private office, he spent his time hatching schemes and keeping busy. He had agents in the field, friends of his, people like Sidney Skolsky; they sent in reports, not necessarily about Hellinger himself, what someone or other said about him, but news in general, about big events back home in New York or notables in Hollywood, so that he'd be the first to know. From his lair, he organized bogus

with Cagney, Rita Hayworth, De Havilland, and Jack Carson; and *Four Daughters*, with John Garfield and the Lane sisters, the picture that made Garfield a star. The Epsteins couldn't seem to miss. Nobody believed they could miss. At one time they were trying to get out of their contract with Jack Warner. They read a heap of stuff out of the morning newspapers to their secretary. She turned it in and in time the word came back from the front office—the boys have done it again!

I worked with Faulkner at Warners. Jerry Wald put me in with him. How this came about, this sudden collaboration, one of Wald's fast ideas —Wald was the locomotive on the lot. He made a good number of the pictures the studio turned out, and was always on the run. He was afraid Faulkner would be too literary or artistic for the work to be done, so he teamed me up with him as a leavening influence, to show him the ropes and educate him; so, in effect, I was supposed to do for Faulkner what Mushy had been supposed to do for me. I couldn't get close to him. It was my fault. I was intimidated. He would walk down the studio path, erect, wearing a tight blue double-breasted sports blazer that was too small for him, always, alas, the same blue jacket, looking straight ahead, his face showing absolutely nothing. There was a silent, secret tumult going on in that man. I'm positive I was right about that. Al Bezzerides took over with him. Al took care of him, drove him around—Faulkner had no car—did what he could to help make him comfortable in the horrible motel room he lived in while he worked at Warners. The motel was on the Cahuenga Pass, on the way to Warners in Burbank, right alongside the steaming traffic of the Hollywood Freeway, or what later became absorbed into the Hollywood Freeway. Al urged me to cotton to Faulkner and be friends with him. Al was big and hearty and loving— as he still is—and could get along with anybody. I was from Brooklyn and Faulkner from Oxford, Mississippi, and I was devastated by a paralyzing awe I had for his novels and short stories. I didn't know how to talk to him. One Saturday after work—people used to work half days on Saturdays—I drove Faulkner to the factory district in downtown Los Angeles. He was having something made to order, a suitcase—it was for a present for somebody—but he couldn't get it done the way he wanted. I think the trouble was with the monogram; the initials weren't satisfactory. Faulkner and the workmen couldn't understand each other. The workmen finally got it through that they didn't do monograms in that section, that we had to go to another part of the factory to have the initials removed and the proper ones applied. We were high up in the lofts of the buildings and it was a maze—the workrooms in this factory cut through the walls of the adjoining buildings, and we wandered from point to point in that great hollow space. We couldn't find the monogram department and none of the workmen would tell us. They didn't know what we wanted. It became nightmarish. It finally got to me and I'm ashamed to say I bolted and left Faulkner high and dry—one of those things you later force yourself not to think about.

The assignment for Faulkner and me was to do some rewriting on a picture that was already shooting and in trouble. Raoul Walsh was the director. The time was short and Walsh did most of the rewriting himself before Faulkner and I could get into it. The picture was based on one of Eric Ambler's spy-thrillers, *Background to Danger.**

Metro bought a *Collier's* story of mine and wanted me to come out and work on the screenplay—that was how I got to Hollywood; it was part of the sale. I had been writing commercial short stories for some years at the time—this was after I had stopped writing novels, after I had stopped teaching. It started with the sale of a short story to *The Saturday Evening Post*, the first one I attempted for a mass-circulation magazine—

---

* PPS: Two recent accounts of Faulkner's life (Tom Dardis, the section in *The Thirsty Muse*; Frederick R. Karl, *William Faulkner: American Writer*) throw light on an elaborate fraudulent role Faulkner created for himself after World War I —that he had been a Royal Air Force pilot, had been shot down in France, had been badly wounded, that he wore a silver plate in his head. This surprised me. In a rare, brief social conversation with him (I can recall only one other, very brief, such occasion), Faulkner told me freely, unasked, that he had had heroic notions as a young man in Mississippi, had gone up to Canada to enlist and train as a war pilot, had promptly crashed his training plane and "got a wood splinter in my ass seven inches long, which was the total extent of my career as a flight officer and my contribution to the war." (I paraphrase as best I can, from memory.)

Frederick Faust, who also wrote under the name Max Brand and, I believe, other names too, came on at Warners while Faulkner was there, and the two became friends or, at least, were seen walking down the studio paths, going to lunch together, Faust, thoughtful and adult in manner, Faulkner, as usual,

they sent me an acceptance and the check ten days or two weeks after the story was submitted to them. We were living in Saratoga Springs when all this happened. I had been teaching school as what was known in those days as a Permanent Substitute, a classification the Board of Education had installed during the Depression. It was a beautiful, happy school—in Brighton Beach, Brooklyn, P.S. 225—but people don't understand what hard work teaching is under the best of conditions. You're up there on stage doing five hours, performing. When the Board of Education finally got around to appointing me—with permanent tenure, starting at fourth-year salary on the payscale—I took the occasion to turn them down and leave teaching. I guess I was afraid of getting locked in. I wanted to be a full-time writer. I asked the publisher I had for an advance, so that I would have something to live on, and went on working on what would have been my fourth novel. The publisher, in his good time, told me he would give me no advance. He said it was against his policy. This publisher one cold winter gave the star writer on his list a used, worn overcoat. So I wrote the story for the *Post*. It was about wrestling. I called it "Elephants with Shoes." It sold. I broke up the novel I had been working on into three or four short stories, the stories from the broken-up novel sold, other stories too, and all was well, the reprieve we get. I wrote stories mainly for *Collier's* and *The New Yorker*. We moved

---

stone-faced. They both carried those old-time tin lunch boxes, the ones with the thermos bottle clamped to the underside of the lids. Faulkner's and Faust's thermos bottles contained whiskey. After Faulkner finished on the lot and they were cleaning out his office, they found his old rocking chair in the room and, in the drawers of his desk, clutters of empty pint whiskey bottles.

Faust went to the war from Warners and was killed in the fighting. I went into the Navy at the end of 1943 and was assigned, after recruit training in San Diego, to the OSS, the cloak-and-dagger intelligence agency. During the period of indoctrination, a group of us were assembled in a projection room and were shown a film to help orient us in the field of espionage. The film was *Background to Danger*, the one Faulkner and I had worked on.

The story, set in Istanbul, was intricately plotted, and the picture, as I've said, already shooting, was giving us a great deal of trouble and worry. We were packed in Jerry Wald's office one day, talking fast, each of us pitching ideas, trying to figure out what to do and how to grab hold of the problem. "Ah know what's the matter with this story," Faulkner said. We all held up as if a gunshot had gone off, and waited. "Too much runnin' around," Faulkner said.

to a farmhouse in Pennsylvania—we had a child by then—and got ourselves settled in. We didn't want to go to California. As it turned out, we really hadn't had to. The agent I had then had worked a ruse to get us out. He met us at the station in Pasadena and laughed at us as we got off the train. Twentieth Century–Fox had wanted the story, too, the agent said, and had even been willing to pay a little more, but they didn't want me as part of the deal, so he had closed with Metro. "Oh, Jim, why did you tell him?" my wife said, as I started railing at him.

We rented a house for three months, and then another for three months. I went from Metro to Warners, was kept on contract there, and we stayed on. A number of other writers started here in the same way. They'd come out to work on a book or play they had sold, intending to do just the one assignment, and then they'd go from studio to studio and make their home here permanently.

Sometime in the Twenties, the singer Ruth Etting was involved in a turbulent relationship with her so-called gangster-type manager (I don't think he was a gangster at all), a man with a badly crippled leg, Moe "The Gimp" Snyder. The relationship ended in a shooting at a house in the Hollywood Hills, in which the other man in the triangle suffered a flesh wound, and in a scandal that became the basis for *Love Me or Leave Me*, a sizable hit movie, which still holds up, is talked about for remakes, and is alive. That was Cagney, Cagney and Joe Pasternak, the man who succored Hungarians. Pasternak was a top pro producer, an all-around human being, as he still is. He stayed away and yet controlled every part of the script. The ending is his. Pasternak and I had our offices on the same floor in the building, the Thalberg Building at Metro-Goldwyn-Mayer, and he would stick his head in the door as he went flashing by. "How can you sit there doing nothing?" he called out to me from the door. "I'm not doing nothing. I'm thinking," I said. "Don't you get bored?" he said, and kept going. A friend of mine, who also worked at Metro and often dropped in, one day broke out in a fit of feeling for me, unable to stand the sight of me laboring over the story—that I was exhausting myself for nothing; that the story was hopeless, downbeat; it would never be made; the script would go straight on the shelf. My friend and I kept seeing each other over the years. We never mentioned the incident.

A strange thing happened along the way on this assignment. I had been given a beat-up mass of old Ruth Etting newspaper clippings as source material and it took me a while to work up a story line. We sent the story treatment upstairs, and while I was waiting to hear from them and go on with the screenplay, an agent walked into my office. This man had considerable clout on the lot through a major family connection — and told me straight out he was going to knock me off the assignment for one of his clients, letting me know in advance of the dirty work he was going to do behind my back. I've often wondered about this peculiar confession and what to make of it. What did he think he was doing? He looked at me and sadly searched my face, as if with pity for the harm he would be causing me. I think it must have been plain stupidity, a seizure of senselessness. Such things happen. I mentioned the visit to Lazar, my agent, which I knew was all I had to do. Lazar went ice-cold with anger at the insult to him personally in the matter. The relative never had a chance.

The picture was originally intended to center on the singer; the working title was *The Ruth Etting Story*. But as we got into the work, Pasternak and I were soon taken with the character of the man, the so-called gangster. The emotion went with him and it was what we had to have if the audience was to follow the story line and be held. After many delays and disappointments and much involved dickering, Pasternak managed to secure Cagney for the part. Cagney made the picture what it was. In the end, you're at the mercy of the actor who speaks the lines. I never discussed the story with Cagney or talked to him. I never met him. The writer, as may be known, is long gone by the time they get to shoot his script. I once caught sight of him standing by himself in front of a hotel on Central Park South. It was very early morning. My wife and I were in a cab on the way to the airport, going home after a trip to New York. The street was empty. The sidewalk was swept clean. He was at the curb, no doubt waiting for a driver to bring a car around. He had a smile on his face and was obviously enjoying the quiet and the fresh morning air. The sun was sparkling and in that light he looked angelic.

The things that went on, the thieving and conniving. You lived with it. *Love Me or Leave Me*, in particular, had an unsavory history, if the truth were known, and I guess that's why the encounter with the agent came to mind. But you get absorbed in the picture-making itself. It's a large-scale, generous art or occupation, and you're grateful to be part of it. When I look back, I think of a picture we made a dozen years before *Love Me or Leave Me*—*The Hard Way*, at Warners. Vincent Sherman, who directed the picture, was and is a good friend. I was still at the studio, working on another assignment, while he shot the picture. He let me come down to the set as often as I liked and it was there, looking on, that I got the feel of the business and became permanently attracted. Irwin Shaw was mixed up in this picture too, although you won't see his name on the credits. Jerry Wald made up the story. He would drop in on us at the writers' building, try out the story, improving it from office to office, and it's remarkable how the finished picture is basically what he worked up and shaped on these excursions. He gave the assignment to Irwin Shaw, who wrote the first draft. Something happened. The studio wanted changes, Shaw refused to make them, took off and left town, and the script went on the shelf. It stayed there for six months. Sherman and I were looking around for something to do. We asked for the assignment, got the script off the shelf, worked on it, and in time showed our final draft to Shaw. He hated it. Shaw and I went back to Brooklyn together, to the days when I was teaching grade school and he was writing for radio, but he told me we had mangled his work and ruined it. He laughed and laughed in the wonderful hearty way he had, whacked us both on the shoulder, told us he wanted to have nothing to do with us, wished us the best of luck, and left town again. He told his agent to get his name off the project.

What impressed me about the people on the set as I looked on was the intensity with which they worked. In the late afternoons, which was when I would go down there, it seemed a mood came over them—a group of people huddled in a corner in the barn of the sound stage, lost in what they were doing, oblivious to the world. On one of the early sessions, I watched Joan Leslie and had to smile, entranced by the way she gathered herself together, the way she drove herself into the impersonation of the part—this when she was hardly out of her teens or perhaps still in them. They were artists or talented people—the photographers, set designers, editors, and others whose names you see on the credit lists. They worked with the assiduity and worry of artists, putting in the effort to secure the effect needed by the story, to go further than that and en-

hance the story, and not mar it. In the early session I referred to, the scene
—played by Leslie and Ida Lupino—takes place in the grimy kitchen of
their home in the steel-making city the two sisters live in and want with
all their hearts to escape. The griminess of the setting was essential, it was
what the script called for, but I felt it would repel the audience just as
it depressed me, and I said something of this to the cameraman, who
was James Wong Howe. "I'll do something. You'll see," he said. What he
did, I saw later, was to produce a softness; the kitchen was still there, but
hidden and not there. The black-and-white glossiness centered instead on
Lupino and Leslie, casting a vagary over their faces and bodies, making
them beautiful and their desire poignant—which is as good an example
of what I can find to show what I mean here (which may also show why
moviemakers object to "colorization"). James Agee, in his review of the
picture for *The Nation*, gave special attention to the photography and
praised it.

The moviemaker has to hold the whole line of the story in his mind
—just as the good novelist holds the whole novel in his head—but the
chore with the movie is much more onerous since we shoot in fragments,
out of continuity, and the balances and values go flying and grow lost.
The Hard Way was particularly troublesome because the story is aver-
age, with no strong central line to follow: Lupino strives and struggles
for Leslie, ruins Leslie, ruins Leslie's husband (Jack Carson), and, in the
end, herself and her hopes. The story is aimless, witless, an accident in
the making and would take us nowhere—except for the providential presence of Dennis Morgan in the cast. This is an enigma to me, a story-
telling mystery. Morgan has nothing whatever to do with the plot. He is
in no way involved with the people in the triangular action. He is ever the
bystander, sometimes uttering a rueful word of warning to his vaudeville partner Carson, most often just looking on with understanding and
forgiveness as the human drama unfolds. And yet he controls the picture. What is it? Morgan makes you believe he is part of the milieu, but
you know he doesn't belong there, that some warp of fortune has put
him in with these people and that he is superior to them; and it is, I
think, the innate grace and courtesy in this cool, elegant actor—the thing
that was born in him—that gives the picture its point and sorrow.

The picture had a nice success; it is the one I am fond of. People liked
it. During the war, in the flurry of military orders and mix-ups, Irwin

Shaw and I fell in with one another for an hour or so in Paris. He told me they had just shown the picture to his outfit in the ETO and so he had finally seen it. He said he still hated it, but when I asked him how the show went over with the men in the outfit, his whole face broke out in a grin. "They loved it!" he said, laughing and laughing, against himself, happy for me, for Wald, for Sherman, and our success. "They went crazy over it and ate it up," he said. He was a grand man. It is a wrench to think that he is gone. He was honorable, to be looked up to—a "delectable mountain," to use the phrase in the French novel by Alain-Fournier, *The Wanderer.*

For a long time I carried around with me the setup for a novel about a woman, an actress—perhaps the woman I recognized that day in the street and who I thought recognized me, too, as she went past, crying—who, in a spate of despair, after many husbands, many mistakes, can only go seeking refuge with the wife, or ex-wife—now the owner of a Palm Springs hotel-resort—of the man the actress once lived with and took away from her. My idea with this novel was to write it in such a way that it would be, not fiction, but the concealed, inside fact behind the fiction—the actuality that readers avidly search between the lines of the text to discover for themselves, dispensing with the fiction. The book, *West of the Rockies,* was a failure. It didn't do what I wanted for it. I turned back to the novel because I thought it was a great story. I had had it with me for years and finally decided to write it. I won't say how much time I spent in writing it. I never knew many movie actresses but I knew people who did and I've heard the stories. These actresses are vigorous characters; there is so much, so much to be had, that when it slips away from them, the breakdowns can be intense and absorbing to follow. While I was trying out this story in my mind, I would think of a screenwriter friend of mine, a paraplegic, from polio, now thirty years dead. His boat, which he kept at Newport Beach and ran down to Ensenada and La Paz, was his car. His apartment was fitted out as a ship's cabin. When the movie-writing jobs failed and he lost the boat, the apartment, the Lincoln Continentals, he refused to bear it and took his life, fumbling once, succeeding the second time. There was no contest, no hope, in my screenwriter friend, so I exchanged him for the actress, whom I called Adele Hogue, and worked up a licorice-bitter story of a man, Burt Claris, who is drawn to use her in her fright or, in fact and as he soon suspects, is drawn by Hogue herself to use her. It's a good story. Maybe, in twenty years.

What makes a story good? How do we manage it? What is the secret elixir that we must look for, the thing that gives a story life? I'm no good with these speculations, with literary theories in the abstract, and am uneasy in talking about them. What use are they? Does anybody benefit from them? Half the time I think we don't really know what we're talking about. There is the story Professor Morris Cohen at City College used to tell, to show, I suppose, the frailty of ideas, how exasperatingly elusive and unsatisfactory they are—the Jewish tailor whistles Dixie and then says to the Devil, taunting him, can you sew a button on that? O, these Jews, forever seeking. There is the line, the story line, the line of action, the run, the continuity, the plot, the mystery of form, the razzle-dazzle from the beginning to the ending—it is the same in movies or the novel. At City College there was this little fellow with his heavy violin case always banging at his knees. He played in ships' orchestras; he went out from cruise to cruise and I never knew how he managed to fit them in his schedule of classes, but he did. He wrote a piece for the college literary paper, *The Lavender*, in which he said it all boiled down to the melodic line. He was writing about music, but it's the same for me for fiction. It's the melodic line—when it all comes together, when it sings. I wrote in an account years ago that a good story was so hard to come by that you didn't really write it; that it existed, that it was out there, somewhere, and you found it. I once said to a famous editor—he has more books dedicated to him than any other man I know, living or dead—that I thought a good story was a matter of luck. He dusted me off, said I was speaking nonsense. Of course he was right. But maybe there is room for my idea too. When Irwin Shaw came out with that sun-splashed piece of wizardry, "The Girls in Their Summer Dresses," and I asked him about it, he was honestly taken aback. He was honestly puzzled. His words, as I recall them, were: "I don't know. I write the story. If it's no good, then I write another." Joseph Mankiewicz, whose work I respect, said in an interview that the most electrifying thing happens in the movie house when you give them the truth. I know what he meant. I have been there. Of course, he didn't mean the word "truth" literally. He meant the indivisible, the indissectible, the stab, the catch at the heart, the indefinable.

You know when you have it. It has sometimes happened to me, and at night, when I can't sleep, I will recite the story to myself passage after passage, word after word; I believe there isn't a writer who hasn't done the same. Here is an example of the perfection I look for. My granddaughter, eleven, writes to my wife: "Don't tell Grandpa, because I don't want him to worry, because I have a little cold and a rash on my neck. Actually, you can tell him. I feel much better." This is wonderment. The "rash on my neck . . ." The calm. The naturalness. It's enough to make you believe in prayer.

I get phone calls—an admirer, unknown to me, in San Francisco, another in Cleveland, young writers at universities, solicitous and polite. They ask, shyly, am I currently writing? Better than ever, I tell them. I've got hold of it. They think I'm joking, making conversation, but I'm completely serious.

SOURCES AND ACKNOWLEDGMENTS

This volume of Hollywood stories by Daniel Fuchs brings together six works of fiction and three memoirs published between 1937, when Fuchs was twenty-eight, and 1989, when he was eighty.

"Writing for the Movies: A Letter from Hollywood, 1962" first appeared, as "Writing for the Movies," in *Commentary* (February 1962).

"Dream City, or The Drugged Lake" first appeared in the third and final issue of *Cinema Arts* magazine (Summer 1937).

"A Hollywood Diary" first appeared in *The New Yorker* (August 6, 1938). It was reprinted in Fuchs's miscellaneous collection *The Apathetic Bookie Joint* (London & New York: Methuen, 1979).

"Florida" first appeared, as "Toilers of the Screen," in *Collier's* (July 8, 1939).

"The Golden West" first appeared in *The New Yorker* (July 10, 1954). It was one of three Fuchs stories reprinted, together with groups of stories by Jean Stafford, John Cheever, and William Maxwell, in *Stories* (New York: Farrar, Straus & Cudahy, 1956). It was also reprinted in *Stories from The New Yorker, 1950–1960* (New York: Simon & Schuster, 1960) and in *The Apathetic Bookie Joint.*

255

"Triplicate" first appeared in *The Apathetic Bookie Joint*.

"The Aftershock: A Letter from Hollywood, 1971" first appeared, as "Days in the Gardens of Hollywood," in the Sunday *New York Times* (July 18, 1971). It was reprinted, as "The Earthquake of 1971," in *The Apathetic Bookie Joint*.

"West of the Rockies" first appeared as a book published by Alfred A. Knopf, New York, in May 1971.

"Strictly Movie: A Letter from Hollywood, 1989" first appeared, as "Strictly Movie," in *Commentary* (September 1989). This piece started life as a *Paris Review* interview proposed and conducted by the writer Aram Saroyan, one of the admiring young strangers Fuchs refers to in the final paragraph here. Although it was only a forty-minute drive from Saroyan's home in Thousand Oaks to Fuchs's in Los Angeles, Fuchs insisted that the interview be done entirely by mail. In February 1989, Saroyan submitted twenty-seven questions to Fuchs, who worked on his answers throughout the spring. Saroyan recalls that everything seemed to be going fine until Fuchs learned that the interview was to be copyrighted not in his name but, like all the "Writers at Work" interviews, in that of *The Paris Review*. Unappeasably outraged—and perhaps also seeing a canny way to turn an unpaid interview into a paying article— Fuchs declined to submit his answers and instead fashioned them into an essay for the editors of *Commentary*, who published many of Fuchs's later stories, memoirs, and book reviews.

I would like to thank Aram Saroyan for providing this anecdote, and for encouraging me to undertake this book. I am deeply grateful to Jacob and Thomas Fuchs, the sons of Daniel Fuchs, for permission to reprint these Hollywood pieces and to take a few liberties with their original periodical titles. Thanks too to John Updike, a longtime champion of Fuchs's fiction, for writing the introduction, and to the reference staff of the Boston Athenæum for their always-cheerful bibliographic assistance.

—CHRISTOPHER CARDUFF
Editor and Publisher
Black Sparrow Books

ABOUT THE AUTHOR

"I was born in New York City in 1909," wrote Daniel Fuchs, "in a house on Rivington Street, on the Lower East Side. We moved into Williamsburg, Brooklyn, when I was five; the tenement, 366 Second Street, was just completed but it was called a tenement from the start. . . . I attended the Eastern District High School, where I was editor-in-chief of the Eastern District High School *Daisy*, how about that? Then I went to New York City College, where I was on the swimming and water polo teams and on the college literary magazine. I taught school for seven years, most of them at P. S. 225, a wonderful elementary school in Brighton Beach, whose principal was about the most brilliant man I ever knew, Mr. Sol Branower. . . .

"I used to go on long walks by myself, to Broadway under the El (the Brooklyn Broadway), drawn to the shop windows there—the ties, the haberdashery. There was a pool parlor on Grand Street Extension, a broad, cobblestone thoroughfare running at a slant from the Williamsburg Bridge Plaza; almost every night a group of young men would be practicing complicated tap-dance steps on the sidewalk there. . . . I had a route. I took in the street sights at night, the Mary Sugar bums at the garbage cans with their bags of belongings, the men fornicating with women pushed up against the wall in the dark doorways of vacant stores. . . . I cannot really explain why in time I was impelled to write pieces about these long walks, the things I saw on them, and the things I liked to make up and imagine. One of these pieces, a forty-page account, was submitted to *The New*

Republic. They accepted two thousand words of it, and the editor kindly suggested that I expand the account into a novel.

"I freely used the sights and happenings, which had absorbed me, in the three books I wrote in my twenties: *Summer in Williamsburg* (1934), *Homage to Blenholt* (1936), and *Low Company* (1937). . . . The books didn't sell—400 copies, 400, 1200. The reviews were scanty, immaterial. The books became odious to me. [I decided to] put it all behind me—the teaching, the novels, the disappointments. I struck out on my own and was successful from the beginning. I wrote story after story. I broke up my unfinished [fourth] novel into stories. The money that came in delighted me.

"The stories I wrote for *The New Yorker* put me in a company I admired with all my heart and brought me esteem. The ones I did for the large-circulation national magazines were even more rewarding. . . . One day I read of a horse-trainer who as a boy was a pigeon-fancier. I got the notion of a group of cab drivers who band together, buy a racehorse, and turn it over to train to one of their number who has tended pigeons all his life. *Collier's* called the story 'Crazy Over Pigeons.' My original title was 'The Day the Bookies Wept,' and this was the title RKO used on the movie, in 1939, with Joe Penner and Betty Grable. It was the first thing of mine to be filmed, the first connection I had with Hollywood and the motion-picture studios. . . .

"How fast the time goes. We are given only a few decades apiece. I didn't become rich. I went to Hollywood. I worked on screenplays, in collaboration or alone, from my own original material or from source material, for movies like *Panic in the Streets, The Hard Way, Criss Cross, Storm Warning, Jeanne Eagels,* and many others. I received the Academy Award in 1955 for *Love Me or Leave Me.* . . .

"The popular notions about the movies aren't true. It takes a good deal of energy and hard sense to write stories over an extended period of time, and it would be foolish to expect writers not to want to be paid a livelihood for what they do. But we are engaged here [in Hollywood] on the same problems that perplex writers everywhere. We grapple with the daily mystery. We struggle with form, with chimera. . . . 'Poesy,' my father used to call it, and I know I will keep at it for as long as I can, because surely there is nothing else to do."

The Williamsburg books were collected, in hardcover, as *Three Novels* (New York: Basic Books, 1961); the comments above were drawn from Fuchs's introduction to this volume, from his own dust-jacket bios, and from an essay he contributed to Gale's *Contemporary Authors Autobiography Series* in 1987. Fuchs's final novel, *West of the Rockies,* appeared in 1971, and his miscellany, *The Apathetic Bookie Joint,* in 1979.

Daniel Fuchs died in Los Angeles in 1993, at the age of eighty-four.